The House on Curzon Street

The House on Curzon Street

by Alan Caillou

William Morrow and Company, Inc.   New York   1983

Library of Congress Cataloging in Publication Data

Caillou, Alan, 1914-
    The house on Curzon Street.

    I. Title.
PR6053.A347H6   1983   823'.914   83-48
ISBN 0-688-01845-9

Printed in the United States of America

First Edition

1 2 3 4 5 6 7 8 9 10

BOOK DESIGN BY LINEY LI

Chapter One

In this spring of the year 1806, the garrison town of Arcot was a fine and pleasant place in which to be stationed.

Some sixty miles inland from the Bay of Bengal and the squalor of Madras, the city was cool, two thousand feet above sea level in the gently rolling foothills at the base of the Ghat Mountains; deep and narrow rivers flowed here at all seasons of the year. The granite mountains were parched and gray, but cumulus clouds hung over them always in a brilliant blue sky.

The garrison was set by the bank of the river and consisted of eleven long barracks, which housed the British and the Sepoy troops, and a three-story building, which was the Officers' Quarters, with its own large Mess Hall and gymnasium. There was a compact group of bungalows which were the offices, a long row of well-kept stables, a very solidly built armory, and a small church. Interspersed among these widely spaced buildings were smooth lawns of an astonishing green, kept close-mown daily by native gardeners with scythes, and rose gardens in circular, square, or oddly asymmetrical shapes. There were fruit trees everywhere—peaches, apricots, oranges and lemons, pears and even apples, and huge walnut trees;

there were masses of bamboo, and towering conifers of a dozen differing species.

In the center of the complex was the parade ground, a dry and dusty place but shaded on its borders by orderly rows of sandalwood trees. In one corner of it was the main flagpole, where the Union Jack would be raised at sunup and lowered at sundown, with the Guard in attendance, spit-and-polished to perfection as the bugle sounded its call; they wore white sola helmets, and scarlet jackets with crossed straps of white leather, white breeches, and black leather knee boots.

And for the officers the sunset bugle call was the sound that heralded the most important event of the day—the pouring of the evening drinks; sometimes it went on for a very long time.

The servants would troop out onto the main lawn where the deck chairs had been set out, beaming their courtly smiles and carrying the glasses and the decanters on highly polished silver trays. The officers, in their dress uniforms, would gather in little groups, while their ladies, in flowered dresses, lounged among them; and the talk would always be of England.

Nowhere, in the whole of the far-flung British Empire, could there be more of peace and serenity than there was at Arcot. And when the sun had gone down and the flares danced in the cool breeze that came down from the Ghat, the peace seemed almost sublime. The officers were mostly young and fiercely handsome, with ruddy faces and bristling moustaches, slender-waisted and fit (the result of constant hard riding over the surrounding hills). Even the Commanding Officer, at sixty-two years of age, was muscular and lithe. And as they strolled the lawns in twos and threes, their evening blues immaculately pressed, their dress swords shining in their gilded scabbards, the picture they presented was one of military excellence.

The ladies too, flouncing their crinolines around the canvas chairs set out for them, seemed to vie with one another in the splendor of their gowns, the elegance of their coiffures, and the refinement of their grooming.

This day had been a particularly good one. The garrison at Vellore, twelve miles distant, had sent over its crack polo team, considered to be the best in the whole of Madras State, if not in all of India, and Arcot had roundly defeated the famous visitors. The game had been followed by a riotous party, with an alfresco dinner on the lawn, on trestle tables set out and covered with cloths of the finest Irish linen.

When the dessert of sliced mangoes and cherries in brandy had been served and cleared away, the ladies retired to the rooms that were set aside for them, to see to their faces and discuss their husbands, and the long sequence of the mandatory toasts began.

It was half-past nine o'clock when Colonel Sir Bryan Dawson rose to his feet to propose the first of them. He raised his glass of port wine high and said, his strong voice ringing out across the gardens: "Gentlemen, I give you now, the pony that won this splendid match for us, the lovely Mirabelle, only twelve and a half hands high, but every hand filled with mischief and cunning."

Major John Entwhistle, second-in-command at Arcot and a man of robust character and physique, stood up quickly and said, his bright blue eyes alight with excitement: "No, sir. With due respect, Colonel, I give you instead . . . the *first* of those hands!"

They drank to the first hand, and the second, and third and fourth, always with mock seriousness, interspersing the toasts with bawdy jokes as the night wore on and sobriety slipped away. And as the moon rose in the silent sky, the colonel said, more gravely now: "The President of the Mess Committee is . . . ?"

Captain Hendrix, gray-haired, red-faced, and battle-scarred, turned to his commanding officer "My turn this week, sir."

"I think the time has come for the brandy, Mr. P.M.C."

On Hendrix' order, the servants changed the decanters, and all the officers stood straight and solemn as the colonel wiped at his gray whiskers with a wine-stained napkin and raised his glass. "Gentlemen," he said, "His Majesty the King, God bless him."

The murmur ran round the table as they echoed the sentiment: "God bless the King . . . His Majesty . . ."

"And now," Sir Bryan said, "shall we join the ladies?"

By half-past eleven, there was not a sober officer in the garrison. And a little after midnight, two of the servants helped Major John Entwhistle to his quarters as he shook their solicitous hands free and said quite firmly: "No, I don't need your help." But he was not very steady on his feet as they guided him slowly up the broad mahogany staircase and into his bedroom, and the senior of them, Sambru Atallah, dismissed his assistant and said quietly in Hindustani: "Go now, Akra. I will take care of the Major Sahib."

Akra left discreetly, and as the major flopped back onto the bed, Sambru undressed him, pulled the sheet over him, and said softly: "There is a woman if you wish, Major Sahib. A new one." As he hung the uniform over a high-backed chair, he laughed, showing his white teeth, gleaming against a heavy black beard. He was a *sudar-behra*, a head servant and a man of privileged position, proud of his status and knowing that he was regarded also with great affection. He said happily: "She is a child, pehaps no more than fifteen years old, and very beautiful. Her name is Darchini. It means cinnamon."

"I know what *darchini* means," the major said, not unkindly. "I speak your bloody language better than you do. All right, send her to me."

"*Ekh bargee*, Major Sahib, at once . . ."

Sambru padded softly out, and John Entwhistle arose and went out onto the tiny veranda that overlooked the gardens and the parade ground and the moonlit mountains beyond. He gripped the woodwork with powerful hands and gulped in deep breaths of the cool night air, sobering up. He fancied that he saw down there the cantering horses of his Dragoons, wheeling in orderly formation, the pennants waving, the moonlight glinting on the blades of their lances; he could almost hear the call of the bugle, the sounding of hooves on the hard ground, and he knew that here, in this well-ordered garrison, was almost everything that he held dear.

He was a big man, standing well over six feet in his socks, narrow at the waist and hips, with broad, strong shoulders and heavily muscled arms and legs. His face was florid, his hair thick and very fair, his eyes a vivid blue under stern brows. He was a martinet, a strict disciplinarian, both with his men and with his family.

His family . . . He thought of them now, counting the months to his next leave, when he would see them all again. Amanda, the beautiful wife he loved so dearly; Peter, growing out of his youthful gawkiness now and causing his parents the deepest anxiety with his stubborn questioning of all the old values; the sweet, kind, and utterly charming Susan, fourteen years old and unaffectedly complaisant; the twelve-year-old child Hilda, older than her years and somehow a stranger to him, a dark-eyed, silent, and introspective beauty whose coloring brought him unwanted thoughts he was ashamed of; and James, the youngest of them at the age of eight, a bright and cheerful boy who played incessantly with his lead soldiers. For six months in every three years, the period of his home leave, his family brought a different kind of joy to him. But he knew that his true home and his destiny were in India, where his talents could best serve his country.

He wondered, missing them now, if he were after all wrong in refusing to bring them all out here. But deep inside he knew that it would be a mistake. They had discussed the question together during his last leave, and Amanda had said, pleading: "But darling, there's perfectly good accommodation out there for the officers' families!"

He had half agreed. "I'm quite sure that you yourself could brave it out, but the children . . . ?"

"They would love it. Even Peter."

"Peter?" He laughed shortly. "There's only one way to hasten the change in that boy's philosophies, which will come sooner or later I'm convinced, and that is to keep him as far away from India as possible. Susan, yes, Susan would love it, and she'd rapidly endear herself to everyone out there. Hilda? Perhaps." (He did not want to talk about Hilda.) "But James is the one we have to think of. In the course of time, James will go up to Sandhurst and learn the responsibilities of an Army officer."

"But John dear! Sandhurst is twelve years away! Good Heavens, darling, in twelve years' time I'll be an old woman. I can't even bear to think of it!"

His arms were around her, pulling her closely to him. "No," he said. "You will never be old, Amanda. Twelve, twenty, fifty years from now you'll be as young and well favored and as spirited as you are today."

"Oh, darling! That sounds exactly like a description of one of your horses!"

He sighed. The night air was cool on his naked body, and when the quiet tapping sounded on the door to his room, he padded softly over and opened it for the lovely, doe-eyed child-woman Darchini.

"*Undur ao,*" he said. "Come in." He took her by her delicate hand, and led her to the bed.

It was nearly four o'clock in the morning when the messenger arrived at the officers' quarters.

He was a young captain named Aaron Snow. There was a fearful saber cut across the side of his head, and the shoulder of his scarlet jacket was stained a deeper crimson. He was in a foul temper, and he said to Sambru furiously: "I don't care if he's got every Babylonian whore in history in bed with him! Get him out of it! I have to speak with him now! What's your damned name, fellow?"

"Sambru, Captain Sahib." He was terribly upset by the sight of that dreadful wound; the captain's ear and part of his scalp had quite gone, and Sambru said unsteadily: "Perhaps I should wake the doctor instead, Captain Sahib . . ."

Captain Snow was already striding to the bedroom door. He hammered on it briefly and threw it open. He walked quickly to the oil lamp and turned it up, and in the yellow light the major sat up in his bed and stared at him: "Good God! Captain Snow, isn't it?"

The young girl beside him was covering herself up quickly with the sheet, and the captain saluted and stood rigidly at attention. "Yes, sir," he said. "Captain Snow reporting from Vellore garrison. We have a mutiny, sir. The Sepoys at Vellore have rebelled."

"*What?!*"

"Fifteen hundred men, sir, in revolt."

The major wasted no time. He was cold sober now, already on his steady feet and wrapping a sheet around him. "Casualties?"

"No final count, Major, but they are considerable."

Sambru said quickly: "I will lay out your uniform, Major Sahib—" The major interrupted him brusquely: "Forget my uniform. Find the Officer of the Day. Tell him I want an Officers' Call immediately. Wake the colonel, give him my compliments, and ask him to meet me in Company Headquarters at once. Find a medic and have him report to me quickly. Tell the Orderly Sergeant to stand by for General Call. *Juldee!*"

Sambru touched his fingertips together and left, and the major reached for his clothes.

"Well," he said, dressing quickly, "We have a mutiny on our hands. The details, Captain."

"At midnight, sir," the captain said, "the Sepoys opened fire on the British barracks. Two hundred British soldiers were killed immediately."

John Entwhistle felt the blood draining from his face. *"Two hundred?* he whispered. "That's half of the British contingent there. . . . You'd better sit down, Captain. I don't like the looks of that wound."

"With your permission, Major, I will stand." There was a twisted smile on his boyish face. "As long as I can stand, sir, I know I'm not too badly hurt."

The major was dressed, and they hurried together down the broad staircase, and Captain Snow, at the major's prodding, said: "As soon as the first shots were fired, the men of course in their beds, the officers came running out of their bungalows to see what it was all about. There were several squads of Sepoys waiting for them, and they just . . . mowed them down. Eleven of them were killed instantly, many others wounded." He said dryly: "We've trained the Sepoys well, Major. It was a very efficient operation. And now the fortress is theirs."

"And Colonel Haskell?"

"The commander is dead, sir. Major Treehorne is badly hurt but was still alive when I left him. He ordered me to ride for help."

"And the time was . . . ?"

"Midnight, sir. As the garrison clock finished chiming . . . that's when the firing started."

In a few moments they were seated at the long trestle table in Company Headquarters under the hard and watchful eye of the colonel; two field officers, four captains, and the lieutenant who was Officer of the Day. They listened while

Snow made his report, and the colonel said at last very calmly: "Well, gentlemen, I need hardly remind you that the specter of revolt is a fearful one indeed. We are a long way here, both in place and time, from England, and the success of the British raj in India depends very heavily on the loyalties of our Sepoy armies. This means, of course, that any attempt at mutiny must be stifled *immediately*." He looked at Major Entwhistle. "John, I think I'll put this in your hands. What options do we have?"

"We have two, sir," Major Entwhistle said promptly. "The first: we can move a massive force from here to Vellore, surround the fortress, and demand their surrender. If we maintain a siege far enough away from the walls, we'd have no casualties and it would come down, perhaps, to a question of starving them out. And I don't really like it too much."

"No," the colonel said. "We don't know how many survivors there might be, but however many there are . . . they'll be hostages. They might even be slaughtered while we're sitting there. I won't have it." He turned to the messenger: "What about the survivors, Captain Snow? Do we know what's happening to them?"

"They were being herded, sir, the last I saw of them, into the dungeon under the guardroom."

"And that's large enough to hold, what? Fifty or sixty men?"

"Not as many as that, even."

"We must assume that they've taken two or three hundred casualties out of a total establishment of five hundred and sixty British officers and other ranks, which leaves perhaps three hundred survivors."

Sir Bryan's face was tight with anger. "That means we may have the Black Hole of Calcutta all over again. Your second option, John?"

The major said slowly: "I like the second one very much, though it's admittedly risky."

"I'd say a great deal of risk is justifiable, under the circumstances."

"Yes, of course. I'm sure we can assume something like the Black Hole again, and this can be to our advantage. It means that our own officers and men will be underground, and safe from anything we care to throw at them." He turned to the other field officer present, Major Blair: "What do you think, Angus? You know these people better than any of us. Will they or will they not realize that in case of a battle, our own people will be *safe* if they're held underground? Or will they keep them up on the walls, a kind of shield?"

Blair was a quiet and thoughtful man who had spent all his adult life here. He was smiling: "They've no' the capacity for deep thought that you and I have, John. It's my belief that in the euphoria of their success, they'll simply be manning the walls and waiting for us to hit them. And I'll tell you something else. They'll already have their runners out, carrying the news to other garrisons. We've no' a great deal of time, John."

"Agreed. Then what we should do, Colonel—" He broke off and said in a moment: "Before I expand on the second option, let me tell you why I like it. We have a certain psychological question here. We have to show the Sepoys that our own superiority is such that we do not *need* a massive force to put them down. We have to show them that we can take care of a contretemps like this almost offhandedly. We have to display, in very full measure, a kind of *contempt* for their arrogance."

The colonel was worried. "That's a very interesting point, John," he said. "Go on. I can't wait to hear the rest of it."

"What I propose then is that I ride to Vellore with a single troop of British Dragoons and two field guns, no more. And that with them, I retake the fortress."

The colonel was frowning darkly. "You'll need more than a single troop to scale Vellore's walls. That fortress is very nearly impregnable."

"We will not scale the walls. To do so would mean bearers to carry the scaling ladders, and our bearers carry knives. This rebellion may be part of a larger effort, and I have no wish for any of my men to be stabbed in the back as they start climbing."

"Disarm them, then?"

"No, sir. That would undoubtedly precipitate a very unpleasant reaction on their part. We can't afford to trust them now, but we can't afford to show them that we don't either. We must move with no bearers, no Hindis at all. This has to be an entirely British operation."

He rose to his feet and began striding impatiently, stabbing at the air with his hands when he wanted to emphasize a point. The colonel and the others listened, knowing that John Entwhistle was a very good soldier. "First of all," the major said, "we blow open the main gates with artillery, and all we need for that is a brace of twelve-pounders. They won't stand up under a concentrated barrage for more than a minute, if as long as that. Immediately, we go in at the gallop in column of four, and we'll cut them to pieces with lances and sabers."

"A single troop? One hundred and twenty men?"

The major nodded. "In truth, sir. I'd be happier with half that number, but I fear we'd take too many casualties. Once we're inside the gates, we'll split up into two columns, one to the right and one to the left. I'll send six men to break into the armory and get weapons to carry down to the dungeon, where another six men will be breaking in and releasing the prisoners. I expect it to be all over, Colonel, half an hour after the artillery begins its barrage."

The colonel's voice was heavy: "But you realize you'll be up against fifteen hundred Sepoys? They're not mountain savages, you know, armed with homemade weapons. They're highly trained fighting men, disciplined and competent, because that's the way we made them."

"Precisely," the major said. "*We* trained them. And the

teacher is invariably more competent than his pupils."

Colonel Sir Bryan Dawson made up his mind. He got to his feet and said shortly: "Then go to it, John. And good luck."

It was only one hour later that the column thundered through the narrow gorge that cut the mountain two miles from Vellore. In the lead, Major Entwhistle rode his favorite mare, a fine chestnut standing nearly seventeen hands; her name was Khuruba, which meant amber in Hindustani and perfectly described her gleaming coat. Behind him, drawn by six draft horses each, were the two twelve-pounder cannons carried on six-wheel limbers. In the storage under the driver's box of each, there were twenty-four cannon balls, each fastened to its own four-pound cloth bag of powder, so that charge and missile could be slipped together down the barrel and rammed home for firing.

Behind the guns, the Dragoons rode at the walk in two files, with the officers beside them and the scouts out on the flanks. They carried lances and sabers, and the sergeants and officers wore revolvers and their swords.

The gorge, cut by a once-violent river, soon dwindled to a shallow gully only six feet or so deep and scarcely wide enough to permit the passage of the gun carriages. Here the order was given to dismount and lead the horses. Movement now would be slow, careful, and quiet; before proceeding, the men bound their horses' hooves in rags. And in a little while, they had gone as far as they safely could if they were to avoid detection. A halt was called, and by word of mouth the major called the officers and the senior sergeants to him.

He said quietly: "Gentlemen, we are roughly half a mile from the main gates of the fortress. As we all know, the area within two hundred yards of the walls is kept clear, the ground beyond that is well grassed, but it affords very little cover. It is my intention to follow this gully for another four hundred yards, at which point we will be directly between the sun, when it rises, and the fortress itself. We will then be some six hundred and fifty yards from the gates, not an unacceptable distance for a charge if our timing is correct and the sun is behind us. Mr. O'Brien."

"Sir." Lieutenant Brendan O'Brien, twenty-three years old, was the Gunnery Officer, and the major said quietly: "I don't want the draft horses out in the open. They make too much bloody noise. That means that from here, the carriages have to be manhandled, silently and under cover of darkness, to within two hundred yards. There is a heavy clump of bamboo right at the edge of the cleared area, a little to the south of the position from which we begin the charge. That's where you'll be. Use the cover to its best possible advantage. You'll need another twenty men to handle the guns. Sergeant Bream will give them to you."

"Sir. And the order to open fire?"

The major smiled in the darkness. "The Sepoys themselves will give you the order, Mr. O'Brien. When they discover you, as they will when the sun comes up, they will undoubtedly direct rifle fire at you from the walls, possibly four-pounder fire as well. The moment they start firing, that will be your signal to begin your barrage. And if the sun has come over the horizon by then, you can count me a very satisfied man. Six rounds from each gun, I believe, will be sufficient to make firewood of those gates, but keep up the barrage until they are utterly demolished. Now, the moment your work is completed, watch for us. Leave two men to guard the guns, and get the rest of them out there at the gallop behind us. They can follow us into the fortress. Is that clear, Mr. O'Brien?"

"Yes, sir. Perfectly clear."

By the time the first thin red sliver appeared low on the

dawn horizon, the guns were in position under the cover of the bamboo. Two hundred yards away, the Dragoons were standing to their horses in the gully, well concealed as the red changed to gold, and the sky, with that peculiar Indian intensity, began to lighten.

And when the first sporadic shots rang out from the fortress walls, the major looked at the tip of the blinding sun as it slowly climbed up, and he said softly: "Perfect." He drew his saber and tested its blade on his thumbnail; it was razor sharp. Then the cannon fire rang out, and he counted the rounds, each following on the last with admirable speed, no more than forty seconds for the twelve-shot barrage. Sunlight was gilding the upper part of the stone walls now and creeping quickly down to its base. He saw that the gates had indeed been splintered into matchsticks and that beyond them a hundred or more Sepoys were desperately rolling wagons up to fill the breach, just as they had been trained to do. The firing from the walls was settling down now into steady, ordered volleys. The major swung into the saddle, heard the shouted order from Captain Quartermaine, officer commanding Number Seven Troop, saw the men settling their lances. He called out: "We canter, Captain, for the first one hundred yards."

"Yes, sir!"

Captain Quartermaine was the finest horseman in the Arcot garrison. He was thirty-one years old, brawny, agile, bushily moustached, and a terrible man with the ladies. He fell in on the flank of the twin column, raised his saber high, and looked at the major. The major was shielding his eyes against the great golden ball of the sun, its nether tip clearing the horizon now. He turned back and said quietly: "Now, I think, Captain Quartermaine."

The captain raised his voice: "Seventh Dragoons . . . at the canter . . . for-*ward!*"

The sound of the hooves on the hard sand was a comforting and even a friendly sound, as though the riders were out for a morning canter over the English moors.

As they came to within five hundred yards of the walls, Quartermaine raised his sword high and shouted out the final order: "Seventh Dragoons . . . at the gallop . . . for-*ward!*"

Now the sound of the hooves lost its gentle aspect and settled into a rhythmic pounding. The pennants were flying, the red, white, and blue flag held proudly aloft, the bugler (carried away by his own exuberance) sounding the charge which had already been ordered. The men, well trained, were riding easily, turning in their saddles from time to time to check their positions, giving the equally well-trained horses their head; the thunder of the charge was hypnotic as the distance rapidly closed. For a while, the shooting from the walls had stopped; the Sepoys were waiting, now, for the riders to come within better range of their muskets. And at a hundred and fifty yards it began again, an ordered volley, followed by another and another, from muzzle-loading rifles that could fire no more than three or sometimes four rounds in a minute.

A few men, hit, fell from their saddles. But now the columns were pouring through the gateways, jumping the piled-up wagons, swords and lances flashing. Some circled the huge courtyard, seeking targets of opportunity; some slipped from their saddles and ran up the steep stone steps to the walls (some, showing off, were racing their horses up them).

The sounds of the battle were intense. The screaming of dying men, the awful sibilation of steel slicing into flesh, the constant firing of the rifles, a revolver shot here and there, the excited shouting of the combatants:

"*Behind you, Harry . . .!*"

"*Ten men to the tower there, Number Two Squad . . . !*"

"*Get that damned door open, you men . . . !*"

"*All right, I've got him. . . . Watch out to your right . . . !*"

"No, you don't, you savage . . . !"

"Your lance, Charlie, right above you, watch out . . .!"

For ten minutes the battle raged over the walls, across the compound, into the storerooms and offices. A fire was raging around one of the smaller buildings, and a wounded dragoon, the blood pumping out of his neck, was lifting a Sepoy over his head and hurling him into the flames.

Major Entwhistle sat his horse, alone, in the middle of the square, using his sword from time to time almost casually; a musket ball had embedded itself in his thigh, and another had creased his left forearm. The fine red mare, Khuruba, was prancing under him, smelling the sour stench of blood.

There was no time even to release the prisoners before white shreds of cloth were waving everywhere; and in less than fifteen minutes it was all over.

Four hundred of the rebellious Sepoys had been killed, and nearly three hundred and eighty of them suffered wounds of varying severities. The remainder were rounded up and placed under guard, squatting on the ground like peasants and knowing that the honorable profession of the military would now be denied to them forever.

By nine o'clock in the morning, the garrison carpenters were already at work fashioning new gates of heavy teak and strap iron; the dead were being counted and set out for burial; the wounded filled the little hospital and its broad green compound; and Major John Entwhistle, leaving his entire force behind him to assist in the reestablishment of order, was riding hard back to Arcot to report that the job was done.

He had suffered casualties. Eight men had been killed, including Lieutenant O'Brien. Forty-one men had been wounded, most of them with knives in hand-to-hand combat.

But Vellore, was secure once more; and such exploits quickly became legends, to be recounted in one military garrison or another across the state of Madras—and in the course of time, across the whole of the British Empire as well.

The legend would grow with constant retelling; and the name of Major John Hayes Entwhistle would not quickly be forgotten.

Chapter Two

Seven thousand miles away, in London, England, news of Major John Entwhistle's historic little feat of arms would not arrive for more than seven weeks.

But there were other victories of empire to be celebrated, not the least of which was the recent seizure, in South Africa, of Holland's Cape of Good Hope. Sir David Baird, England's commander in South Africa, had achieved this extraordinary victory with fewer regiments than might have been thought necessary merely to hold the coastline.

In the upper-class circles of England's military establishment, it was an occasion for great jubilation; and from the sheltered confines of the Empire Officers' Club, the invitations went out.

In the Small Library of her beautiful Curzon Street house, Amanda Elizabeth Genevieve Entwhistle picked up the vellum card and read it again for the benefit of her eighteen-year-old son Peter:

> *The President of the Empire Officers' Club Presents his Compliments to Mrs. John Entwhistle, and is pleased and Honored to Request her Gracious Presence, together with that of her Honbl. Escort, to a Dinner to be held in the*

*Robert, Baron Clive Chamber of the Club's Premises at
One Hundred and Four St. James Street, London, Com-
mencing at Eight o'clock in the evening of Saturday May
the Fifteenth in this year of Our Lord 1806, to Honor
General Sir David Baird and his recent Remarkable and
Valorous Achievements in South Africa, which have re-
stored Two Hundred and Seventy-Eight Thousand Square
Miles of the Globe to the Benevolence of British Rule.
Decorations will be Worn*

She said, delighted: "It will be a simply marvelous party!
And I have splendid news for you. You will be my escort."

Peter stared at her. "Oh, Mother! No!"

"Yes," she said firmly.

She was not a woman who could easily be denied. At the
age of thirty-nine, she was already a matriarch, holding together a family of four children whose father came home from
India only once in every three years. Her strength of character
was very great, and her intellectual capacity was high. She was
the kind of woman people listened to—though sometimes with
a kind of bewilderment at the radical idea that a woman
should have something to say that might be worth paying
attention to.

Physically, Amanda was a creature of quite startling
beauty. She had preserved, by careful devotion to the task, not
only the peaches-and-cream complexion of her skin and the
voluptuousness of her figure, but also her youth and her desir-
ability. She was not, by any means, promiscuous; but as an
"Indian Army widow," she had perhaps *slipped* once or twice,
though very discreetly. And she was greatly devoted to her
absent husband, largely because the major represented the
British raj at its best; it was not a quality lightly to be
dismissed.

Peter sighed. "It will be nothing but a lot of pompous
asses," he grumbled, "interminably holding forth on empire.
I'll hate every minute of it."

Amanda peered at herself in the mirror over the fireplace, studying her coiffure intently, wondering if her new bedchamber maid was really as competent as she was supposed to be; the glorious dark auburn hair hung down in ringlets over the bare shoulders of her empire gown. She said tartly: "Well, if you make up your mind that you're going to hate it, you probably will. Why don't you decide, instead, that you'll enjoy it? You might find it very, very satisfying. The dinner, undoubtedly, will be excellent, the wines well chosen, and there'll be a number of attractive young ladies there whose company you might find stimulating in the extreme."

"Ah . . ."

"So that's settled, then."

But Peter said, the slightest edge to his voice: "Though I've never understood why it should be that all your friends seem to have such intolerable daughters. I can't, offhand, think of a single one of them who's capable of arousing a virile man's passions to the satisfying peaks of perversity."

Amanda was shocked. "Peter! What a dreadful thing to say!"

Motionless and very regal, she looked at his reflection in the mirror and said coldly: "I suspect that when you speak of my friends' daughters, you really mean women of our own class. And if I'm right, then it's greatly to be deplored."

Somewhat to her astonishment, he was laughing suddenly. He said, making a joke of it: "As always, Mother, you're absolutely right. Call it one of my very few weaknesses that I really prefer women without quite so much pretension. . . . And as for the dinner, yes, I'll be your Honorable Escort. Though I can't think why you don't go with Captain Reynolds. They'll all be expecting you to arrive on his arm anyway."

Amanda looked at herself in the mirror again, set the ringlets of her hair just so, and said quietly: "That is precisely why I prefer to walk into the Great Hall on the arm of my son."

He was conscious of her hurt, and he went to her and put his arms around her and kissed her lightly on the cheek. He said: "I'm sorry, Mother. I didn't really mean that."

She was quite composed now. "Never listen to gossip, Peter," she said. "It does *no one* credit. It can sometimes do great harm." She embraced him warmly and held him at arm's length to smile at him, a tall and somewhat awkward young man of very strong opinions, always absolutely sure that everything he believed in was *ipso facto* true. She said: "And why don't you go and change. It's nearly dinnertime."

"Yes, I'll do that."

He went to the door and turned back, and he said quietly: "You're a wonderful woman, Mother. You'll never know how much I love you."

She was standing with her head a little to one side, her eyes shining, a woman of exquisite loveliness. She said: "And I love you too, my darling. I'm so very proud of you. . . ."

Suddenly his thin, ascetic face was wreathed in smiles. *"Proud of me?"* he echoed. "Mother! You know damn well that you hate everything I believe in!"

Amanda laughed, a laugh of genuine amusement. "Of course I do!" she said, "and it's only right that I should. You're a monster! Now go and change. I won't have dinner kept waiting."

He did not move. "You really think there'll be some attractive young ladies there?"

"I'm sure of it, Peter."

"Name me a name."

"Oh. So that's the mood you're in! Well, both of Colonel Antrim's daughters will be there, certainly."

"I'm sure of it. Looking for husbands, as always."

"And Alice St. John . . ."

"She looks like a horse."

"Peter!"

"Not even a racehorse. A dray."

He held her eyes again and said deliberately: "Alice St. John is a stuck-up *prig*! And the Antrim girls expect everyone who wasn't well born to get on his knees before daring to speak to them. It's not a philosophy I relish. The groundlings are people too, you know! And it's all very simple: I just want them to enjoy the kind of human dignity they're not always allowed."

Amanda said carefully: "Peter, I hope I've always taught you that the lower classes should invariably be treated almost as if they were our equals." She patted the ringlets into place and murmured: "Though never, of course, as if *we* were *theirs*."

Peter had heard the thought enunciated before, and he hated it.

Out of the blue, he said glumly: "Do you remember Farnham, Mother?"

She frowned, drawing those marvelous eyebrows together. "Farnham? Of course I do, darling. She was one of our kitchen maids. But you were only ten years old when she had her accident. You still remember her?"

"I remember her, Mother. . . ."

It had left an indelible impression on him; and yes, he had just celebrated his tenth birthday.

With the inherent mischief of his age, he'd been climbing up the kitchen ladder to slice off some of the sausage hanging over the stove for smoking, to test the blade of the fine pocket knife his father had given him for his birthday. ("A young man," John had said sternly, "must always have a good knife in his pocket.")

The ladder had fallen, and he had fallen with it quite safely to the floor; but the wooden rungs had caught the handle of the big iron pot and by a strange set of consequences had splashed its boiling oil up into the face of the tweeny who had run to his assistance; to this day, he could still hear her screams ringing in his ears.

He remembered how he had crouched over her thrashing body, his own hysterics almost worse than hers, wondering why the kitchen should be so empty of staff at this crucial moment. He'd found one of the footmen, who had taken over in great competence.

Above all, he remembered her slurred words to him as she sat, later, on one of the wooden kitchen chairs, her dreadfully burned face swathed in wet rags, her thin belly filled with the analgesic brandy the butler had filled her with. She had even reached out, in a kind of stupor, to clasp his hand, wetly whispering: "It ain't that bad, Master Peter, truly it ain't. And the likes of you, sir, honestly don't 'ave to fuss over the likes of me . . ."

And then the fatal words: "After all, young sir, I'm only a skivvy."

Only a servant; he'd never forget it.

From somewhere below stairs, the gong sounded to announce that dinner would soon be ready for serving.

"We took exceptional care of Farnham," Amanda said a trifle testily. "We retired her on a pension, half her wages. She has more money coming in every month, very regularly, than any woman of her class could ever hope or expect to receive. I'm not heartless, darling."

"A beautiful young girl disfigured for life . . ."

"Peter! She's well cared for! And I honestly don't understand how poor Farnham crept into this discussion! The only question at the moment is . . . will you escort me to the Empire Officers' Club dinner willingly, or not? Because if you don't want to, I swear I'll *drag* you there, screaming."

He was a young man of unpredictable moods, and he laughed suddenly: "All right, then. I will! If only for the satis-

faction of knowing that the only truly beautiful woman there
. . . is my mother."

And then the laughter had gone as quickly as it had come,
and he said seriously: "A child's memories are very persuasive,
aren't they? But I remember her so vividly. . . ."

"Remember whom, darling?" The curls were still not
right.

"Farnham, Mother! Was she really as lovely as I imagined
her to be? Or is it just a childhood recollection?"

"That's exactly what it is," Amanda said, "a recollection
somewhat distorted, as most of your thinking seems to be
these days. Now go and change, for heaven's sake. The gong
has sounded, and I won't have dinner kept waiting."

"Yes, Mother."

When he was gone, Amanda sighed and looked at the
splendid portraits that hung on the library walls, moving
slowly from one to another, thirty-seven in all, a visual history
of the family that reached back to the fifteenth century. The
last rays of the pale evening sun were slanting through the
casement windows, their old-rose velour curtains tied back
now with gilded cords; they were picked up by the polished
oak of the library shelves and fell across the latest of the portraits, that of then Lieutenant John Entwhistle, resplendent in
his dress blues, painted by no less a luminary than Sir Joshua
Reynolds himself.

She sat down at the little escritoire to write her beloved
husband a letter.

The days slipped by, and the dinner at the Empire Officers' Club was upon them.

Amanda dressed for the occasion in a fine French-inspired
gown of green silk, very tight at the waist and flouncing out
over her seven petticoats, decorated with blue forget-me-nots

and purple violets made from tulle, with frills of pale pink organdy along the very low décolleté which was meant to show off her splendid bust and succeeded in doing so admirably.

There were more than seventy guests in the anteroom to the Robert Clive Chamber, and she paused at the door, conscious that many enviable eyes were on her, knowing that she looked absolutely at her best this night. The majordomo tapped his staff on the floor three times and announced in sonorous tones: "Mrs. John Entwhistle and Mr. Peter Entwhistle."

General Lord Balcombe, the seventh duke of that title, was waiting to receive them, leaning heavily on his cane, a very dignified old gentleman who was president of the club. His sideburns and his hair had been heavily oiled, the skin of his face was yellow parchment, and his eyes were deeply sunk in sockets of exaggerated bas-relief. He said, coughing rheumatically: "A great pleasure, ma'am, and an honor too." He turned his myopic eyes on Peter, and Amanda said: "My son, General, Peter Entwhistle."

"Ah, yes, of course," His Grace said. He shook hands and mumbled: "Your father, sir, I know him well, serving now . . . where is it? Ah, yes, in Africa, with that idiot David Baird, never really understood how he got to be a general, no sense of military tactics at all. But I'm sure your father, sir, Henry, er, yes, Henry Entwhistle, I believe, will be an invaluable aide to him. Keep him on the right path, don't you know. Yes."

"My father, Your Grace," Peter said clearly, "is presently serving in the state of Madras, in India. And his name, sir, is John, not Henry."

"Of course, of course, and how thoughtful of you to remind me. Then he's with Bryan Dawson, isn't he? Bloody place called, what is it, Arcot? Spent some time there meself, a dreadful place." His eyes, floating in their sockets, were on

Amanda's breasts, and he said, sighing: "I was a lot younger, then. Well . . . I promise you both a fine old time tonight. We've got a new wine in from Portugal. The club's buying into the winery."

The majordomo was hammering the floor again with his staff, and the resonant tones rang out: "General Lord Percy Stanford and Lady Daphne Stanford . . ." Amanda excused herself, and Peter said mildly, looking around him at the immaculate uniforms and splendid gowns: "I can't help thinking, Mother, that you're going to have a perfectly wondeful evening. And that I am going to be bored stiff."

"Oh, nonsense!" Amanda said. She was swept away almost at once on the arm of a young cavalry officer, and Peter accepted a glass of champagne from a passing waiter and sat on one of the huge, red-upholstered, high-backed oak chairs to sip it moodily and wonder why almost every stalwart and highly polished officer he studied seemed to be twirling the ends of his moustache, why almost all the young ladies ("attractive," his mother had called them, and "stimulating") seemed to . . . *simper* when they were spoken to.

A lone piper from one of the Scottish regiments was playing his plaintive pibrochs for them, half hidden up on the gallery high by the vaulted ceiling among the carved wooden buttresses, from which regimental flags were draped. There were pikes and swords and lances and ancient muskets everywhere. And when at last they all followed the general into the chamber for dinner, they found it to be quite spectacular.

The guests were seated at a single mass of tables placed in a quadrangle, which was meant to be symbolic of the famous "British Square"—historically so efficient against the enraged onslaughts of the savages.

There was onion soup, followed by an excellent salad of Dungeness crab, cos lettuce, watercress, tomatoes, and pickled beetroot. Then there was sole with a sauce of shallots, parsley

and anchovy, and a truly magnificent mutton curry, the recipe
for which had been brought home from Madras, India, by no
less a personage than the young Arthur Wellesley, soon to be
named Duke of Wellington and himself a gourmet of some
note. There were great glass bowls of trifle set out on the table,
and then huge plates of cheeses—single and double Gloucester,
Cheddar, Cheshire, Dunlop from Scotland, and six huge, nap-
kin-wrapped Stiltons, their centers already scooped out and
filled with port wine.

When the long meal was over, there was the single mandatory toast to the ladies—the intimation that it was time for
them to retire and await the later company of the gentlemen.

Now the drinking began in earnest. Toast after toast was
drunk as the port was passed around; to Robert Clive, who
had conquered India by the purest happenstance; to Sir David
Baird, to the Marquis Wellesley, to Lord Cornwallis and Lord
Minto, to Major Lawrence, and to all the other heroes of the
empire. . . .

By the fourteenth toast, Peter Entwhistle was *drunk*, there
could be no denying it. He hung on stubbornly to the rem-
nants of his sobriety and said to his neighbor at the table: "For
a man, sir, who does not . . . not habitually drink more than
. . . more than a glass or two of wine a week, the miserable
business of . . . of toasting all our heroes is . . . is a matter of
some concern."

The neighbor was the Earl of Redhill, an elderly colonel
of Lancers. He turned his very cold eyes on Peter and said:
"The *miserable* business, sir?"

"Miserable, Colonel, to those of us who . . . who are not
accustomed to . . . to an . . . an excess of wine that almost
surpasses the . . . the excess of our adulation for these . . . these
paragons of English virtue. And each of the names we are . . .
is 'honoring' the word? Each of them represents . . . how many
unfortunates slaughtered for their own personal glory?"

There was the tiniest silence, and then the colonel said: "I gather, sir, that you are one of the Entwhistles? Peter Entwhistle, is it not?"

"At your service, sir."

"And yet . . . it seems that you are not a military man. I find that very strange, sir. I would have expected you to be up at Sandhurst."

"No, Colonel, I am *not*, as you perceive, a military man."

The little silence again. And then those hard eyes boring: "Would it be presumptuous of me, sir, to ask the reason for your deviation from a path set down for you by very many illustrious forebears?"

The wine was flowing fast in his veins, and Peter said truculently: "I don't think it's any of your damned business, Colonel."

Three, four, five, or six chairs away, heads were turning toward an incipient confrontation, and in this little section, all other talk had stopped.

The colonel said, tight with an anger he had no wish to suppress: "I am a military historian, Mr. Entwhistle. I know of your father, by excellent repute, of your grandfather, Sir Richard Hayes Entwhistle. . . . I could recite the names of your family, soldiers all of them, back to the fifteenth century. You are aware, I am sure, that in the year 1415, one of your progenitors was a renowned Commander of Archers at the Battle of Agincourt?"

Peter drained his glass and watched it being refilled at once. He turned back to Redhill and said: "There is a portrait of him, sir, in the Small Library of our Curzon Street house, one of very many soldierly portraits. And though I am no historian, I know the particulars of Agincourt well enough. With the loss of one hundred and twenty men-at-arms, we slew five thousand of the French. Most of them were prisoners, who were slaughtered because King Henry had not enough men to guard them. That renowned commander, as you call him, my ancestor, was the man who supervised the massacre."

The colonel was raising his voice; he wanted others to hear this. He said coldly: "I am convinced, sir, that I detect a certain sympathy for the French, who are our natural enemies. Are you then also sympathetic to Napoleon's cause? Are you one of England's damned Napoleonic faction?"

Peter said firmly: "I belong to no *faction*, sir. I do not need the company of others to convince me of the truth of my philosophies. I do, however, believe that a Europe under Napoleon is preferable to an Europe governed either by . . . by mobs or by monarchs."

"*What?*" The colonel's choler was apoplectic. "You dare to defend France? *Here?*"

"I argue for peace, Colonel," Peter said stubbornly. "Nothing more, nothing less. Dialogue is always more sensible than battle."

The voice was rising higher; more heads were turning. "And our own monarch, *Mr.* Entwhistle? The *only* king in Europe who is prepared to stand alone against Napoleon? What do you think of him?"

"I greatly admire him, sir. Poor Farmer George is above all a family man, a kind and gentle man. Though perhaps I should reserve the phrase 'above all' for another of his admirable qualifications. And that is—that he is not a soldier."

The colonel rose to his feet, and he shouted angrily: "Waiter!"

One of the soldier-servants came running, and the colonel said, controlling himself now: "Give me a glove, fellow."

"Yes, sir." Perplexed, the waiter stripped off his white cotton glove and held it out, and Colonel the Earl of Redhill took it and drew it twice across Peter's face. Now almost half of the assembled guests were listening, wondering, watching him. He tossed the glove down on the table and said contemptuously: "Well? I await your reply, sir."

Peter, white-faced, answered him coldly: "I do not approve of dueling, Colonel. I will not fight you."

"You will not . . . Must I insult you more, Entwhistle?"

"It would do no good, sir. I will *not* fight you."

"Coward!"

"Yes. By your standards, I am perhaps a coward. I do not
accept those standards."

"*Coward!*" The harsh voice rang out now, and the general
was cupping a hand to his ear.

Peter too was on his feet, swaying only slightly, the
drunkenness forced away by his anger. He said, his voice very
tight and constrained: "You have chosen, Colonel, to offer a
physical duel as the solution to an intellectual dispute. I suggest this is foolishness."

He was conscious of the staring eyes around him. Some of
them were shocked, some horrified, and some frankly delighted at the liveliness of the occasion, and he said quietly: "I
am opposed to everything you stand for, sir, and if you wish to
convince me of your opinions, there are better ways than
pistols at twenty paces. But that's the essence of military philosophy, is it not? Bow to the flag, or we'll slice you open with
a saber?"

The earl tried no longer to control his fury. His face was
flushed and his eyes were goggling. "You *dare* to lecture me,
sir? A mere whippersnapper still in school . . . ?"

At the far end of the table, the general, now had become
half aware of what was happening. He said, leaning to his
neighbor: "Good God! Did I hear a challenge?"

The neighbor was one Captain Reynolds of the Cold-
stream Guards, and he answered: "Yes, General, Redhill has
challenged Peter Entwhistle to a duel. And the young man has
refused it."

"In God's name! A *duel*, you say? On what grounds? A
lady, no doubt . . ."

"No, sir." Reynolds, a very worried young man now, shook his head. "I fear it is far worse than that, sir. From what I could gather, Entwhistle has offered insult not only to the military, but to His Majesty as well. *Pro-French* insult, it seems."

The general was speechless. Reynolds rose quickly to his feet and said urgently: "But by your leave, sir, there is something I must do at once. . . ."

"Yes, yes, of course, dear boy. My God, a duel! If Redhill wants me for a second, tell him . . . tell him I will happily oblige. Fascinating thing to watch, a duel. . . ."

Reynolds had already left him.

He went to the Blue Room, where the servants were preparing the coffee and liqueurs, and he knocked hesitantly on the door that gave on to the ladies' lounge, and waited, and knocked again even when someone called out, "Come in."

The door was opened at last by a pretty young girl with staring brown eyes, wondering at this intrusion on female sanctity, and he said apologetically: "Your pardon, mistress. But if I could speak with Amanda Entwhistle? It is a matter of some importance."

Those highly amused eyes were mocking him. "Amanda? Yes, she's here. Why don't you come in, Captain?"

"I would prefer not to, mistress," he said awkwardly. "If she could perhaps step outside for a moment . . . ?"

"A dashing captain, afraid of twenty or thirty ladies? Is that the case?" She was laughing at him, and Reynolds said desperately: "Mistress, it *is* a matter of great import."

She turned her head and called: "Amanda, darling! That gorgeous Captain Reynolds has come to claim you. And he's not much of a lover, is he? He won't even fight his way in here."

"Captain Reynolds?"

Amanda was hurrying to the doorway, surprised rather

than alarmed. She whispered, chiding him: "Edward, how could you? You really must *not* be seen with me! Darling, it's so terribly indiscreet."

He interrupted her, conscious of the young girl's rapt attention. "Amanda, we have to talk *now*. Peter is in the direst trouble. That idiot Redhill has just challenged him to a duel."

Her face was suddenly very white. "Oh, my God! Whatever for?"

"A stupidity," he said impatiently, "and Peter has refused him. That's bad enough, but there's far worse to follow. Come. The Blue Room is empty now, and we must talk."

"All right."

Amanda settled her dress just so as they sat together on one of the leather sofas and he said helplessly: "I don't know what you can do, Amanda, but you have to do *something*! There's no one else who can handle that rambunctious young man. And you have to do it *now!*"

She was pulling herself together by an effort of will. "I can and will do *nothing* until I know *everything*. So tell me, Edward, as quickly but as fully as you can, how it all came about, how it began, how it ended."

"I will. From where I was sitting, I couldn't hear all of it, but by George, everyone within earshot was positively straining. Even the general heard part of it."

She was very calm now. "And what did Peter say, exactly?"

He ran a worried hand through his tightly curled brown hair. "He was holding forth like—forgive me, Amanda, but I must say it, like the immature young schoolboy he is. It seemed to me, as it obviously seemed to Redhill, that he insulted the King. . . ."

"Oh, God, no! He would never do that, Edward, *never!* He greatly admires Farmer George."

"I don't know. It was a trifle oblique. Whether Redhill took it as an insult to His Majesty, or to himself personally, I don't know, and frankly, it matters little. He also spoke out in favor of Napoleon . . . *that* I heard very clearly."

Her voice was tight with anger. "In this . . . this inner sanctum of the military establishment?"

"Yes."

"And so . . . Redhill challenged him?"

"Fellow took a glove from a *waiter*, can you believe it? And struck him across the face with it."

"Oh, God! The general saw this?"

"The general is as blind as a bat, Amanda. But in matters of military honor . . . yes, he saw it."

There was a little moment of silence, and then Amanda rose to her feet. She said clearly: "Do not come with me, Edward. I am about to make a spectacle of myself."

She swept imperiously out of the room, went to the Clive Chamber, and stood there in the doorway, looking across the great table and waiting as all eyes turned to her.

A *woman?* Encroaching on the sacrosanct after-dinner hour? Even the waiters were appalled.

Peter was still on his feet, and his voice was raised in anger, filling the room. He was saying furiously: ". . . and we are expected to subscribe to the philosophy that the only way to change the mind of a humble native who may not agree with what we say is to cut off his head, and if I live to be a hundred I will never believe that! If we had any sense at all of what is right, we'd get out of India, get out of Africa, let the local peoples decide their own destinies! The whole history of empire is filled with our arrogance."

In the awful silence, he picked up his glass of port and drained it, he raised his voice and shouted, hoping desperately that *somebody* would listen to him: "The Earl of Redhill has challenged me to a duel. And what? Will you all gather at dawn in the nearest glade to watch me take a pistol shot in my chest just because my opinions are not yours? Will you watch me bleed to death just because I disagree with your philosophies? This is insanity, and I'll have no part of it, I refuse to give you—"

He broke off, conscious that he was no longer the center of attention. He saw Amanda standing there, and in the awful, expectant silence, the Earl of Redhill said coldly: "Your mother has come, child, to spank your bloody bottom and take you home. And we will be well rid of you."

He wanted to speak to Amanda and drive home the insult, even though he knew her to be a woman of quality; but after the ladies had left the table, protocol would not permit the mention of a lady's name in the mess; heads had rolled for lesser contraventions of accepted military behavior.

Amanda said, her voice very low and steady: "I crave your indulgence, General, for an intrusion that must seem unwarranted. But I felt that my coming here was necessary, if only to ask your pardon for my son's disgraceful sentiments."

The general, not quite sure what that protocol called for now, had risen to his feet, and all the other officers had followed suit; they stood there, a jury. He said, mumbling: "You will agree, ma'am, that the presence of a lady in the mess after dinner is disconcertin', to say the least. Indeed, in the long and honorable history of the Officers' Club, I daresay it's never happened before. And I am quite at a loss."

Amanda's head was tilted up in that little gesture of imperiousness she sometimes affected. She said quietly: "And I apologize for it, General."

"Yes, yes, of course. Not quite sure what I'm supposed to do about it, no precedent, y'know. But the matter in hand . . ." He was aware of all those eyes staring at him and tried to steel himself by recalling those long-gone days when he was a general in more than name; his years were very heavy on him now. He said: "That is to say, the matter of your son, ma'am. The presence of a young man of military age in civilian clothes at a reception of this nature is, of course, acceptable. I can think of a dozen reasons for a young man *not* being in one of the services. Er, well, one or two at least. Yes. But his apparent aversion to military service seems to be only part of the difficulty we now find ourselves in. A very . . . *painful* difficulty, I might say."

His voice was quavering, the voice of a tired and very old man.

He left his place at the table and walked steadily to her, and took both her hands in his and said gently: "Your husband, ma'am . . . his father, his grandfather, and many others before him have served our country well. We are all proud of the Entwhistle name, of the family record. I am sure that you are aware, there's a bad apple in even the best of the barrels. I am equally sure that this remarkable young man has said his piece and would wish to leave us now."

Amanda was about to answer him but he raised a white, skeletal hand before she could frame the words. "But no opprobrium attaches to you, ma'am, and it is my fervent hope that you yourself will stay. We are about to drink His Majesty's health, and shortly after that we will all join the ladies in the Blue Room." He was wheezing, coughing rheumatically. "I will be personally pained, ma'am, if you choose not to be among them."

"I thank you for your kindness, General. . . ." Amanda turned her eyes, cold and hard now, on her son, and said clearly: "Go home, Peter. You are no longer welcome here." She turned on her heel and swept away.

Peter could not control his emotions. Trembling, he strode away from the table, opened the first door he came to, and slammed it shut behind him.

The officers were taking their seats again, in ones and twos, and the buzz of excited talk was quickly stifled; the general stood and raised his glass and said: "Gentlemen, His Majesty the King!"

* * *

The corridor in which Peter found himself was narrow and dimly lit, a taper in its glass bowl only every twenty paces or so. He threw open another door and found himself in one of the kitchens, where a dozen serving maids were at their work washing the dishes. Four or five husky young men were carrying more in from the chamber. The open grates of the huge iron stove that ran down one length of wall were flaming brightly in reds and golds, and there was the smell of cooking everywhere; it was a friendly place to be. Great copper pots hung on the walls, with long strings of Spanish onions and a dozen hams suspended over the stove.

Peter closed the door behind him and leaned into it, looking over the people there and wondering why they all seemed to be staring at him. A young girl said anxiously: "Are you all right, sir?"

She was quite pretty and very buxom, dressed in a long gray woolen skirt and a cotton blouse loosely tied with a length of black ribbon at her full white breasts; there were wooden clogs on her feet. Her eyes were dark and bright, and she was frowning, wondering about him.

He nodded. "Yes, I thank you. I am all right."

"If you're looking for the latrine, sir, it's out be'ind the 'all."

"No. No, I don't quite know what I am looking for. For solitude, perhaps."

"Ah . . . we all need that once in a while, don't we, sir? But you won't find it 'ere." She was laughing now, a very sweet young child, and he said: "What is your name, girl?"

"My *name*, sir?" The question seemed to puzzle her, but she giggled suddenly. "We don't really 'ave names 'ere, sir, it's just a matter of: '*you there* . . .' But my name's Ivy, sir."

"Well, Ivy, I trust that you are not as unhappy this night as I am."

"Un'appy? Well, no, sir. I don't 'ave nothin' to be un'appy about. I does me work, I gets me four shillin's an' tuppence a week. . . . I'm 'appy."

"Four shillings and tuppence? Good God, that's not very much, is it?"

She was more serious now and even a little frightened; it seemed to her that she was being invited to *complain*, and a complaint could mean instant dismissal. She said quickly: "It's enough, sir. I mean, I'm only a skivvy, like, and I get two meals a day, me dinner and supper before I go 'ome. I mean, it's food that costs so much these days, ennit?"

Only a skivvy . . . Where had he heard that comment before?

He sighed. "I still don't know how you manage. And that's something I really ought to know about, isn't it? How the lower classes can stretch four shillings and tuppence a week into an adequate subsistence? I'd have you know it distresses me, Ivy."

A middle-aged matron across the room called out: "You there! Get on with your work!" The young girl looked at her hesitantly, and back to Peter, and wasn't at all sure what to do now, and to her surprise he dragged up a chair to the long scrubbed oak table and sat down. He said: "And where would home be? Don't you have quarters here in the club?"

"Oh, no, sir. I got me own place on 'Erbal 'Ill."

"Herbal Hill? I don't think I know it."

"Off Clerkenwell Road, sir, just a short street with four 'ouses in it. I got a basement room in one of 'em."

"And may I say, Ivy? . . . You're very pretty."

She was blushing, and she pushed a lock of untidy hair back into its place under her bonnet. "I am? Well, thank you, sir."

"Yes, indeed. No resemblance to a horse at all."

She was out of her depth, and she said, stammering: "I

don't think . . . I don't think I understand you, sir."

"I'm quite sure of it," Peter said cheerfully. "The upper classes have a very recondite sense of humor. One might almost call it . . . unconscious humor."

She blinked at him for a moment and said at last: "I'm trying to understand what you're talking about, sir. Really I am . . ."

She broke off as the matron approached them and scuttled off quickly to be about her business. The matron said sternly: "I don't know why you're here, sir, but you're not supposed to be, you know."

Peter's spirits were returning fast. He said amiably: "I'm quite sure I'm not. . . . But I had a bit of a set-to at the dinner, and I flatter myself that I may have upset some of their ridiculous notions." He thought about it for a moment and said at last, glumly: "No, that's not true. The end of the world won't change their ideas."

He tried to focus his eyes on the matron, a plump, untidy woman. "Tell me, ma'am, do *you* believe in all this damned nonsense?"

She was very uneasy. "What nonsense would that be, sir?"

"Do you personally believe," Peter said, "that the British should lord it over half the known world?"

"Well, sir," she said (a woman of some spirit), "whether I believe we should or not . . . I mean we *do*, don't we? It's the will of God, sir, and we can't argue with the will of God."

"I wish I could be so sure about that. I find I cannot."

Suddenly the work was beginning again with renewed vigor. Most of the servants had left their chores and were listening to him, wondering what could have happened out there, but now, inexplicably, everyone was very busy.

Peter turned and saw a very dignified old man moving across the kitchen, tall and gray-haired, and very, very thin. He

was dressed in a butler's uniform—a black frock coat not un-
like those the gentry wore, with a high starched collar and a
small black cravat, a gray-striped waistcoat, and very highly
polished black boots. There was a look of determination on
his angular face, framed in white muttonchops as he strode
toward Peter.

He was very courteous, as befitted his station; but he was
firm too. He said coldly: "With your permission, sir, I am
Hawkes, the butler. And if you will be so kind, sir . . . I must
ask you to leave."

Peter leaned back in his wooden chair and stretched out
his long legs. He said mildly: "If you will tell me why, Mr.
Hawkes, I will at least entertain your idea. That's what this
incipient chat was all about, the exchange of ideas."

"Not Mr. Hawkes, sir, save to the other servants. A simple *Hawkes* is more correct, if you don't mind my saying so.
Please, if you would be so good as to take your leave."

"And if I choose not to, Mr. Hawkes?"

"I am sure, sir, that you would not wish to embarrass us
any further?"

The others, obliquely, were watching.

"In the dining chamber," Peter said, "no one would listen
to me. Perhaps here they will. Perhaps I will stay and . . .
subvert your staff, explain to them that we are all men and
women, not lords and serfs."

"If you do not leave at once, sir," the butler said coldly,
"then I will summon a footman and have you thrown out
bodily."

"Ah! You too! If a man doesn't agree with you, break his
damned head!"

Hawkes was not a man to trifle with. For sixty of his
seventy-two years he had been a servant in the mess, for the
last thirty of them in his present elevated position, a disciplinarian who had spent nearly all of his years attending to the

needs of military gentlemen in one capacity or another, first as a twelve-year-old boots, then at the age of eighteeen as batman to a colonel of Hussars, then as footman and finally butler in the Empire Officers' Club.

His face was flushed with anger, and his voice came from the glaciers of his personal dignity. He said quietly: "To my chagrin, Master Entwhistle, I heard all that you said in the chamber, and I will confess that I felt the blood curdling in my veins. Never in all my years have I heard a young gentleman spouting such arrant nonsense."

"*Spouting,* sir?" Peter's blood was rising.

"*Spouting,* sir! Ideas that are anathema to me personally, an insult to the general and to all the other honorable gentlemen present, and yes, to your own respected name as well. In God's name, go!"

Peter, suddenly cold with fury, rose to his feet. He was conscious only that the eyes of the young girl whose name was Ivy were on him as he left the room.

He slammed the door shut furiously behind him and found his way into the gardens and around to the front of the mansion, the anger hammering into his brain. It was a thunderous night to match his temper, a heavy rain pounding the cobblestones. He found the family coach drawn up there with a dozen others, the coachman stolidly sitting on his box under the deluge, against the time he might be needed; the rain was pouring down over the brim of his top hat.

Peter said sharply: "Briggs! I'm going home!"

"Yes, sir!" The coachman climbed quickly down and opened up the carriage door and pulled down the step, and Peter said: "No. *I* will take the reins. Get inside there, Briggs, out of the rain."

Coachman Briggs had been with the family for nearly twenty years. He said hesitantly: "But I can't hardly ride inside, Master Peter, it's not proper."

"Proper or not, that's what you'll do, Briggs."

"I'm all wet, Master Peter, and the mistress will be hopping mad if I get her upholstery dirty. We spent more than an hour shining up the leather today."

"Inside, Briggs! Sit back in comfort, and I'll drive you home."

He was still unsure. "And the mistress, Master Peter?"

Peter's anger had quickly gone, and he was beginning to enjoy the joke. He said happily: "In you get. I'll brook nc argument."

"Yes, Master Peter." He did not move. "If you're sure that's what you want, sir?"

"It's not only what I want, it's what I insist on. Up with you, Briggs. Make yourself comfortable, and I'll give you a drive the like of which you've never had before in your life."

Certain that there would be trouble ahead of him because of this, the coachman climbed heavily in and sat on the edge of the soft leather bench; he was acutely conscious of the water dripping off his cape onto the Wilton carpeting.

Peter clambered up onto the box, took the reins, and yelled a furious: "Giddiup!" The carriage raced off at alarming speed, up into the Circus, swinging on two wheels into Piccadilly, thundering along till it came to Whitehorse Street, up through Shepherd Market, and into Curzon Street. He yelled out a "Whoa there!" and threw his weight on the reins when they came to the house. The horses pranced, as excited as he was, and Peter jumped quickly down before the worried Briggs could open the door, and opened it for him and pulled down the step, and shouted: "There, Briggs! Did you enjoy the ride?"

"Blimey, Master Peter," Briggs said, "I've never been so terrified in all me born days! I thought I knew them 'orses well, but I never knew they could race like that."

"Go back to the club, Briggs, there's a good fellow, and wait for my mother."

"Yes, sir." He hesitated. "What shall I tell her, Master Peter? About the upholstery, I mean."

"Tell her the truth, Briggs," Peter said. "When in doubt, always tell the truth."

"Yes, sir."

Peter stood in the drenching rain and watched the carriage turn around, and as it moved off at a sedate walk, he thought about that damned Earl of Redhill, of the contempt on so many faces when he had said so clearly: *"I will not fight you."*

He thought of the waiter, meekly handing over a white cotton glove to be used for the ultimate insult; and when he turned and strode up the steps to the front door, his anger was beginning to mount again, insupportably.

The butler opened the door to his ring, and his fourteen-year-old sister Susan was there, running across the hall to greet him, throwing her arms around him and squealing at the sodden contact. He hugged her tightly, then quickly pushed her away and laughed with her as she looked down the wet front of her dress, pale blue in silk and organdy, and she asked: "And how was the party, dear Peter? Did you hate every minute of it? Where's Mother?"

"Mother is still there, enjoying it enormously, I'm sure, and yes, I hated every minute of it. And I had far too much to drink. Does it show?"

"Well . . ." But she knew what Peter wanted her to say, and so she said it, laughing: "No, it doesn't show in the least."

"Good."

"Except that you look absolutely dreadful! You must get out of those wet clothes at once, or you'll catch your death of cold. How on earth can an ʳone get . . . get soaked through to the skin like that?"

He said mildly: "It's raining, Susan. It's pissing down."

"So go and change quickly, put on a dressing gown or something, and then come and join us by the fire and get warm. There's a marvelous fire going in the withdrawing room."

"Us?"

"Ranjet is here. We've been having a perfectly marvelous time. He's been reading me some of his latest poems. And they're simply wonderful, Peter. Just wait till you hear them."

"Ah . . ." He looked at the water forming little puddles around his feet and said: "I'm delighted he's here. And I'll confess to you that there's no one in the world I'd rather be with . . . than Ranjet Singh."

Susan knew him well. She looked at him dubiously and said: "Oh. That means you're in one of your moods again."

He nodded. "Yes, my dearest Susan. I am in one of my moods."

She took his arm and went with him across the hall and watched as he ran up the broad Adams staircase, and she sighed and went back to the drawing room, where the young Indian boy was waiting for her.

Chapter Three

The withdrawing room in the Entwhistle house was a quiet and intimate sort of place, decorated with wood paneling which had been painted in white and Wedgwood green.

There were two deep bay windows in one wall which overlooked the lovely old archway of Shepherd Market and were curtained in silk of a darker shade of the same color. There were three large sofas here, deeply cushioned and covered with green-and-white striped linen, with four armchairs and an ottoman in the same material, as well as half a dozen small tables of highly polished oak on which lithographs, flower vases, and other little oddments had been set out; there was a coal fire burning in the hearth now, a brass coal scuttle beside it.

Ranjet Singh was standing with his back to the flames, a sheaf of papers in his hand, a broad smile on his walnut-brown young face as Susan returned.

He was very tall, a darkly handsome boy of sixteen years with an incipient beard and moustache that were struggling still for recognition. He was very slender, and perhaps by English standards a little effeminate, with movements that were strangely *controlled*, as though every muscle in his body were dominated by his intelligence. He wore a very correct and formal frock coat and black trousers; but his hair was bound up in the traditional turban of his caste.

He said, gesticulating with his papers: "That was Peter, no doubt. So where is he?" He laughed. "I was quite sure that he would not survive for very long the rigors of a dinner at the Empire Officers' Club."

Susan flounced down on a sofa. "Yes," she said with a sigh, "it was Peter. And you are right, it was too much for him. What else could we expect? He'll be down shortly, he's soaked to the skin, he'll probably get pneumonia and die before the night is out, and we'll have to bury him. What a terrible bore. . . . Now, where were we?"

Ranjet waved the papers again. "We were at stanza thirty-eight," he said. And your dress is all wet. Get closer to the fire."

She was sitting on the floor, leaning back against the sofa, and obediently she shuffled her way closer to the flames. "Good," she said, "stanza thirty-eight. I want to know what happens to poor Bulbul."

Ranjet sat down on the floor and stretched out his legs. "Very well," he said. "Bulbul the nightingale is in the forest, and the dark is closing all around her. And the dark is a man named Shehr, which means Tiger. . . . Bulbul's wing was broken, you remember, in stanza twenty-one, and she can no longer fly. She is in the unaccustomed humus of the forest floor. So . . ."

He said, reading, his soft voice caressing the words, trying to make the harsh English sounds poetic:

The clouds were not there.
Their comfort no longer about her.
There was only the dreaded forest

Where the predators prowled
In the dark night. . . .
Her poor heart
Was beating swiftly
As the man named Shehr approached her,
And he said, in honeyed tones:
Why do you wander, Maiden,
In the dark of the night,
Where the predators prowl. . . ?

He broke off. Peter, wearing his favorite blue dressing gown, was standing in the doorway, looking at him quizzically. He said, quoting: "Where the predators prowl . . . that's where I've come from, Ranjet. And how are you, dear friend?"

The Indian boy tossed his papers aside and strode to him, hugging him in a tight embrace. "Poor Peter!" he said, laughing. "Was it intolerable for you?"

"No, not intolerable," Peter said. "Abominable, yes. But I have long since learned to tolerate the abominable. At least until I can do something about it."

Susan was pouring lemonade as Peter made himself comfortable on one of the sofas, lying down with his feet up and happy to be among his peers once more. He said cheerfully: "I was challenged to a duel."

Susan's face blanched, but Ranjet said, laughing: "A *duel?* God in heavens! You will of course call on me for your second?"

"I refused him, Ranjet."

The Indian boy stared. "You did *what?*"

Peter said calmly: "I told the idiot I would not fight him. Fellow called the Earl of Redhill, a colonel of Hussars."

"Thank God you had the sense to do that," Susan whispered. "He would have killed you."

"That is hardly the point," Ranjet said tartly. "There's far more to this than the problem of who gets killed. Peter! An Entwhistle cannot refuse a challenge. It's unheard of!"

"It's heard of now. I did it."

"Yes . . . and perhaps it's not too late to rectify the situation. Tomorrow morning you must find out where Redhill lives, call on him, and insult him again. And this time, when he challenges you, you must accept."

"Ranjet, you don't understand."

"I understand perfectly."

"No, you *don't!* I will not fight with this man! I do not believe that intellectual arguments can be solved with bullets!" Peter clambered to his feet and began pacing. "For a moment, I toyed with the idea of accepting his challenge, of choosing pistols, at dawn, at twenty-five paces. Merely so that I could wake up in my comfortable bed long after sunup, and think of this simpleton Redhill striding up and down the glade and wondering where his adversary might be. Of just leaving him there in all of his high drama, with no one to fight. But I decided it would not be a gentlemanly way to behave."

"And refusing a challenge *is?*"

Peter's pale blue eyes were suddenly very hard and cold. He turned them on Susan and she said, her voice very firm: "Of course you can't fight with him. The idea is ridiculous. But I can understand Ranjet's concern too. He thinks, as we all should, in terms of the family honor. It may be that you should go to him, distasteful as it may be, and simply apologize for whatever you did to anger him."

"I will not apologize, because he was in the wrong."

"Then we have a problem on our hands that just has no answer to it."

"If a problem has an answer, dearest Susan, it is no longer a problem."

"Wait, wait," Ranjet said urgently. "This is no time for bickering over trivia. Tell me what the quarrel was about."

Peter was smiling. "Can you believe," he said, "that I have almost forgotten what started it? He had the nerve to ask me why I was not in the Army, and I seem to remember I told him what I thought of the damned military establishment."

"Oh, God. In the Empire Officers' Club?"

"Yes. And they really are a sorry lot, aren't they? I never saw so many bristling moustaches in my life."

"Redhill, Redhill," Ranjet muttered. "A colonel of Hussars, you said. Rather old, with white muttonchops? Recently home from India?"

"Yes, I believe so. You know him?"

"Yes, I've met him on occasion. He's a very good man, Peter."

"Well, that's not the impression he gave me." He laughed shortly. "And I told him the British ought to get out of India. That really rankled. I could see him positively squirming."

"Well," Ranjet said tartly, "I know your views on *that* question, and you know mine, so we will not pursue them. I will simply reiterate, as I have told you a thousand times, I thank God that the British *are* in India, or my people would still be killing each other off with their damned tribal animosities."

"Cant, Ranjet," Peter said angrily. "Pure bloody *cant*, and you know it! Just a lot of damned empire humbug!"

"Remind me, Peter," Ranjet said sarcastically, "I always seem to forget. How long did you spend in my country, that you know it so well?"

" I have spent no time in hell either," Peter said, "but I'm convinced nonetheless that no one is very happy there."

"There are very many of us in India who welcome the British presence. My family have governed Ambala for far more generations than even your family can begin to count. And it is only since the arrival of the British that they have been able to govern in peace."

"Your family is as privileged in India as the British are."

"That was not a very nice thing to say, Peter." He was very angry now.

"Perhaps not. But I hope that you will recognize it as the truth. Your father the maharaja is a servant of the British, no more than that."

Ranjet Singh was a very gentle man, but he felt the blood draining from his face in a sudden access of rage. He lashed out at Peter, inexpertly struck him hard in the face, knocked him to the ground, and shrieked: "My father is no one's servant! Shame on you!"

Susan screamed, and dropped to her knees beside her fallen brother. She shouted: "Ranjet! No . . . !"

Ranjet too was in complete shock, and crouching beside him. He whispered: "Oh, God . . . I hit you, I hit the dearest friend I have. . . ." He produced a handkerchief from his pocket and wiped at the blood at Peter's nose. He was almost weeping. "Will you forgive me, Peter? An insult to my family. I am sure that you did not mean it."

Peter said, sulking a little: "No. I did not mean it. I'm sorry."

"Did I hurt you badly?"

Peter sighed. "Perhaps it is my fate to be hurt by my friends whose ideas are not my own."

There was the ticking of the grandfather clock, and suddenly its chimes boomed out across the room. Ranjet said quietly: "It means, Peter, that in spite of Susan's understandable fears, you must *not* go to Redhill and apologize. No, of course not! Instead, you must go to him. Insult him again—and since you will be quoted by every young blade in London, choose your words very carefully, even wittily. And then . . . then meet him. And who knows? You might, by chance, even shoot him dead."

"There will be no duel!" Peter shouted, exploding. "The

matter is finished, it will rest as it lies now!" He picked up his glass and hurled it furiously into the fireplace.

Susan was in tears. "Peter," she whispered, "it *cannot* rest where it is now! Think of Mother! Think of the scandal she would have to face. Why, tomorrow it will be all over London, unless you do something about it at once. Never mind what Ranjet says. Make up your mind to go to Redhill first thing in the morning, call on him and leave your card, and when you see him, tell him . . . tell him you were carried away by too much . . . too much to drink. Please, it is the only logical solution."

Peter's immature anger had quite gone. With the point of his boot he was slowly brushing shards of broken glass from the carpeting into the grate, and for a long time he did not speak. He could feel their eyes on him.

He said at last, brooding: "Amanda, our dear mother Amanda . . . Frankly, after what she did to me tonight, I don't care anymore. She held me up to ridicule in front of fifty or so scarlet toy soldiers whom she knows I detest. She took their side! She apologized for me! And now you want *another* apology, is that it?"

He held her by her shoulders and looked down into her tear-stained eyes. "You are so convinced," he said quietly, "that I am wrong?"

"Yes. Utterly convinced."

"Convinced too, as I am, that when Amanda returns tonight, she will not expect me to be here?"

She stared at him. "Not . . . not expect you to be here? Peter, I don't understand."

"No, of course not. How could you? You did not hear her, hear the little speech she made to all those assembled moustaches. 'You are no longer welcome here,' she said."

There was a terribly bitter tone to his voice. "I can only assume that I am no longer welcome in her house either."

Susan's eyes were wide, and there were sudden tears there. "No, Peter, no!"

Ranjet Singh laid a hand on his shoulder and said: "No, that is simply not true. And this is not the time for rash decisions. When you've cooled down a little—"

"I am *not* a rash man," Peter said, interrupting him, "and there's no question of cooling down. I know what I have to do now." He took Susan in his arms and whispered: "I must leave this house, tonight."

"Peter, *please . . .*" The tears were streaming now.

"I *must.*"

"But . . . to go where?"

"I don't know. I only know that I must not be here when Amanda returns. I can't face her, Susan, it's as simple as that."

He turned away to hide his own emotion and went quickly up the stairs to his room. Susan sank down into a comforting sofa in which she found no comfort at all. Ranjet dropped to his knees beside her and took her hand and he said, not at all sure that he was right: "In a few days, Susan, he'll come to his senses, I'm sure of it."

Her eyes were angry now. "You mean he'll come crawling back? Peter never crawled in his life."

"He's as stubborn as any of the Entwhistles, but he's not a fool. And it won't be long before he realizes how wrong he is. A week or two perhaps, no more."

"Oh, God . . ."

There was a strange silence as Peter came down the stairway, dressed now in his workaday clothes and carrying a small leather suitcase. He put down his case and went to Susan to embrace her, pulling her to her feet and throwing his arms around her; she fancied she could feel his trembling. "It will not be forever," he whispered. "And however long it may be . . . we will always be close, wherever I am. Good-bye. And God bless you, darling."

He gripped Ranjet's silent hand and said: "Goodnight, Ranjet."

"Good-bye, Peter." The black eyes were burning.

They watched him stride to the front door and open it, and when it closed behind him, a dreadful pall seemed to settle on them. But with a kind of instinct that was peculiarly his, Ranjet turned and looked up to the far end of the balcony that ran halfway around the library from the top of the staircase to some of the upper rooms, conscious that there had been a witness to their exchange.

A silent bundle of pink flannel was crouched there, half hidden by a small escritoire, her huge eyes wide with silent sadness.

He felt a sudden tightening at his heart, and he forced a smile with great difficulty and called out: "Hilda! What are you doing there, child? You should be asleep! Do you know what time it is?"

She unbundled herself and ran quickly down the stairs to him, her arms outstretched, reaching for the comfort that she knew only he could give her.

Hilda was twelve years old now, and for a curious reason was being kept out of the mainstream of the Entwhistle family life; she was not quite as English-looking as she ought to have been . . .

Her eyes were very dark instead of the family blue, her skin olive-colored and lacking that peaches-and-cream look that might have been expected; her hair was almost black. Even at this tender age, Hilda was well aware that she was "different." She was quiet, introspective, and terribly unhappy.

Ranjet Singh scooped her up in his arms and held her tightly, and there was great pleasure for her in his embrace. She tucked an escaping lock of his hair back under the turban and said, not seeming to be very upset about it: "Why did you hit Peter, Ranjet Singh?" It was a search for information more than a reproach.

He set her down and sat beside her on the bottom stair, and smiled at her, stroking the back of her head. "Oh, you saw that foolish thing too?" It was so easy to talk with Hilda.

She was not in the least upset, and she nodded: "Yes, I saw it. His nose was bleeding."

He threw a quick look at Susan and saw the worried look in her eyes, but he did not lose the smile. He turned back to Hilda and hugged her and said gently: "Well, what can I say? I suppose I have to admit that I lost my temper, and that is something a gentleman really ought never to do. And the moment I had done it—I was sorry and thoroughly ashamed of myself." He sighed. "Unhappily we sometimes do things that, only a few moments later, we are sorry for, and this was . . . well, one of those times. I promise you I'll never do it again. Will you believe me?"

"Of course, Ranjet. Why shouldn't I?"

"Good. Now you must go back to bed. Where's your brother? Is he up there too, watching us?"

A child, she laughed suddenly. "James is a baby, Ranjet. He's only eight years old! He's fast asleep."

"And you should be too."

"So tell me why Peter left us. He's gone forever, hasn't he? I mean, for absolutely ever?"

He shook his head. "Not forever," he said emphatically. "Peter was in a temper too, a different kind of temper, and when he loses his anger, as I lost mine, he will come back to us. It is a question of *time*, Hilda. And that is something that you must learn also, that time cures almost everything."

She sighed. "I hope so."

"And now, back to bed. Would you like me to come and tuck you in?"

"Yes. Oh, yes!"

"Very well." He turned to Susan, smiling still. "Give me a few minutes," he said, "and I'll rejoin you. All right?"

Susan touched her eyes with her kerchief. "Yes, of course, Ranjet. Good night, dear Hilda. Sleep tight."

"Good night, Susie. Do you believe Peter will come home soon?"

"Yes, very soon. And please don't call me Susie. You know I don't like it."

"I'm sorry, Susan. Good night."

"Good night, darling."

She watched as Ranjet carried Hilda up the broad staircase to her room. Susan, older than her sister by two years, was only fourteen; but there were already stirrings of jealousy in her.

It was perhaps because of the physical differences in their personal aspects. For the first five or six years of her life, Susan had been what was called "an adorable baby," pink and dimpled and chubby and curly-haired. But her hair, now, was taking on a mousy sort of color and was no longer bundled around her head in tight ringlets, but rather straggling and a little untidy. The baby fat had not left her, but had turned into excessive weight. She was still sweet and charming, but the charm was of a different kind now.

And Hilda had developed from inauspicious beginnings into a very special kind of beauty. The luminous dark of her eyes was filled with a strange mysticism; when she was spoken to, they were always fixed unwaveringly on the speaker, disconcertingly so in such a young child, taking in every word that was said and seldom answering anything at all, as though she wanted only to receive and never to impart; all that she heard was tucked away in a receptive mind and never disputed or agreed with, one way or the other.

At the age of twelve, her young breasts had developed to a most un-English fullness, ready to burst out of her confining bodice, and Ranjet was conscious of them now as he tucked her solicitously into the bed. In his own country, she was ready for marriage, and he wondered if she *knew* how close she really was to that country of his. How much, at such a tender age, could she know of India?

For the children of the Anglo-Indian military establishment, that distant world was very much a part of their own, nourished by the exciting tales their too-seldom-seen fathers recounted to them, and distorted by their own imaginings. He wanted to talk to her about this, but he could not, though in India he would have felt no qualms at all.

"I'm so fond of you, Hilda," he whispered. "So very, very fond of you. The sweetest child in the whole world. I love the others too, Susan and Peter, and even James, though James is really a bit of a prig sometimes, isn't he?"

"Yes, he really is just that. A dreadful prig."

"And most of all, your mother. Amanda's a truly wonderful woman. But you . . . well, you're someone very special for me. You know that, don't you?"

"Yes. And is it because I'm . . . different?"

"Perhaps. Does it make you unhappy?"

"Does what make me unhappy?"

"That you're so different from the others?"

"No." She shrugged her little shoulders. "It happens, I s'ppose."

She reached up and hugged him and laughed suddenly. "Your beard tickles so!"

He pulled the blankets up under her chin and kissed her cheek again and wondered what he could do or say to make her less desperately unhappy.

Did *anyone*, save Amanda, know the true circumstances of her conception? He himself did not dare to think of them. He worshiped Amanda, and the idea of infidelity on her part would not rest easily with him. And yet . . . it was not only

Hilda's coloring—her *mind* was more Indian than English! Could there perhaps be some other reason? Some strange genealogical trick played in response to an atavistic blunder in the far-distant past?

He thought not. John, that excellent man, came home from India every three years, and Susan and Hilda were only two years apart. What, then, were *his* thoughts? And what would Amanda's reply to them be, even though they were undoubtedly never spoken?

He sighed; was it any of his business? He thought it was; the sweet little Hilda was left out in the cold, and he was closer to her than he was to any of them.

She was asleep, and he tiptoed out of the room and went downstairs to rejoin Susan, and to comfort her as best he could.

It was after three in the morning before Amanda returned to the house on Curzon Street, long after Ranjet Singh had left. She was a little put out, because, in spite of Briggs' efforts with bundles of rags from the club's kitchens, the fine leather seating of the couch was still wet.

In spite of the hour, Susan was still up, though fast asleep in a chair in front of the fire. She awoke at once as her mother entered, and ran to meet her, throwing out her arms and clutching at her with the desperation of her years. "Mama," she wailed, "Peter's gone!"

Amanda raised her eyebrows; she was not really surprised. She laughed prettily, as though to say: *Oh, what nonsense!* "Gone?" she said. "But gone where, darling? It's awfully late for anyone to go anywhere."

"I don't *know*, Mother. He's just . . . *gone.*"

Susan pulled a little square of white cambric from the silk pocket at her waist and dabbed at her tears. She caught a glimpse of herself in the mirror and said glumly: "I look a sight." It seemed to her that her red-rimmed eyes were an emblem of tragedy, and Amanda said calmly: "Yes, you do, darling. And you're crying for absolutely nothing, a storm in a teacup. Without any doubt at all, Peter will be striding furiously up and down Curzon Street in the pouring rain and convincing himself that he's a martyr. He'll be home before morning, you'll see."

She went to the fire and warmed herself and patted her hair into place and said, watching her daughter's reflection: "I imagine you already know what happened at the club?"

"Yes, he told me. About the challenge. He was terribly upset about it."

"Give me leave to doubt that, darling," Amanda said. "It would be very much out of character for him."

"But Mama, he was! That's why he went off in such a huff."

"And Ranjet was here?"

"Yes."

"And what did Ranjet have to say about it?"

"He wanted Peter to challenge the Earl of Redhill all over again, and this time accept."

Amanda scarcely hesitated. "Oh, for heaven's sake! You know how fond I am of dear Ranjet, but sometimes he's a little too empire even for my tastes. Though has it ever occurred to you that one of the finest things we have done in India is . . . we've turned their upper classes into gentlemen? They never were before, you know."

"Oh, Mother . . . !"

"It's absolutely true."

She swung around, a woman of the most imposing regality. "Well, be that as it may, don't worry unduly about poor Peter. He'll be back very soon with his tail between his legs, and everything will be marvelous again. And as for that foolish duel, tomorrow morning I will call on dear Redhill myself and have a quiet word with him. I don't want this scandal all over London, and between us we'll put a stop to it."

"Yes, Mama." It was a great relief for her.

"Hilda and James?"

"Both sleeping, Mama."

"Good. And you should be too, darling. But it was nice of you to wait up for me."

"Was it a good party?"

"Except for that one dreadful incident, yes, it was a perfectly lovely party. David Baird has taken over almost the whole of South Africa. You remember David Baird?"

"No, Mama, I don't think I do."

"He called on us a few years ago. He's a general now, and he's snatched South Africa right under the noses of the French. Everyone is delighted about it. Can you imagine the *French* in South Africa? What a dreadful calamity that would be!"

She embraced Susan gently and stroked the hair at the back of her head. "And now, my darling, I will go to bed and so will you. It's really been a most exhausting evening for me. That dreadful Lady Arnot was there, with her even more dreadful daughter, and you know how easy it is for those two to upset me. She wore the most unflattering dress imaginable. . . . Come to bed, it's very late."

They went together to Susan's room, and Amanda sat on the edge of the bed and watched her daughter undress and get into her nightclothes, wondering where all that loveliness of infancy had gone, a blond, curly-haired, and dimpled baby turning year by year into a . . . was the word *frump?* She sighed. "Susan, darling," she said, "you really must learn to take better care of your hair. You look so very pretty when it's nicely done."

"Yes, Mother."

"If you brush it one hundred times exactly every morning when you get up, and again when you go to bed . . ."

"Yes, Mother."

There was the smallest silence. And then: "Don't worry about Peter, darling. He'll be back."

"Yes. Yes, I hope so." She held her mother's look. "You really believe that, don't you?"

It startled Amanda. "Yes, darling," she said. "Of course I believe it. You mean . . . you don't?"

"No. I think he's gone . . . forever."

"Oh, pish-tosh!"

Susan sought her hand, clutched it, and said desperately: "But don't you *understand*, Mother? I know him so much better than you do."

It cut her to the quick, and she wondered if the hurt in her eyes would show through, but she smiled gently and said: "No, darling Susan, that is absolutely not true. And now you really must go to sleep. How often have I told you, a good night's sleep cures all vexations. Well, most of them, anyway. Good night, my love."

"Good night, Mama."

She snuggled deep down into the clouds of the feather mattress as Amanda drew up the blankets. "I do so much hope you're right. About Peter, I mean."

"Of course I'm right. I almost always am. Do you have a hot-water bottle?"

"Yes. Yes, right under my feet, the stone one. Robbins put sand in it instead of water, and heated it in the oven. Really, it holds the heat for much longer."

"Ah, good." She forced a little joke. "Mind you, don't kick it out of the bed. You might break the chamber pot."

Susan sighed and closed her eyes as Amanda kissed her on the cheek, and thought about her stubborn brother, wondering where he was now and worrying about that suitcase he had been carrying; it did not indicate the wandering on the streets that her mother was so sure about. Would he write to her and let her know where he was?

She was sure that he would, very soon, and on this comforting note she fell asleep.

Amanda went to James' room and stepped gingerly over the marvelously intricate lead soldiers that were spread out on the carpeting, the night-light in its little saucer of water standing among them. The soldiers were set out in very orderly arrays, and there was a card there lettered in James' childish hand that said: *1790, Lord Cornwallis' assault on Bangalore.*

She retrieved the tallow and set it on the bedside table, and looked down at her sleeping son; James Entwhistle, eight years old, bright, inquisitive, and already precociously knowledgeable about the more famous battles of the British Indian Army. She kissed his soft, smooth cheek and whispered: "Good night, Entwhistle . . ."

She went to Hilda's room and found the younger of her daughters sleeping soundly. The flame from the squat, round candle was lining her features with an edge of yellow light, and there was great serenity on that sleeping face; the dark hair was darker still against the snow-white linen of the pillow, tumbling loosely in great abundance, framing a dark and somber visage in which it was very easy to imagine the eyes open and staring wide; sleep seemed to leave her very vulnerable.

Amanda touched the olive cheek lightly, pulled up the bedclothes against the cold of the night, and tucked them under that innocent chin.

She dropped to her knees at the bedside, but it was almost a gesture of helplessness, as though all of her formidable self-control had left her completely; it was not even an ordered movement, but rather as if she were going to faint.

There was an oppressive silence in the room.

Did Susan truly know Peter better than she did? The tears

were streaming down her face as she thought that it probably was true, and she whispered: "John, John, my darling, where are you when I need you so badly?"

She reached for a child's warm hand and found it; the arm was wrapped around a black rag doll that was called a "gollywog," with staring white eyes of felt and shoe buttons, a very popular kind of doll that was meant to represent the natives of Africa and India and to teach the proper British children a certain protective condescension for the unfortunate natives of the far-flung empire. She took it in both hands and stared at it, and it stared back at her in the flickering flame of the nightlight; she wanted to tear it apart.

She could not remember who had given it to Hilda, five years ago, she remembered, a birthday present. Was there perhaps mockery in the giving? No, she thought not; it was Mrs. Arnold, of course, a devoted and dedicated teacher and a good, good woman to boot, who undoubtedly guessed why Hilda was not going to Susan's school but was discreet enough—or knew her place well enough—never even to *think* of such alarming and deeply personal matters.

"A gollywog!" Hilda had shrieked delightedly, pulling it from its wrapping and hugging it; and Amanda had smiled her smile of thanks to bloody Mrs. Arnold; too late now to throw it into the fire.

Amanda replaced the doll carefully in her daughter's arms and knelt there, unmoving and staring at nothing, quite in control of herself now, her eyes dry. She wondered, was she quite fair to her children? Did she spend too much of her love on Hilda, at the expense of Susan and Peter and even James?

"But don't you understand, Mother? I know him so much better than you do."

She touched that luxuriant hair, rose to her feet, and whispered: "*Damn* you, Cedric! Cedric? Damn you, damn you, may God damn you forever for what you did to me!"

The tears were streaming again as she moved quietly out of the room, and she was not aware that those huge black eyes had opened and were watching her as she gently closed the door behind her.

Cedric was Lieutenant Cedric Martin Prendergast, thirty-four years old, assistant camp commandant at the garrison in Arcot, state of Madras, India.

This night, Lieutenant Prendergast was Officer of the Day. It meant that till his turn of duty was up, at 0600 hours, he was expected to remain relatively sober even after the sun had gone down. It was midnight, and he was on the third of his rounds to make sure that the sentries were all wide awake and alert and that those doors which should be locked were properly bolted, that the garrison was secure.

He was in the kitchen of the Officers' Mess, where seven or eight tallows were burning. (It was laid down in Standing Orders that no room in the garrison building should be left unlighted after dark; there were too many enemies constantly prowling the fortress' borders.)

He heard the unexpected sound of a key in a lock, and he frowned and drew his sword quietly and concealed himself in the shadows as the door opened.

But it was only Nayak Shama, a corporal of the house staff whose main duty was to discipline the mess servants. And there was a young girl with him, hiding her face behind her grubby gown, only the dark, suspicious eyes showing.

Prendergast sheathed his sword and said: "Nayak, you damn nearly got your bloody head sliced off."

The corporal was short and thick-set and heavily bearded, and he was grinning broadly, his oversize teeth incredibly white, his black eyes gleaming. "I am sorry, Lieutenant Sahib," he said, "that you find me here. Major Sahib said to me, 'Shama,' he said, 'take care no one sees you.'" But you saw me, Lieutenant Sahib, and how will I explain this to Major Sahib? Isn't it?"

"Who's the *larkee*, Shama?" Prendergast asked. "Who's the bloody girl, and what the hell's she doing in the garrison at this time of night? I've got a sneaky feeling you're up to no damn good, Shama. I've a feeling I should put you smartly under arrest. What do you say to that?"

The wide grin was still there. "Oh, no, Lieutenant Sahib," he said happily, "a very bad idea, I think. Isn't it?"

"The *larkee*, Shama. What's she doing here?"

It was a ridiculous question and he knew it, and he sighed and said: "All right, then, she's for Major Sahib." He looked at the woman, shrouded from head to foot with only those dark and angry eyes showing, and he said to her in Hindustani: "Show me your face."

Slowly, her eyes not losing his, she dropped the headcloth down to her chin, and he saw a very young girl of quite startling beauty, with fine and delicate features and a lambent olive skin. He was tempted to tell her to show him her body too, but he thought better of it; Major John Entwhistle was not a man to trifle with.

He turned back to the corporal. "And her name?"

"Her name is Bunda, Lieutenant Sahib, and she is the wife of a Sepoy whose name is Ukab Gara. But poor Ukab is on a distant patrol tonight, a very *distant* patrol, isn't it? And so Major Sahib will take her to his bed. And if I may say, Lieutenant Sahib, he is *waiting*. 'Bring her to me *juldee*,' he said, 'at once.' And 'at once' has already gone into past history, Lieutenant Sahib, isn't it?"

"All right, then," Prendergast said, "be on your bloody way, Nayak. You may forget that I saw you. *Juldee kuro!*"

The corporal was bobbing up and down. "*Han*, Lieutenant Sahib," he said. "I am going, we are both going . . . *now*, isn't it?"

He took the young girl nmed Bunda and hurried off with her, out of the kitchen and up the stairs to the splendid, immaculate Officers' Quarters. And ten minutes later, Major John Entwhistle lay with her under the saffron-colored bell of the mosquito net that was draped around the polished mahogany bed. Her skin was nut-brown against the startling white of the sheets; her breasts were small and high-set, and in her eyes there was just a touch of trepidation. There was a great delicacy in her movements, a softness that he found quite irresistible; when she smoothed her long black hair—so very long, down to her waist and below it—it was the languid, controlled gesture of a ballet dancer, like those he had seen in Paris and London, a calculated gesticulation that seemed to tell a story even with so ordinary a movement.

They whispered together in Hindustani, though she did not wish, it seemed, to talk very much.

"You are truly very beautiful, child."

"Thank you, Major Sahib."

"And your name, I believe, is . . . Bunda?"

"Yes, Major Sahib."

"And how old are you, Bunda?"

"I am sixteen, Major Sahib."

"Nayak Shama tells me that this is your first time with a British officer. Is that true?"

"Yes, Major Sahib."

"And I think that you are frightened. . . ?"

She shook her head vehemently. "No, Major Sahib, no . . ."

He smiled. "I will not hurt you, child. I am a very gentle gentleman."

"Yes, Major Sahib. Nayak Shama told me so."

"A gentleman very far from his home, and sometimes in need of the comfort that can only be found in the body of a beautiful woman. You bring me that comfort, Bunda."

"I am glad of it, Major Sahib."

The odor of her body was strong, and he wondered idly why he had not told Shama to have her bathed first; but the smell was part of her womanhood, and it aroused him strongly.

There was nothing unusual in this assignation. There was not an officer in the garrison who did not have a local girl brought to him once or twice a week. It was the natural outlet for all the stifled emotions that were brought on by the never-admitted but considerable dangers of their day-to-day existence, and by their loneliness. It was not considered correct for a gentleman to sleep with the native women, and the practice was frowned on, but the common joke was: *The longer you've been here, the whiter they seem to get.*

In the compound itself, there were only other officers' wives and daughters, and to take them to bed would have been considered even more reprehensible, even if a virile man could stomach the cold acquiescence of an English lady, to whom any form of sexual endeavor had its overtones not only of wickedness but also of *permanence,* which was not to be tolerated.

There were indeed many quite good-looking young Englishwomen in the garrison; but beautiful or not, they were not particularly desirable.

John Entwhistle remembered now, caressing those amber thighs, a depressing encounter he had suffered only a few weeks previously. He had found Daphne Harris, the daughter of a Ranker Captain, bathing almost half naked in the stream that ran past the fortress walls. He had slipped out of the saddle to approach her and had helped her gallantly out of the water, putting an exploratory arm around her and had said, laughing: "Why don't we turn this fortuitous meeting to account and lie together in the grass for a while?" (Since her father had been promoted from the ranks and was not a gentleman, it was permissible.) But she had said, laughing too: "Oh, John, don't be so very ridiculous. . . ."

Ridiculous? It was a terribly British response, and he shuddered at the memory of it, all the excellence of her young body disappearing with the utterance of a single word. He had made a desperate attempt at recovery, laying a hand on the wet chemise over her breast, and she had not even tried to brush it away. Instead she had said, smiling: "Come now, John, that's not the way for a gentleman to behave. . . ."

He thought of this awful endeavor as he turned his attention now back to the warm Indian girl and made hasty love to her, wondering why she sucked her thumb as he lay on her. In a little while he stretched out beside her and stared up at a tiny lizard that had been put into the net to catch any mosquitoes that might find their way into it, cupping the child's breast.

She whispered: "Shall I go now, Major Sahib?"

"No. In a little while, I may need you again."

But it was not to be.

Her Sepoy husband, only three weeks married, was supposed to be on a patrol that was making its way into the Ghat Mountains to search out snipers there. But having been also detailed, by administrative bungling, to search for a local plant named *gasra* that could be tucked into kitchen recesses to kill cockroaches, he had missed his patrol.

The British sergeant had said to him: "Ukab Gara, it looks to me like you got lucky. Your patrol left an hour ago, and they're all going to get killed off in the mountains. So why don't you go back to that pretty little new wife o' yours and give her the old pork sword. It's what you married her for."

Beaming, touching his hands together, Ukab Gara had gone to the squat, low, married quarters. He had learned from his neighbors there that Nayak Shama had taken Bunda away, and he knew *exactly* what the corporal's duties were. Nayak

Shama now lay dead in a pool of his own blood; but before he died, he talked.

Ukab Gara burst into Major Entwhistle's room. He found his lovely young wife straddling the major in the light of the tallow, and he killed them both with his dagger.

Attemptimg to escape from the fortress, he was shot and killed by the Officer of the Day, Lieutenant Cedric Prendergast.

Chapter Four

Colonel Sir Bryan Dawson called a meeting of his officers and made a little speech.

They gathered together in the colonel's own office, only the field officers finding seats in the somewhat starkly furnished room. He had ordered the chief clerk to set out glasses and a decanter of brandy—no servants were allowed in here—to give the meeting an air of informality; because what the colonel had to talk about, though well within the bounds of military tradition, was not entirely without its aspects of impropriety.

"Gentlemen," he began, "the Entwhistle name is an ancient and very honorable one wherever the expoits of the British Indian Army are celebrated. I have given the matter of John's death some very considerable thought, and I have arrived at a certain conclusion, of which all of you must be informed."

He found that he could talk more easily on his feet, and he left his chair and began pacing, a stern and white-whiskered gentleman of imposing aspect, his scarlet uniform impeccable, his ruddy face shining.

"I will *not* have it known," he said, "that John Entwhistle, whom we all loved and admired, died in circumstances that I can only describe as unfortunate. If word of this tawdry affair were to reach the War Office, it would mean dishonor to an honored name, and I will not have it. It is my intention, therefore, to inform the War House in London that John died in battle. And if there be anyone among you who disagrees with my intention and thereby ends his illustrious career as an officer and a gentleman, let him speak *now*."

Unexpectedly, someone—was it Lieutenant Prendergast?—said loudly: "Hear, hear . . ."

There was a moment of silence, and then Major Blair, who had been a close friend of John's, said softly: "It seems to me, Colonel, that ye hav'na read the report I submitted to ye this day. Or maybe I forgot to submit it, I canna remember. . . . It was to the effect that John was"—he cleared his throat noisily and took another sip of brandy—"it was to the effect that John was returning from Madras, where he had regimental business, ye understand, when he found one of our patrols under attack from a very superior force of heathens. He led a fine and noble charge against the enemy and took a musket ball in the head for his trouble. It was a glorious way to die. Did ye no' get the report, Colonel? Ah, well, it'll be on y're desk within the hour."

The colonel was looking around at their bewhiskered faces; they were all nodding their assent.

"Very well," he said. "The Officer of the Day will write up a report, and I will so inform the War Office. My intention is clear to you, Mr. Prendergast?"

"Yes, sir, it is. And if I may be permitted to say so, heartily endorsed."

"Good." He turned back to Major Blair. "I suggest, Angus, that you confer very closely with Prendergast to get the, ah, supportive detail, as much of it as possible, agreed upon, and let me have a copy of your report at once."

Major Blair nodded. He was even smiling slightly. "Of

course," he said. "And have no fear, Colonel, dissemination comes right easily to an honest Scot. Ye'll have all the corroborative detail ye could wish for, and more."

"I thank you, Angus," the colonel said. "I myself will write a letter of condolence to Amanda Entwhistle, whom many of us here have had the great privilege of meeting, informing her of the circumstances of her husband's untimely and heroic death. And if I may suggest, gentlemen, those of you who have had that honor might wish to write to her too. Making quite sure, of course, that you first acquaint yourselves with the true facts as set down by Major Blair. Let us have no discrepancies. And now, if Mr. President of the Mess Committee, in the absence of any servants, will be good enough to pass the brandy, we will drink a toast to the memory of Major John Entwhistle, who died bravely in battle against the superior odds that arouse the fighting spirit of any good Englishman, defending the British raj in India."

The colonel hesitated. He said at last, and his eyes were very hard, the eyes of a martinet who knew that he could command instant obedience from his subordinates:

"I am sure that my final comment is quite unnecessary, but I will make it nonetheless. We are privileged in this garrison to enjoy the company of a number of ladies, the wives and daughters of the officers and sometimes even of the other ranks. Should any of these estimable ladies ever find cause to believe that John died under conditions other than those which will be set out in Major Blair's report . . . gentlemen, I will personally track down the originator of such calumny, and I will drive him from the garrison in disgrace that will follow him to his dishonorable grave. And now . . . Mr. P.M.C.?"

Lieutenant Hardcastle, an excessively young and bewildered subaltern who hailed from the North of England and was not well accepted in the mess, passed the brandy bottle around, being very careful to do so in the strictest descending order of seniority.

They drank to John Entwhistle, seven toasts in all. First to him; then to his lovely wife, Amanda; then to his family; then to the suppression of the Vellore revolt; then to the British Army in India; and then . . .

They drank solemnly to John's latest exploit, in which he had led a ferocious charge against an as yet not decided number of heathens and had died in the effort; and they drank, finally, to His Majesty King George III.

Before they left, the colonel had a final word for them. He cleared his throat and said: "I'm aware, gentlemen, that I am now dealing with one aspect of garrison life that my authority cannot easily control, because it concerns activities that always take place in the strictest privacy. But control it I will. It is against standing orders to bring a native woman into the compound for these purposes of nature, and I won't have it. Apart from the considerations of decency and morality, the inevitable result is *chi-chi* children. Good God, the regiment's been here less than fifteen years and the town's full of them! There is not a stew in the village, not a bawdy house within ten miles of us that doesn't have a half-caste girl for every one of its beds, some of them nine years old and less. It's unconscionable! Mr. Prendergast!"

"Sir." He was taking firm hold on himself.

"Not for Standing Orders, Mr. Prendergast, but a written note to whomever takes Nayak Shama's place, stating: *The practice of smuggling native women into the garrison after dark will cease forthwith.* Is that clear?"

"Yes, sir."

"Good night, gentlemen."

The colonel turned on his heel and stalked out, and the other officers finished off the three bottles of brandy and left Lieutenant Cedric Prendergast, at last, to his thoughts.

He stared morosely out of the window as the servants behind him cleared the glasses away, and he thought about that terrible word *chi-chi.* . . .

It was a word that every British Indian Army child knew almost as soon as he could walk, and it meant . . . *contumely*. *Chi-chi*. . . .

Was it only two years ago? It seemed like a lifetime.

His father, Colonel Stephen Albert Prendergast, camp commandant in Madras, had come visiting, and within sight of Arcot's walls, a Pathan's lead ball had torn its way into his stomach. He had been carried by a patrol into the garrison, and after the surgeon major had done his best, had been taken to his son's quarters to die.

It was a moment Lieutenant Prendergast would never forget. The awful stillness, and that ashen face—he had not known what to do or to say.

"The pain, Father, is it intolerable?" (What a damn fool question! A lump of lead an inch across just recently carved out of his bowels?)

The old man was strong. He took his son's hand and tried to clench it but could not. He said weakly: "There's not much money, boy, but what there is . . . it's all yours."

"You'll recover, Father, I know it."

"Don't be a fool! It's a miracle I came off the operating table. Might even call it a *vicious* miracle, because, yes, it hurts like hell. And there's something you must know."

"Don't talk now, Father, please."

"I must. I *will*." The voice was weak, but that strength was still in his eyes. "Something . . . something I have to tell you. Can you hear me, boy?"

"Yes, sir, I can hear you."

"They pumped me so full of some damned drug or other . . ."

"Father, it can wait . . ."

"No. I'll be gone . . . gone within the hour. It's about your mother. . . ."

The voice was trailing away, and Prendergast waited, wondering. At the age of six, he had been told that she had died shortly after he was born, and he remembered only the aunt who had brought him up.

The old man's eyes were closed, but he opened them now and said: "She didn't . . . didn't die, y'know. She just . . . just went back to her village. I thought . . . thought it was the best thing."

Prendergast stared. "Her *village*, sir?"

The old man moaned. He reached out a shaking hand and stammered: "The pills there, boy, the pills . . ."

"Yes, sir . . ."

He shook out a pill from the bottle and poured a glass of water and helped his father take it; and when the shuddering had stopped, he said hesitantly: "You were saying, sir, Mother went back . . . to her *village?*"

There was a long, long silence. Then, very quietly: "Yes, her village. She was a Pathan, from somewhere up in the North-West Frontier Province, sweet little thing. Can't really remember quite how she came to . . . came to share my bed, but she did, for more than a year. Ran off when her belly began to swell, and I swear to God I missed her sorely. Came back a few weeks after you were born, and showed me . . . showed me . . ." He grimaced with pain, morphine or no morphine. "Showed me a baby so British-looking I couldn't bear the thought of him crawling around naked in the dust of a damned Indian village, wanted to put you down for Sandhurst there and then . . ."

The blood was draining from Prendergast's face, and he could not speak.

The colonel said: "You're *chi-chi*, boy. Thank God it doesn't show a bit, it happens sometimes. But if you marry . . . you'll find that your children, . . . some of them will be as black as the ace of spades, it's the pattern . . . Don't . . . don't ever . . . ever marry."

The old man's eyes were glazing over, and he tried to reach out and could not; he seemed to *stab* at the air as though seeking support, and he whispered urgently: "Keep, keep . . . keep the secret for me, boy . . . there's . . . there's a good fellow . . ."

The old head dropped back, ashen-skinned. The thin-lipped mouth was open wide, and the eyes had lost their vision. There was one brief sound; and then Colonel Stephen Prendergast was dead.

The lieutenant sat by the bed for a very long time. He went to the window and looked out at the Dragoons there, charging in column across the parade ground with their lances lowered. He heard the bugler sound the retreat, the regroup, the column of fours, the charge again, the trot, canter, and the gallop. . . .

He shouted for the orderly and told him without emotion: "Tell the Officer of the Day that Colonel Prendergast is dead."

He went down to the mess and drank himself into a stupor. And from that day forth, Lieutenant Cedric Prendergast, who spoke Hindustani far, far better than the Hindis themselves, who could read and write it fluently, who could even translate the abstract poems of Gondhar Singh into English, would not allow a Hindi word to pass his lips. The whole mess wondered about it; talking to a servant in English was unheard of; it was . . . just not done.

He even consciously changed the way he walked. There was hardly a young woman in the garrison who, at one time or another, had not mentioned—admiringly—the way he moved, with the sinuous grace of a tiger.

Or of a Hindu; or a *chi-chi*; it was the one thing that could give him away; and blond as a Saxon, he changed it.

Keeping his promise, Colonel Bryan Dawson wrote to Amanda, though it was five months before the letter reached her. It read:

My Dearest Amanda.

It is with the deepest sense of grief that I take upon myself the very heavy duty of informing you of the untimely death of your husband and my dear friend, John Entwhistle.

You know me, Amanda, as a simple, rude man, a soldier who lacks the ease of articulation that would serve me better now. You know me as a blunt man who cannot easily find the kind of language that might perhaps soften the blow and make it easier for you to bear. But what words can help now?

I write this letter as though it were the sole source for you of heartbreaking tidings, even though I know that you will long since have received from the War Office that shocking little notice which is sent out by some unnamed bureaucrat to inform you, in cold and correct military terms, of your husband's death. I am trying—so very hard—to convince myself, to imagine, if you will, that you have heard nothing, and that this first knowledge comes, as it should, from a dear and respectful friend.

There can be no grief approaching yours, dear Amanda. But mine is heartfelt too. I recall with both pleasure and sadness the occasion when John's leave and mine happened to coincide, and he took me to your beautiful Curzon Street house and said, with such pride in his eyes: "Amanda, darling, this is my commanding officer and good friend, Bryan Dawson." He was showing you off! And letting it be known how dearly he loved you.

The other officers of the mess know that I am writing to you. Indeed, they have urged me to recount to you the very valorous and honorable circumstances of his death.

He was returning, accompanied by only five dragoons, from Madras, where he had regimental business to attend to. He found that one of our patrols had been ambushed

*in the mountains by a very strong force of Pathans who
had pinned them down in a quite untenable position and
were slowly picking them off one by one. Not prepared to
accept this attrition—he was above all a soldier!—John led
a charge against the enemy position. And with a total of
only twenty-two men he succeeded in breaking them up
and driving off more than two hundred tribesmen, all well
armed with those homemade muskets of theirs. It was an
exploit that would well rank with his defeat of the muti-
neers at Vellore, and one which brings yet more honor to
the Entwhistle name.*

*He took a musket ball in the head, Amanda. It was
quick and without pain, though I know that had he not
been killed instantly your name would have been on his
lips when he died.*

*What more can I say, dearest Amanda? I am a soldier,
and death is part of my life. It should not be part of yours.
You have my sympathy, and the compassion of all of us
here in Arcot.*

In the deepest, heartfelt devotion,

Bryan Dawson.

Like all women of natural strength, Amanda wept readily
whenever her comfortable, secure world fell apart. That "cold
and correct" military notification had indeed been sent to her
nearly three months previously: "*Madam, we regret to inform
you that Major John Entwhistle was killed in battle, fighting val-
orously for his country . . .*" And Bryan Dawson's letter was a
twist of the knife in her side.

But the pain went on. There was the simple matter of the
return of the major's possessions, undertaken with casual inef-
ficiency by the military forwarding office, a total of seventeen
trunks, lockers, and portmanteaux arriving over the course
of a month, each delivery bringing with it all the painful
memories.

One of the lockers contained the journal, volume eleven, which John had been keeping. Amanda clutched it for a while, thinking how much of history and the family would be recorded in it. She opened it at random and read a few pages in silence, punishing herself with John's reflections, and she handed it almost reverently to her son at last and whispered: "It is yours to keep now, Peter, the eldest surviving male Entwhistle. Remember that it is not so much a history of empire, but a *family* history. . . ."

"Yes, of course." Peter took the book and placed it on the shelf with all the others and said, not quite sure how he could phrase his thoughts without hurting her: "But it won't be quite the same, will it? The first of the family who's not a soldier."

"Don't be ashamed of it, darling," Amanda said, somewhat to his surprise, and he answered quickly: "Believe me, I'm not."

"Good. Your father was always as proud of you as I am."

It was a lie and he knew it, but he said nothing. He went on with the unpacking, the uniforms, the saber, the dress sword, the Wellingtons, the sola topee and the cape, the two revolvers in their cases, the medals and the miniatures in the mahogany box lined with red velvet. He tried to shake off the feeling that all these possessions somehow constituted a reproach.

And now Peter was gone, and the months had seemed interminable as they slipped quickly by.

Amanda had taken to sitting up very late at night by the window of her room, open whatever the weather, and trying half the time to persuade herself that she was not listening for the sound of a carriage. She thought also of John on those long vigils, as well as of Peter. John could never return to her, the only man she had ever truly loved, in spite of that awful . . . *infatuation* that had brought her so much distress. She was sure, however, that Peter, one day, would come home, shame-facedly as he always was on those rare occasions when he was forced to admit that he was in the wrong. And, please God, would it be soon now?

Amanda's dejection deepened as time went on and there was still no word from her son. Had she truly wounded him so deeply? Irrevocably? Surely, none of her children was so overly sensitive!

"I know him so much better than you do." She could not forget Susan's innocent words.

She was taking daily walks in the park now, quite alone; there were very few of the splendid receptions for which the Curzon Street house had previously been so well known. And ever since that fatal night, she had never once spoken to Captain Reynolds. Four times he had come calling and she had simply sent word that she was not at home; four times he had left his card, and then, recognizing defeat (a most unmilitary accomplishment), he had simply given up.

On the anniversary of John's death, driven by a kind of despair for which she hated herself, she went to Scotland for three months, to stay with distant relatives in their frigid stone castle, leaving Susan, Hilda, and James in the care of the good Mrs. Arnold, who had agreed to expand her tutorial activities and take over the management of the house in her absence.

She had no excuses for leaving. She merely said to Susan, a very down-to-earth and pragmatic young woman of fifteen now: "I'm falling apart, darling, and I have to pull myself together. But please keep in touch. Write to me every single week, will you do that? The mail coaches are very fast now and really quite reliable. They reach Edinburgh in less than two days."

"Yes, Mama, of course."

"Do you have the address written down?"

"Yes, Mama."

"Always do as Mrs. Arnold tells you. . . . You are quite fond of her, are you not?"

"No, Mama, not really. But it doesn't matter."

"Oh, I thought you were, though I know that Hilda thinks she's a little severe, which she has to be, children these days. . . . But then, Hilda's only a baby, isn't she?"

Susan was staring at the patterned carpet, examining the design intently. "Mama," she asked, "why can't Hilda go to school with me?"

"Because I think it best," Amanda said calmly, "that she should have the benefit of private tuition. She's really very bright, far brighter than all of you, even Peter, and I have the highest hopes for her. So she will have private tuition."

Susan shuffled her ungainly feet. She said, stumbling over the words: "It's not just because . . . because she's *chi-chi?*"

Amanda felt the blood draining from her face. Almost subconsciously, she found her hand on the desk, seeking for support. She was trembling. But her capacity for what she liked to call "pulling herself together" was very strong. She said steadily: "I don't know where you heard that dreadful word, Susan, and frankly I do not wish to know. But never, *ever* use it again. Do you understand?"

"Yes, Mama. I'm sorry."

Amanda went to the window and pulled back the heavy drapes to look down on the street below her. There were a few carriages there, no doubt on their way to the exhibition in the park, where the band of the Royal Fusiliers would be playing this afternoon. Sitting on the box of one of them, a young lieutenant in the uniform of one of the British Indian regiments was celebrating his leave and unsteadily driving the horses; a bewildered coachman was beside him, trying vainly to contain the young officer's exuberance.

The lieutenant was tall and fair and very sunburned. He saw Amanda staring down at him, brought the horses to an untidy stop, and shouted: "A good afternoon to you, lady! A

splendid day for the frivolities ahead of us! Come with us!"
Showing off his proficiency in Hindustani, he shouted: *"Kya
kuhteh ho?"*

Amanda caught her breath. *Kya kuhteh ho?* What do
you say?

It had been one of Cedric Prendergast's favorite expres-
sions. "Shall we have dinner now, *kya kuhteh ho?* Shall we ride
in the row together, *kya kuhteh ho?* Shall we make love again,
kya kuhteh ho?"

Cedric, where are you now?

She was biting her lip, forcing away the memory of a
treacherous indiscretion; and was it truly thirteen years ago?
At twenty-seven years of age, she'd been far more susceptible,
less sophisticated than she was now, and married only seven
years to a man who came home only once every three years.

And the young lieutenant, home on leave, was attentive,
charming, and very persuasive indeed. He moved gracefully,
like a tiger; and like the tiger, he knew when to pounce. It was
an affair that swept over her furiously, as violent as a whirl-
wind and as short-lived too. And still, the memories would
not leave her . . .

She turned away from the window and said clearly:
"Susan, my darling . . . you must listen very carefully to what I
have to say now. Hilda is *not chi-chi,* as you put it so vulgarly.
Yes, she is a little different from the rest of us . . ."

"And I still love her, Mama . . ."

"As indeed you should. She is your sister. And now that
your father is dead, you must know that I can speak freely, as I
will. I swear to you on the memory of your father and my
devoted husband that I never once betrayed him. Are you old
enough to understand what I am saying, darling?"

"Yes, Mama. I am older than you believe."

"Yes, perhaps you are. Are you old enough to know how
babies are made?"

Susan was blushing furiously. "Yes, Mama. The girls at school . . ."

"Good. And do you know what a bastard is?"

"Yes, Mama, I know."

"Then be assured that your sister Hilda is a true sister. She is *not* a bastard. Her coloring, yes, is not like ours, and neither your father nor I were ever able to explain it, though we discussed it often." (This was a lie, too; those terrible thoughts had never, ever been enunciated.) "It is perhaps some . . . some genealogical throwback to ancient times, an atavistic accident, no more." Her lovely eyes were on fire. "An accident," she said again. "Your father . . . is Hilda's father."

"Yes, Mama, I am sure of it." The tears were rolling down Susan's cheeks.

"Good. As long as that is thoroughly understood, I will say no more." She embraced her daughter and said gently: "And while I am away, will you miss me?"

"Yes, Mama, very much."

"Will Ranjet Singh call on you often?"

"Yes. Yes, Mama, I think so."

"I am very fond of that young man. He's very good for you, even though he is . . . well, an *Indian.*"

"He is a very nice man, Mama. I think I'm in love with him."

"Oh, pish-tosh! At fifteen years of age? Well, I suppose that's the most impressionable of all the ages . . ." Her hand was suddenly on her daughter's arm. "You haven't . . . gone to bed with him, I hope? Have you?"

Susan was aghast. "Mama, no. . . !"

"Good. And that was a very foolish question, wasn't it? Forgive me. I know him to be a very honorable young man, and I should absolutely not have said that. But it just . . . slipped out."

Susan was still very young, and she giggled. "Mama," she

said, "I have a feeling that never, ever in your whole life have you ever said anything that just 'slipped out.' "

"Well, be that as it may. But watch your language, darling. Never say 'love' when you mean to say 'like.' It can give quite the wrong idea."

"But I do love him, Mama. I hope that one day he's going to want to marry me."

"Oh, my God." Amanda fluttered her fingers at the neckline of her gown, setting it just so. She said carefully: "That, of course, is unthinkable, but you're a very sensible young woman and I'm sure you realize it's just an infatuation you'll grow out of in time. I'm sure Ranjet knows that too, he's such a bright young man . . ."

Before she left for Scotland, she said, whispering: "And if you should hear from Peter while I am gone . . ."

"I know, Mama. Two days for the mail to Edinburgh."

"Good-bye, my darling. Take good care of Hilda and James."

"Of course."

"And if he should . . . Good-bye, dear Susan."

An hour later, she left for Scotland.

She had not told her daughter of the notice she had placed on three different occasions in the personals column of the *Times* of London, a simple plea saying: *"Peter, please come home. We all love you. Amanda."*

Peter, these days, was not reading the *Times* of London.

Chapter Five

There were times when Peter thought that his break with the family should be permanent and decisive. It was a question of pride, and therefore foolish; he knew that the pride was part of a heritage that had suddenly become quite distasteful to him.

He wanted to write to Susan—so badly—but could he write to her and not to Amanda? It was a question to which he could not easily find the answer, and so he put it off from day to day until the days became weeks and even months; and time itself made any possible reunion more and more difficult.

He had found a modest room in the White Hart Inn on Borough High Street, a rambling old place of great antiquity, where the gentry from across the river often came to spend their evenings, the top-hatted aristocrats mixing with the cloth-capped working classes.

And it was at the White Hart that his first introduction came to the writings of a certain William Cobbett, in a newspaper left behind by a previous patron. He looked at it curiously; he had heard, vaguely, of Mr. Cobbett, but his *Political Register* was hardly the kind of journal that would ever find its way into the Entwhistle house. Cobbett was a radical of virulent attitudes, attacking Whig and Tory alike and crying out for economic reform and an end to the dreadful privation of England's working classes. Peter read,

> *Disgusted with the miserable condition of London's poor, your correspondent, to his shame, decided to leave the squalor of the City behind him and search for solace in the countryside, at a farm in Hampshire. . . . But the change opened his eyes to the misery of the rural poor who are not better off than their urban brothers and sisters in London, Sheffield, Leeds, or—the most offensive hellhole of them all—Manchester. . . .*

Peter was sitting on a bench in the tavern's saloon, his ale on the copper-topped table in front of him. All around, the candlelights, at least a hundred of them, were dancing reflections in highly polished copper, brass, and oiled mahogany. The air was thick with cigar and pipe smoke. He put down the paper and leaned back, his eyes closed as he thought about what he had heard of William Cobbett. *"The only articulate champion of the working classes,"* he had written of himself, *"and a man who has learned that God is not good to all of us. . . ."*

There was noisy chatter all around him, and raucous laughter as the young bloods who came here for an evening exchanged their boisterous gossip; snatches of broken conversation came to him:

"A bloody *footman*, mark you, and I threatened to whip him to within an inch of his life . . ."

". . . laborers, who can't read or write, and they want representation in Parliament . . . Insanity gone rampant!"

He studied the paper, and a customer sitting beside him, an impeccably dressed young man of twenty-five or so with sharp aquiline features, nodded pleasantly at him and said, his eyes on the *Register:* "A strange choice of journals, sir, may I say? For a gentleman, that is."

"Strange, sir?" Peter raised his eyebrows. "I take it you don't approve of Mr. Cobbett's writings?"

"Well, hardly!" His companion laughed. "I have on occasion skimmed through the *Register* myself, in the belief that a sometime dose of righteous anger is good for the soul."

Peter nodded. "Yes, indeed it is. But do you speak of your own anger, or of Cobbett's?"

"My own, of course." He said languidly: "I really cannot concern myself with the indignation of a maniac." Suddenly he shot out a hand and said: "Whitley, sir, Ambrose Whitley at your service."

"Peter Entwhistle, sir." The hand was cold when he took it, the soft, cool hand of a woman. The girl was bringing his ale, and Whitley drained his tankard and said to her: "Another. Put them both on the slate for me."

"Yes, sir."

Peter said, frowning: "And we were talking of Mr. Cobbett's indignation. . . . Is he truly a maniac in your estimation?"

"Worse," Whitley said happily. "He's a Whig, supports all those parliamentary do-gooders. England's fast becoming a place where it's a crime to be a gentleman! You think they'd learn from the bloody French, wouldn't you? Give people like Cobbett a free hand and they'll be setting up guillotines on London Wall, mark my words."

"And yet," Peter said mildly, "his arguments are persuasive, to say the least." He read aloud from the paper: " '. . . *the wages of a workingwoman in service are about five shillings a week. How can anyone live decently on such a pittance?*' And he's right, you know." He said, brooding: "I had occasion recently to talk to one of those serving girls myself."

What was her name? Ivy? He could not remember. He could only remember sparkling eyes in a work-weary face, and yes, the white, swelling breasts under a loose gray blouse.

"Four and tuppence a week," he said, "it's all she earns. It's not enough."

"I pay my kitchen maids a little less, I think," Whitley said, "though I can't be sure. It's hardly the kind of household detail one pays much attention to." He saw that Peter was not of like opinion, and he said earnestly: "But don't misunderstand me, sir, I consider myself to be . . . well, quite liberal in this respect. Take my butler now, rattlin' good fella. I like to treat him almost as if he were my equal. And as for Cobbett, the word you chose was exactly right, *persuasive*. Trouble is, he persuades the wrong people! Well, give him his due, he's a *thinking* man. And you know what that means, don't you?"

"It means that he deserves our respect, I'd say."

"Perhaps. But it also means—" He broke off as the girl came and placed his drink on the table. Whitley patted her behind and was not aware that her smile was only on her lips. He raised the tankard and said: "Your health, sir, and to the downfall of bloody Cobbett and his ilk." He drank deeply and set down his mug, and he took the copy of the *Register* and said cheerfully: "Only one thing to do with a rag like this, dear boy . . ."

He held a corner of the newspaper to the candle's flame, and when it was well alight, he dropped it on the floor and said, laughing: "Expiation by fire. We were *right* when we burned that damned Maid of Orléans. . . ."

The landlord, one Mr. Welks, was there at once, from behind the bar, and he picked up their tankards, poured the ale on the flames, and said lugubriously: "We can't have that sort of thing, sir, now can we? The White Hart has survived a number of fires, and we don't want to start a new one, now do we?" He stomped on the dying flames and held up their tankards and said: "And if you'll allow me to refill these for you? On the house, of course . . ."

"Chalk them up, Welks," Whitley said coldly. "I have no wish to be beholden to a publican."

"Of course. Thank you, Mr. Whitley, a real gentleman."

Peter sighed, and Whitley laughed. "Where was I? I was about to make a point."

"The point being," Peter said, "that in your estimation Mr. Cobbett's capacity for thought means . . . ?"

"Ah, yes." He was smiling, a very smug smile indeed. "His capacity for thought, as you phrase it, means that when England's revolution comes, as it undoubtedly will, Cobbett will be put up against the wall with the rest of us. But whereas you and I will go there with a certain amount of dignity, Cobbett will be dragged there, screaming."

The landlord was back with the ale, and Whitley said grandly: "Have one yourself, Welks."

Welks bowed, bobbing his bald head up and down. "You're very kind, sir . . ."

Peter drank heavily and rose to his feet. He said, only a trifle unsteadily: "That must be my sixth or seventh pint this evening, Mr. Whitley, and Nature calls. In one ear and out the other. By your leave . . ."

"Of course," Whitley said gravely. "Even a gentleman must piss when the time comes. It's the one thing we have in common with the rabble."

Peter went outside and urinated into the gutter, and as he stood there listening to the euphoric sound of the mighty splashing, he was aware that he was not alone. He turned his head and saw a shadow detaching itself from a dark doorway, a woman.

He tried to clench his muscles so that he could button up, but seven pints demanded their release and he was in anguish as she approached him, a middle-aged prostitute of unappetizing aspect, blowsy and unkempt, her lank hair, not even confined by a bonnet, hanging down over shoulders that were almost naked, the string of her torn blouse so loose that her heavy breasts were half exposed; the sound of her wooden clogs on the cobblestones was sharp and incisive.

She said, a smile on her melancholy face: " 'Ello, ducky, 'ow are you this evenin'? Do you feel like a bit of the old in-and-out? It'll only cost you a shillin', an' all me customers tell me I'm a ray of sunshine in the middle of the night, and a lot of them gentry too . . ."

Peter turned away, wondering if the streaming would ever come to its end, and he said awkwardly, trying not to show his distaste: "No, no, though I thank you . . ."

"Ninepence then," she said, whining. "Ninepence can't be too much for the pleasures I can give you, sir? Ninepence? And nothin' for the room, I've got me own place, just round the corner on Mermaid Court."

It was not the first time he'd been approached by a prostitute, and he almost never knew what to do or say. He fumbled in the pocket of his trews and found a shilling and gave it to her, and said, any excuse better than none at all: "It so happens . . . so happens . . ." He searched for the words. "Just an hour ago I left my mistress. There's really nothing I could do now."

"Oh."

"I mean . . . a man has only so much energy, it's limited."

"Oh."

"So . . . if you'll forgive me . . . ?"

There was that desperate shaking of the last few drops and the buttoning up, and as he moved away she called after him: "I'm 'ere every night, ducks, right outside the White 'Art, and all of me customers are gentry, 'onest they are . . ."

He was suddenly aware that he wanted no more of Mr. Whitley, whose butler was almost his equal, nor of the pub, and he kept on walking. The night was cold, the moon bright in a clear sky, and he walked off the intoxication, moving more briskly as he crossed the Thames over London Bridge, breathing in great gulps of the fresh night air. He found himself in Cannon Street and moved north onto Cheapside, finding pleasure and relief in the walking though he could not forget the

woman who had approached him. He walked on to Clerkenwell Road and was suddenly aware that the footsteps behind
him had been with him for a very long time. . . .

He stopped, and the footsteps stopped too, and when he
continued on his way the sound of them, more restrained
now, came to him once again. Street-robbers, then. He was not
far from the confines of London's historic walls, where the
dregs of humanity fought each other for survival. He waited,
listening, and suddenly there was a flurry of activity in the
darkness. A body came at him, leaping onto his back and pin-
ioning his arms to his side, and there were two other fists
driving relentlessly and in silence into his face and his
stomach.

He twisted himself around and fell to the ground, breaking free, but a cudgel came down ferociously on his head, and
as he almost lost consciousness he was aware that hands were
exploring his pockets. He screamed "No! No!" and fought,
driving his fist into a pale white face and hearing a bone crack.

And then they were gone; he heard their footsteps racing
away in the night to search out more compliant victims.

He got to his feet and leaned heavily into the stone wall
of a building. He felt in his pocket for his time piece and
found that it was still there, and he flipped open the case and
saw that it was half past nine. He sat down on the curb, his
feet in the gutter where water was gently flowing, carrying
with it on the way to the Thames all kinds of stinking refuse—
potato peelings, human excrement, apple cores, scraps of fetid
meat trimmings, dead rats, and fish heads from the market on
Goose Yard. . . . This was the gutter where Clerkenwell's poor
washed themselves when the dirt on their bodies became intolerable.

He looked up at the street sign carved into the stonework
of the corner building: *Herbal Hill.* And he wondered: Had he
consciously or even subconsciously guided his steps in this
direction?

No, it could not be! He had never heard the name Herbal Hill before that awful night in the Empire Officers' Club. And yet . . . "off Clerkenwell road" *she* had said, and what strange force had brought him to this narrow, slum-festered street? He rose heavily to his feet and explored the alleyway; four houses, as she had said, and one of them was abandoned, wooden planks nailed over its doors and its windows. And of the other three, only one had a basement.

He stood there for a long while, staring at the yellow light that came from its narrow window, set close to the ground. There were iron bars over it, and what looked like a piece of old blanket had been placed in position to serve as a curtain. He made up his mind at last and walked down the six steps that led to the door and knocked on it and waited . . .

There was a long, long silence, and then a muffled voice: "Go away, nobody's 'ome. Go away."

He said clearly: "Ivy? Is that you?"

The silence was shorter now. And then: "Yes. Who is it?"

"You won't know my name," Peter said, "but it's Peter Entwhistle, and we met in the kitchen of the Empire Officers' club. I'd like to talk with you, please?"

"The Empire Officers' Club? Well, it's where I work, but I don't remember ever . . ." She broke off, and he could hear her sudden gasp. "Yes, I do! 'Old on, sir, 'old a minute. . . ."

There was the sound of chains and bolts, and when the door opened at last, there she was, staring at him in shock. She said, her voice hushed: "Oh, my Gawd, what 'appened to you, sir?"

"Can I . . . can I come in?"

She stepped back quickly and closed the door after him, locking it again with a chain and a padlock, and she reached out and touched his face and said again: "Oh, my Gawd . . ." He was not really aware that he had been so badly hurt, but she said quickly: "I ain't got any proper disinfectant, sir, but per'aps a little biddy'll 'elp . . ."

She was leading him to an overstuffed armchair, its upholstery torn, and sitting him down there. He said "Biddy? I
don't believe I know what that is."

"Red biddy," Ivy said. "It's a spoonful or two of boot
polish in a lot of red wine, a good drink if you're not too fussy,
and a powerful disinfectant too. Just sit still . . ."

His unexpected arrival seemed not to disconcert her at all
as she found the bottle and moisteneed a rag and dabbed at his
bruised face with it; it smarted and burned him abominably,
but he suffered in silence. He said awkwardly as she held the
rag against his split lip: "I wish I knew what I'm doing here,
Ivy. But I don't, you know. I think I just . . . *gravitated* here,
for no reason at all."

"Oh, I knew you'd come, sir," she said nonchalantly.
"Sooner or later, I knew you'd be 'ere. I mean, when you
asked me where I lived. . . . It makes sense, don't it?"

"Yes. Yes, I suppose it does."

"I mean . . . the way you looked at me."

"I did?"

"Oh, yes. I can tell when a gentleman has designs. Why
don't I pour you a glass of biddy? Only I don't 'ave no glasses,
it'll 'ave to be a tin mug. I'm sure you won't mind."

She had dispensed with her club working clothes, the
long black skirt and the cotton blouse and the gray bonnet,
and was dressed in a simple shift and nothing else, a sheath
that covered her body and still seemed to expose it. She was
really quite pretty, he thought, a sweet and gentle face, and
eyes that gave promise of great understanding. He watched her
pouring from the bottle into two small metal cups, liking the
way she moved, enjoying the free movement of her breasts
under the cheap homespun.

He looked over the tiny room, no more than ten feet
square. A simple brass bedstead, propped up at one broken leg
with bricks, a broken-down armchair in which he was sitting
now, a washbasin with its pottery jug and bowl in a corner, an

iron bucket of water beneath it, a pine-plank cupboard, a shelf on the wall on which there were a dozen books . . .

He rose and went to look at the books; a Bible, three penny dreadfuls, an *Old Moore's Almanac*, a dilapidated volume of bound copies of *Strand* magazine, a copy of *Mr. Winter's Travels in Arcadia*, and several romances by authors he'd never heard of.

Ivy said proudly: "I like to read, sir. When there's nothing else to do, I just . . . read a book."

There was also a copy of a novel called *She Liked to Be Whipped*, and he flipped its pages and looked at the lurid illustrations. He said, not turning to face her: "Are you a prostitute, Ivy?"

"No, sir."

Her voice was very steady. "I entertain me gentlemen friends sometimes, but not very often. And I don't like to take money from them unless I 'ave to. Me wages don't go very far, not with the prices like they are today. But I'm not a whore, sir, even though there's lots of them livin' around 'ere, if that's all a gentleman wants from a girl. It's just that . . . well, a girl can't starve to death, can she?" Her voice was a little uncertain. "It's a question of keepin' 'er self-respect, sir, and not finishin' up in the gutter, which 'appens all the time. And I've never in me life, sir, taken money from anyone 'oo respects me, never."

He turned to face her now and saw that her eyes were sad: "Potatoes are a ha'penny a pound now and beef drippin' is three farthin's for enough to fry them in, a girl 'as to have more than her wages. . . . But I don't take money from people I like, sir. It wouldn't be right."

She was across the room, a little distance from him, and he found that she was quite enchanting. He said slowly: "May I stay here tonight, Ivy?"

"Yes, sir."

"I mean . . . sleep with you?"

"Yes, sir, I know what you mean, sir."

"Good. That makes me . . . well, a very happy man."

He closed the book and put it back on the shelf and noticed that the author was apparently a man named Cecil Flogg. He picked up his mug and drained the red biddy, feeling it searing his throat, and said amiably: "Could I have another, do you think? Tomorrow, I promise you, I will go out and buy you some wine."

"Yes, of course, anythin' you want, sir, anythin' at all."

"And you really mustn't call me 'sir,' " Peter said. "My name is Peter, Ivy."

"Yes, sir, Mr. Peter sir."

The bed was unmade, and she went to it and smoothed it over, and said, ashamed: "I don't always make it before I leave in the mornin', the way I should, you know 'ow it is, by the time I've made me tea I'm goin' to be late for work already, and I'm very fussy about not bein' late for work. It's a long walk to St. James from 'ere."

She straightened up and turned to face him. "And would you like me to take me clothes off now, sir? Or would you like to sit and talk first? You're upset about somethin', ain't you? Aren't you?"

"No, not really. Just . . . no, not upset at all. You're a very attractive young woman, Ivy, did you know that? Very . . . yes, attractive indeed." That awful drink was going to his head very quickly.

She pushed the straps of her shift off her shoulders, let the garment drop to the floor, and lay down on the bed, quite naked. He stripped off his clothes and tried to pass the time by folding them meticulously and setting them down just so, and he said at last, his voice a little hoarse: "The first time I'm afraid it will be very fast. I'm terribly excited."

"That's all right, sir, I don't mind."

"Please, please don't call me 'sir.' "

"No, sir. Yes. I mean . . . Yes, sir, Peter."

Her body was soft and white and very comforting, and her eyes were wide and wondering as he loved her. There was a kind of euphoria for him here, and all his worries seemed trivial in her embrace. He lay beside her at last and stared up at the ceiling where the plaster was peeling off and there were great patches of damp, a basement room that drew in the moisture from the foul gutters of the street.

She whispered: "Was it good for you, sir? I mean, if there's anything else I should have done. . . ?"

His hand was at her young breast. "Yes, it was good . . ."

"And will you stay all night? I mean . . . you don't 'ave to go 'ome, do you?"

"No. I don't really have a home, Ivy. Not anymore. A family, yes, but they are far removed from me now, perhaps irrevocably so. But not a *home*."

He was to stay with her for nearly four months.

The next day, he walked back to the White Hart and collected his suitcase and just moved in with her as though it were the most natural thing in the world. There was no spoken arrangement about money, but he found himself buying the potatoes and the beef dripping, and once a week or so even an aitchbone.

Every morning at half-past six Ivy would leave for the long walk to the Empire Officers' Club, and Peter would relieve her of the chore of cleaning up the tiny basement room. By ten o'clock he would take his morning constitutional, stopping off for a tankard of ale at the Pig and Whistle before returning to sit in that dreadful armchair and read Cobbett's *Register*, imbuing himself with a kind of anger that was only partly intellectual and mostly heart.

Then one day there was an experience in store for him that he could only think of as traumatic. . . .

Ivy had returned from her work at nine o'clock or so, and

she said casually: "You never go around to the Swan and Sugar Loaf these days, Peter. You should, you know."

He smiled. "I'm happier in your company, Ivy."

"Yes, and I'm glad of it. But . . . why don't you go and have a pint or two this evening? It's good for a man to get out of the house once in a while."

He laughed. "Are you trying to get rid of me?"

But he saw that her eyes were very somber, and she said, her voice tinged with an unaccustomed hardness: "There's someone coming to see me, Peter."

He stared at her. "Coming to see you? I'm not sure what that means."

"Major Lord Lovell. He offered me a pound. I can't afford to say no. A pound. Twenty shillings."

The blood was draining from his face. "You mean . . . ?"

"Yes. You 'ave to be gone, for an hour or two. He mustn't find you 'ere. Arthur Lovell of the Grenadiers, a very rich man. It's just . . . just a question of money, Peter, nothin' else, really it isn't."

For a long time Peter was silent, and his heart was beating so hard he wondered if she could hear it. Trying to keep any harshness from his voice he said quietly: "I *have* told you, Ivy, very many times, that when you need money . . . I have enough."

"No!" she said desperately. "No, no, no! I've *never* wanted to take your money, you know that! I mean, it's . . . different with us, I've always told you that!"

It was an argument he could not counter. He had been with her for a very long time now, never, after the first two or three efforts, offering her any money at all, contenting himself with paying all the household expenses just as a husband would—the food, the rent, the candles, the coal, and three warmer blankets for their bed. All these weeks he had been happy, if that was the word, spending his evenings writing pamphlets which he sometimes had to pay to get published; the profession of pamphleteer was not a happy one and was sometimes even downright dangerous. Cobbett, Arnold, Whittaker, Frank, and now Entwhistle . . . these were the names whose crudely printed sheets were passed out by street urchins to anyone who would accept them. And sometimes they found their way into the hands of that nebulous entity known as the authorities . . .

He wrote a long and angry article one night about the meanness of this existence and took it to the *Register*'s office the next morning in the hopes of persuading the editor to publish it, scurrilous though it was. But he found the office to be in shambles, its windows broken, its furniture smashed, its ancient printing press being wrecked by a dozen burly young men with crowbars.

He had stood there in astonishment, not understanding at all what was going on or why this should be. Until, that is, one of the men—was he their leader?—snatched the sheaf of papers from his hand, reading laboriously and at random, and quoting aloud to his fellows some of its passages:

> . . . *it is a matter of the deliberate suppression of the working classes, most of whom seem not to work because there is no work for them, in a calculated endeavor, bolstered by acts of Parliament, to ensure that the legitimate complaints of these unfortunates will never be heard, that they themselves will never leave the squalor in which they were born. . . . In God's name and the name of justice, is there not one voice in Westminster that will cry out in their defense. . . . ?*

He tore up the pages, dropped them to the floor, and looked at Peter with a frightening malice in very hard eyes. "What's your name, fellow?"

"If you tell me by what right you ask," Peter said coldly, "I will give you my name. Not otherwise."

There was just a moment of mildness. "What right? The *constables* sent us, scum!" And then a massive fist shot out and buried itself in Peter's stomach. He doubled up in pain and righted himself before he was ready, striking out in his own defense, finding his arm caught and twisted up behind his back. Another of them was driving the heavy end of a cudgel skillfully into his chest and groin, and he fell to the ground, vomiting. He heard them laugh, and then he was picked up bodily and thrown like a rag doll through one of the broken windows onto the street. He lost consciousness for a while, and when he came to and went stubbornly back into the building, they had all gone, and the *Register's* offices had been reduced to a shambles. A water pipe had been wrenched off the wall, its faucet twisted off, and everything on the floor was sodden with ink-blacked water.

Back in the Herbal Hill room, he had let Ivy tend to his bruises with a hot bread poultice, and that night he began another of his articles:

> *I was witness this morning to the destruction of Mr. Cobbett's offices and presses by a gang of Irish bully boys who claimed they were hired by the constables for this vandalism. I can only suppose that this, too, is a matter of deliberate policy on the part of the magistrates and their hirelings. . . .*

In the morning he collected his things from Herbal Hill and caught the midday coach to Manchester.

Chapter Six

It was a grimy, sodden town, where the factories were cheek by jowl, belching out their noxious gray fumes.

This was the color of Manchester—the gray slate roofs, the gray stone walls, the gray-cobbled streets; even the sky seemed constantly gray. And when he saw for the first time the undernourished young children in their gray rags streaming out onto the streets at the sound of the factory bells, children as grimy as the city itself, he knew that if his voice were ever to be raised, it would be on behalf of these sad urchins and their families.

He found a bed-sitting room in the house of one Mrs. Brice, who eked out a meager living by renting out the four small rooms of her cottage. "One and fourpence ha'penny a week," she said. "It's not too much for a right clean room, now, is it?"

Peter nodded. "A very fair price, I would say."

"Ye get a plate of porridge brought to the room every morning at six, which is the time ye'll have to be up and about if ye've come here lookin' for work. Ey, there's not much of it around these days."

"I'm not really looking for work at the moment," Peter said. He wondered why he should feel so guilty. "At least, not factory work."

"Oh? Then would it be presumptuous of me to ask what it is ye do for a livin', sir?"

He sighed. "Well, I have . . . I have a very little money of my own set aside, not very much, but enough to live on for a while. And I write . . . pamphlets. I'm a pamphleteer."

The Mancunians were known for their suspicious nature, and the good Mrs. Brice was no exception. "And ye get *paid* for that, sir?" she asked.

"Very rarely, I'm afraid."

"Well . . ." She shrugged her bony shoulders. "It takes all kinds to make a world. And will ye be stayin' long, sir?"

He was standing by the window, staring down at the damp street, where little groups of men in baggy clothes and caps stood on the corners in threes and fours, saying nothing, doing nothing, just . . . standing disconsolately there. "I think so," he said wryly. "I've seen very little of Manchester as yet, but what I have seen . . . Yes, perhaps for quite a long time."

It was cold and damp in the room, the moisture seeping through to his marrow. "And is there a Mr. Brice? If so, I'd very much like to chat with him when he comes home. Perhaps over a mug of ale?"

"Ey, Mr. Brice died three years ago, sir, an accident at work. There's just me and the children, three of them."

"Oh, I'm sorry." How old is she? he wondered. Fifty, perhaps? "And the children?" he asked. "Are they working?"

"Only the girl, sir, the eldest, she's ten. She works a loom at the Livingstone place, it's not a bad job for a young girl. The boys are five and seven. And if I could trouble you, sir, for the money, I like to get paid in advance if I can."

"Of course." As he counted out the one and fourpence ha'penny, she said: "The privy's out in the yard, and there's always a brolly kept at the back door in case it's rainin'. I'll bring you a cup of tea at four o'clock, and supper's served at half-past six."

"Thank you, Mrs. Brice. Do you have any other guests here? Factory workers, I mean."

"Mr. Hoskins, he's over at the Britannia Company, woolens, though he can't rightly be called much of a factory *worker*. He's in packin', or supposed to be, but he spends most of his time on strike, or demonstratin', or just . . . just raisin' hell, if you'll pardon the expression, sir. He's a nice enough man, but he never rightly knows when to speak up, and when to shut up." There was an unexpected laughter in her gray eyes, and he smiled, catching her mood.

"Then he might be just the kind of man I'd like to speak with," Peter said; and when he met with his fellow guest that evening he was surprised to find a quiet and very soft-spoken man in his forties who did not in the least look like a hell-raiser. Hoskins was slight and wiry, with gentle, intelligent eyes that seemed to catch fire from time to time and at others were almost veiled over, as though everything behind them had to be hidden from the outside world.

They sat together in the public bar of the Star and Garter and drank the local bitter; the bar was full, but Peter noticed that the ale was not flowing very fast. Many of the men there were waiting for someone to buy them a drink, some more fortunate fellow who'd put in a full fourteen hours' work this day.

As though reading his mind, Hoskins said quietly: "There's nothing for an honest workingman quite as sad as the sight of empty tankards in a crowded bar, Mr. Entwhistle. Ey, Mancester's not what it used to be."

Peter offered his cigarette case. "And is it really the hellhole that Cobbett says it is, Mr. Hoskins?"

"Cobbett? Our Willie Cobbett? You know him?"

"No. I know *of* him, and once I almost met him, but not quite." He told Hoskins of the brush with the Irish who had been wrecking the office, and his new friend listened in silence till he had finished, looking thoughtfully into his beer. He said at last: "Then you could say the day was won by the magistrates."

"Yes, I suppose so. When I came around, I went back into the office to . . . I don't know what for, I just felt I wanted to hit back."

"One of you against so many?"

"Foolish, of course."

"They could have killed you."

"I was angry, very angry. An angry man seldom thinks clearly."

"That's not true, Mr. Entwhistle," Hoskins said mildly. "I'm one of the angriest men you've ever met. And my mind's as clear as a bell. Will you let me tell you why you lost out to them?"

"I think I know the answer to that."

"Because they were using force, and you wanted to use reason. It's unequal combat, and that's always been Willie Cobbett's mistake too."

"How so?"

"He thinks words will change our condition. They won't."

It worried Peter a little, but there was something else that intrigued him; in spite of the rough clothes, the threadbare jacket, the torn trews, the rag at the throat of the collarless shirt, and the cloth cap, Hoskins was somehow . . . out of place. He said slowly: "I trust you won't think it rude of me, Mr. Hoskins, but . . . you're not really a workingman yourself, are you?"

A thin smile spread over Hoskins' face. "Are *you*, Mr. Entwhistle?"

"No, sir, I cannot so class myself."

"And yet, unless you're feeding me a passel of lies, you're on our side."

Peter said hotly: "A passel of *lies?*"

Hoskins waved a nonchalant hand. "Oh, don't take offense," he said, "this is a time for frankness. I'll take a small bet that you've not yet reached the age of twenty-five, which makes me old enough to be your father, but you've decided to try to help the underprivileged, and that's something I started doing a long, long time ago, back in the days when girls were employed as spinners in the cotton gins at one and ninepence a week, at the age of *six.* I'm an old hand at this work, Mr. Entwhistle, and if you're truly on my side, then I welcome you with open arms. And to answer your question . . . yes, I *am* a workingman. But I have the benefit of a tolerably good education. Which, I flatter myself, I put to good use."

"A rare quality in the factories," Peter murmured, and Hoskins said at once: "Yes! And do you know, sir, the three qualities which the workingman lacks above all else? In ascending order of importance, he lacks education, food in his belly . . . and gumption."

"Your priorities surprise me."

"They should not! By gumption, I mean the will to *fight.* And not with words either. Action, Mr. Entwhistle! We have to make our presence known, *unforgettably* known! There is no quality in the world more important for a rebel than this! And if you stay with us in Manchester for a very few years, you will see what Mancunians can achieve when they're driven too hard."

He lowered his voice; even here, it seemed, there were secrets. "It is in Manchester that the revolution will start. When? God alone knows! I know only that I will be part of it. And it is my hope that you will be too."

He drained his tankard and raised a finger to the landlord:

"That's two pints of bitter, Ramsbotham." He looked over the crowded room and said: "And a half for Renck in the corner there, and for Charlie Ray. Give Mrs. Billing a best port and lemon too, compliments of the league."

Peter said, puzzled: "The league?"

"Why, the Workingmen's League," Hoskins said. "That's what we all are, workingmen, aren't we?"

"And the League buys port and lemon for its members? I find that strange."

The cloud was over Hoskins' eyes again. He said softly: "Don't push too hard, Mr. Entwhistle. You'll find out where we get our money from when the time is ripe. Not before."

He lay awake one night in his cold and dreary room, wondering how he could make himself more acceptable a part of a local society which, he knew, tended to distrust him as an outsider, and worried too much about their certainty that violent confrontation with authority was inevitable. It was an argument he fought vehemently against, but there were very few among the workers who would listen to him; and one of those demonstrations over which they argued so strongly took place two weeks later.

At shortly after eight in the morning, Hoskins came to his room, smiling gently, and said: "Am I disturbing you, Entwhistle? I hope not."

"Of course not," Peter said. "Come on in. I just made some tea."

"Ah . . ."

He had learned how to boil a small kettle of water on his open hand warmer, blowing on the smoldering charcoal in the brass container from time to time to coax it into flame.

He chipped at the ice on top of the milk bottle, poured, and said: "Almost my only weakness. I never leave the house in the morning without three cups of tea in my belly. It's a great fortification against the day's disasters."

Hoskins picked up the book Peter had been studying, and said: "French? You read it fluently?"

"Oh, yes. I've been studying for a long time now. I like to think that it keeps my mind active. French, Spanish, Italian, even German. When it rains so hard a man can't even step out of the house . . . that's what I do. Study. Well . . ."

"And are you planning on going out today?"

It was a surprising sort of question. "Yes," Peter said. "I found a very good secondhand bookshop in Market Square."

"Stay out of Market Square this morning. It's not a healthy place to be today."

Peter stared, "Oh?"

"The Britannia Company's on strike today, four hundred and eighty workers demonstrating."

He was smiling gently, and he took his timepiece from his fob pocket and said: "One hour ago they smashed the last of the looms. Now that's where they're gathering. Stay off Market Square."

"But . . . but we should be there, Hoskins! If only to control them! You've told me yourself, your Britannia people are very easily aroused."

"My tutelage," Hoskins said smugly. "That's the way I taught them to be."

"Well," Peter said, gulping his tea, "I'm going over there to see what I can do to stop a demonstration from becoming a riot."

"No," Hoskins said. "They have guns, Entwhistle."

Peter felt his blood curdling. *"What?"*

"Three rifles, two revolvers, all in the hands of ex-soldiers who know how to use them."

"Oh, my god . . ." He said wrathfully: "And how long do you think it will be before the magistrates find out? Hoskins, for God's sake! The news will be out within the hour, and they'll have the militia there . . ."

"Not the militia," Hoskins said. "The Dragoons."

"The *Dragoons?*" Peter felt that his face was white. Hoskins put down his cup and took him by the shoulders. The smile had quite gone now, and there was only a dreadful earnestness in its place. He said heavily: "You will not approve of this, Peter, I know it. But you're a very young man, a boy, unskilled in these matters, and now . . . you must listen to your betters." He took a long deep breath and said slowly: "The Dragoons have been warned. They'll be there. I warned them myself. We need martyrs now."

It seemed to Peter that all of common sense was gone, that the whole world was falling about his ears. He shouted: "Damn you, Hoskins, damn you!"

He rushed from the room and ran all the way to Market Square, pushing his way under the bellies of the Dragoons' horses lined up in ordered array at all the four entrances to the square. The square was packed tight with screaming, sweating bodies, all yelling imprecations at the show of military might, which had taken them by surprise. He eased his way slowly toward them, leaving the line of troopers behind him, half fearful of the sound of a shot at him which might mean his death.

But the sound that came startled him out of his wits: "*Entwhistle!*"

He turned and saw the Dragoons' commander sitting his horse in front of his men, less than twenty yards away, a face he knew very well indeed, the last time from the Curzon Street house four or five years ago. It was a red-whiskered face, red-cheeked, red-nosed, and in his memories red-eyed too, with too much hospitable whiskey. The voice called again: "Entwhistle!" and then: "Peter Entwhistle, by all that's holy! What the devil are you doing here with this rabble, boy?"

Peter stared up into a face that was far from friendly but still a link with the past. He said hesitantly: "Major Murdoch, is it not, sir?"

"Of course it's Major Murdoch!" the major roared. "Who the bloody hell else would I be? Jesus bloody Christ? Answer my question! What are you doing here with this rabble?"

"I am trying to prevent bloodshed," Peter said testily, not trying to mask his anger.

A lieutenant came cantering up and saluted with a swift movement of his drawn saber. He said: "We've just been informed, Major, there are fifty rifles among them somewhere."

"Not fifty!" Peter said at once. "They have three rifles and two revolvers, I *know!* . . . That's why I came here, to make sure they don't use them, and invite your response! It's been *arranged*, Major Murdoch! They want martyrs!"

There was a long silence, and then the major said, very quietly: "You know me, Peter. I'm a field officer in the Lancers, and if what you say is true . . ."

"It's true, sir."

"I won't be drawn into this kind of a trap. I'll slaughter the bloody heathen Pathans till the day I die, but I don't want to open fire on honest Englishmen, however misguided they may be. . . . But if they fire one single shot, boy . . ."

"Yes, sir, I understand."

"Do you have any authority with them?"

"No, sir."

"Can you assume it?"

"I can try."

"Then do so."

"Yes, sir."

Peter turned, walked toward the screaming mob, and held up his hands for silence. Not to his surprise, it made no difference at all and he shouted at the top of his voice: "Listen to me! Listen to me! I am Peter Entwhistle, Hoskins' close friend! Listen to me!"

At the sound of Hoskins' name the shouting died down somewhat, and he yelled: "There are four hundred of you . . . and three hundred of *them*! And *they* are armed to the teeth with muskets, swords, and lances! If one single shot is fired, they will charge you! And how many of you will die? Twenty? Thirty? Forty? This is a battle we cannot win! Go home! The odds are too high! We must learn . . . *must* learn . . . never to start a fight that we cannot win!"

The shouting had reduced itself to discontented rumblings, and he turned on his heel and strode back to the major. He said: "You heard what I said, sir. I think they are half convinced, but no more than that. Will you withdraw your men?"

"What?" The major was almost apoplectic. "Withdraw them? Are you mad? My orders, sir, are to put an end to a riot before it begins."

"Which we have done."

Peter turned and looked back at the crowd, milling about now in disorder and uncertainty. The lieutenant was still there, his horse prancing, and the major turned to him and said: "The bugler, Mr. Hardcourt. Send him to me."

"Yes, sir."

When the bugler reined in, Major Murdoch said to him: "Sound the retreat, the regroup, the column of fours."

"Yes, sir."

"And if a single shot is fired from that rabble," the major said testily, "you will not wait for the order, you will sound the charge at once. A single shot will be your command."

"Yes, sir!" He raised the polished brass bugle to his lips and pursed them, and the melodious notes of the retreat filled the air. As the troopers swung their mounts around, a great shout went up from the crowd; it was a notable triumph for them. And as the horsemen regrouped into their column of fours for the ride back to the barracks, the square slowly emptied of its press of bodies, till Peter found himself quite alone,

save for one black-skirted woman he had seen before somewhere. Where could it have been?

It was in the pub, with Hoskins. Mrs. Billing, a lady who
liked port and lemon bought for her by the Workingmen's
League.

She came to him, laid a hand on his arm, and whispered:
"I'm so glad, Mr. Entwhistle sir. My son Harry had one of
them guns. I've never been so fearful in all me born days.
They'd have killed him."

"Yes. Yes, it's quite possible. It's a rule of survival, Mrs.
Billing, that if you curse a lot of men with guns . . . they're
quite liable to curse you back, with bullets. And another rule
is, never fight at all unless you have a chance to win. Here
there was no chance at all."

Could he tell her that her son had been detailed as . . . a
martyr? He thought not.

"Let's call it *half* a victory," Hoskins said that night as
they sat together in the Star and Garter. "I should be very
angry with you. You used my name in quite the wrong con-
text. But I'm not." He said sardonically: "It's one of the advantages of that education of mine which you find so strange
that it enables me to recognize a man of goodwill when I see
one. A rare creature, I assure you. And perhaps we need them
almost as much as we need fighters. Men of *gumption*. Let's
have another pint of bitter, shall we?"

When Peter went back at last to his freezing room, he sat
down to compose a long letter, not to Amanda, but to Susan.
He wrote:

My Darling Susan,

    *I dare not try to count the long years that have passed
since that awful night when, in a fit of pique, like the*

*spoiled child I always was, I stalked out of our beautiful,
friendly house into a world that I have found to be filled
with hostility. . . .*

He found it hard to continue. He had forgotten to buy
charcoal for his hand warmer, and he held his cupped hands
over the candle flame until they warmed up a trifle. Then he
took the two blankets from the bed and draped them over his
shoulders as he sat in the armchair to think for a while.

Susan! In God's name, how old was she now? Had she
forgotten him altogether? And James? And poor Hilda? He
said to himself: I am not stubborn. I simply made a wrong
decision that cannot easily be rectified, not after all these
years.

He strode briskly around the little room for a while and
then took the big glass jug from the shelf and went out into
the drizzle and across the road to the Star and Garter. Hoskins
was there with Mr. Renck of the United British Company,
cotton and yard goods, but he contented himself with a wave
of the hand and said to the landlord: "A jug of brown, Mr.
Ramsbotham, if you'd be so kind."

The landlord pulled on the polished ebony handle. "A
night at home, Mr. Entwhistle?"

"Yes, a letter to write."

"Mrs. Brice has the coldest house in all of Manchester.
Thank God you're not a brass monkey."

Peter laughed. "Yes, I think it must be. Perhaps a half of
bitter here before I go, to warm up."

"Make it a pint, Mr. Entwhistle, on the house. We heard
what you did today."

"We were lucky. A ghost out of my past."

"A ghost?"

"A ghost with red whiskers and a whiskey nose. A major
I once knew was in command of the Dragoons. It helped."

"Well, we're all glad of it. Tom's a good man, but . . ." He lowered his voice. "Don't tell him I said so, but he does get a bit rambunctious once in a while."

"Tom?"

"Why, Tom Hoskins, Mr. Entwhistle."

"Oh." In all this time, he had never before known Hoskins' given name. He raised his tankard and said: "Here's to you, Mr. Ramsbotham. And to men of goodwill everywhere."

"I'll drink to that. Your good health, sir."

Within the hour, his bones unfrozen now, he was back at the wooden table and writing again, the most difficult piece of composition he had ever attempted:

I am tempted to devote this letter to what might be called news of my adventures, but the awful weight of my own stubbornness precludes the recounting of such trivia, and the true reason for it is to ask for forgiveness, both from you and from Amanda. And what this means, my darling Susan, is that I want to come home. . .

He put down his pen and rested his head in his hands, worrying about what he had just written. Did he truly wish to return to Curzon Street and all that it stood for? To his family, yes! But the one was inseparable from the other. He sipped his beer and then began gulping it; and in a little while he went down onto the street to relieve himself. A steady sleet was falling, and the darkness was absolute. He thought of London's West End, where the new gaslights in the streets were turning night into day and delighting everyone; up here in Manchester, even the moon was obliterated by dank and heavy clouds.

He went back upstairs and warmed his hands again at the candle, noticing for the first time that there were chap sores across his knuckles. He wondered if it were perhaps a kind of delight in self-punishment that kept him here. He read through what he had written and knew that his letter would never be sent.

And in a moment he held it to the candle flame and watched it burn.

He was to spend eight years in Manchester.

In spite of the very marked differences in their philosophies, he had become very friendly with Tom Hoskins. "Rambunctious," the landlord at the Star and Garter had called him, and this was certainly true. But his mind was bright and imaginative, and the ends he was trying to achieve, if not the means to them, were laudable.

From time to time there were other demonstrations, food riots, protest marches (some of them very highly organized). And always, forewarned, the constables or the militia were there; Tom Hoskins was still searching for his martyrs.

In this period, seven of Manchester's factories closed down, put out of business by vandalized looms, the owners just giving up and putting their money instead into Spanish and Portuguese vineyards; the exchange of cotton piece goods for Iberia's wines had long been an established and highly profitable trade.

During these years, too, Mrs. Brice's eldest daughter, Nellie, died at the age of fourteen after losing her arm to one of the new machines in the Livingstone Mill. Abel Livingstone, the sole owner, paid Mrs. Brice four pounds in compensation while not admitting responsibility for the accident; it was enough for her to live on for two months now that her major source of family income was gone. (Both of the boys, old enough to be on the job market, had been able to find only casual work shoveling coal on Manchester's docks.)

The firebrand Renck died, from the intake of too much drink, at the age of fifty, and the Workingmen's League was making itself felt very strongly, centering its demands ("outrageous," the establishment called them) for representation in Parliament.

All this time, Peter had immersed himself in what he thought of as his "calling," writing virulent pamphlets against the injustices of the day, paying more often now for their publication from his rapidly dwindling resources, and sometimes—to his surprise—being paid a few shillings for them. Some found their way into the pages of the *Political Register*, still functioning sporadically between periods of vandalism and mayhem; some were merely passed around the factories in a conscious effort to bring home to the workers the misery of their condition and persuade them that with unity they might be able to alleviate it.

As a result of these writings, he was immensely popular.

It was the summer of 1815, the time of Napoleon's final defeat and of his incarceration on the island of St. Helena, and Peter was twenty-seven now, no longer an immature youth but a man filled with the fire of his vocation. He had taken to affecting a battered top hat as he sat every evening in the Star and Garter, always at his own table, which Mr. Ramsbotham kept for him, making notes on scraps of paper as they occurred to him, enjoying the friendship and yes, the admiration of his fellows. His beard was long and full now, and like a kind of resident sage, albeit still young for that elevated position, he would accept the pints of ale that were offered him, saying: "Thank you, Mr. Pollock, and we will talk about the number of accidents in your mill over the last three months . . ." Or: "Your health, Mr. Murphy, and what can you tell me about the fines being levied in Harcourt's Gin for not meeting management-imposed quotas?"

And always, at the end of the night's drinking: "If you'd pour drinks all round, Mr. Ramsbotham. . . ?"

His limited money was disappearing very fast.

*　*　*

It was in November of the year 1816 that Hoskins invited him to return, for a quick visit, to London.

They were sitting together in their habitual meeting place, the saloon bar of the Star, detached from the working-men over on the other side of the partition in the public bar, where ale was a farthing less for a pint.

The candles shone in the incised glass, and there were little advertising signs everywhere: *What we want is a Watney's*, and, *Guinness is good for you*. The ebony handles of the pumps, with their mahogany inserts, were in constant use as the bartenders pulled up the foaming brews.

Hoskins said, in that conspiratorial way of talking that he had: "It's not been easy, Peter, but at last we've brought London into the fight. They're soft down there in the South, they don't have the gumption of the Mancunians. But they've agreed to join with us now, and it's a great day for the working-man all over England. I'm off to a meeting there. Will you come with me?"

"Well," Peter said cautiously, "if you'll tell me what the meeting's about."

"It's about the most important of our demands," Hoskins said, an edge of triumph in his voice. "It's about . . . representation for the industrial towns of the Midlands in Parliament."

"Ah . . . it's been long overdue! Yes, I'll be glad to come with you. If only to keep you out of trouble, Tom."

He laughed. "Representation? If it can ever be achieved, and it won't be easy, it'll be the first step toward an industrial revolution. A bloodless revolution, of course."

"Of course," Hoskins said. "They've promised me near a thousand people. But it'll be peaceful, no one to get hurt. You'll see."

"So be it, then. When?"

"Tomorrow morning," Hoskins said. "We leave on the six-o'clock coach." He took the two tickets from his pocket and waved them at Peter. He said happily: "And believe you me, we'll set the bloody Houses of Parliament on their bloody ears this time!"

But there was a warning bell ringing in Peter's mind. He said slowly: "In the past, Tom, and you know that I've always disagreed with you over this, you've often warned the authorities yourself."

"Once or twice, Peter," Hoskins said smoothly, "no more than once or twice. In a justifiable endeavor to build a mountain of what is all too often a bloody molehill."

"Whatever the reasons, I disapprove. This time. . . ?"

"This time the magistrates will know *nothing*, believe me." He called for a refill of their mugs and said, suddenly very serious: "It's being called by the Spenceans, Peter, and they don't play games. Perhaps we'll learn something from them. You know who they are?"

Peter shook his head, and Hoskins said cryptically: "Well, you'll soon find out. The one thing the Spenceans truly believe in is making their presence *felt*."

 # Chapter Seven

In London, the winter of the year 1816 was particularly savage. There was more than a foot of snow on the streets of the City. But it had none of snow's pristine purity; it was gray-black, covered with a thin film of soot that clung to a man's boots when he ventured through it. The soot covered the snow like a dismal shroud. To Peter, it seemed little better than Manchester.

The warehouse was filled with machinery destined for shipment to the New World, but not one of the laborers was here this morning; reporting for work before the sun was up, they had been turned away by guards at the gates, brawny men armed with cudgels and ready to use them, who had simply stated: "The Spenceans are here, comrades, be on your way. Get back to your wives and warm them up on this cold morning." The speech of the guards was affable, but their mien was menacing, and so half a hundred laborers, wondering where the pennies would come from to recompense them for the loss of a day's work, turned grudgingly away; the Spenceans were not to be taken lightly.

When the two of them entered the small warehouse—

Hoskins, Peter saw, merely flashed a printed card—they found that more than eight hundred of these angry men, very many of them from the North, were gathered here, crowding over packing cases, squatting on the floor, perched on shelving that seemed ready to collapse under their communal weight; some of them were even up in the rafters, drinking sour ale which they had brought with them in any kind of container they could find; this was to be a great occasion for them.

The so-called Spencean Philanthropists were listening now to a speech from their Leader, one Mr. Spence from Yorkshire, a schoolmaster turned politician and agitator. He was a small and fiery man who wore a bedraggled frock coat of black wool and very tight knee breeches of the same material, with a gray cravat around his throat. He carried a tall hat which he used to emphasize his gestures as he spoke, and he was striding up and down a dais made from packing cases, haranguing the crowd.

He said, shouting: ". . . and I will tell you, my good friends, the evil of this age lies in . . . the *machine!* The machine that is putting so many of your good friends and mine out of work, and if a man does not work, how will he eat? How will his family eat? His wife, his children? Must they all *starve?*"

There was a roar of approval from the crowd, and he went on, waving his hat for silence: "It is a cornerstone of the Spencean philosophy that all machines must be outlawed by acts of Parliament, *all* of them! No more of the damned mechanical looms that take the bread from the hungry mouths of your families and mine! We *must* destroy them!" There was the applause again, and he shouted: "You all know me well, an honest and God-fearing man, and I tell you, one stocking machine is now doing the work of forty-two men! One single loom! And how many stocking looms are there in Manchester alone?" He paused for effect and answered his own question: "There are seven thousand of the new looms now in operation in *our* industrial North! And if you want a figure, I will give you one! It means . . . two hundred and ninety-four *thousand* men out of work!"

Over the deafening applause, a single voice was raised, and it was Peter's. He was standing on a crate, a little above the crowd, and he called out: "By your leave, sir! May I speak?"

The applause died down, and there were very many eyes turned on him, aware that it was the voice of an educated man and therefore suspect.

Peter went on: "Can those two hundred and ninety-four thousand men, displaced from their hard labor at the stocking looms, not find work manufacturing the very machines that have displaced them? Will there not be even *more* work for them in a more progressive industry—the manufacture of such machines upon which our economic future depends?"

There was a small silence, and then Mr. Spence said very clearly (he was conscious of his northern audience): "By your speech, sir, you are a Londoner, I think?"

"Yes. Yes, I am. Though my home now is in Manchester."

Hoskins, beside him, whispered urgently: "Let him talk, Peter! What he says is . . . what they want to hear. . . ."

"And I want them to hear what will serve them better," Peter said angrily. "He's talking poppycock!"

But the schoolmaster was not fazed in the slightest; he knew well how to turn aside any unwanted reasoning. He said, mocking: "And will you tell me, sir, where is your home in London!"

"My home is . . . *was*, in Curzon Street. I left it some years ago to devote my energies to the improvement of the working man's condition."

"Curzon Street!" Mr. Spence made a wide, sweeping gesture with his hat as he turned back to the crowd. "Curzon

Street!" he said again. "And there is not one man living in
Curzon Street who has to eke out a paltry living on less than
five hundred pounds a year!"

His heavy sarcasm was not lost on the crowd, and they
roared their contempt for all that Curzon Street stood for.
When it died down, Peter said coldly: "I have, sir, the benefit
of an education and perhaps even of . . . of privileged birth,
though no longer of wealth. These advantages do not disqual-
ify me from a cause to which I am prepared to devote my life,
if need be."

Spence was laughing, a very happy man with the crowd
on his side. "And will you tell me your name, sir, if you are
not ashamed of it?"

"My name is Peter Entwhistle."

"Not *Lord* Peter Entwhistle?"

"No, sir. A plain mister, as in *Mr.* Spence."

"Well, *Mr.* Entwhistle, will you listen to a humble workingman?"

"I came here, sir, for that purpose. To listen to arguments, I was given to understand, concerning representation
in Parliament for the industrial North. And, indeed, to add to
them. I have heard no such discussion as yet . . ."

Someone shouted from the depths of the crowd: "Ey,
shut up, man! Sit down and shut up!" And the crowd roared
its agreement.

Mr. Spence raised his arms and called out: "We move out
now, my good friends! You all know your leaders! Follow
them! You all know our slogans! Shout them! You all know
our cause! Be prepared to fight for it!"

As the mob fought its way out through the warehouse
doorways, Spence jumped down from his dais and elbowed his
way among them. He said to Hoskins, furiously: "Who the
hell is this man, Tom? What's he doing here?"

Before Hoskins could answer, Peter said mildly: "I'm a

pamphleteer, Mr. Spence, working with a different weapon for the same cause you spoke of."

"Oh." Spence grunted. "Words, words, they've never helped us yet."

"They will, Mr. Spence. We must have patience." He turned away to join the crowd, but Hoskins' hand was on his arm, restraining him, and Spence said, a thin smile on his face now: "Patience means *following* a mob, Mr. Entwhistle, rather than leading it. It's always the people in the front who get hurt."

"Oh, God . . ."

They moved with the tail of the column, and Peter said, anguished: "For God's sake, Tom, what are they planning?"

For once, it seemed, Hoskins was unsure of himself. "I don't know," he said. "All I can say is . . . sharpen your pencil, Peter. You'll have plenty to write about before this day is over."

Ahead of them, a dozen burly men who wore armbands battered down the barricaded doors of a gunsmith's shop, and the mob milled about as they looted the assorted guns they found there, forty-seven of them all told. Peter tried to reach them, to calm them down, to plead, to reason with them, but two other men, wearing armbands, were holding his wrists behind his back as they propelled him forward, and he heard Hoskins' anxious voice: "Don't try to fight them, Peter . . ."

They moved on down Lombard Street and into Great Tower Street. And there the Dragoons were waiting for them.

The sharpshooters were on the rooftops, the tightly disciplined companies drawn up on the streets. The confrontation was short, sharp, and decisive. Eight of the rioters were killed and more than a hundred injured.

On the outskirts of the fray, Peter saw an old man being savagely beaten with rifle butts. He went to his help, and as he struggled with a trooper he saw a musket, swung by its barrel, raised high over his head. He threw himself to one side, but he was not expert in this kind of skirmish. The weapon came down on his skull and knocked him unconscious.

The stars were still blinding him.

He opened his eyes and tried to steady the seething motion of the cold stone walls around him but could not. He touched his pounding head and felt the crude rag bandage there. A voice came to him out of limbo, a voice with a laugh in it, and a strange accent too: "You're goin' to be all right, friend . . ."

He closed his eyes again and let the coma sweep over him; it was more comforting than the reality. And when he came back to his senses, he was lying on a coarse mattress of straw instead of the flagstones he had felt under him before. There was a face peering into his, an old man's face twisted into a kind of wry humor, and that strangely accented voice was saying: "Do you hear me, son? No, you don't hear a damn thing I say, do you? Well . . . time, me boy, it's all a question of *time*, the greatest cure in the pharmacopoeia. Are you awake now? Are you *compus mentis?*"

If only that awful throbbing would stop!

Peter looked up into a friendly face and took comfort in it, a man in his fifties, perhaps, with a gray-brown and drooping moustache and a beard that was only there because he had not shaved in quite some time. The hair was lank and unkempt, but the face was cheerful, and one to be welcomed. The eyes were very dark, and they too were laughing, as though there were great humor, somewhere, in this situation. He said: "My name is Cobbett, sir, William Cobbett. And yours?"

"Entwhistle . . . Peter Entwhistle, Mr. Cobbett." The pain was intolerable.

"And by your speech, a gentleman." He was chuckling. "Will you tell me who Amanda is?"

"*Amanda?*"

"Amanda. For nigh on three hours Mr. Entwhistle, you've been raving about a lady named Amanda, and another named Susan . . . your mistresses, I'll be bound. It's remarkable how a fellow's thoughts will fly to his ladyloves when his poor skull has been battered open."

"My mother and my sister, sir," Peter said stiffly. "And I spoke of them in my . . . my . . . ?"

"Delirium? Yes, you spoke of them. Your family, you say? Then I tender my apologies for a crass thought and even more foolish words. It's my hope that you will accept them."

"Of course. Will you tell me where we are, sir?"

He tried to struggle to a sitting position, and Cobbett said gently: "No, not yet, just rest awhile, there's a crack in your skull it would take a strong man to jump across. And where are we? Why, we're in Newgate Gaol. It's not a bad place, really. They give us the run of it, no discipline at all. It's known among those of us who have enough experience on the subject, as a 'good' jail. Place is constantly full of tinkers and cobblers, whores and children wandering about, all kinds of riffraff. But there are precious few prisoners here a gentleman can talk to. The gentry incarcerated here—and there are many of them—seem to talk about nothing but the debts that put them behind bars. It's not an easy life . . ."

There was a thought hammering at Peter's mind, and he said suddenly: "But . . . Cobbett, you said, sir? *William* Cobbett?"

"Ah . . . you've heard of me. I'm delighted."

"Yes, of course! And in God's name, sir, what is a gentleman of your stature doing in Newgate Gaol?"

"My second home," Cobbett said wryly. "I've lost count of the number of times they've thrown me in here. Whenever I'm careless enough to be caught in me office when they wreck it . . . But you, sir? You were brought here with a dozen of those poor, misguided Spenceans. Are you one of them?"

Peter shook his head, and he grimaced at the pain it brought him. "No. I was just . . . interested in their aims. Hopeful, perhaps, that they might achieve them. I was foolish enough to be drawn into one of their demonstrations."

"Protest, Mr. Entwhistle," Cobbett said gently, "is only of value when it has at least a chance of achieving its ends. Otherwise . . . it's a boneless wonder."

"Yes, I'm sure you're right."

From the poacher's pocket in the tail of his long gray coat Cobbett produced a half loaf of bread, an onion, and a hunk of cheese, and he said: "I'm sure you must be hungry. This is not a fit meal for a gentleman, but it's nourishing, sir. Have you read much of my work, Mr. Entwhistle?" He was cutting up the food with a pocket knife, and Peter said, smiling: "Yes, indeed. A great deal of it is mandatory reading for any honest-to-God radical, I'd say."

Cobbett speared a piece of cheese and offered it on the blade of his knife. "The best English Cheddar," he said. "I hope you'll enjoy it."

"It's very welcome, Mr. Cobbett, and I thank you for it."

It was a little moldy in parts, and Peter scraped off the gray-green patina with his thumbnail. He stared up at the small barred window and the gray sky beyond it. A crow was on the sill, its head jerking from side to side as it stared down on them.

At the age of forty-four, Robert Banks Jenkinson, second Earl of Liverpool and now Prime Minister, was becoming a little testy; the paralysis that was to bring about his death was already beginning to cripple him.

He was a man of sound judgment and manifest integrity but not much liked by the ordinary people of the new industrial England. For more than twenty yers he had been a member of the India Board, which technically oversaw the operations of the British Indian Army, and he was now its head.

And on this bitterly cold morning he sat in his chambers in the House, wrapped up in top coat and woolen muffler; the coal in the fireplace was wet and would not burn at all.

He shuffled the papers he was studying and rang the little silver bell to summon his clerk, a frail and elderly civil servant named Bradley, and when the old man came in Liverpool waved a document at him and said, worried: "Bradley, this damnable nonsense on Great Tower Street, I've been going through the names of the people they arrested. One of them seems to be a fella named Peter Entwhistle. That wouldn't be one of the Indian Army Entwhistles, would it?"

There was deep anxiety on that weathered old gray face. "I really don't know, Prime Minister . . ."

Liverpool threw the paper down and said angrily: "Well, find out, man, damnit! Let me know at once."

"Yes, sir, of course." He shuffled out and came back scarcely an hour later and said hesitantly: "Prime Minister . . . ?"

"What is it, Bradley?"

"Peter Entwhistle, sir."

"Who?"

"Mr. Entwhistle, sir, who was arrested in the Great Tower Street riot . . ."

"Ah, yes, of course. Well?"

Bradley put on his spectacles and read from the notes he had made. "It seems, Prime Minister, that when he was arrested, he was hurt and unconscious, and no one quite knew who he was until another of the arrested rioters, one Frank Watson, a millhand from Manchester who is well known to the constables, I'm afraid, a man of very violent persuasion . . ."

Liverpool interrupted him testily: "I asked you about

Entwhistle, Bradley. I'm not interested in damned millhands."

"Yes, sir, of course. But it was Frank Watson who gave the constables Mr. Entwhistle's name, an effort, it is believed, to give the demonstration an aura of, shall we say, somewhat wider social scope than it really deserved . . ."

"Oh, for God's sake, Bradley!"

"Yes, sir. To answer your question, it appears that Peter Entwhistle is the son of the late Major John Entwhistle of Arcot in the state of Madras, India . . ."

"I know where Arcot is, man!"

". . . and Mrs. Amanda Entwhistle of Curzon Street."

The Prime Minister rose heavily to his feet and moved painfully to the fireplace. He stood with his back to it, his hands clasped behind him, and wondered why the room was so cold. He thought about the problem for a while and said at last: "Take a letter, Bradley, to Bowers-Wright over at the Cockpit."

The old man found a pad and wet the point of his pencil with his tongue, and the Prime Minister dictated slowly:

> *Reggie,*
>
> *I learn to my great distress that a member of one of our most illustrious families is in Newgate Gaol as a result of the unfortunate disturbance on Great Tower Street.*
>
> *I have reference to Mr. Peter Entwhistle, whose father was none other than the legendary John Entwhistle of Arcot.*
>
> *I will not have this, Reggie. England's great debt to John Entwhistle is of far greater importance than any foolish peccadillo his son may have committed.*
>
> *Get him out of there at once. Have them give him a sensible dressing down, and then release him.*
>
> *Let me know when this has been done.*
>
> *Yours, et cetera,*
Liverpool.

"Mark that 'Private,' Bradley, and sent it over immediately, by special messenger. See that it is handed to the Secretary personally."

"Yes, sir."

"And have Trent fetch me in some hot tea. It's positively arctic in here today." He glowered at the fire and said: "British coal is the finest in the world, and the damn stuff won't burn."

When the old man had shuffled out, the Prime Minister sat at his desk and turned his attention to more important matters.

And only two days later, Peter was released from Newgate Gaol. He suffered the "dressing down" in silence and went back to the yard to say good-bye to his newfound friend, William Cobbett. They had quickly become very close.

"And will you too soon be out?" he asked. "I hope so. This is no place for a man of sensitivity."

Cobbett shrugged, smiling gently. "I learn on the grapevine they won't keep me here much longer, Peter. They're afraid of making a martyr of me, and there's nothing like a martyr to push a cause forward."

"Yes . . . I have a friend in Manchester who believes that. I think you know him, Tom Hoskins. He calls you 'Our Willie.' "

"Ha! And we call him 'Mad Tom.' Well, at least he tries hard enough. When I get out, will you come to see me at my office?"

"Of course."

"Perhaps we should put our heads together. There are phrases turning over in my mind that will set the whole country on its ears."

"Yes, and in mine, too . . ."

"Prison's a great device, is it not, for setting an honest man's brain to work. And you? What will you do now?"

Peter fell silent for a moment. Frowning, he said: "So

much to be done in the Midlands . . . but I might stay for a while in London. It's my home, after all."

"And if you do, where shall I find you?"

"I'm taking digs in Swan Lane, next to the Old Swan Tavern. A Mrs. Henderson has a boardinghouse there."

The two men embraced, and Peter set off with a strangely heavy heart, moving westward steadily through the fine, cold drizzle of the night. He was soaked to the skin when he arrived in Curzon Street, and he sheltered, shivering, under the arch-way of the market for a while, self-doubting and hesitant. He walked around the corner and down the cul-de-sac and stood outside the house, on the opposite side of the street, staring up at the lighted windows. The soiled bandage on his head was wet through, and he pulled off the bandage and dropped it to the ground. He stood there for a long, long time, trying to persuade himself to cross the road, mount those few steps, and hammer on the door for a fine, spectacular return to the fold.

Fine and spectacular indeed! His clothes were in rags, his body smelly and washed only by the rain, beating down more heavily now. His hair was unkempt and filthy, and he knew that the itching there came from Newgate's lice. He felt the stubble of his beard and imagined how he looked; he knew that he had found the flimsy excuse he was searching for.

He turned on his heel and walked away.

Ten days later, as he was packing his frugal belongings into his single suitcase, a message came to his digs, carried by a boy from the *Political Register*: Mr. Cobbett was back at work, and would Mr. Entwhistle please call on him at his leisure?

He found that Cobbett too was packing.

There was a gentle smile on that genial though ravaged face, and Cobbett said, embracing him warmly: "I'm glad you came, Peter. I've no wish to leave without saying my farewells to a fellow jailbird."

"Leave? For where, William?"

"America, where else? It's the only place these days where a man can feel free to speak his mind without fear of arrest."

"But you've only just been released!"

"I know it. But that abominable Home Secretary of ours has finally succeeded in pushing his gagging bill through Parliament, and it's a dreadful weapon, Peter, loaded and aimed at people like you and me! Habeas corpus has been suspended, you must know that. It means there's nothing we can do to safeguard our rights."

"But the Midlands need you, William! Come with me to Manchester. They'd welcome you with open arms up there!"

"The arms of the law! No!"

He was suddenly very earnest. He took Peter by the shoulders and said gently: "With the wisdom of my greater age, Peter . . . what you've been trying to do up there does you credit. What you've actually *done* . . . that's another matter altogether. Don't allow yourself to be deceived by people like Tom Hoskins and his kind. There's a peculiar social disease up North, and it's called 'looking out for yourself first and to hell with everyone else.' It might just be that there's *nothing* you and I can do for them, that we're just . . . pissing against the wind. No, I've made up my mind, and I'm off to America again. I'm leaving some good men behind me to carry on with the work I've started, and it's a forlorn hope of mine that you might be one of them."

"Of course, of course! Anything that I can do . . ."

They walked down to Wine Office Court, where a famous old tavern stood, and drank very heavily together. The fame of the Cheshire Cheese rested almost entirely on the excellence of its home brew, and this was a very special occasion. At the end of three hours, when the landlord called out his cheerful: "Time, gentlemen, please," as he rinsed out his pewter mugs, Peter was barely conscious that they were almost the only two customers left.

The cold air of the night was a shock to him, and he heard Cobbett calling up a carriage, wondering why his friend seemed so unsteady on his feet. He remembered flopping down into the leather seat, and then nothing more till he awoke in his own bed in the morning. He shook the sleep from his eyes and went to the window to draw the curtains and found that a watery sun was shining on a new day.

There was a note on the table where Mrs. Henderson brought him his meals, and he smiled as he read it, the image of that genial face still in his memory:

> This was quite a night, Peter, and when I return, we must have more of them, they're good for a man's soul. I've a feeling I shan't be gone for much more than a year, and if that be so, then perhaps I'll join you up North. I'll still be sending articles to the Register while I'm away, so you can read them and sharpen your indignation on the honing stone of my prose. Never lose that indignation, good Peter, it's the basis of all intelligent protest. My thoughts will be with you always.
>
> William.

The next day, Peter left once more for Manchester. He took with him a copy of the *Times* of London to wile away the dreariness of the long journey, and reading it from cover to cover he found an item of great personal interest that clutched at his heart.

It was part of a somewhat rambling article on the emergence of women, in these modern times, into areas that till recently had been denied them:

> The field of nursing has historically, because of its some-times abominable nature, been left to men, the only exceptions being among those women who are in Holy Orders. Today, however, we are faced with the surprising spectacle

of laywomen who are taking this remarkable step in a direction that might not be as calamitous as, at first sight, it would appear. In view of the large number of hospitals springing up in our fair City today, almost all of them grossly understaffed, perhaps the appearance of female nurses in the offing—nurses who, it seems, are to be trained exactly as men are (and do not throw up your hands in shock, dear reader; this training seems to be acceptable to them) may, in the long run of events, turn out to be advantageous indeed. Your reporter spoke to one of these extraordinary ladies recently—one of the so-called lay female nurses—whose name is Susan Entwhistle. Miss Entwhistle, who lives on Curzon Street, is the daughter of the late Major John Entwhistle of Indian Army fame. (Her brother James is up at Sandhurst, following in his father's footsteps.) She reports that she knows personally of eleven other ladies, from varying walks of life, who are embarking on this extraordinary course. She herself, having completed that training we spoke of, devotes fourteen hours daily to her new vocation, in Guy's Hospital, on the south side of the river. Dr. Mayberry, surgeon-in-charge at the hospital, is most enthusiastic about her work, vigorously postulating that he has seldom encountered such dedication, even among a staff that is known throughout London for its excellence. . . .

Peter leaned back into the seat in the grip of deep emotion. He was conscious that a friendly fellow traveler was peering at him anxiously, and he took out his handkerchief and dabbed at his eyes.

"Not bad news, I hope, sir?" the fellow asked.

Peter shook his head, and he was smiling. "No, sir, though I thank you for your concern. Just . . . news that I find opening up an old wound and yet . . . filling me with pride."

And Hilda, he wondered? How was Hilda coming along? She'd be twenty-two years old now, a grown woman. And the lovely Amanda? Dear, dear Amanda; he could not bear to think about her, and the steady clop-clop of the horses was a token of his distant sadness, carrying him far away once again.

Chapter Eight

When he arrived and settled in with the estimable Mrs. Brice once more, Peter discovered that his friend Tom Hoskins was in hiding; the magistrates, it seemed, were after his blood because of a speech he had made in which he referred to His Majesty King George III as "that straitjacketed madman"; sick or not, Farmer George was greatly loved by everyone, and this was going just too far.

He wanderd through the sullen streets by day to see if Manchester had changed at all in his absence. It had, but only for the worse. (Why is it, he wondered, that change is so seldom for the better?) And at night he continued writing his pamphlets and pursuing his language studies.

One day he sat on a broken wall and watched a demonstration filing past him, a thousand ragged workmen and their ragged wives and ragged children in an equally ragged column, shouting out their slogans. It was the beginning of a food riot, one of the many that were becoming the pattern now. There were placards waving everywhere; one of them, carried by a pretty but undernourished child, caught his eye, and it read simply: IS FOOD TOO MUCH TO ASK FOR? She was ten years old, perhaps, and her free hand was holding onto that of a man who might have been her father. Peter had seen him before. Where was it? In Newgate Gaol? What was his name? Frank Watson? It was a sad and toil-worn face, the face of a man who'd been beaten down to the ground and wasn't really strong enough to bounce back; and for the life of him Peter just could not place it in its proper perspective.

But it was the face of the child that was fixed in his mind. He saw her as sweet and charming; but it was her *vulnerability* which affected him so deeply, a frightened look in those huge, staring eyes that made him want to weep.

Her little snub nose was red with the cold, and she was sniffling; she wore a coat made from the cheapest kind of cotton instead of wool, and she was shivering.

How much of the shivering was the cold, and how much was sheer fright, he would never know.

The food riots were becoming far more frequent now as the months passed with no relief. They were larger, better organized, and far, far angrier. The people, quite simply, did not have enough to eat; and there was nothing more dangerous in the lexicon of protest than empty bellies. Though they affected him only vicariously, Peter worried about them insofar as they affected other people, many of whom were fast becoming his friends.

And then, one night when the winter had given way to a spring that was only minimally less cold, an event took place that was to bring his understanding of poverty down to a far more personal level: He was robbed.

He had drunk three pints of ale that evening and awoke in the small hours of the morning with the urgent need to relieve himself. For some little time he lay between sleep and wakefulness, wondering if he could bring himself to put on his coat and his boots to go out into the yard; it was raining cats and dogs. And as he lay there, he slowly became aware that there was someone in his room—he heard sounds so infinitesimal they were almost inaudible, and quite unidentifiable.

But there was someone in the room with him, there could be no doubt about it at all. He raised himself up on one elbow and shouted angrily: "Who's there?"

There was a lithe shadow racing to the door, and he heard it flung open, and then there was only silence. He leaped out of his bed, followed to the top of the dark stairway, and fell as he tried to run down three steps at a time, banging his head painfully against the banister as he tumbled.

The front door was open, and when he recovered he stood there for a moment, staring out into the deserted street, freezing in the chill night air.

In a little while, a small circle of candlelight appeared behind him, at the top of the stairs, and Mrs. Brice was there, white-faced and frightened, and she stared down at him and whispered: "What . . . what happened, Mr. Entwhistle?"

He told her of the intrusion, and as she came down the stairs in her woolen plaid dressing gown, she said, her voice filled with shock: "Eh, it was one o' they Gypsies, I'll be bound . . ."

"The Gypsies?"

"Aye, the constable warned us against them. They've moved into Ramsey's Field, more than forty of them. But I can't for the life of me think how he got in! Ma doors are bolted, the windows shuttered . . ."

"If what I've heard of the Gypsies is true," Peter said drily, "locked doors won't stop them, nor barred windows either."

"Aye. It's true enough. And shall I make ye a cup o' tea? I really feel like one meself."

Peter nodded. "If it's not too much trouble, Mrs. Brice, then yes, a cup of tea would be very acceptable now."

* * *

When he returned to his room at last, as the early light of a chill morning was beginning to creep through the window, he went at once to the aspidistra pot under which the envelope was hidden that contained all his money, one hundred and four pounds ten in banknotes. And he was not entirely surprised to discover that it had been taken.

In a little while, he went back to bed, to try and sleep, restlessly, in the knowledge that he was now a pauper and one of *them*.

There was only one awkward moment.

At the end of the week, terribly embarrassed, he said to Mrs. Brice: "If I could pay you in just a few days' time? I've applied for a job and have every assurety that I'll get it . . ."

She was a good woman, but she too was poor and lived from hand to mouth. "Eh," she said, and there were tears in her eyes, because she was really quite fond of him, the only one of her tenants who gave her no trouble at all: "I'll keep your room for you, Mr. Entwhistle, for a week or mebbe even two." But she was also a Mancunian, with a stern eye for common sense. "But with no money coming to me, I can't feed you . . ."

He nodded vigorously: "Yes, I understand that. And I'm very grateful to you."

When the other guests sat down to their supper that night, he went for a walk in the pouring rain and came home and went to bed hungry, just as so many of *them* were. There was no porridge and jam the next morning, and no supper either; and at eight o'clock, even though his pockets were empty, he went to the Star and Garter just to get warm, wondering how long he could bring himself to enjoy its comfort without buying a drink. And Hoskins was there, sitting alone in his habitual corner.

His eyes lit up when he saw Peter, and he shouted boisterously: "Eh, come and join me, Entwhistle, this is a great day for all of us, and I've no great liking for drinking alone. Sit down and have a pint or two or three." He grinned broadly: "On me, of course, I heard the sad news. Those damned Gypsies . . . The only good thing the constables have done in the past ten years, they've turfed them out, all their caravans are heading for Bolton, we don't need them here. What'll it be, bitter?"

"I have to tell you," Peter said evenly, "that for the moment at least I cannot reciprocate."

Hoskins waved an airy hand: "We're all broke once in a while. At least most of us are. It'll be your turn when you're on top again."

He had five pints with Hoskins as the night wore on, and they talked about the strike at the Holloway works, where the new looms had all been smashed with sledgehammers, and of the trouble at the Bellingham plant, where strikebreakers had cornered three strikers and had beaten them half to death.

And when at last he returned to his digs, very unsteady on his feet, he found that the good Mrs. Brice had left a quarter loaf of bread, two small onions, and a sizable piece of Cheddar cheese on his table for him. Mrs. Brice, though a Mancunian, was not entirely heartless.

He wolfed the unexpected food down voraciously, and for the first time in almost a week, he slept like a log.

Two days later, he started work with Abel Livingstone and Sons, jobbers to the trade, translating the voluminous correspondence that, with the end of the war against Napoleon, was now coming in from France; Manchester exported a great deal of cotton to the Continent. He was paid tuppence an hour for this skilled labor, but there were only eighteen hours or so a week of it. He was paying Mrs. Brice one and fourpence ha'penny for his digs, but after a long and friendly chat with her one evening, over a very small glass of sherry which she offered him, she agreed to move him to a smaller room; it was only a windowless cupboard under the stairs, but the bed, though excessively narrow, was comfortable enough, and the sheets were always fairly clean. And by skipping the midday meal altogether and agreeing to eat only bread and cheese for supper, he was able to bring the price down to ninepence three farthings for the week, including a breakfast of good porridge and jam, all that he could eat.

His first payday was of the greatest relief to him; and to his astonishment, it was accompanied by a two-shilling bonus; Abel Livingstone was an employer of great perspicacity and knew when he'd been fortunate enough to hire someone who was worth coddling. He paid his debt to Mrs. Brice, and in the light of his new security of income stalked across the road to the pub to pay off his debt to Hoskins too.

And when he called for his bitter, Landlord Ramsbotham swabbed at the copper-topped table and said, not meeting his eye: "I'll bring it to you in the back room, Mr. Entwhistle."

It surprised him. "The back room?"

Ramsbotham gestured. "The door on the left."

He hurried back to his place behind the bar, and Peter went, wondering, into the back room. It was almost dark there, a single candle burning, and he heard Hoskins' voice: "Close the door, Peter . . ."

He shut the door behind him, and then Hoskins was there, gripping his hand and shaking it with Mancunian effusiveness. "Peter, it's good to see you! Come, we've got great news for you!"

Peter blinked at the half-dozen men gathered there, tankards of ale at their table. "We?"

Hoskins said: "You've no need to know their names, nor they yours. It's enough that we're all friends. Come, sit down and drink with us."

It was almost a ritual invitation. *Break bread with a man,* Peter thought, *or take salt with him. Or drink his ale . . .*

The faces around the table were shadowed in chiaroscuro,

angry, suspicious, and not happy at all with the intrusion. But Hoskins said, raising a placatory hand: "A man we *need*, friends."

He looked at Peter and laughed suddenly. "Very well, yes, they know your name. And this is"—he gestured with his tankard—"Boggs, Klaus, Weymann, Andrews, Hare, and O'Shaughnessy, six of the finest boyos you'll ever meet. We're all committeemen from the league. And most of us"—he laughed—"most of us in hiding from the magistrates."

Peter pulled up a chair as Mr. Ramsbotham came in with a tray filled with tankards of ale. As he set them down on the table, he said: "Petty just came in, Tom. But don't worry, we'll fill his belly with best brown till he can't even stagger home. and if that's not enough, then some of the boys will be waiting for him outside."

"Ah, you're a good man, Ramsbotham," Hoskins said. He turned to Peter. "Ben Petty," he said, "a spy for the militia. He thinks we don't know." He turned back to the landlord. "When he's well in his cups," he said, "tell him confidentially that we're meeting tonight over on Moss Side. Let him take the militia there. Let them find *nobody* there."

"Aye, I'll do that."

When he was gone, Hoskins said with great satisfaction: "The time has come, Peter. There's to be a meeting tomorrow fortnight in Petersfield. And this time . . . it's going to be *big*."

"Meetings, meetings, meetings," Peter said wearily. "They never seem to advance our cause one whit."

"This one will," Hoskins said. "There'll be a hundred thousand people there."

Peter stared. "*A hundred thousand?*"

"Aye. That's why it's taking so long to organize. And our demands this time have been put down in black-and-white, with the notice that they're not negotiable."

"And they are . . . ?"

"We want a rise, all the way down the line, ten percent.

We've got it figured out in pounds and shillings, ready to throw at management." He sipped his ale and said: "They pay us now an average of half a crown a week for twelve, fifteen, sometimes eighteen hours of work a day. Ten percent means an extra threepence a week, and we believe that won't hurt the owners too much. And we also want . . . overtime."

"Overtime?" Peter frowned. "What might that be, Tom?"

"If a man works more than seventy-two hours a week," Hoskins said, "he gets paid more for his overtime."

"Well," Peter said dubiously, "that would seem, on the surface at least, to sound like a reasonable idea. You mean . . . if he works more, he gets paid more? Is that it?"

"That's it exactly."

"Well . . . it's a very strange concept. But it should not be discounted merely because of that."

He thought about it for a moment. Then: "You'll never get them to agree to such a radical idea. But it might have a certain value as a bargaining point."

Hoskins spun the wheel of his tinder and blew on the touchwick till it was glowing. He put it to his pipe and puffed out a cloud of smoke.

"Two weeks from tomorrow," he asked, "will you address the meeting? We need a few more speakers, and the ones we've got . . . nary a one of them ever had more than a year of schooling, most of them none at all. And if a man of your education spoke to them . . . it would give them hope, Peter, and that's a commodity we're all sorely in need of."

There was a long, long silence. At last, Peter sighed. "How often have I talked with your people in the past, Tom? They don't usually listen to me, do they?"

"What, *my* people? They're yours too, Peter! And this time they'll listen, believe me. A hundred thousand men and women to address! If only by the law of averages, there'll be *some* brains among them."

The silence again. And then: "Very well. Just tell me where and when, Tom, and I'll be there."

Hoskins' eyes were shining. He said quietly: "The field at Peterloo, on the sixteenth of this month. And this battle . . . we are going to win."

Chapter Nine

On August 16 in the year 1819, Peterloo was a disaster; it was to be recorded in history as "The Manchester Massacre." It would live forever in the history books and never be forgotten.

The dreadful lesson of the French Revolution, with all its terror, was too recent not to have left its imprint firmly in the minds of English authority, and Lord Liverpool, together with most of his peers, was convinced that much the same kind of thing could happen in England—if it were not to be stopped in its very beginnings. And when word was brought to him of the Peterloo meeting (only a few days after its initial planning; there were spies enough in the North) he determined to put an end to the foolish aspirations of the working class once and for all.

He called Bowers-Wright of the Home Office over to his chambers and said heavily, leafing through the sheaf of documents that had been brought to him for study: "They say there'll be more than a hundred thousand people there, Reggie. I don't like it a bit."

"A question of degree, Prime Minister," Bowers-Wright said. "It's the same old complaint, merely a louder voice than we're accustomed to."

"I know it." He sighed. "I've always thought of my ad- ministration as a benevolent one. We've got the very young children out of the factories and almost into the schools . . . or at least working shorter hours now; we've recognized the exis- tence of the Workingmen's League—and that, I don't mind telling you, was a mistake, we've allowed them to bargain for more pay than they deserve—but I will not allow illiterates any voice in Parliament! Good God, they can't even sign their own names! I won't allow it, Reggie!"

"I say again, sir, a question of degree. Peterloo should be no threat at all to established order."

"I want them stopped. Whatever has to be done . . . do it."

"Yes, sir."

And so, once the meeting was well under way, with eighty thousand men, women, and children gathered together in St. Peter's Field, the Mounted Militia cantered into place with drawn sabers, three columns of them at strategic in- tervals.

The speechmaking had already begun, and Hoskins was on the improvised timber rostrum, surrounded by a dozen men in rolled-up shirt sleeves, and he was shouting, his hands cupped to his mouth: "and Mr. Peter Entwhistle, whose pam- phlets many of you will have read . . . a man who has given up the life of luxury to which he was born, in order to serve your cause and mine . . . a man I am honored to call my friend . . . a friend of the downtrodden everywhere . . . Peter Entwhistle . . . pray silence . . . will now address us on the evils of Lord Liverpool's oppressive administration!"

It was not at all what Peter had decided to talk about.

He had written, as his speech, a long and quite angry article for Cobbett's *Register* describing the inequities of the "Six Acts" which, though intended to alleviate the sufferings of the poor, had been so altered in their passage through the Houses of Parliament that in the end they merely gave the authorities broader powers with which to stifle all opposition and dissent.

But as he mounted the dais, his papers in his hand, he was alarmed to hear the sound of a bugle.

The commander of the Yeomanry, alarmed by the sheer size of the crowd, had ordered his bugler to sound the charge. If the poor had been marching on London with muskets, pikes, swords, and cudgels, they could not have created a greater fury of passion and of panic in official circles. White with fury, Peter stood in shock on the rostrum and saw the three columns spur their mounts into the gathering, seemingly oblivious to the fact that none of the enemy was armed and that there were many women and children among them. The crowd was screaming and fleeing wildly in all directions, and he saw a very sweet-looking child whom he had noticed once before in a much smaller demonstration, still carrying the same crudely lettered placard that read: IS FOOD TOO MUCH TO ASK FOR? The same man was with her, trying to drag her away from a horse that was prancing over them. He saw him go down to a saber cut that nearly amputated his arm, and Peter screamed and ran forward, forcing his way through the shrieking, terrified mob. He grabbed the child by her skinny arm and fell with her to the ground, covering her body with his own. Her eyes were wide with fear, and she was bawling her frightened heart out.

The line of horses passed over him, and he dragged her to relative safety and tried to catch his breath. All around him, the crowd was running, thinning out now as they fled, and the horses, still in that ordered phalanx, were coming back at great speed. He gathered the child up in his arms and stood there facing them, cradling her and knowing that there would be no hope at all in flight now. The young girl was clutching at him fearfully, no longer screaming, though her tragic eyes were wide with terror. He stumbled and fell as he tried, quite inexpertly, to throw himself to one side as a horse leaped easily over him. And as he got to his feet, the flat of a saber caught him a cruel blow across the small of his back and he lost consciousness.

He was not to know it till much later, but in this fearful confrontation, eleven people—eight men, two women, and a nine-year-old boy—were killed; and the number of injured, many of them very seriously hurt, was in the hundreds.

When he awoke at last, he found himself in a cart with twenty or thirty other men lumbering over a gravel road he did not recognize. The rain was pouring down, and he was coughing furiously; every racking at his throat tugged at his back, and he was sure his spine was broken. He struggled to a sitting position and looked at the stolid, uncomplaining faces about him; some of his companions were gripping the wooden bars of the cage that covered the cart. He tried to change his position and found that his feet were shackled with iron chains. The broad back of the man seated next to the driver was uniformed, and it turned; there was a plump and cheerful face looking down at him and laughing, and Peter said, stammering: "There was a girl, a child . . ."

The man did not stop laughing, nor did he answer him. He said, instead, leering: "It's London Town and Newgate for all of you, matey. You don't want to learn your lessons, do you?"

The jail cart rumbled on, and fifteen hours later Peter found himself in prison again, and there was no Cobbett here to comfort him now. A doctor grudgingly examined his back and declared it to be whole, and said, not unkindly: "Just rest it, fellow. Don't try to lift anything heavy, lie on your back for a week or two, and you'll be right as rain again."

Peter asked him hesitantly: "Can you tell me, Doctor, how long I'm likely to be here?"

The medic looked away. "Next."

They took him back to the yard, and for three months he lived on prison slop.

Newgate was known for the confined freedom of its inmates. There was very little control of the prisoners here, and when fights broke out, as they often did, the guards stood by and jeered, cheering this or that contestant until the struggle was decided, sometimes with considerable mayhem. Visitors came and went, men and women alike, and the wonder of it all was that no one ever seemed to attempt escape, perhaps because it would have meant the leg-irons.

In one such fight, Peter was involved for no good reason at all; someone had simply mistaken him for an informer who had reported minor infractions of the prison rules to the guard in exchange for a larger ration of soup. He was badly beaten, and when he came to his senses again he found himself in a corner of the yard with a woman cradling his head in her lap as she sat there on the gravel and dabbed at his forehead with a wet rag. By her speech, she was a Londoner from south of the Thames. She was of indefinable age, perhaps in her early thirties, and passably attractive. She said: "It's Mr. Entwhistle, sir, isn't it? I mean, I 'opes it is, what with all this trouble an' all."

"Yes," Peter said. "Peter Entwhistle . . . and if I may know your name?"

"I'm Amy. Just Amy. I seen you in the White Hart, sir, it's a pub I work sometimes. And I brought you a piece of meat."

He stared. "You brought me . . . ?"

She said quickly: "I come 'ere every week, sir, to see me old man, 'e's been 'ere for nigh on four years now, 'e's a pickpocket, and not very good at 'is trade, 'e's always gettin' 'imself arrested. But when I 'eard you was 'ere, I thought to meself: well, that nice Mr. Entwhistle . . . So I brought you somethin' better to eat, I know 'ow awful the food is 'ere."

She held up a small leg of mutton; it was covered over with a black patina of flies, but that was undoubtedly what it was, a cooked leg of mutton. He took it from her gratefully and said: "How very, very kind of you."

"Not at all, sir, I'm only too pleased, I'm sure."

Her large, hazel eyes were holding his. "And. if there's somethin' else I can do for you, sir . . ." He blinked at her, and she said quickly: "I read one o' them pamphlets you wrote, you know, about gettin' the vote for women, what an idea! But there ain't many gentlemen who speak up for us, Mr. Entwhistle, sir. It did me poor 'eart good to read what you wrote, even though it's like what the Bible calls kickin' against the pricks." She giggled. "A joke, sir," she said. "Kickin' against the *pricks*."

"Yes, yes, I'm aware of it." He was terribly embarrassed.

Those wide eyes were very bold, and she said, knowing that he was still unsure: "I'm a whore, Mr. Entwhistle. It'll be dark very soon now, and it won't cost you a penny."

The need was very strong in him; was it just the enticing curve of her breast? The expectation in bright hazel eyes? Or merely the fact that in this sordid condition any relief at all was to be desired?

But he was hurt, and he said awkwardly: "I don't . . . don't think I could perform very well at the moment, Amy. Though I thank you."

"Oh, you leave that to me, sir. But if you'd just like to talk, I'm very good at listenin', Mr. Entwhistle, really I am. And you'd be surprised at what a little of the old 'eart-to-'eart can do for a man."

In spite of the notorious freedom of Newgate Gaol, it was still a very lonely place, and he lay with his head in her lap and *talked.* He told her of the misery he was trying so hard to counter; of William Cobbett, who had been forced to flee the country because of his opinion; of England's dire straits in the aftermath of the war with France . . .

And she was indeed a good listener. The darkness came, and he found himself fondling her as he talked. In a little while, they moved to a secluded corner of the yard, and he whispered: "Oh, God, what am I doing? The guards . . ."

Her hands were all over him, skillfully. "Don't worry about the guards, Mr. Entwhistle, sir. There are ten, fifteen, maybe twenty whores in here tonight, the same like any other night. We pay the guards off."

He loved her passionately for more than an hour, and when she had gone he found the cell he shared with two other men, its door never, ever locked; he sat on the straw mattress and with a knife carved up the meat that Amy had brought him so that the three of them, at least this night, would have a decent meal; and then he slept, forcing all thought of Newgate away from him and thinking only of Curzon Street and of the life that had once—so very long ago!—been his.

He worried about Amanda, and Susan, and even about James, until sleep, blessed sleep, overtook him.

And it was not until three weeks later that a guard came to him and found him playing draughts with a prisoner he had befriended, a wiry little fellow named Maskin; he had found out that Maskin, a professional pickpocket, was Amy's father, but he kept his silence. The guard was jangling his keys, the ubiquitous emblem of authority, and he jerked a thumb at Peter and said, peering: "Entwhistle, is it?"

Peter nodded. "Yes. Peter Entwhistle."

"On your feet then, matey, you're gettin' out of here."

There was no elation in him at all. He followed the guard out, and into the cold, bare room, and he stared in shock at the woman waiting there, a plump, motherly-looking woman in her late twenties, dressed in a very elegant but modest and rather old-fashioned gown of pale blue organdy, with a matching hat richly decorated with feathers, and a cashmere shawl. He stared at her, unbelieving, and she ran forward and threw her arms around him, the tears streaming down her homely face. "Oh, Peter," she whispered.

"Susan!"

He could not believe his eyes. "Susan, is it really you?" The cavalcade of the years was tumbling through his mind, and he could not bear to think of the time that had passed by so uselessly. "Susan, Susan, Susan!"

Nor could he let her go. But she had grown into a very practical woman, and she took his hand and led him away, saying fiercely: "First we must get out of this awful place. . . ."

The guard opened a series of doors for them, and at the last of them, which gave onto the street, he held out a small notebook and a stub of pencil and said gruffly: "Here, make your mark here, and you're a free man."

For no reason at all, Peter began to laugh. He made a crude cross where the grimy finger was marking the spot, and said cheerfully: "I thank you, officer, for your hospitality. Perhaps I may return it for you one day."

The guard stared as he took Susan's arm and moved off with her to where the carriage was waiting. It was the same carriage, with the same old coachman sitting on the box and staring at him, his mouth open in astonishment. He leaped to open the door, the grin on his face a little restrained. "Welcome home, Master Peter," he said.

"Briggs? Well, I'll be damned!"

Briggs was heavier now, and his hair was gray, but it was still the same old Briggs. He said slowly: "Though it's a sad house you come to, sir."

Peter looked quickly at his sister. Her face was pale and drawn, her eyes, red, and she said quietly: "It's Amanda, Peter."

The blood left his face. "Oh, God! Not . . . ?"

"No, not yet. Come, get aboard and I'll tell you as we drive home."

"No!" He was shouting, and he seized her by the shoulders roughly and said: "You'll tell me *now!* What's happened?"

"Very well. She was knocked down on the street by a runaway horse."

"When?"

"A week ago."

"How badly is she hurt?"

Susan bit her lip. "She's dying, Peter, I'm sure of it. She's only holding on by . . . by that willpower of hers. Because she knew you'd be coming home."

"She *knew* I'd be coming home? But in God's name . . ."

He broke off, knowing that this could wait but that the other could not. He pushed Susan aboard in sudden agitation, slammed the door shut on her, and leaped up on the box and gripped the reins and the whip. He shouted: "Giddy-up there" over Briggs' protests, lashed out with the whip, and drove like a Jehu through the streets, conscious of Susan's screaming behind him as she was thrown from side to side of the carriage as it careened around the corners on two wheels.

They covered the two and a half miles to Curzon Street in less than five minutes, and Peter leaped down and ran up the stone steps and hammered on the door with both fists. Susan, her bonnet awry and her hair disheveled, was hurrying up behind him, and she said crossly: "Peter, for God's sake . . . !" She unlocked the door for him, and he ran furiously up the fine old staircase to the door to Amanda's room and stopped. There was an awful premonition in him, and he felt that his heart was no longer beating; he waited, ashamed of himself, trying to find some sort of composure.

Susan was beside him, her arm around him, and she sank her head on his chest as he embraced her.

He whispered: "I'm so sorry . . ."

"Yes, I know. You must pull yourself together." It was Amanda's constant phrase.

"Yes, I will. Is she awake?"

"She will be. She knew that I went to fetch you."

"Yes, she knew . . . I must find out about that too."

They were whispering together like conspirators. "Shall we go in?"

She nodded silently, and Peter straightened himself as best he could and tapped lightly on the door.

Amanda's voice came to them, strong and self-assured: "Come in, Peter."

He opened the door and stood there looking at her, trying to control his emotions. His eyes went briefly to Hilda and then to James, and he could not believe the difference in them. They were almost strangers to him. He turned his eyes back to Amanda and moved toward her very slowly for the first few steps, then lost his resolve and ran the rest, to drop to his knees at her side to clutch feverishly at her hand. It was warm, thank God, and he pressed it to his cheek and tried to speak but could not.

He felt her hand slide under his chin, lifting up his face to look into his eyes. Though she was smiling, there were tears in her eyes now, and they were sliding slowly down her cheeks unheeded. She said quietly: "There are no words, Peter, to tell you how happy you have made me."

"Amanda . . . Mother." He could not keep the sob from his voice.

"And will you stay now?"

"Yes, yes, yes! Oh, Mother!"

How drawn her face was! He thought he could detect a touch of rouge on her cheeks, and a very light brush of pink powder to hide, not quite successfully, the dark lines under her eyes. She was still very beautiful. Was she in great pain? He dared not ask.

"Come," Amanda said, "put your arms around me, but very gently. I'm a little fragile now, and that's a detestable thing to admit to."

Carefully, he embraced her; her shoulders under the layers of chiffon were trembling. But her eyes were bright, suffused with a very great pleasure. She whispered: "Hilda and James . . ."

"Yes."

It was hard to release her, to break the contact that had been remade after so long a time. He got to his feet and greeted Hilda first, smiling at her and throwing his arms tightly around her. He said quietly: "I always knew you'd grow up to be a great beauty. Save for Amanda . . . I think I never saw a more lovely woman in all my life."

It was true. She was *stunning.*

She was tall and willowy, her dark eyes larger than ever, her skin smoother and the color of very old ivory, her hair jet black and carefully piled on top of her head with small ringlets hanging down. She wore silk, very décolleté and high-waisted, with no pelerine to hide the splendor of her body.

She was smiling, and she said quietly: "I'm glad, Peter, so glad."

James came around the bed and his arm was over Peter's shoulder. James was a very fine figure of a young man now, in full dress uniform, though it was only six o'clock in the evening, the blues of a lieutenant of the lancers. He took Peter's hand in a strong grasp, and he was grinning broadly. He said happily: "And by God, sir, you look a mess! Where *have* you been?" He embraced him warmly and said: "And also by God, it's damned good to see you home again, damn place hasn't been the same since you left."

"The man of the house, now! You look well, James, marvelously well! Not only well, but the spirit and image of our father, too, rest his soul."

"Yes, so they tell me. And if I can live up to the reputa-tion he set for all of us, I'll be a happy man indeed." He thumped Peter on the back. "Welcome home, Peter. This is a great day for all of us."

Peter dropped to his knees and sank down beside Amanda again. He took her hand and said: "It's foolish, I suppose, to ask for forgiveness, but . . . I cannot credit my own stupidity. And worse . . . my cruelty. Please, please Mother? Forgive me. *Please.*"

Oh, the softness in those still-wondrous eyes! Amanda said very, very quietly: "Where there is absolutely nothing to forgive, I forgive you absolutely. You are my son, Peter. My *son.* And I love you very dearly. Now more than ever before."

"How could I have been so . . . so hateful?"

"But you are still not so old that you can afford not to do as your mother tells you, Peter. So for God's sake get out of those dreadful clothes and into something more suitable. After, of course, you have washed away the grime and that positively *awful* smell."

Peter said, close to tears: "It's the smell of Newgate, Mother. The smell of Newgate Gaol."

"Yes, I have been informed. And it's really quite disgrace-ful. An Entwhistle in prison! Shame on you, Peter!"

But her eyes were still laughing, and Peter said wryly: "The price we have to pay, Mother dear, if we want to change the course of history, as the Entwhistles, one way or another, have always been destined to do."

"Yes, yes, and I'm proud of you. Your dear father died for what he believed in, James is fighting for it now, and you . . . yes, dear Peter, I am more proud of you than I ever dared think I would be."

"Mother . . ."

Her breath was coming a little faster now, almost in gasps, and it alarmed him. Her hand was clutching at his, without much strength in it, and she whispered, as though aware that she could not hold her composure much longer: "You must leave me now, all of you. . . . The doctor tells me that I must sleep as much as I can, and I will admit to feeling a little tired, though I can't think why. I suppose it's the excitement of your homecoming. It really can't be anything else."

Indeed, her voice was becoming weaker. Peter rose to his feet. "Yes, of course, you must get all the sleep you can, it's the quickest possible way to full recovery, I'm sure of it. As soon as you're well rested . . . ?"

"Yes. In the morning we'll talk again."

"Later tonight, may I tiptoe in and kiss you good night, as I used to? Even if you're asleep? I promise I won't awaken you."

"I'd like that very much indeed. My *son*, home again . . . and there's nothing in the world more important than *family*, is there? I've always believed that very strongly. Always . . ."

Her voice was gone, and she was asleep.

Peter leaned down and kissed her lightly, sure that there was the lightest of smiles on her face. The others followed him out.

There was a surprise waiting for them in the Great Hall of the house. Bateman, the butler, was there, and the other servants were lined up as though they were on parade.

Peter stared at them, a smile of pure delight on his face, and the butler cleared his throat and said carefully: "Master Peter, sir, from the pinnacle of great privilege that my forty-seven years of service in this house entitles me to, I have taken it upon myself, sir, to, ah, to let the staff know that the master of the house is home again, and to offer you, sir, a very heartfelt welcome from all of us. It's been some years, if I may say so, Master Peter, and I'm an old man now, though still a good servant, I like to believe. And I hope, therefore, that you will forgive this, ah, this little liberty."

Peter was touched. The old man took him down the line of servants and spoke their names one by one: "Robbins I'm sure you remember, sir, he's head footman now, Black passed away. Hawthorne too was here when you left us, but not Scott, he is quite new here. Louise the cook I'm sure you well remember . . ."

Peter was shaking their hands, and he grinned at Louise and put his arms around her plump shoulders and said happily: "Some of your pork for supper tonight, Louise, or I'll pull your hair again, the way I used to . . ."

She curtsied and squealed her delight: "It's already in the oven, Master Peter."

Bateman went on: "Millicent is new, she's the upstairs maid; Mary you perhaps remember, from the kitchen; Helga has been with us for only a short while, she's foreign but does her work very well, she's upstairs too. . . . And finally Dora, who came to us, ah, some four years ago."

Peter made a little thank-you speech to them and they all trooped out, the girls giggling delightedly. Bateman looked a hundred years old, Peter thought, a nice, doddering old fellow spending the remaining years of his life in a position that he found important and honorable and was therefore satisfactory to him.

James was at the sideboard where the decanters and glasses were set out. "What's your drink these days, old man?" he asked. "Whiskey? Brandy?"

"Brandy, James, please."

Susan was poking the fire into brighter flame, and she said slowly: "It's quite incredible. I haven't heard Mother talk like that, so easily, since her accident."

"And does it perhaps mean," Peter said, "that she's on her way to recovery after all?"

James handed him his drink, a very large one. "No," he said, "though I wish to God that were true. I'm a blunt man,

Peter, and I'll tell you. We've a new doctor now, a very good man indeed, his name's Townes, lives on Harley Street. He's wise enough not to try to hide the truth from us. I believe she perked up like that because of sheer willpower, nothing else."

Susan sat and stared into the fire. "Her rib cage was crushed," she said miserably, "her back broken . . ."

"But she can move her arms!"

"Don't ask me how. It's the first time I've seen her do that."

"Willpower," James said flatly. "She's quite indomitable, as we always knew."

"Her pelvis," Susan said, "is shattered. There was a great deal of internal bleeding. Dr. Townes gave her a day, perhaps two, but no more. And on the second day, we were all sure she was slipping away. And then . . ."

In tears, Susan could not continue. "Tell him, James. I can't."

James sighed and began striding about, just as his father used to when he was worried. "On the second day," he said, "a fellow named Reggie Bowers-Wright came calling, from the Home Office, very decent sort of fella. He brought us news of you, Peter."

"Of me?" Peter was startled. "I don't think I've ever heard of him."

James smiled. "Oh, but you have! Not for some time, though. It seems he knew Amanda and John very well some years ago, lost touch with the family, you know how these things happen. Said he used to bounce you up and down on his knee. Said you used to call him Uncle Reggie."

"Oh, Lord! I remember!"

"Anyway, it turned out that some years ago the Prime Minister himself told Bowers-Wright to get you out of jail, couldn't bear to think, very properly, of an Entwhistle rotting there. So the second time it happened he took it upon himself to put the release in motion. And then he called here to ask Amanda for God's sake to see it didn't happen again. When he learned of her accident, he insisted, positively insisted, on going upstairs to pay his respects. I made him wait till I could warn her, feeling sure she wouldn't allow it, but . . . well, she agreed to see him, for old times' sake."

"Because she knew she was dying," Susan said.

James went on: "Sue and Hilda and I were all with her, of course, and she really looked awful. Immobile, and white as a sheet, though she'd had Hilda make her face up for her. . . . Bowers-Wright told her that you, Peter, would be home within a day or two. I couldn't believe the way she suddenly seemed to come to life."

Silent and feline, Hilda was curled up on a sofa, listening. She spoke at last: "He didn't tell Mother where you were, but he told the three of us later. He wanted James to pick you up and bring you right home . . ." She broke off, as though she'd already said enough for the whole evening.

James said: "But I was on regimental duty, couldn't get off. And we all decided that we'd better tell her what had happened to you, if only to prepare her for the way we were sure you'd look. And you really do look pretty awful, old boy."

Peter said moodily, sipping his drink: "I'm not at all convinced about Mother. She seems so . . . so bright. Her eyes are clear and sparkling . . ."

"Morphine," James said tightly. "Physically, she can't feel a thing. Thank God she can't."

He looked at the misery on Susan's face and said gently: "She told us that when she goes, she wants no tears. And by God, I won't allow weeping in this house for her while she's still alive. Let's at least pay her that courtesy. The greatest woman who ever lived! Now let's see what we can do about long-lost Peter."

He came over and thumped Peter on the back and said: "God alone knows where we're going to find clothes for you till we can get a decent tailor around here. My stuff won't fit you, but some of Father's mufti might. . . . But a good hot tub first, you know where the tub is, and Bateman will already have had the hot water carried up there. And if you want someone to scrub your back, I recommend Helga, she's a saucy little piece . . ."

Susan said, shocked: "James!"

James grinned. "Well, she is."

Before he went upstairs, Peter kissed Susan and Hilda and embraced James again, and said to him, smiling: "You know, James, I always thought, when you were very young, that you were the most abominable child in history. But you're really a very stout fella, aren't you?"

He looked back when he reached the top of the stairway and saw them all looking up at him as though they could not believe he was home again; he could *feel* their pleasure.

He sat in the hot tub that had been prepared for him and luxuriated till the water was getting cold and dressed in a robe and went to find something to wear. Robbins was in the fine old room that John liked to use on his periods of leave, and he was going carefully through the clothes; a few pairs of trousers and some shirts were laid out on the bed, and the footman said cheerfully: "Mr. Bateman, sir, he told me to find you something to wear from among the major's mufti. I've laid out some breeches that I think you might get into. If you'll forgive me saying so, the major was a mite lighter around the waist most of the time. But he always seemed to swell out marvelously at the end of his furlough, Louise's cooking, you know. And if I might echo Mr. Bateman's sentiments, Master Peter . . . there's not a dry eye below stairs this night. Even Mr. Bateman himself . . . first time I've seen him take more than his one regular glass of brandy in ten years. He's just sitting there in his armchair with a big, big smile on his face. And getting drunk."

"Thank you, Robbins," Peter said, laughing. "And I hope you'll do the same before the night's over."

"I will indeed, sir, with your permission."

He held up a pair of buff-colored breeches for Peter to step into, and said, chatting away amiably: "Briggs has his orders, sir, to go to Savile Row first thing in the morning and bring the major's tailor here. He'll whip up some suits for you in no time at all."

The breeches were a little tight at the waist, but Peter struggled into them and found a white silk shirt that fitted him well enough, and long black stockings and shoes. He used the silver-backed brushes that bore the family crest and the initials R.H.A.E.; they had originally been the property of Peter's grandfather, Sir Richard Hayes Arthur Entwhistle, who had died in the dreadful flu epidemic that swept London in 1794. He thought of Amanda's words: *There's nothing in the world more important than family, is there?* There was a kind of continuity in even so simple a thing as a pair of silver-backed hair brushes, and it pleased him greatly.

He went to Amanda's room, opened the door silently, and moved silently across the deep carpeting to the bed. The tiny night tallow was in its saucer on the bedside table, flickering. He stood looking down at her for a moment, marveling that in such a dreadful state she could still be so beautiful. Her face was turned to one side, as though done deliberately to pick up the light of the candle to illuminate her loveliness; and yes, it was powder under the eyes, and rouge on the cheeks.

He bent down and touched her lips very lightly with his own, and he froze. His heart skipped a beat and there was a lump in his throat.

He sat for a long, long time on the floor by the bedside,

his knees drawn up, his arms around them. He stared out at nothing and did not move. He rose to his feet at last and pulled the sheet up over her face.

When he went downstairs, Susan and Hilda and James were still there, waiting. Susan and James had a chessboard between them, and Hilda was still curled up on her sofa as though she had not moved a muscle in his absence. He saw the smiles leave their faces as he approached, and he stopped halfway down the broad staircase and said quietly:

"She's gone. Amanda is dead."

Chapter Ten

The Year of our Lord 1820 dawned on a vastly troubled England; and it was the time, among other momentous events, of a curious and quite scandalous happening which became known as "The Cato Street Conspiracy."

A certain Mr. Thistlewood, it seemed, had conspired to murder *all* of Prime Minister Jenkinson's ministers in one fell swoop, with a bomb of formidable potency to be set off while the whole Cabinet was dining at the Grosvenor home of Lord Harrowby; protest against the government was becoming very fashionable.

Poor fellow. Mr. Thistlewood was caught before he could detonate his bomb and was quite properly hanged for his presumption.

But for a while, London society was talking of nothing else, and it was Ranjet Singh who brought the news to Hilda in the Curzon Street house. He found it hard to contain his boisterous laughter.

"Two hundred pounds of dynamite!" he said, quite convulsed, "placed under the dining table in the foolish hope that no one would ever notice it! My God, had it exploded, it would have destroyed half of May Fair!"

Hilda had never been able to understand the awful separation of England's classes that led, on occasion, to this kind of violence. Kind and gentle by nature, she lived in her own secluded world, far removed from otiose protest like that of poor Mr. Thistlewood's; hers was a more stable ambience, built on the granite foundation of privilege.

She said sadly: "Will you tell me the why of it, Ranjet? Will you tell me *why?*"

She was curled up on the sofa, like a leopard in repose; and Ranjet looked at her and thought that he had never known a more beautiful woman in all his life.

At the age of twenty-six, the silent and secretive Hilda was a woman of singular loveliness. She was quite tall and very slender, with a waist that, even without its customary whalebone corset, Ranjet could easily put his hands around and have his thumbs and fingertips meet.

She liked to go for long walks by herself, and on the streets and in the park there was seldom an eye that did not turn to admire her, sometimes even in awe. She dressed very fashionably and well, with a penchant for deep colors that complemented the splendid luster of her skin.

But she spent most of her time at home, quite content to remain there alone. Susan was always busy at Guy's Hospital, James was more or less permanently installed at the barracks, and Peter was forever dashing up North on one pretext or another, though he was never away for very long at a time. "Curzon Street is my home again," he would say. "I never want to leave it."

Hilda was usually to be found in her own upstairs room, or in one of the two libraries on the ground floor, studying hard; the years of tutoring under the fiercely dedicated Mrs. Arnold, long since gone, had left her with deeply ingrained study habits, and she was teaching herself Hindustani, Gujarati, and Sanskrit, with the enthusiastic help of Ranjet Singh, a more frequent visitor than ever now.

At a tap on the door, she said absently: *"Undur ao."*

Peter opened the door and came in, laughing. He said: "I only hope that means: Come in! How are you, Hilda?"

She ran to embrace him, throwing her arms around his neck. "How am I? I'm thoroughly perplexed!"

"Oh? And why should that be?"

"I'm trying desperately hard to decipher some stanzas written by a fourteenth-century poet named Namdeo. Do you know about the *Adi Granth?*"

Peter said cheerfully: "Nothing whatsoever."

"The sacred book of the Sikh gurus. Ranjet has given me some lines from it to study, and they're really awfully difficult. And I thought I was coming along so nicely!"

"Well, take an hour or two off and come for a walk with me. Will you do that?"

"Yes, I'd love to! If only because you're the only person in the whole world I can really feel comfortable talking to. Except Ranjet, of course." She hesitated. "Do you find that strange?"

He smiled. "Sometimes. Do you realize that all through dinner last night you said not a word to anyone?"

"Not even to you? Oh, that's dreadful! Where are we going?"

"To Mother's grave, with flowers. Then to the park to look at the rhododendrons."

"Ah, good. Can I have an hour to change my dress?"

"No."

"I can come like this?"

"Of course. You look marvelous."

"I've been slouching around in this awful gown all day long. Oh, well."

They walked together to the little churchyard where the

grave was, and Hilda whispered, her eyes moist: "I should have worn black."

"No, Amanda would not like to see you in mourning for her."

They went to the park together and walked hand in hand, and Hilda fell into one of her long silences. It was not till they reached the massed pink, mauve, and purple rhododendrons, in full and magnificent bloom now, that she spoke again.

She said quietly: "Ranjet will be coming to the house tonight, Peter."

It was splendid news. Peter said happily: "Well, good! I can't wait to see him."

"And he too."

Every time Ranjet came visiting, it seemed that Peter was off on one of his trips, and on his return, Ranjet was in Bath, or Southampton, or Dover, about his own affairs; he was sole owner now of a small shipping line for the East India run.

Peter was aware that something was troubling Hilda; perhaps not exactly *troubling* her . . . He searched for the word and could not find it, and so he waited.

"He was here last week," she said, "while you were in Manchester."

"Yes, I know. Susan told me how sorry he was that we missed each other, time after time." He hesitated. "Susan is very, very fond of him, isn't she?"

"Yes."

"When I left home she was still a child, but . . . even at that tender age, I think she was truly in love with him."

"Yes."

"And is she still?"

"Yes."

"And is it really . . . serious for her?"

"Yes."

"She still loves him?"

"Yes."

He thought about it for a moment, then: "There's a great deal that is said against mixed marriages, Hilda, though I don't really know why it should be so. Is it some atavistic fear bred into us? A fear that everything outside the clan is dangerous?"

"Perhaps. We are all guided by forces we don't truly understand. It may be that we shouldn't fight them. It may be that they're for our own good and it may be that if we did resist them . . . we would lose anyway."

"Yes, it's true. And Ranjet? How does he feel? Will they marry one day?"

He thought she was never going to answer him, but he was very close to her, loved her, knew her well, and so . . . he waited and said nothing.

They were sitting together on a bench, and she took his hand and rose, and he went with her closer to the splendid blossoms; there were bees circling among them.

"They're lovely," she said. He did not answer her. And then the bombshell: Hilda said quietly: "Ranjet has asked me to marry him, Peter."

"Oh, my God! I mean . . . no, I don't know *what* I mean! Have you accepted him?"

"Yes."

"And have you told Susan?"

"No, not yet. I wanted to tell you first "

She had turned to him and was staring up with wide and lustrous eyes; he had never before realized how slanted they were.

As though reading his thoughts, she said, holding both his hands feverishly: "I'm *chi-chi*, Peter! You know it, I know it, everyone in the family has always known it, even your father knew it! And never a word has ever been spoken about it, because we're too . . . too damnably *polite!* Well, it's time we faced it! Somehow, Mother had a lover once, and I love and respect her memory nonetheless for it, you understand what I am saying? *None the less!* And I'm more Indian than English, and Ranjet is Indian, and it will not . . . not really be a mixed marriage, whether that be good or bad, and I don't know that either! All I know is . . . yes, I love Ranjet Singh with all my heart, and I have accepted him. And soon, very soon now, I will go to India with him. We'll be married there in a Sikh ceremony at his father's Palace." There was a little silence. Then: "Will you help me tell dear Susan?"

"Of course. Though I don't believe for one minute that you need help in anything . . ."

"Oh, but I do!"

"Then I will help you."

He took hold of himself and said, hoping he was right: "And you have no cause for worry. Susan is a very sensible woman, more sensible than any of us. And James . . . James will make a great joke of it and break open a bottle of champagne. You have no cause for worry at all."

A little silence. Then: "And you, Peter?"

He was smiling, and he raised her hands and kissed them. "I'm happy for you, Hilda. I think it will be a perfect match and I wish you long, long years of happiness together. I'll only be sorry that you're so far away."

"And you're sure about Susan? Yes, you are, I'm certain of it. You know all of us better than any of us, don't you?"

He laughed. "Yes. That's absolutely true. All of you, better than any of you."

The meeting with Ranjet was a great success.

It seemed that they spent an eternity clapping each other on the back, and Ranjet said emotionally: "Peter, dear Peter! You cannot begin to know how glad I am to see you home again! Over all these long years your family missed you so much, as you must have learned, and I myself . . . yes, perhaps even more so."

They were in the hall with Hilda, and Bateman was standing patiently by; he had taken to walking with a cane now, even though he was only a butler, a necessity he could think of only as a terrible presumption.

Hilda said: "Let's go into the parlor, Susan and James are there, and Peter has an announcement to make."

"Oh?" There was an inquiring, even a mischievous sort of look in Ranjet Singh's intelligent eyes. At the age of thirty, he wore a rich beard now, tightly curled, and his handsome face was a little more swarthy. He had grown taller and very strongly chested, a man of quite imposing aspect in his Savile Row clothes. He said, amused: "Can I guess what the announcement might be? You told him, Hilda?"

"Yes, I told him. Come, they're waiting."

James, back at the house on a week's furlough, poured drinks for them, and for a few minutes they talked of nothing until, seeing the anxious light in Hilda's eyes, Peter said clearly: "Let me propose, first of all, a toast." He raised his glass. "To the memory of Amanda."

The toast was answered as they gathered about him: "To Amanda, God rest her soul."

"She is up there looking down on us, and I know that she will approve of what I have to tell you."

They were all very silent now; Ranjet was drawing closer to Hilda. Peter's eyes were on Susan and he said:

"Hilda and Ranjet . . . are to be married. Ranjet is returning soon to India, and Hilda will go with him. And with my blessing, as head of the family now, they will be married there in a Sikh ceremony at the Palace of Ambala. I drink to their happiness together."

His eyes had not left Susan. She was smiling, and she went to Hilda and embraced her, and said, a whisper: "I'm so happy for you, Hilda . . ." She moved to Ranjet Singh and kissed him and said: "I always knew this would happen one day, I was sure of it . . ."

James was shouting happily: "My God, my sister is marrying a bloody savage! This calls for champagne!" He strode first to the door to yell for Bateman: "Bateman! Down to the cellar with your old bones and bring us some bubbly!" And then to Hilda; he took her in his arms and said: "He's a damn decent sort of fella, Hilda, be happy with him." He took Ranjet's hand and shook it vigorously and shouted: "By God, I'm off to India meself in a few weeks, but to Madras, and you'll be where? Up in the savage North? Well, perhaps I'll try to wangle a transfer up there. With my sister a daughter-in-law to the maharajah, they'll either make me a colonel overnight or cashier me."

"Then perhaps," Ranjet Singh said cheerfully, "I'll have my father ask for you as military adviser to his court. It's a much-sought-after posting. And at least I won't feel guilty for breaking up the Entwhistle family altogether."

Bateman brought the champagne, and Peter told him the great news and said: "I'm sure the staff would like to drink to the health of the happy couple, so break open a few bottles of wine for them, Bateman, there's a good fellow."

The old Butler nodded. "My . . my . . . congratulations, Master Peter. And there are indeed a few bottles in the cellar of 1800 Pouilly Fouissé which are not as good as they should be. Perhaps this is, ah, the occasion I have long been looking for to dispose of them."

"As you see fit, Bateman."

"And have you heard the bad news, sir?"

Peter frowned. "No, I think not, Bateman. But on this happy occasion, perhaps bad news can wait."

The old man was wheezing; his voice had almost gone now. "Robbins was on an errand, sir," he said, "and he heard it on the street. His Majesty is dead."

"Oh, God . . ." A hush fell on them as they listened to Bateman's unhappy tale.

It seemed that King George III, England's most-beloved

monarch, a family man of the deepest devotion and the only ruler in Europe to stand firm against the violent onslaught of Napoleon, had finally given up the ghost.

Totally blind, totally deaf, and totally insane, he had spent his last days wandering from room to room in his white gown as he plucked at his long gray beard, reciting the works of Milton to himself.

> *"Oh thievish night,*
> *Why shoulds't thou, but for some felonious end,*
> *In thy dark lantern thus close up the stars*
> *That nature hung in heaven, and filled their lamps*
> *With everlasting oil to give due light*
> *To the misled and lonely traveller?"*

The lonely traveler was gone; England would never be quite the same.

But the sad news could not be allowed to interfere with the young lovers' plans, and in two weeks' time, only two days after James' posting not to India, as he had hoped, but to Greece, the day of excitement was on them.

The parting was a grievous one.

It had begun as a sensible and very happy celebration *en famille* for the couple, a great deal of champagne being drunk, as though it might help stave off the awful feeling that soon the sound of the carriage that was to take them to Southampton would signal the breakup of a deeply devoted family. The servants were all lined up to bid them farewell as Hilda and Ranjet, accompanied by Susan and Peter, set off on the long journey with very mixed emotions. They spent the night in the pretty country town of Guildford and continued the next morning in a slight drizzle that cleared as they passed Winchester.

There was more champagne on board, where they were joined by the ship's officers and the senior members of the crew; they were sailing on the *Bilgee,* the flagship of Ranjet

Singh's own line, a splendid vessel of eleven hundred tons, operating very successfully now that Lord Liverpool had abolished the monopoly held for so long on this route by the East India Company

And then, at the awful moment when the shout came to them—"All ashore, please, going ashore"—there was the final realization, held back for so long by deliberate effort, that this was to be for all time, a parting for *always*. Susan, the sensible one, was clutching at Hilda and saying: "Oh, God, oh, God, will you ever come home again?" She embraced Ranjet warmly, and it was very hard for her to let him go.

Peter threw his arms around his Sikh friend and clapped him on the back and said somberly: "Hilda is very precious to all of us, I know she's in good hands. Let her be happy, always."

"She will be, I promise you both," Ranjet said.

They shook hands, and the Indian turned again and kissed Susan quickly on the cheek and said: "Dear, dear Susan. God bless you."

She held herself together till the ship was moving smoothly down the bight, the white sails billowing against a clear blue sky, a picture of awesome beauty. And then, quite suddenly, she turned to clutch at Peter, burying her head in his chest; and she was crying. "Oh, God," she murmured. "Oh, God, oh, God . . . I feel so *empty*."

"Yes. I know."

He held her tightly; she was very dear to him. "Shall we find a teahouse? Would you like tea?"

She drew away from him and produced a slip of lawn from her reticule to dab at her eyes with, and said: "I'm not normally such a fool, Peter."

"You were *never* a fool."

"Oh, yes, very frequently! Did you know that I've always been in love with Ranjet?"

"Of course."

"And yet . . . look at the two of us. Hilda is without a doubt the most beautiful woman in the whole of London, the most gorgeous *animal* who ever lived. And look at me! Can you imagine any man in his right mind desperate to get me into his bed?"

"Susan! Thats really quite a shocking remark!"

"Yes, it is. But can you? I mean . . . look at me!"

He sighed. "Let's go and have tea."

"No. We'll have coffee, there must be a coffee shop here somewhere, and this is very definitely a coffee occasion."

"Very well, we'll find one."

Coffee shops were springing up all over England now, pleasant little places with open terraces where the customers could sit when the weather was fine, with always a small orchestra of very elderly gentlemen (and sometimes a lady musician too) screeching out their favorite set pieces on not very worthy strings.

They found one close to the docks, where they could sit in the open air and watch the ships and still hear the sounds of the pleasant music that came to them from inside the building. The little orchestra was happily playing a piece by Johann Sebastian Bach that was very popular in the coffee houses because of its name and its theme; it was called the "Coffee Cantata" and had been written—for reasons which surely only he and God could understand—nearly a hundred years ago to portray what he had called *"the protest of the fair sex against the claim that their use of coffee makes them sterile . . ."*

Peter knew the piece well, and he laughed and said happily: "Susan dear, there's nothing in the world more foolish than utterly useless protest."

She blinked at him, not knowing in the least what he meant.

With Hilda gone and James in Greece, the Curzon Street house would never again be quite the same. There were just the two of them left as the years slipped inexorably by.

News came to them from time to time from an India that was still part of their existence. In 1824, the victory of the East India Company over the neighboring Burmese (with its attendant reparations to the company by the King of Burma to the tune of one million and one pounds) was a champagne occasion in which even the servants took part. On a more social level, the opening of England's first railroad some two years later almost convinced Peter—but only momentarily—that with Mr. George Stevenson's new locomotive and its attendant demands for manufacture, the problem of constant unemployment would be solved for thousands of workingmen.

And in 1827, that kindly old cripple Bateman the butler went to join his ancestors, gentlemen's gentlemen all of them; and the new butler was Robbins.

Searching the hall one day for any slight trace of dust, running his finger along every high ledge he could find, he went himself to the front door to answer the ring of the iron bell and found a waif there. There was no other word for it; she was a *waif*.

She was in her late teens, and without a doubt very pretty indeed, but dressed in clothes that he could only think of as rags. And she was frightened. She said hesitantly, as though plucking up courage: "Your pardon, sir, is this the right house where I might find Mr. Entwhistle? Mr. Peter Entwhistle?"

He looked her up and down and said sternly: "Well, you might, girl, and then again you might not. But I can't think what the likes of you would want with a gentleman, so be on your way."

She said quickly: "Sir. My father was a friend of his, in Newgate Gaol. In the prison? I *have* to speak with him . . ."

Newgate Gaol? So much of past history. Robbins thought about it for a moment and said at last, making up his mind: "The back door is on Market Mews. Go there."

He closed the door in her face and stalked in high dignity to the tradesmen's entrance, wondering what this grubby but fetching little girl could want with the master, and there she was, waiting; she must have run all the way, he thought. Her face looked as though it had not been washed in a week.

He said: "Very well, girl. Before I let you into this house you'll tell me what it is you want. I won't have the master bothered by people out of a past that's best forgotten."

"I'm sorry, sir, it's just that . . . I *know* he'll see me if he knows I'm here."

"What's your name?"

"It's Dorothy, sir, Dorothy Watson, and my father was Frank Watson, only he's passed away now, he was with Mr. Entwhistle in Newgate." Her voice was a whisper. "I know that he's a gentleman, sir, but I *have* to talk to him."

"Yes. Well, Newgate is something we'd all like to forget about in this house."

"Please? *Please,* sir?" She was swaying slightly on her feet, and Robbins was alarmed. As a child, he had been brought up on very hungry streets, and he knew the signs. There were dark lines under her eyes, and her cheeks were hollowed. He said gently: "When did you last eat, girl?"

She reddened, and said defiantly: "I'm not hungry, sir."

"When?"

"I had bread this morning, a lot of bread, and cheese too."

He knew it was a lie, and he turned to Louise, standing there and clucking her tongue, and he said gruffly: "Feed her, Louise. There's stew aplenty on the stove."

He took Dorothy's arm and propelled her to the scrubbed plank table and sat her down. He said: "It's not easy for the likes of you to get past a good butler, Dorothy. But I think you did it."

She sniffed very hard when she saw the plate of food that

Louise slipped in front of her, saying: "There's nothing to be ashamed of in being hungry, girl. Just eat slowly, or you'll have pains in your stomach all night long." She sat down heavily beside her and patted her arm with a pudgy hand and said: "You're not the only one in London who's hungry these sad days, and I know that's precious little consolation for you. Go on, girl, eat your fill, there's more where that came from."

Robbins found Peter playing chess with Susan in the small library, and Peter was saying gleefully: "Two more moves to mate, Sue . . ."

Robbins said hesitantly: "Begging your pardon, sir, there's a *person* to see you, a young woman. Says her name is Dorothy Watson, says you knew her father, Frank Watson."

"Frank Watson? No, I think not."

"If you'll pardon the expression, sir, she says you were in Newgate together."

"Ah, yes . . . of course! Show her in, Robbins. I'll see her in here."

"Very good, sir."

Frank Watson! It had been a long, long time, and he'd met him only once or twice, a thin, angry man who was not very articulate and was scorned by all the others in the various movements as never knowing quite what it was he wanted.

He said to Susan: "Shades of Newgate Gaol! She probably wants money, and if I think it'll be put to good purpose, then I'll give it to her. Your move."

"You're right. Mate it is." She tipped her king over.

He turned as Robbins brought Dorothy in. He went to her and took her hand and said pleasantly: "Dorothy Watson? I'm Peter Entwhistle, and I remember your father well. He's a . . . a millhand, I believe?"

"Yes, sir, he was a millhand. But he's gone now."

"Gone?"

"Passed away, sir."

"Oh. I'm sorry, very sorry. He was a fine man, Dorothy."

An image came to him suddenly, an echo from a very distant past . . . *There was a roan stallion prancing over him, its hooves flailing savagely over the body of a skinny, undernourished child who was screaming out her terror,* and he stared at her and said: "My God, I remember! At Peterloo Field, what was it, eight years ago? That miserable business with the horse, was it . . . was it *you?*"

She nodded eagerly. "Yes, that was me, sir. You dragged me out from under, you saved my life. Yes, that was me. And they hit you with a saber, the yeomen did, and carried you off, and I remember screaming because I thought . . . I thought you were dead."

"My God!" He hardly knew what to say. "You've, ah, grown since then."

"A girl does that in eight years, sir."

"When did Frank die, Dorothy?"

"I don't know, sir."

"You don't know?"

"No. He died in Newgate. I went to visit him there and all they'd say was that he was dead and buried in Pauper's Field, they wouldn't even show me where his grave was."

"Oh, God. What was it they arrested him for?"

She said tightly: "For speaking his mind, sir. And he'd lost an arm, you know, at Peterloo, one of the mounted yeomen hurt it so bad it had to be cut off. He never really recovered from the shock."

He felt foolish standing there, remembering old horrors that he, at least, had escaped from. "Come," he said, "sit down, and we'll talk about it."

She perched herself on the edge of a chair, her hands in her lap, her eyes cast down; it appeared that she was a little apprehensive of Susan, and when she would not speak, he said awkwardly: "I don't remember where Frank was living. Was it in Manchester?"

"Yes, sir. But with him gone, they've taken the cottage

away. I mean, what I mean is, I can't live there anymore."

He frowned. "The landlords were the millowners?"

"Yes, sir."

"Then where do you live?"

"I don't live anywhere, sir."

Susan had moved toward them, drawing up a chair, and she said gently: "Then where do you sleep, Dorothy?"

The voice was almost inaudible. "In doorways. There's nowhere else. I can't find work, I've tried everywhere . . ."

"And no other family?"

"No, ma'am."

Peter exploded. "Then for God's sake how do you eat?"

There was an uncomfortable silence and then a whisper: "I beg, sir. But it's not easy to put up with being a beggar, taking something for nothing. I was brought up to be honest. And the last time I saw Dad, he was . . . I think he knew he was dying, he was terribly sick, and he said to me: 'If anything happens to me, child, there'll be no money and there's no one for you to turn to, except the only truly honest man I ever met, and his name's Peter Entwhistle, I hope he remembers me. You'll find him either up in Manchester with the Livingstone Mills, or maybe down in London in a house in May Fair somewhere. Go to him, child. Perhaps he'll be able to help you.' "

The words were tumbling out now, unconstrained: "He said: 'He's a gentleman, and gentlemen always have servants, and maybe he'll know someone who needs an honest kitchen maid. But don't take charity from him, mind, I'd not rest in peace if I thought you were living on charity.' And I won't do that, sir. It's not money I'm begging for. I'm begging for work. Any kind of work. My back's strong, and I'm willing. Willing to do anything at all, just so's I don't have to . . . to beg. Anything at all."

Susan patted her arm. She said: "Then the problem is

over and behind you, Dorothy. Louise in the kitchen is always complaining that she doesn't have enough help, so . . . all right, Peter?"

"Yes. Yes, of course." He was vaguely ill at ease. He said: "Would you like to work here, Dorothy?"

"Oh, yes, sir, yes."

He summoned Robbins and said: "Dorothy will be working here now, Robbins, with Louise. She may need a little training, but . . . you'd better have Helga find her some clothes, some shoes, see the seamstress in the morning and have her stitch up some uniforms. And . . . see that she's made to feel at home here."

"Very good, sir." He looked at Dorothy and said gruffly: "Well, come along. Don't just sit there, girl, you've been dismissed."

But her eyes were on Peter, and she was biting her lip with some strange emotion that he could not understand. She whispered: "I don't . . . don't hardly know what to say, sir. Except . . . thank you."

When she had been led out, docile and uncertain, stopping briefly at the door to look back at him with solemn and appealing eyes, Peter turned back to Susan, frowning, and he said heavily: "Now tell me, if you can, why I am suddenly so depressed."

Susan held his look, her pale blue eyes very thoughtful. She said slowly: "I think I know why. You're a rich man again, Peter, after a brush with poverty that . . . changed you. And now that you see it again at such close quarters . . ."

He sighed. "I wish I could do more."

"She's very sweet, isn't she?"

"Sweet? Yes, I suppose so. Though it's hard to find sweetness in abject misery."

"And so frail. But she'll be all right now."

"Yes, I hope so."

He knew the cure for the dejection that was on him; it was to throw himself furiously into his work. He went to his room and sat down to write an angry article, all about Frank Watson, a man he had scarcely known.

And when at last he had finished, he looked up to find Susan standing there at the door; she was tired, he thought. "Supper?" she asked. "You must be starving."

He pecked her on the cheek and shook his head. "No, I'm not hungry tonight."

"You never are when you're bothered. But it won't do, Peter! Let me have Robbins bring you some soup."

"No. And you?"

She gestured vaguely. "I'll have a little something."

"Then read this, tell me what you think of it."

He waited while she read the article through carefully, standing by the open window and looking down on the dark mews, listening to the distant clopping of a carriage on the street. She handed it back to him at last and said: "That poor girl's really upset you, hasn't she?"

"Yes, she has, though I don't know why. In truth, I hardly knew her father, but . . ." He sighed. "She said she was willing to do anything at all, just so she would not have to beg. You know what she meant by 'anything at all,' don't you?"

"Yes, of course I do. I'm not a child anymore, Peter." She was smiling, and his anger went.

"And the article," he said. "Is it good?"

"Well, it's a little *harsh*, perhaps. If a few phrases there are not deleted, they'll come looking for you again, you must know that. And there's only Cobbett's *Register* that will accept it."

"Yes, I suppose so." He flipped the pages and scowled at them. She said again: "Are you sure I can't send you up some supper?"

He shook his head moodily. "Go to bed, Susan dear, get a good night's sleep. You look terribly tired."

"As indeed I am. Good night then."

When she had gone, he sat down and rewrote the whole article, making it a little stronger, and when the clock on the mantelshelf struck midnight, he got up and stretched his legs, flexing his cramped muscles. He locked the papers in a drawer of his desk and decided to sleep on the vexing question of where to place them, a newspaper with a larger circulation, perhaps, than the *Register.*

He went downstairs to pour himself a nightcap, and to his surprise he had scarcely entered the library when Dorothy followed him in; it was almost as though she had been waiting for him, watching. She carried a silver tray on which a plate of meat had been set out, together with some slices of bread.

He stared at her in surprise: How she had changed! She was wearing a neat gray uniform that he thought might belong to Helga, a little loose on her, with a white pinafore and a bonnet, and her face was scrubbed and shining nicely, her eyes bright. She looked very attractive indeed, and the sight of the transformation cheered him up instantly. He said, smiling: "Dorothy, how nice you look! But you should be in bed. It's late."

She set down the tray on the buffet and said quietly: "Miss Susan said you didn't want anything to eat, sir, but Mr. Robbins told me you were partial to a little meat before you went to bed, so I thought . . . I mean, Mr. Robbins said it would be all right if I stayed up to bring you something."

"Well, that was very thoughtful of you."

She picked up the brandy bottle, took a glass, and said hesitantly: "He said you like a glass of brandy too, but . . . I really don't know how much to pour. And that you like your bread toasted." She began pouring, drop by drop. "If you'll say when, sir?"

"When. Thank you, Dorothy."

She gave him the glass and took the plate of bread to the fire and used the long brass toasting fork that hung there, holding a slice on its tines over the red embers till it was nicely done. She was crouching down on the floor, a picture of domesticity, the firelight flickering over her profile. Her forehead was good, her nose delicate, her lips full. She saw him examining her and turned her eyes quickly away. And when the bread was done on both sides, she wrapped it carefully in a linen napkin and set it down on the tray and said, like a well-trained servant of long standing: "Will there be anything else, sir?"

He shook his head. "No. No, thank you, Dorothy. Go to bed. I'm sure Louise will want you to start early in the morning."

"Good night, then, sir." She paused at the door and looked back at him. "There's just one thing, sir. Miss Susan told me you were writing about my father, for the newspapers. I want to say . . . to say thank you, sir."

He grimaced. "It won't do any good at all. And Miss Susan's in bed?"

"Yes, sir. I took her up some good soup, but she's asleep already. I wrapped a cloth around the bowl to keep it warm in case she wakes up. I hope that was the right thing to do?"

He said gravely: "Exactly the right thing to do. You're learning very quickly."

She blushed. "I want to do the best I can, sir. And Mr. Robbins is helping me." Her eyes were lowered, and she raised them to look at him briefly, and then dropped them again. "Good night, Mr. Peter, sir."

She was gone, and he sat down with his cold meat and toast and found that he was very hungry indeed.

He saw her on occasion in the days that followed and always took pleasure in the way she smiled at him shyly as he passed her by. She had her own uniform now, the same long gray skirt and blouse but made to fit her very slight body, molding her breasts under the top of the pinafore. He noticed that her hands were always well scrubbed, even her nails kept neatly cut and very clean.

He was sitting with Susan at dinner one night as Robbins served them, and he said to him: "How is Dorothy coming along in the kitchen, Robbins? Is Louise satisfied with her?"

The butler nodded enthusiastically. "She's a treasure, sir," he said. "And if you don't mind me saying so, there's a very surprising thing about her. She can read and write, and very nicely, too."

"Oh?"

"She tells me that she didn't have very much schooling, but her mother, before she died, was a woman of a little education, grammar school, I think, and she taught her."

Peter said nothing. He was aware that Susan's eyes were on him, questioning and perhaps even a little amused, and when Robbins had gone and they were alone with their thoughts, nibbling on biscuits and Stilton cheese, she said: "I can't help feeling, Peter, that you have a rather proprietary interest in that young girl. Am I right?"

He smiled. "No. Not really. I just think that she's a very bright and intelligent creature. I don't really like to see her as a servant. I wish I could find her something better to do."

"Such as?"

"I don't know. Even in these modern times there's very little a woman like her can do, outside of domestic service."

"We could find her a job as a nanny somewhere," Susan said. "Or a governess, it's a higher station in life for her. And yet, if we do that . . ." She broke off, looking at him with her eyebrows raised.

He nodded. "Yes, if we did that, it would be like . . . like packing her off, out of the way. It would sadden her, I'm sure."

"Do you mean, perhaps, that it would sadden *you?*"

"Yes, perhaps I do." How very well Susan understood him! He said quickly: "She was a child of ten years at Peterloo, and I dragged her out from under the hooves of a miitiaman's horse, saved her from very grave injury, maybe even saved her life. I feel responsible for her now. I won't just pack her off to a better job with someone else. I won't do it."

She pushed her chair away and came around to plant a kiss on his cheek. "Peter," she said, "you're a very nice man indeed, and you're absolutely right. Let's see what happens." It was a solution very typical of Susan.

"Very well. If you say so."

"Will you work tonight?"

"Yes, I must."

He had taken the famous article, after all, to the *Register*, and Enoch Mulligan, editing the paper in Cobbett's prolonged absence across the Atlantic, had read it with glee and then tossed it back at him across the desk, shouting: "Hit them harder, Peter, *harder!* You can do it!"

Mulligan was a big, rough man in his fifties, with a shock of untidy gray hair and muttonchop whiskers; he had survived an aggregate of no less than twelve years of his life in prison, had seen the *Register* office raided and wrecked four times, and he still would not be tamed, but bounced back always for more and still more trouble. He had a slight limp; his left leg had once been broken in a scuffle with three or four guards, and it never properly set. His voice was as big as his body; he'd never said a quiet word in all his life.

And now Peter was at work in his room. He polished off the last few sentences, and locked the article away till the morning. He threw open the tall windows and stood on the tiny iron balcony, grasping the rail as he looked down on the mews; there was a charcoal brazier burning there, a watchman asleep beside it, guarding the stalls for tomorrow's market. He gulped in great deep breaths of the cold night air and was suddenly conscious that he was not alone.

Very close beside him, no more than six feet or so away, a shadow was there, a woman standing on a second tiny bàlcony, quite similar to his own but somewhat smaller; it was the balcony at the end of the corridor that led past his room to the cubicle that Dorothy and Helga shared half a flight above. There was very little light, and he stared. The clouds scudded their way from the moon, and he saw that it was Dorothy. She was in her night chemise with a robe thrown over it, and her long hair was no longer piled up under a bonnet but cascading down over her shoulders; he could see her surprised eyes gleaming as he looked at her.

He said quietly: "Dorothy? Is it you?"

The moon brightened as the clouds moved on; there was a line of blue light down her profile, and she whispered: "Yes, it's me, sir. I'm sorry, I couldn't sleep, and I came for air. I'll go now."

She turned away, and he said urgently: "No, wait."

She turned back, and he looked at the gap separating the two little balconies, and he went to the corner and said softly: "I do this often, when I lock myself out of my room . . ."

He swung a leg over and reached for the other railing and her hands were on his arm, helping him as he clambered over. He shook his head and ran a hand through his hair and said: "You don't have to go, Dorothy, just because I'm here."

She was very hesitant. "I thought perhaps I should, sir. I mean . . . if you want to take the air too . . ."

"Yes, but not necessarily alone. It's a beautiful night, and it's not my private property. Even if it were . . . No, that's rather silly, isn't it?"

How sweet she looked in the moonlight! And she was tiny! She was barefoot and dressed in a loose robe that he saw now was blue, gathered at an infinitesimal waist with a sash, very slightly open at the throat, the long hair shining and the eyes very wide and solemn, even expectant. Of what? he wondered. The sudden stirring in his loins discomforted him; he longed to touch her, but he would not. Trying to find words, he said: "And your room, it's comfortable?"

"Oh, yes, sir! And Helga and me, we really get along very well together."

"Good, I'm glad of it. She's very, er, very nice, Helga."

"Yes, sir, she is."

Silence. Then: "I don't really know her too well. Mr. James, I know, thinks very highly of her. Of her work, I mean."

"Yes, sir."

"And . . . and Miss Susan too."

"Yes, sir."

He turned away from her and started down on the street. The watchman had wakened and was stirring his coals in the brazier; he lay down on the pavement again and covered himself with his coat.

Not looking at her, he said: "Well, I suppose I'd better be getting back."

Her voice beside him was a whisper: "If there's anything I can do for you, sir . . ."

"No. No. Thank you, Dorothy. Good night."

He clambered back over the twin railings, cursing himself for a fool, and as he stepped into his own room he looked back and saw that her grave eyes were still on him. He closed the windows behind him.

He went to bed and lay down on his stomach for the comfort it gave him, thinking and yet not thinking. and when the first rays of the sun came in through the window, he fell asleep.

He woke up at ten, shaved and dressed, and went to deliver the article to Enoch Mulligan at the *Register*.

Chapter Eleven

Robbins came to the breakfast table and said: "A Mr. Cobbett to see you sir. A Mr. William Cobbett. I told him the hour was not opportune, but he convinced me, sir, that you would wish to see him."

Peter was both astonished and delighted. "Wish to see him I do!" he said. "Show him into the library, Robbins. No, in here, perhaps he'd like some breakfast too." He turned to Susan. "You know the name?"

She grimaced. "Of course I do! The company you keep, Peter! All those dreadful people up North, and now Cobbett ... He's a perfectly appalling man!"

Peter said happily: "Yes, I suppose that to your way of thinking, he is. But he's a man after my own heart."

He could feel a kind of rekindling of his revolutionary spirit at the thought of seeing his old friend again, and when Cobbett appeared, looking somewhat older, in this year of 1828, than his sixty-five years, it was a joyous and emotional reunion. They embraced warmly, and Peter said: "My God, how good it is to see you! And you never looked better in your life."

"And never felt better, though a little . . . down at heel now, to the devil with it! How are you, Peter?"

"In the best of spirits. How else? May I present, Mr. William Cobbett, my sister Susan."

She held out her hand, and he kissed it with an old-fashioned kind of elegance. "A pleasure and a great honor, ma'am," he murmured, "that you receive an old reprobate like me in your house."

She smiled. "Well, at least you *know* what a reprobate you are. . . . You are very welcome here, sir."

"Come, sit down, have breakfast with us, and tell us of all your adventures," Peter said. "Where've you come from? Long Island, was it not?"

"Most recently from Jamaica."

Robbins came in and placed a thick slab of cured Wiltshire side before the old man, and he tackled it with gusto, tearing at the bread too and wolfing it down. He said: "But I have news and advice for you, Peter, news you might find alarming, and advice you'd better take." He paused and drank some tea and said with satisfaction: "The Frank Watson article, Enoch and I are both in agreement on one thing, it's going to be construed as an attack on the King himself, and Parliament today is in no mood to be trifled with. It's going to mean bad trouble, Peter."

"Good. It's time we stirred the pot up again."

Cobbett hesitated. "But let me tell you what will happen. First of all, they'll raid the *Register* and close it down again, and I'm resigned to that. This time it won't be easy for them. I propose to hire still more bully boys, Irishmen all of them, to guard my presses." He laughed. "A broken pate to an Irishman is like a pat on the back to a civilized man, and they'll lose out in the end, but they'll break a few heads before they all get carted off. And as for the presses, well . . ." He grimaced. "We'll find new ones, we've done it before."

Susan was very quiet, and Cobbett went on: "The next thing they do is . . . they'll come looking for you, and the necessary advice I have is, leave London, Peter, for a month at least. I'll be in hiding, and you have to be too."

There was a long, long silence, broken only by the rhythmic *swish-swish-swish* of steel on steel as Peter sharpened the long carving knife and sliced up more of the bacon; he was conscious that Susan's worried eyes were on him.

He said at last, very quietly: "No. I'll be damned if I let them force me out of my own house. This is my home, William, I'll not be chased out of it by their damned constables. No. I'll not run away."

"Peter," Cobbett said, urging, "for your own safety . . ."

"No! And there's no more to be said about it."

"But in God's name, how can you fight them!?"

"I'll find that out when the time comes . . ."

"A storm breaking, and you don't have the sense to take cover?"

"I've the sense to know when there's no other recourse than flight. I'll not take it now, and I won't listen to another word on the subject."

His anger left him, and he said calmly: "Have some more bacon, Willie. It's very good, isn't it?"

Cobbett sighed. "Yes, it is indeed. And you're a stubborn man, Entwhistle. Too stubborn for your own good . . ."

"So they tell me," Peter said equably. "They say it's a family weakness."

The storm broke three days later.

In the very early hours of the morning, an advance copy of the *Register* was delivered to Curzon Street by a runner, together with a note from Cobbett himself:

I'm hiding, Peter, in Kensington Village, just riding out the tide; have you notice that tides disperse their fury very

quickly if you ignore them? And I say to you again: Run!
Good luck, dear friend.

He sat in the library and read the offending article through three times, and thought about it for a long, long while. There was a phrase he was particularly proud of: "*. . . and if an Englishman may not speak his mind, does it mean that England is to be governed by the mindless?*"

And when at last Susan came down, surprised to find him there so early, he gave it to her to read and waited for her comments.

There was only one. She said, awed: "My God, Peter! They'll hang you for this!"

He said morosely: "If it reaches the ears of the Commons, and perhaps of the Lords too, then it might almost be worthwhile. There must be some among them who'll be moved, there *must* be!"

"They'll be battering our door down!"

"On Curzon Street?" he asked dryly. "In spite of all we've done to them, the lower classes, of which the constables are part, still have an inherent respect for their betters."

At midday, he summoned Robbins and said to him, quite cheerfully: "It may be, Robbins, that we should expect a modicum of trouble in the near future, from the constabulary."

Robbins was far too good a servant to raise his eyebrows; he inclined his head instead, and murmured: "I'm quite sure we'll be able to handle it, Mr. Peter."

Peter gave him the paper and said: "If you'll find the time to read my article, you'll know what I'm talking about."

A slow smile was spreading over the butler's rough, peasant face. "If you'll pardon me, sir, we all know, below stairs, what this is all about. I read the article before you came down this morning. I hope you won't think it presumptuous of me."

"Well . . ." Peter scowled. "Well, yes I do. I won't have

the servants reading my paper before I get to it. This was quite uncalled for."

"I'm sorry, sir." Robbins was quite chagrined, but he said: "With deference, Mr. Peter, when the constables arrive, as they surely will, it might be best for me to tell them that you're, ah, in France? For a short holiday!"

"No. If and when they come, I will see them."

Robbins said stubbornly: "They won't be calling, sir, just to pay their respects."

"I know it."

"They'll be wanting, if you'll pardon the expression, sir, to drag you off. To Newgate Gaol again."

"And I will not allow it. That's all, Robbins. And thank you."

"Yes, sir."

When he had gone, he found Susan in her room at work on some tatting, and he told her of his conversation with Robbins and of all he had read between the lines. He said: "When they come, I want you to stay here, out of sight. I'll deal with them myself."

She tried to mask her deep anxiety: "All right. If you know what you're doing, Peter . . ."

"I know what I'm doing. Believe me, I'm *never* going back to Newgate Gaol. Father had a shotgun here somewhere. Do you know where he kept it?"

Her eyes were wide with sudden fright. "Oh, no . . . !"

"Where, Susan?"

She fought it for a moment, but then, very hesitantly: "In . . . in the small wardrobe in his room, on a rack behind his dress uniforms. But Peter, please . . . ?"

He said furiously: "I'm just not going to put up with this damned nonsense! They say that an Englishman's home is his castle, and by God, if they're going to lay siege to *my* home . . . then I'm going to defend it!"

* * *

They came at eight o'clock of a thunderous evening, four burly officers full of their own importance, and their first setback was when Robbins, answering their hard knocking, opened the front door to them and said coldly: "The tradesmen's entrance is at the back, on Market Mews. Go there." And he slammed the door in their faces.

Peter and Susan were seated at dinner over a fine rack of lamb, and as he passed through the dining room, Robbins said—his eyes shining with a fiendish delight—"The moment is on us, Mr. Peter, sir. I sent them around to the kitchen, four of them."

"Good thinking, Robbins. I'll see them there."

He set his plate of succulent lamb aside, kissed Susan on the cheek, and said: "Just stay here. This will be over in no time at all."

He took the shotgun from its place by the hearth and went to the kitchen with Robbins. Dorothy and Louise were there, with the two other kitchen maids, as well as the two footmen and the four gardeners; and he saw with surprise that the men had all armed themselves with heavy ash cudgels.

Robbins threw open the back door with a flourish; and there they all were, just standing there under a ferocious rain that pounded down from the heavens in buckets . . .

Peter said, holding his shotgun loosely: "Well, gentlemen, what can I do for you?"

Their leader cleared his throat. He was short and squat and very powerful-looking. He said: "Peter Entwhistle Esquire, is that you, sir?"

Peter nodded. "Yes, I'm Peter Entwhistle."

There was the throat-clearing again, and then reading from a sodden sheet of paper: "Under the authority vested in me as a constable subservient to the magistrate of May Fair, to wit Colonel Lord Malcolm Fetter, and under the Sedition Act of 1792, it is my duty to place you under arrest, and to ask you to accompany me to the court of said Magistrate Colonel Lord Malcolm Fetter, to hear charges against you under said Sedition Act of 1792, and what say you, sir?"

Peter said: "What say I? I say categorically that I refuse arrest, and what's your abominable name, fellow?"

Under the pouring rain, sad eyes were blinking. "My name, sir? It's Modge, Mr. Entwhistle, sir, Charlie Modge."

"Well, Charlie Modge," Peter said equitably, "I am *not* going to accompany you to Lord Fetter's bloody court, and if you should be foolish enough to try and take me by force I'll blow your bloody head off."

He gestured with the shotgun, quite languidly, and said: "I mean it, fellow."

Poor Modge looked down the twin barrels of the gun, looked at the ash cudgels, seeming to close in on him now as Robbins and the other men moved into a half circle behind Peter; Modge was conscious that his own men were shuffling their feet uncertainly. Seizing the moment, Robbins said: "So be on your way, Modge, or there'll be broken pates tonight, I promise you!"

Peter said sharply: "Robbins! Leave this to me!"

"Yes, sir."

Modge pulled at his ear, and said, worried: "I'm sorry, sir, but I'll have to report that you resisted arrest, and it means another seven years in Newgate on top of what you'll get for the sedition you'd been charged with . . ."

"Oh, shut up! Lord Fetter's court is not in session at this time of night, I know His Lordship well, and he never held court after dark in his life . . ."

"That's true enough, sir, it reconvenes at ten in the morning . . ."

". . . so when you report to him tomorrow, present my compliments and tell him, if he chooses to send you back here, then he'd better have the Dragoons to back you up."

Modge was deeply distressed. "Well," he said, "with due

respect, sir, I can't hardly tell His Lordship that. He'll have my neck."

"I think not," Peter said dryly. "The days when the bearer of bad news was killed are gone, Modge. And I fancy His Lordship won't want an armed confrontation on Curzon Street any more than I do."

"Well . . ."

Desperately, Modge searched the faces of his dour companions for encouragement but found none. There was a loud rumbling burst of thunder to explode the eardrums, and sheet lightning lit up the sky as the rain redoubled its ferocity.

Suddenly Peter was conscious that the constables were not wearing the new mackintoshes which were slowly being issued to them now, but wore instead simple overcoats of sodden wool. One of the men was visibly shivering, blowing on his chapped hands to warm them; in the lightning, his running nose was red as a radish. Peter sighed and said: "God in Heaven is pissing down on you, Modge, because He knows what foolishness you're about, and it's a freezing night. But the kitchen's warm, so come on in and have some refreshment."

He turned to Robbins: "Do we have ale in the house?"

"No, sir, but I can send out for some . . ."

"Then we'll all have whiskey, before these poor bedraggled fellows drop dead from pneumonia. I don't want it on my conscience."

He stood back and said, happily now: "Come in and dry out, Mr. Modge, and bring your men with you."

Modge was astonished; but long years of service with the constabulary had taught him that the gentry, with whom he came into occasional contact, were always quite unpredictable. He murmured: "You're very kind, sir," and touched his forelock.

Peter said: "By God, Robbins, we'll use the hunting

chairs. If ever there was an occasion for them, this is it."

"Yes, sir."

There was precious little hunting from Curzon Street. But the hunting chairs had come from the family's cottage down in the forest of Hayward's Heath when it had been demolished to make way for the new London-to-Brighton road, much of it surfaced now with tarmac to make the ride easier for the carriages of the upper classes.

The hunting chairs, made of turned oak, were tall and spindly and on casters, their woven-rush seats some five feet high. When you came in from the shoot, soaked to the marrow with the constant rain, you climbed up onto the chair and draped your soggy cloak over your head, and the servants wheeled you up to the big cast-iron kitchen stove to dry out as they poured the whiskey and cooked the ducks you had brought down; it was a very civilized endeavor indeed.

The four intruders were perched up there, sniffling in the steam that rose around them, as Dorothy and Louise and Robbins kept their glasses replenished from the heavy stone whiskey jar. Peter, too, pacing back and forth below them, was drinking very heavily now.

Modge said somberly: "I'm an educated man, Mr. Entwhistle, I had nearly four years of schooling, I can read and write very easily indeed, even though I say it myself. And I read most of your article, it took me a little time, there were a lot of words I didn't understand. . . . But I have a lady friend, if I may make so bold, she's a schoolteacher, and she helped me with it. And you were right, sir, absolutely right. There's not many of the aristocracy will speak out for the likes of us."

"So if you agree with my thinking," Peter said, "how can you possibly work as a constable? A *constable,* for God's sake! You're an enemy of your own natural philosophies!"

"Why? Because they pay me six shillings and tuppence-three a week, that's why. It's almost enough to live on."

"*Almost?* I'll agree, it doesn't sound like very much."

"I pick up an extra two shillings a week from the whores on Stew Lane, just to leave them alone. I'm not proud of it, sir, but I've got a wife and eleven kids to feed . . ."

Dorothy said, hoisting up the jug: "More whiskey, Mr. Modge?"

He beamed down on her; he was getting very drunk. "Well, I don't mind if I do. And you're a very pretty little thing, now ain't you?"

The comforting steam was rising from their bodies as they huddled up there, close to the ceiling, slowly being dried out. And this was exactly what those hunting chairs were supposed to do.

Peter had drunk too heavily with Mr. Charlie Modge and his cohorts.

He stood in his robe on the little iron balcony of his room, trying to find sobriety by taking in great gulps of the damp night air.

"You're drunk," Susan had said accusingly, and he'd been sober enough to admit it. How much had they imbibed? He trid to count the glasses and knew only that among the five of them they'd polished off a gallon jug of Mr. Dewar's warming Scotch before the constabulary had staggered off home.

The heavy rain had given way to a steady London drizzle, a fine mist hanging in the air; and once again he became aware that he was not alone. On the adjacent veranda, Dorothy was standing; the clouds were drifting, and momentarily a moonbeam limned her, and he could see that her bright eyes were very anxious. She whispered: "Are you all right, sir?"

He nodded. "Yes, I'm fine. And you?"

"Just taking the air, sir. The storm's leaving us now, it'll be a splendid day tomorrow. And it's a very beautiful night, isn't it?"

"Yes, it is. I think I never saw a brighter moon. May I . . . may I join you?"

He clambered clumsily over the twin railings of the balconies and almost fell the three stories down to the mews below. But her arm was around him, surprisingly strong, helping him over. He straightened himself, determined to be absolutely sober. He put his arm around a waist that was so fragile he could not believe it; his hand dropped a little, onto the tip of a pelvic bone that lay in his palm for a while.

The moonlight was etching that silhouette of her sweet face again, the high forehead, the slender line of her nose, her lips, her chin, her throat, all caught in a pale blue light. Her gown was wrapped carelessly about her, far more open than it had been the last time, in spite of the cold, and he could see the curve of a high-pointed breast; he fancied that he could even see a nipple but knew that it was only wishful thinking; it was hidden by a fold of cotton stuff.

He *thought* about her breasts, obviously very small and tight; and he wanted desperately to touch them, fondle them, perhaps even kiss them.

He said, searching for the release of conversation: "My brother, James. He's in Greece, you know."

Her voice was a whisper. "Yes, so I believe."

"And do you know about my sister Hilda? She's in India, married to a maharajah."

"Oh, really?"

"Yes. Married to a maharajah. It makes her a maharanee."

"That must be wonderful for her, sir."

"She was always regarded as one of the most beautiful women in London. Perhaps in the whole of England."

Dorothy was laughing suddenly. "And the way you handled that Mr. Modge this evening, sir! It was really very impressive."

"It was?"

"Oh, yes, indeed! But . . . will they really come back tomorrow with the dragoons, sir?"

"No."

He shook his head. "I know the chief magistrate, he's not the kind of man to countenance a gun battle on Curzon Street, which is what I promised him. He'll back away, I'm sure of it."

His hand was creeping slowly up her incredibly slender body, till it had reached the underside of her breast, just enough to feel the beginnings of the resilience there. He said, stifling his natural emotion: "Mally Fetter's not very bright, but he's not an absolute idiot either. He knows, he *must* know that a man can be driven just so far before he turns and fights. . . . And he'll back off, you'll see."

He had raised his hand just a little, and it was cupping her breast now. She made no attempt to brush it away, but she said steadily: "I think I should go to bed now, sir. With your permission, of course."

He dropped his hand to her waist instantly. "Yes, perhaps you should. It's very late, isn't it? But let me see you to your room." Forcing a joke, he said: "There may be ghoulies and ghosties and long-leggedy beasties prowling the corridors . . ."

Her eyes were shrouded in the blue moonlight. "That's very kind of you, sir."

He took her arm and shepherded her down the long passageway and up the half flight of stairs to her room. His hands were on her hips, not moving, and he said: "May I come in for a moment or two? For a chat?"

There was a moment of silence, almost as though all this were not preordained. And then a whisper: "Helga's there, sir. We share the room."

"Ah, yes, I forgot . . ."

"But she's a very heavy sleeper. Last night, with all that thunder, I thought the house was going to break apart. But Helga slept through it all. If we talk very quietly . . ."

She pushed open the door. There was a night-light burning by the big double bed, a small cylinder of wax in a saucer of water, and on one side of the bed, Helga's naked arm was draped down to the floor.

"She likes the edge of the bed," Dorothy whispered.

They sat down together on the other side of the bed, and for a moment neither of them spoke; they both just sat there, knowing what was going to happen now. In a little while he touched her breast and then slipped his hand under her gown to savor the nakedness of it. He was beside himself as he pushed her gently down and found her lips, kissing her passionately; she did not refuse him.

He opened her gown and found that she wore nothing underneath it, and he covered her body from head to foot with little kisses. Still she would not fight him; instead, she moaned gently as his lips found her.

The emotion he felt was bolstered by a genuine and very honest affection; he knew that Dorothy, now, was not just another woman, but someone very special indeed. He opened his own robe, and in a fury of excitation broke the cotton draw string of his pajamas when the knot resisted his efforts to untie it. He felt her unaccustomed hand on him, heard her moaning, and rolled on top of her.

There was a sound from Helga in the same huge bed, a four-poster that had come too, he remembered, like the hunting chairs, from the Hayward's Heath cottage; he threw her an anguished glance, but the sound was merely a sleep-induced moaning. Gingerly, he turned his attention back to Dorothy, knowing that the circumstances were hazardous but that nothing could stop him now.

He entered her slowly, carefully, gently, and he caught his breath when he heard the sudden gasp of pain, knowing what it meant even though he had never heard it before.

He rolled back from her at last and lay on his back,

watching the dancing shadows of the night-light on the ceiling and wondering if the guilt he felt was apparent to her.

It was.

She stroked his cheek and whispered: "It's all right, sir, I don't mind, really I don't."

"You don't *mind* . . . Oh, God."

There was blood, quite copious, more than he had ever imagined, and he mumbled: "I should have known with absolute certainty . . ."

She was upset, just because he was. "It's all right, sir," she whispered, "really it is. I don't want to see you unhappy because of something that was bound to happen one of these days."

"Bound to happen? It was?"

She said earnestly: "Yes, I'm sure of it, sir. I remember the time when I first came to the house, when Mr. Robbins said: 'Don't just sit there, girl, you've been dismissed.' I remember the way you looked at me then, and I *knew*. I knew that sooner or later we'd finish up in bed together."

"Even though you were a virgin . . ."

"Yes, sir." She was searching desperately for ways to comfort him. "It's not that important to a girl, really it isn't. And in the morning I'll wash the sheet, and no one will ever know."

No one would ever know?

He was suddenly aware that Helga, on the other side of the bed, was awake. Worse, she was propped up on her elbow, one full and quite naked breast carelessly exposed, with no attempt made to cover it; and she was staring at him, her pale blue eyes filled with amusement.

Awake? She was *wide* awake. She said, politely: "Good evening, Mr. Peter, sir. And are you well?"

Hastily he covered himself, aware that he too was exposed to the cool night air. He left the bed and wrapped his robe tightly around him. These were servants' quarters; he was an intruder here, and he knew that these were very important matters of protocol.

He said tightly: "Good night, Dorothy. Good night, Helga."

He strode to the door with all the dignity he could muster and knew that their eyes were on him as he closed it behind him. There was just time to hear that Helga was laughing softly; and it infuriated him.

# Chapter Twelve

Peter's affair with Dorothy proceeded apace.

It had started almost inconsequentially, perhaps even triggered by too much whiskey from that persuasive stone jar. But he had lain awake all the rest of the night trying to persuade himself that the sudden passion was not really very important; and he could not.

He stared at himself in the glass the next morning as he shaved and saw the face of a man who had seduced one of the servants in the sanctity of the house that had once been Amanda's; he wondered what that gracious matriarch would have thought about it. He remembered James and Helga; but surely this could not be compared to James' constant whoring? Or could it?

He saw Dorothy a little later from his bedroom window as she gathered bay leaves from the tree in the tiny kitchen garden. One of the gardeners, a young man named Jennick, was setting out roots of bergamot nearby; some of the servants preferred it to ordinary Indian tea.

He went out and said to the young man: "The lavender by the front gate, Jennick, it needs a copious application of horse manure. See to it, please."

Jennick was about to say: "I've already done it, sir," but he threw a quick look at Dorothy and said instead: "Yes, Mr. Peter, I'll see to it at once." Helga, that Scandinavian baggage, had been talking her head off in the kitchen that morning, enlivening the servants' breakfast table, in spite of Robbins' constant and angry warnings to hold her peace, with lively and sometimes quite hilarious accounts of last night's escapade.

"Mr. Peter's such a nice man," she had said. "I'm glad, truly I am, that he found someone to sleep with . . ."

Jennick scurried off, and Peter watched Dorothy for a moment. Her eyes cast down, she was picking the bay leaves one by one and threading them with a needle, to be hung up over the kitchen stove to dry out. He moved to her and said quietly: "It's about last night, Dorothy. Would it embarrass you to talk about it?"

(What would James have said under like circumstances? *Nothing!* He would have looked at her and laughed!)

She was quite surprised. "Embarrass me? No, sir, not one bit."

"I have . . ." He gulped. "I have given the matter some considerable thought. Indeed, I lay awake all night thinking about it. And what can I say? I took advantage of you."

Her heart was beating fast. Three more bay leaves on the needle and she said: "But not without my consent, sir. There's no blame."

"No blame?"

"No, sir, none at all."

"But it was a monstrous thing to do!"

"No, sir. It's not my place to argue with you, sir, but . . . no, it made me very happy."

"It did?"

"Yes, sir, very happy indeed."

"But . . ." He was unaccustomedly unsure of himself. "But if we were to do this again . . ."

He began pacing, even circling the carefully shaped little

tree as he searched for the words he knew had to be spoken; from time to time, the dense mass of oblate leaves hid her inquiring eyes almost entirely and somehow made it easier for him.

He said at last, brooding: "There's really nothing I can offer you in exchange, Dorothy. What, *money?* No! I can't even raise your wages now. It would be tantamount to turning you into a whore. I won't do it!"

"I'm happy with my wages, sir," Dorothy said calmly. "And perfectly happy to lie with you again if you ever feel that you need me. I mean it, sir. There was pleasure for me, too. You really don't have to think that you owe me anything."

Her eyes were wide and honest. He took her hands and whispered: "Then will you sleep with me tonight, Dorothy, in my own bed? I want so much to wake up in the night and find you beside me, to touch you, to know that you are there. . . . Will you do that? Please?"

"Yes, oh, yes!"

At midnight, she crept secretly down the half flight of stairs to his room and shucked off her robe as she approached the bed; her body, lit by the wax night-light, was tiny and slight and flawless, and he reached out for her in a kind of delirium. He loved her three times during the long night, and she was gentle and receptive to him, giving and not always taking.

And when he awoke in the morning, she was gone; he took comfort in the thought that the servants' morning call was for half-past five, at which hour they were expected to polish the big iron stove with bootblack and dust all the rooms that might be used that day and set the table for the eight-o'clock breakfast . . .

He lay on his back and thought about her and wondered about Susan too.

Would she, with her usual perspicacity, know what was

going on? And if so, what would she think of it? It was a problem he did not really want to face.

The next night and the next and the next, Dorothy crept silently down from her room to share his bed, and they became constant and devoted lovers. And yet, outside the close confines of their very personal little world, her attitude was immaculate.

At breakfast she would say: "May I make you more toast, Mr. Peter, sir?" Or, "I think the tea is cold, sir. Should I make another pot?"

And always, Susan would smile and say nothing; but he was convinced that she *knew*.

He said to Dorothy one night as he lay beside her with his hand cupping her young breast: "Dorothy, my love . . . I've come to the conclusion that we can't, and mustn't, hide this from Susan."

She propped herself up on an elbow, her eyes very wide as she stared down at him. "Yes, I know it. And I've always felt that she *knows* about us. I'm sure of it."

"Yes, so am I. Even though she's never said a word."

"She's waiting for you to tell her, I think."

"Yes. That's Susan exactly. But how can I find the words? What are you now, my mistress? I suppose that's the term. Does it alarm you?"

"Alarm me? No, of course not! Why should it, dear Peter? You've given me so much happiness! And I don't want it to end, ever!"

She was a bright and clearheaded young woman, and she said gently as she caressed him: "You'll *have* to find the words, Peter, you'll *have* to tell her, sooner or later, that we're lovers. We can't go on deceiving her. Just . . . tell her that I'm your mistress. I promise you . . . it will never interfere with my household duties. Not one whit, I swear it."

Peter sighed. "I'm convinced it's a matter of confirming

what she already knows. Knows and won't even hint at out of her sense of propriety."

"Yes, I think so." She snuggled closer to him, her slender, naked body fitted to his angular frame as though they were one. "She'll understand. And I don't think it will disconcert her in the least. She loves you very dearly, Peter, and all she wants for you is . . . happiness. She'll know that I'm bringing it to you. She must already see it in your eyes, in your moods . . . even in the way you eat your food."

He laughed and fondled her. "In the way I eat my food?"

"Yes indeed! Lately, you have never once said, as you used to so often: 'No, I won't eat tonight, I'm not hungry. . . .' "

It astonished him to realize that it was true, and she went on earnestly: "Your eyes have never been brighter, even the way you move—there's a positive *bound* to your step now."

"There is?"

"Yes. And Susan must surely have noticed it and wondered about it. She'll know that it's my doing."

She embraced him, her arms tight around him as she dreamed her personal, erotic dreams. "I greatly admire Susan," she whispered, "perhaps even love her. And not the least of my reasons is that I have seen how much she adores you, thinks of you, wants nothing but good for you. And shall I tell you something else? As soon as you tell her what there is between us, she'll call me in for a heart-to-heart talk, just to assure herself that I'm not . . . not a designing woman. She must already know that, I'm sure. But she'll want to be absolutely certain."

Peter nodded. "Yes, I'm afraid you're right. Will that worry you, Dorothy, my love?"

"No. I'll welcome it! I want her to know that I ask for nothing more than I have now. I want her to know that the happiness she wants for you is what I want too. And that's *all* I want, Peter."

"And nothing for yourself? It's not very fair, Dorothy."

"*Everything* for myself," she said fiercely. "Do you think I merely *accept* you now? Yes, that first strange night I did, even though from the first time we met this was one of my fondest dreams. But no longer."

She was crying suddenly. "Dear, dear Peter. I'm so terribly in love with you . . ."

Under her caresses he had become terribly excited again. She raised herself and straddled him and guided him into her and leaned down so that he could suckle on her breasts the way he so much liked to.

And all their worries were lost in the excitation of the moment as he thrust up into her.

Robbins said happily: "We have kippers for breakfast this fine morning, Mr. Peter. Louise went to Billingsgate at sunup and came back with some fine kippered herrings."

He set the plates before them, and Susan said: "Let me take the bones out for you."

"Ah . . ."

When Robbins had retired to the kitchen, Peter said, a little hesitantly: "Er, Susan darling. There's a matter of great import we have to talk about."

She was fiddling with the bones, two forks expertly employed. "About Dorothy?" she did not even raise her eyes, and he was shocked.

"Well, yes, it's about Dorothy. Sooner or later I'm sure you'll find out, and it's better that you hear it from me. I'm afraid I've been sleeping with her for the past month or so now. I just don't want to hide it from you anymore."

"Yes, I know," Susan said calmly. "And why *should* you hide it from me? At your age, you simply have to have either a wife or a mistress, a dozen mistresses if you want . . ."

"Susan!"

"And I'm glad for you. Will it surprise you if I say I'm very, *very* fond of her?"

She stared at him now and said earnestly: "In spite of her station in life, Dorothy is a young woman of the most admirable character, I might almost say a woman of *quality*. And she's very sensible and down-to-earth too, just as I am. And really, she's very beautiful." She laughed suddenly. "Peter dear! I'm not blind! I've seen what's been going on, of course I have. But—far more importantly—I've also seen how it's changed you. You just don't . . . skulk around looking miserable anymore. She's good for you, darling! And she really shouldn't be just a servant—you said as much yourself once."

"Yes, I believe I did."

"She's intelligent, and devoted, I am convinced, to your welfare. She speaks well, as you must have noticed, though perhaps that is not important anymore, the times are changing very fast these days, but really, she's very well spoken. And I saw the way she looks at you, Peter. I don't know exactly what your feelings are toward her, but I will tell you . . . Dorothy loves you to the limits of desperation. She's even *awed* by you. And it's not because you are an Entwhistle, it's because you are the Entwhistle she loves."

There was a new light in his eyes, and he said, perhaps a little wryly: "It did occur to me that perhaps I should think of her in more decisive terms."

"Peter, that's a very obscure remark."

He sighed. "If I were to think, to *think* only, mind you, in terms of marriage, what would your feelings be?"

"Oh, God . . ."

Susan ran to him and threw her arms around him and kissed him and said: "Peter, for a man of erudition you can be so foolish sometimes! What business is it of mine whom you want to marry? But it seems that it is, and I think I know why, so I will tell you—and I say it with all conviction, Peter! Dorothy will make you a wonderful wife, and I will welcome her into the family with open arms. There! I've said it! So go and propose to her, now!"

He hesitated only briefly before he stalked to the door. He turned back, leaning into it, his face alive with pleasure, and he said, scarcely able to restrain his emotion: "It's what I want so badly, Susan dear! And yet . . . I want your approval too." His mind was made up, and there was the opportunity to banter with her now. He said, a wonderful sense of good humor on him: "Does that mean that I cower in the pocket of your apron, like a worried lover? Does it mean that our relationship, yours and mine, borders on the incestuous?"

"Peter! For God's sake! Mother was right—you're a monster!"

"Almost the only virtue I have."

"Peter, you talk too much! Go to her! Now!"

He almost ran out of the room and up the stairway to the bedrooms and found Dorothy in his own, turning down the covering, as Helga blew on the charcoal of the copper warming pan and slipped it between the sheets. They both turned to look at him, and they were startled by his flushed features. He threw a look to Helga, whom James had always liked to call "a saucy little piece"; and he looked to Dorothy and said, forcing upon himself a calm that he did not feel: "Dorothy . . . there is something I must say to you, a question I must ask."

Helga threw the sheet and the blanket over the warming pan, curtsied, and said: "I'll be about my business, sir."

"No, Helga! It is not a secret. Stay."

"Yes, sir."

She could only stare, sure that she was about to witness events of momentous importance.

He put his hands on Dorothy's shoulders and turned her to him, holding her close, and he said clearly: "Dorothy, you know how much I love you, do you not? And I think that you love me too. Will you then consent to be my wife? I ask you in all humility. Will you marry me?"

He heard Helga gasp. Then Dorothy was clutching at him, burying her face in his chest and trying to control her sobs. "Yes, yes, *yes!* Oh, Peter, I love you so dearly."

"My darling."

She drew back from him suddenly. "And Susan? What will Susan think?"

He looked down at her, happy and smiling broadly, and said, gently reproving: "Dorothy, my love . . . I make all the important decisions in this house, as befits my position here. But to set your mind at rest, I will tell you. I informed Susan only a few minutes ago that I was about to ask you for your hand in marriage, and she was *delighted,* as delighted as I will be if you accept me as your husband."

"Oh, Peter, I do, I *do!*"

She would not let him go, embracing him tightly as though this change in her fortunes might, by some trick of fate, somehow elude her.

"Will you come down with me now and tell Susan the news she is waiting for?"

There was a moment of inconsequential concern. "But your bed isn't properly made yet . . ."

"Helga, I am sure, can finish it. Come, my love, and off with your bonnet and apron."

She cast them aside and went out with him, throwing a bemused look back at Helga, conscious of a light in those Nordic eyes that might almost have been of mischief.

When they reached the Small Library, Susan embraced her and said simply: "I welcome you to the family, Dorothy dear. I know that you will make a good wife for Peter. I know that you will make him as happy as you have made me today, as happy as James and Hilda will be when I send them word of this truly splendid news."

A brief three days later, they were married at the little Church of St. Vedast on Foster Lane, a quiet wedding, with a reception to follow that was attended by only a dozen or so of their closest friends. Cobbett was among them, up from his Kensington farm and talking happily and at great length about his maize, and the seedling trees he was importing from the Americas, and not once mentioning the scurrilous articles his *Register* was still publishing—many of them Peter's.

He said, drinking copious draughts of the beer that Robbins had brought from the King's Head especially for him: "She's a beautiful girl, Peter. You're a very lucky man. A tiny, fragile body on her, but the mind of a mature woman of great spirit. She'll be very good for you. If I send you a pine-tree seedling, will you plant it in her honor? There's a little space by your kitchen door that needs filling . . ."

The days, the weeks, the months slipped by, and there was a great happiness in the Curzon Street house. Even the servants were delighted, conscious that what they called, whispering among themselves, "one of our lot" had become a *lady*. They called her "ducks" or "luv" when Peter was not there; and even in his presence they so far forgot themselves as to address her as "Dorothy," without the mandatory honorific.

For Peter, it was a period of the most exquisite wellbeing. He worshiped her, and she worshiped him in return. In her bed, there was a kind of constant delirium, and out of it there was a relationship that belied entirely the differences in their God-given stations. She would take his hand at night and place it on her stomach and whisper: "There, can you feel him kicking? Your son, my darling, is going to be so very, very strong. And what shall we name him?"

Peter said instantly: "Not John after my father, whom I loved and admired in spite of his empire philosophies. Nor even after his grandfather, Sir Richard, who was a family man of some consequence. We will name him, instead, after his great-great-grandfather, who fought against the Dutch in 1664, on the East Coast of America, and changed the name of New

Amsterdam to . . . New York. He was one of the greatest men who ever lived, and his name was Arthur. My child and yours, Dorothy, will grow up to be a great man too, I know it."

"Arthur? A fine name, a name of kings. And if it should be a girl?"

"Why, then . . . Amanda, of course."

Nine months almost to the day, after that first traumatic coupling, their son was born, a lusty, bawling young man with flailing fists who seemed to want to fight the whole world.

It was a difficult delivery—her hips were just too small. And in spite of Susan's expert and devoted care, Dorothy died painfully, in childbirth.

Chapter Thirteen

It seemed to Peter that the Curzon Street house would never again be the same.

He wandered from room to empty room, disconsolately, staring at all the remembrances of her, conscious, so often, that Susan's worried eyes were on him, the blue of them paler than ever as she grew older. She was thirty-five now, four years his junior; and why did she look so old?

He said to her, bitterly: "I feel that it's not my home anymore. For me, Dorothy took all of its attraction with her."

It was a cold, wet afternoon in December 1827, and she was seated by the fire in the Small Library, working with needles and colored threads on canvas that was tightly stretched over her tambour; she was tatting a design of flowers for a small cushion cover.

She whispered: "It's been our home for so many generations, Peter."

"Yes, I know." He said, brooding: "It's suddenly become almost hateful to me."

And then more calamity fell upon them, in the form of a black-bordered letter from the War Office: It read:

I have the painful duty to inform you, sir, that Captain James Hayes Entwhistle died in action this Monday fort-night, in Missolonghi, Greece, fighting against the Turk-ish-Egyptian forces of Governor Ibrahim Pasha. . . .

What? James gone too? The cheerful, ebullient James, whose only real interest in life was the pursuit of willing women?

Susan was in tears, but there were subtle obligations for him as head of the household. When he called Robbins to him and told him to inform them all below stairs, he said gently: "When you break the news to Helga, Robbins . . . remember that she was always very fond of Mr. James." He cleared his throat and said loudly: "In this house, there are no secrets either above or below stairs, nor will there ever be as long as I am master of it. Compassion, Robbins, when you tell Helga."

Robbins was too good a servant to allow himself any show of emotion. He held himself in and inclined his head and said quietly: "My condolences, sir. And there's not much I can say, is there? Except that . . . there won't be a dry eye below stairs tonight. We were all very fond of Mr. James, sir."

"Thank you, Robbins. Grief shared is always a little easier to bear."

"I mean . . . coming right on top of the other, sir."

Peter said steadily: "That will be all, Robbins. Thank you."

"Yes, sir. I didn't mean to open wounds, sir, that can't hardly be healed yet."

"God in heaven damnit!" Peter shouted. "That's all, Rob-bins! God dammit, that's *all!*"

"Yes, sir."

When the butler had gone, Peter, brooding, said to Susan: "We've always been very close, you and I, haven't we? Hilda and I too were always just as dear to each other. But James . . ."

He poured himself a brandy. "When we were children, I always thought that James was an insufferable little prig. I couldn't stand the sight of him. Every time I saw him setting out all those damned lead soldiers of his, lining up for one famous battle or another . . . I swear, it used to make me physically sick. But when I came back from . . . from those foolish wanderings of mine, I discovered the real James, a man of very sterling qualities indeed. He'd matured, hadn't he? Into the good, honest, sensible man he was when he left for Greece. The man he was when he died for a cause he believed in."

Susan's needle, threaded with scarlet wool, was poised. "No," she said. "It wasn't James who matured, Peter. It was *you.*"

He could only stare at her and wonder if, as was usually the case, she was right.

With the death, in 1830, of the worrisome King George IV and the accession to the throne of his genial and easygoing brother William, an entirely different climate had settled on the country; the liberals were taking over everywhere, calling themselves "socialists," and it was no longer a disgrace for a man to be known as a radical.

In short, there was precious little left for Peter to tilt at. Protest about the workingman's condition had moved from the streets to the dining tables of the gentry, who threw brightly shining witticisms at each other in flippancy and mock concern; and it distressed him deeply.

Since the death of his beloved Dorothy, he had not been quite the same. He was morose and terribly moody, and it seemed that the only release he could find was in his daily readings of Cobbett's *Political Register,* as though he were vicariously punishing himself for what he could only regard as the abject failure of his efforts to improve the condition of England's working classes.

Or was it a failure? At least there was a liberal government now!

Worrying about him, Susan said gently: "Peter, darling,
Dorothy's been gone for two years now. You really can't
spend the rest of your life moping. It's just not healthy."

He smiled wearily. "Do I *mope*? It's very hard not to. I was
so deeply in love with her!"

"But now you must find yourself a new wife. A decent
period of mourning has gone by, and there's no reason why
you shouldn't do that *now*. If not a wife, then at least a mistress. I'm a very practical sort of woman, as you know. And
this is at least half of the problem. You're starved for someone
to *love*, and so you bury your nose day and night in that dreadful man Cobbett's complaints about Jamaica, about the condition of the slaves half a world away from here. It's consuming
you, Peter. It mustn't be allowed."

The diagnosis was not only Susan's.

Below stairs, they worried about Peter too, and after a
quiet discussion among the servants about the change that had
come over the whole house since Dorothy's passing, Helga
said to Robbins as they sat at the kitchen table together, dining on the roast pork that Louise had prepared for them: "The
master needs a woman, Mr. Robbins, in bed with him. It's a
cure for every ailment a man can have."

"That's enough of *that!*" Robbins said sharply. "I won't
have you spreading your foreign ideas in *this* house. The master will pull himself out of it in time, and meanwhile, it's none
of your business, don't forget your place."

"No, Mr. Robbins. But he really was in love with Dorothy. And she was one of *us*." She fiddled with the top of her
blouse. "Just once or twice a week, it's all a gentleman needs,
really."

Robbins said sourly: "Well, I don't know what it is

you've got in that foreign mind of yours, Helga, but whatever it is, don't do it."

"No, sir, of course not, Mr. Robbins."

She had deliberately left the copper warming pan between the sheets of Peter's bed, and when she thought the time was just right, she walked into his bedroom without knocking and pulled up in mock surprise when she found him lying in bed and reading sheets of papers by the light of the tallow.

She said: "Oh! Oh, I'm sorry, sir, I didn't know you were in bed already. I'm afraid I left the pan between the sheets. I forgot to take it out."

It was on the floor by the bed, and she picked it up and shook the coals out of the window and hung the pan in its proper place on the wall and turned back and said: "I'm very sorry, sir. It shouldn't have happened."

Helga was no longer the "saucy little piece" that James had dallied with. She was many years older and had filled out a little. But she had kept her youthful good looks and had become very satisfyingly voluptuous, maturing as a woman will to whom her femininity is important. She was very full-figured now and pleasing to look at, her eyes a brighter blue, her blond hair escaping here and there under her white bonnet.

She asked the stock question: "And will there be anything else, sir?"

Peter shook his head. "No. No, thank you, Helga."

She did not move. "I mean . . . if there's anything I can do, sir?"

She took a few paces forward and stood by the bed, her eyes cast down. "We're very worried about you below stairs, sir. I mean . . . it's been a long time since we saw you laugh. And this used to be a very happy house, Mr. Peter, sir."

She would not meet his eyes, but she said steadily: "If Mr. Robbins knew what I had in mind, he'd have fifty fits, but . . . I think you know, sir."

"Yes. Yes, I do, indeed."

He reached out and took her hand; there were chilblains on her knuckles. "I know, and I'm truly grateful. You are a very beautiful woman, Helga, and . . . desirable too. I'm more grateful for your . . . your concern than you will ever know." His voice was a whisper. "But I am . . . restricted by a great love I have for a lady who has left us. Please try to understand me?"

He dropped her hand and turned away, burying his face in the pillow to hide the sudden tears.

Helga went to the door, suffused with shame, and she turned back and whispered: "I'm sorry about the warming pan, sir. I just forgot it."

"It's all right. Good night, Helga, and thank you. And bless you, too."

"Good night, sir."

She was gone.

In the morning, Peter went to find Cobbett. And that gentleman farmer from Kensington was in a fine old fury; the windmill he was tilting at was still Jamaica.

Cobbett said, fuming: "Prime Minister Grey has bullied his antislavery act through Parliament, and it does him credit! But I'd be happier if he were making sure the law's obeyed, which it is not! If I had a few years of life left in me, I'd be back in Jamaica tomorrow, continuing the good work I started there. It's where I belong, Peter. It's where *you* belong!"

They were walking together among the massed seedlings in the Kensington garden, row upon row of them, pine trees for the most part, brought over from the New World. They came to the beginnings of the cornfield, the ears just ripening, and Cobbett said disgustedly: "Ants, look at the damned ants. . . . But if we can ever get this stuff to grow half decently, we'll have gone another step forward toward feeding a starving world. There's great nourishment in those yellow kernels. Maize, they call it, and I still can't get the honest English laborer to eat it. All he wants to do is feed it to his pigs." He shrugged. "Well, it's recovering my fortune for me, even so. And the Entwhistle fortunes, Peter, how are they? Susan, James, Hilda . . . how are they all?"

"Susan . . . flourishing. But James, I'm afraid, is dead."

"Dead? Oh, God, no!"

"Yes, fighting for Greece against the damned Turks, a sad, a terrible thing."

A slight rain was beginning to fall, scarcely more than a mist, and Peter looked up at the sky and said moodily: "James was so very like our father, John, the same military swagger, the same simple philosophies about the way life ought to be. Perhaps we were closer than I always thought. But Hilda . . ." He brightened suddenly and said, laughing: "Dear Hilda! We had a letter from her only a few months ago. May I read it to you? I carry it with me always."

"A sign of true devotion, and yes, please, I would greatly like to hear it."

Peter took the folded and much-thumbed sheets of paper from his pocket, and they moved under a shelter where the youngest of the seedlings were, and he read, very happily:

My Dearest Peter,

So much of time has passed since we last wrote to each other, and how that time has changed! There is so very much I have to tell you! But first, I will say that I am almost deliriously happy, and have been since the day that Ranjet first proposed to me; that, at least, has not changed. But our condition . . . yes, a change indeed! Ranjet's father died four months ago, and he is now the new maharajah, and I am his maharanee. We have four children now, three boys and a girl. The girl, who is the

*eldest, is called Ravi, and—oh horrors!—she is absolutely
blond!*

Peter laughed suddenly. "We always had problems," he
said, "because of Hilda's own coloring. And now . . . a blond
Indian girl!" Cobbett said nothing; he had always been aware,
as a close friend of the family, of those difficulties; but he was
content to know that the passage of time had eased them.

Peter read on:

*How we all wish that you could come to visit us! And
really, why don't you do that, both you and Susan? Why
don't you come and spend a year or two with us? We were
both terribly disappointed when James was posted to
Greece instead of India. Ranjet was very serious about
asking for him as military adviser; and one of the great
pleasures of our dreadfully elevated position is that what
we ask for from the British raj—we get! Does that mean
that we are spoiled? Yes, I will admit it, we really are!*

*The palace is a dream out of the Thousand and One
Nights; money means absolutely nothing at all, we have
more servants than I can even begin to count, elephants
and horses without number. . . . And, after all these years,
I still cannot get used to the number of robes I have,
ceremonial and informal, or the jewels that Ranjet showers
on me almost daily. I succeeded the other day in convincing one of our village headmen to allow a doctor in his
village, and in celebration of this really quite surprising
event Ranjet gave me the biggest ruby I have ever seen in
my life.*

*He is such a good man, Peter! And I am so happy with
him. In all this time, I think that I have wept only when I
think of you, and Susan, and James, and perhaps most of
all, of dear Mother. What a truly great lady!*

It is all so far behind me now. I fear that you would not

even recognize me anymore. I have a small mark on my
forehead to proclaim my caste, and I have become more
Indian than the Indians themselves.

God bless you both, dear Peter and dear, dear Susan.
Do please write to me. It only takes nine or ten months for
a letter to get here these days.

In great love, your devoted sister,

Hilda.

He folded the letter carefully and put it back into his
pocket, and Cobbett said, smiling: "An Entwhistle an Indian
maharanee! We're living in strange times, Peter."

"Yes, we are."

"But do I detect a note of sadness there? A kind of home-
sickness?"

Peter shook his head. "No, I think not. It's not easy to
leave the country you were born in, but traditionally we've
always done just that. As a family, I mean. I sometimes ask
myself what Susan and I are doing in London when there's a
whole new world out there, beckoning."

"Oh?" Cobbett's eyes were gleaming. "Are my words of
wisdom finding a way through that thick skull of yours at
last?"

"Perhaps." He said wryly: "I've come to believe I really
can't survive without something to be very angry about. I
suppose it means that my whole life depends upon . . . obses-
sions. Is that so foolish, do you think?"

"No," Cobbett said emphatically. "An obsession is a driving force, and that's all it is. How *can* a man of spirit survive
unless he's driven?"

"Well, you've given me a very new and important one,
William."

On June the eighteenth in the year 1835, William Cobbett died at the age of seventy-two, struck down by that same

influenza that had taken Peter's grandfather, Sir Richard, forty-one years earlier.

Peter said to Susan heavily: "The dark clouds are all about us, aren't they? With the possible exception of Ranjet Singh, William was the best friend I ever had. And London has suddenly become quite intolerable to me. I want to leave it."

She was alarmed. "Oh, Peter! Not Manchester again, please?"

He shook his head slowly. "No, of course not! Manchester is even darker, more grimy, and more squalid than London has become, and it means nothing to me now. The last time I was there, Tom Hoskins, who was once a radical and a rebel fighting the establishment, had just purchased three long rows of slum houses, a landlord now, calling himself 'Mr. Thomas' and putting up his rents whenever he feels he needs money. No, I've no more wish to help those who think only of themselves."

He poured himself a glass of brandy and said: "The devil take them all! For myself, for *us* . . . I want space, I want room to breathe, I want to feel the hot sun on my face. I feel that my life here is in danger of atrophy, and I want to begin it all over again."

He took his glass and stood in front of the portrait of Dorothy he had commissioned, staring up at it moodily. "Dorothy would have loved Jamaica," he said, "I'm convinced of it."

"Jamaica! It's half a world away!"

"William told me so much about it. It's a perfect place to raise our son! Arthur will love it too."

"Jamaica!" She said hesitantly: "But aren't there cannibals there?"

He smiled. "No, I think not. Black men, yes. But as far as I know, they don't eat each other. At least I hope they don't."

Susan tried to hide her anxiety. "To leave London forever?"

"It's what James did," Peter said, brooding. "And John too." He brightened suddenly. "And so did Hilda! The Entwhistles have always searched out their destinies far away from England, and perhaps we should too. It's mostly for Arthur."

"Well . . . if it's what you truly want, Peter."

"Only with your approval, Susan dear. If you want to stay here . . . then that's what we'll do."

"No. Perhaps after all it might be a good idea to emigrate. Yes, I'll agree, quite readily. Honestly, quite readily."

And so it was decided.

When he had gone to bed, Susan took up her embroidery again and found that she could not concentrate on it at all. She stared up at the family portraits and wandered around, touching the immaculate oak and walnut surfaces of furniture that had been there for more than four hundred years. And when she retired at last, deep in the valley of her feather mattress and shivering against the damp cold of the linen sheets, she quietly cried herself to sleep.

At the end of the year, the family sailed for Kingston, Jamaica, a beautiful jewel set in cobalt-blue waters under a cyaneous sky, where the hot sun was always brightly shining.

Chapter Fourteen

Their first sight of the island was an experience they would never forget; after the rain, the bitter cold, and the winter grays of London, Jamaica seemed to them ablaze with a riot of color under a brilliant blue sky and a burning sun.

They saw it first in the very early morning. They had been told by a friendly third mate the previous evening: "If the wind holds, Mr. Entwhistle, if we can maintain the speed we're making, then by three bells of the morning watch we'll see land." He made the little joke he liked to use on his favorite passengers: "Three bells is not three o'clock, as an intelligent man would suppose, but half-past five. We do that especially to confuse the landlubbers . . ."

For Susan, the initial anxiety had translated itself, once this new adventure was under way, into a quite ecstatic dream of a new and astonishingly different life, which she was not only prepared to accept but was now intensely excited about.

The change in her thinking had come about with the packing of the steamer trunks for a voyage to the New World and a new life; she thought of the hot sunlight and the bright blue skies that Peter had spoken of, and they made her heart beat faster.

Now it was a dream that was about to be realized, as though all that had gone before had not really happened at all because for so long there had been nothing but an expanse of open sea that was sometimes very rough, leading to a distant promise she could not imagine. And for Arthur, a bright and expectant nine-year-old, the excitement was intense.

Just as dawn was breaking, they had left their cabin and found room, together with many others of the passengers, along the railings very close to the schooner's prow. The sky was still dark to the west of them, and they would look back to the east as though they were *willing* the sun to rise and light up their destination for them.

In a little while, the blackness turned to a shadowy gray, the gray slowly took on a glorious red-gold, and the mass ahead of them became a living, vibrant landfall, with high purple mountains and forested hills dropping down to yellow sand beaches where slender palms leaned out over water so brilliantly blue and clear that it took their breath away.

The island was closing on them, and there were masses of scarlet where the flame trees blossomed in voluptuous profusion, and bright yellow creepers clambering everywhere, and great clumps of trees in more differing shades of green than they could have thought possible. The cliffs were the color of saffron, and when the sunlight drenched the island, all of its beauty seemed to explode for them.

The harbor, as they tied up, was packed tightly with three-master trading vessels, and there were black men, almost the first they had ever seen, carrying huge loads on their backs. "Slaves," Peter said tightly. "They look just like you and me, don't they?"

"No," Susan said, "they do *not*."

Not entirely to her surprise, he laughed; this was not a moment for anything but pleasure. "The slaves," he murmured. "Should we try to save them from their manifest destiny? Or would that be arrogance?"

"It would be indeed," Susan said, smiling. "But whatever you feel you have to do here . . . I know you will do it."

The lighters took them ashore, rowed by muscular black men who never seemed to stop shouting to each other in a quite incomprehensible language; they laughed a lot, showing very white teeth, and they all seemed to sweat profusely.

As the family waited interminably for their trunks to be unloaded, they wandered along a spit of rock and watched naked children there diving for lobsters in their hiding places, plucking octopus from their rock lairs and turning them quickly inside out for the evening meal. Others were shrimping with wide cotton nets, scooping up the catch in great quantity.

Peter said mildly: "Well, it seems that a man need not starve here . . ."

Arthur was ruining his best jacket by lying on the rocks on his belly and trailing a hand in the water, and he said: "I think I will learn to swim here."

"Oh, calamity!" Susan said. Ever since the dreaded plagues of the Middle Ages, it had not been customary for Europeans to venture into the sea; they feared waterborne infection.

They walked around the town for a while as they waited, enjoying the balmy air and the new, exciting atmosphere. The sky was unbelievably clear, and the heat of the burgeoning morning was almost insupportable; Peter suffered in his frock coat, but he bore it with good humor. He saw that the local people, black and white alike, seemed to wear only what common decency demanded. Even the Spaniards, who, he had been told, were the elite of the island's population, often wore white silk shirts without jackets, open at the neck; and the blacks were content with short trews or skirts, welcoming the sun's blistering heat.

* * *

It was not long before they found a suitable house, half-way between Spanish Town, the capital, and Kingston, the commercial center at the mouth of the lovely harbor. Their neighbors, spread out along the beach at great distances, were mostly English.

Susan took charge at once with characteristic zeal, hiring half a dozen servants to "clean the place up a bit," as she put it. It was a good house, well built of solid timber, painted white everywhere and roofed over with red clay tiles, with seven bedrooms upstairs and four reception rooms at ground level. There was a vast timbered kitchen with a flagstone floor, an excellent fount in one corner which spouted constant good water from a carved stone ram's head.

The living rooms were large and comfortable, furnished with divans, sofas, chairs, dressers, and *hautes-bois* imported from Spain. Even the privy, which stood behind the kitchen, was well built with mahogany planks, its seat carefully shaped with a spoke shave for the utmost comfort. Just off the large scullery there was a tiny room with a tiled floor for the hip bath.

It was a pleasant place to live in, and there were lawns of the deepest green outside the windows, and gardens in which oranges, lemons, limes, papayas, mangoes, and guavas were growing profusely; there were five huge *coratoe* trees on the property, around which pretty little humming birds buzzed constantly; Susan was delighted with it.

She was forty-four years old now and very matronly. Her problem hair was as tousled as ever, she was heavy and plump-shouldered, and she walked in great long strides of surplus energy like an untidy man. But she was a good housekeeper, and she worshiped both her brother and her nephew.

Almost at once, the neighbors came calling, and they were very friendly indeed; they had quickly discovered that the newcomers were English, and therefore a welcome addition to

the colony of British expatriates there. There was Commander
Ambrose Crenshaw, a retired naval officer who had been with
Captain Cook on his search for the Northwest Passage, together with his two sons, Gerald and Amos, both of whom
were in the sugar industry. There was an elderly lady known
only as Madame Phyllis, whose long-dead husband had left her
with a fortune in gold coins, which he had reputedly dug up
on a beach near Montego; she was sweet and kindly and
seemed to spend all her waking hours baking sugar cakes, one
of which she had brought with her. She rode a strange two-
wheeled contraption called a "velocipede," pushing herself
along on it with her feet on the ground.

There was an Arnold Dawson, a sly and somewhat secretive man of forty or so who, together with his pretty young
wife, Zelda, ran a highly successful chandlering business in the
port of Kingston. And within a few weeks, as a result of this
little group's gossip, Susan knew who *everybody* was who lived
on the stretch of sand that lay between the two towns.

But she had come here to *work*, and within two months
she had refurbished the old coach house on the property and
had turned it into a dispensary, virtually scouring the streets
for the sick, the lame, and the dispossessed who could be
treated here.

Soon the coach house was crowded all day and half the
night with black men, women, and children whom she would
tend with the medicines she had brought from England and—
more importantly—with her desire to help.

One of her patients was a man named Arada Arudu.

He was jet black, very old and wasted, with a fringe of
gray hair tightly curled, thin as a skeleton and walking with
the aid of a long stave. It was late at night when he called, and
the coach house had been closed down till the morning. Peter
answered the door (the servants were long since in their beds),
somewhat surprised that anyone should come calling at so late
an hour. The old man's appearance surprised him even more;

he was dressed in rags, and yet in his bright and intelligent eyes there was a look that could only be described as indicating formidable authority. His chest was bare, and there was a ragged blanket over his shoulders. Like so many other Jamaicans, he carried a machete in his belt.

He spoke exaggerated English, only lightly accented, with the ease of a man accustomed to the uses—and the power—of language.

He said quietly, a faint smile on his ravaged face: "I crave your indulgence, sir, for a call at such an inopportune time, but my duties would not permit me to call earlier. If I may present myself, I am Arada Arudu, and I am a slave. You, sir, are Mr. Peter Entwhistle, I believe?"

A slave? With such ease of language?

Peter nodded. "Peter Entwhistle, Mr. Arudu, and what may I do for you?"

"I had the honor, sir, of being treated a few days ago for a touch of the fever, by the Doña Susana, who I think is your sister?"

"Yes, my sister indeed. I'm afraid she's gone to bed already, a heavy day. If you'd come back in the morning . . ."

The old man held up his hand. "It is not with the gracious Doña Susana that I wish to speak, but with you, sir, if I may."

"With me? Oh, well . . ." Peter hesitated, for no reason he could logically think of, stood back, and said: "Come in, Mr. Arudu."

He indicated a chair, wondering what it could be the old man wanted. But Arudu was not wasting time; it was not his habit, and he came straight to the point. He said carefully: "Several of our people who have visited your sister's dispensary have told me the same thing, but you must correct me if I am wrong. She has mentioned to them, in the course of conversation, that you have come here largely to support us in our revolt. Is that true, Mr. Entwhistle?"

Peter was startled. "No, sir," he said, "it is not! Indeed, this is the first I have heard of a revolt, and the mere thought of it alarms me."

"Why?"

"Why? In simple terms, Mr. Arudu, a revolt presupposes . . . mob violence, which I am opposed to."

"You qualify the word *violence*," Arudu said swiftly. "I take it to mean that you are prepared to defend . . . shall we say, your person? By force, if it is threatened?"

Peter laughed suddenly. He said: "I have done so in the past, Mr. Arudu. But I fear you're throwing a very specious argument at me."

"No, sir, I am not! We too are threatened, each and every one of us. And if physical force is to be excluded . . . do you have an alternative?"

Peter grimaced. "At this stage, no. I am aware of the problem, of course. Frankly, I don't yet know what might be done about it, perhaps because I'm still a newcomer. Persuasion, mediation, discussion . . . these are only words, I admit. But they are not entirely without merit if there is a foundation of good logic in them. I will talk with as many people as I can find who will consent to enlighten me."

"With the slaves themselves?"

"Yes." He smiled. "With people such as yourself, Mr. Arudu, and with many others too, I hope."

"Ah . . . and then?"

Peter threw up his hands. "I don't know. I cannot guess at a solution to the difficulties, if there be one, until I have learned the extent of them."

Arudu was nodding his head, smiling benignly, and he said: "And may I take that, sir, as license to talk *now*?"

"Well . . . yes, of course. I will gladly listen to anything you have to say."

"Then I will say first that we *shall* resort to armed revolt,

Mr. Entwhistle, unless other means are found to improve our condition."

"And those means," Peter said clearly, "are what we *must* find."

For more than an hour, Arudu spoke, eloquently and without passion. He refused the glass of wine that Peter offered him and went on talking, and Peter poured himself a drink and listened. Arudu spoke of the squalor in which the slaves were still forced to live; of their meager rations, which kept them near the level of starvation in a land where food was abundant; of the chains and the cages that were used for their punishment; and above all, of their hopelessness.

His long talk was interrupted, once, by the arrival of Susan. She had thrown a heavy robe over her night chemise and was carrying a candle, and she stood at the door and asked: "Is everything all right, Peter? I heard voices."

Arudu had risen courteously on her arrival, and he half bowed and murmured: "Forgive me, Doña Susana, I fear my voice carries far when it should not, and not far enough when it should."

She peered at him. "Mr. . . . . Arudu, is it not?"

"Yes, Doña Susana, and your servant."

"The fever, has it quite gone? No more of those dreadful aches?"

"Quite gone, thanks to your generous attentions."

"Good, I'm delighted. Keep taking the medicine I gave you for another three days. Peter, if Mr. Arudu would like something to eat, there's cold meat and potatoes in the larder."

"Yes, of course," Peter said, but Arudu made his courtly little bow and raised a hand: "I thank you, Doña Susana, and God's blessing on you for your kindness. But no, I have but a few more words that must be said, and then I will leave your gracious house. And leave you, too, an old man's gratitude for . . . for hope. It is a very precious commodity."

"Then . . . if there is nothing I can do?"

"No," Peter said, smiling. "Go back to bed, Susan. And Arthur?"

"Sleeping like the child he is. Good night."

Arudu resumed his seat. "And if I have moved you, Mr. Entwhistle . . ."

"Yes, you have." Peter was deeply troubled. "I learned in England," he said, "that some of the slaves here have not been freed, as the anti-slavery act demands. It disturbs me that I do not understand why."

"Some of them? *All* of them, Mr. Entwhistle, and that is a very big number. Do you know how many of us there are?"

"No, I have no figures. Several thousands, I'm sure."

Arudu laughed shortly, an angry, bitter laugh. "On the island of Jamaica, four hundred and fifty thousand. In the whole of the British West Indies, the number is . . . six hundred and seventy-four thousand slaves. And if any of us raises his voice—then he is simply shot, by the volunteers of the Planters' Association."

Peter was aghast. "I've heard of the association," he said, "and heard of their excesses too. But the authorities, man! There's a strong force of troops here to keep them in line!"

"No!" Arudu said. "To keep *us* in line, not to enforce the law at all! Oh, they're not all evil. Some of them are righteous, God-fearing men, but they still have biblical ideas about the essential rightness of slavery, and so . . . they don't really want any change and will fight it for as long as they can. Then there are the others who say yes, the slaves should go free, but who's going to work in our fields if they do? And the association has a lot of money that changes hands from time to time."

"Are you talking about corruption in government? I had a friend in London, William Cobbett, who wrote about it."

"Ah, yes," Arudu said. "I had the great pleasure of meeting Mr. Cobbett. That corruption is very rife, I'm afraid."

"In the Army too?"

Arudu nodded gravely. "Unhappily, the Planters' Association is very wealthy, and they have found it easy to buy the loyalties of some Army officers, yes." There was a kind of veil over his eyes, and he said softly: "Only two weeks ago, a patrol of the association's men, led by a certain Mr. Barstow, passed through my village looking for two slaves who had run off into the mountains to fend for themselves. We knew where they were hiding, of course, but no one would tell them. The patrol killed three of the villagers, burned down four huts, and carried off two young girls. That patrol, Mr. Entwhistle, was supported by a lieutenant of the Army with five troopers."

"I find that so very hard to believe . . ."

The old man pulled himself up on his staff. "I must go now to my village, there is a meeting there tonight. And if I were to invite you to my home, would you accept?"

"I would. With pleasure."

"Not tonight. I must persuade the others first of what I know to be your good intentions. These are times of stress, and the presence of a white man in the village would surely be misconstrued. In a week or two? It would interest you, I think, to see the way the slaves are forced to live."

"I am sure of it. And I would be pleased indeed."

When the old man had gone, Peter walked slowly down to the beach and found a small mound of sand under a clump of bull-thatch palms. He lay down to stare up at the darkening sky, listening to the susurration of the surf and wondering about Arudu, knowing that he had been speaking with a man of quite extraordinary character, well spoken though unschooled, bitter about his condition yet shrewd enough to know that it could be changed. Peter eased himself into the shifting sand and worried, both with his mind and with his heart.

There was a strange kind of luxury in the air, a softness, warm and moist, that brought on a lassitude he was unaccustomed to. He closed his eyes and slept for a while, and when he awoke again, the moon was just rising over the water, casting a long trail of luminescence on a sea that was hardly rippling. And a woman was coming up out of the surf, some thirty yards away from him, moving slowly and languidly with a kind of animal grace, a simple cotton dress clinging to her body. She stopped, raised her arms, and twisted this way and that in what was almost a dance.

He felt guilty watching her, and he rose carefully to his feet and began to move away, imagining that her solitude was as important to her as his was to him. But she heard the rustle of the bull-thatch palms and said sharply: *"¿Quién es?"* He turned back and saw that she was walking toward him. She said again: *"¿Quién es?"* and she sounded quite angry.

He said to her in Spanish: "Forgive me, *señorita*. I was asleep under the trees here. I had no intention to intrude . . ."

She was extraodinarily beautiful, with eyes that seemed, in this faint light, to be almost black; they were large and well shaped. Her hair was jet-black, wet and lank now, and she moved with a very lithe and easy motion, a young woman, perhaps no more than twenty-two or twenty-three years old.

As she drew close, he worried that his presence might have frightened her, and he said again, smiling: "Forgive me. I fell asleep here and just . . . just woke up this minute. If I startled you, I hope you will forgive me. My name is Entwhistle, Peter Entwhistle."

"Ah . . ." Suddenly she was smiling too. Her voice was very low and melodious. "The husband, I think, of Doña Susana?"

"Not husband, *señorita*, but brother. Susan is my sister. You know her?"

"I have not had the pleasure of meeting her, but I know of her. Some children she is treating, two black boys whose family name is Celera . . . they are sons of a servant of mine."

She held out her hand, the knuckles uppermost, and said: "I am Isabella Corsia de Sendala d'Alonzo."

He brushed the hand with his lips. *Su servidor, señorita.*"

"You speak excellent Spanish, sir. It is rare in an Englishman."

He laughed, delighting in her company. "Some years ago, *señorita*, I earned a living of sorts translating certain documents, many of them in Spanish, for my employer. I fear you may find my accent a little strange. No doubt it will improve."

"It is already excellent, I assure you. And what do you think of our island?"

"Well . . ." He hesitated. "I have not been here long enough to form any intelligent opinion. But at first sight, it is most remarkably beautiful, we have already met many people here among whom, I am sure, we can find good friends. . . . I do find that quite a large part of the population is not as happy as it might be. We have the same problem, of course, in England. Though in somewhat a different form."

"You speak of . . . ?"

"In England we have a different kind of slavery."

"Ah, the slaves . . ." She sighed. "Yes, there are very many unfortunate people here who live in conditions that can only be described as appalling. I speak as a Spaniard when I say the fault is ours. We brought them here."

"And as an Englishman, I say the fault is *ours*. We freed them, and yet they are *not* free. And is it a sign of the times that at our first meeting we, somehow, choose to talk politics?" He said gallantly: "I find that quite disturbing."

She did not answer but held his look and then said abruptly: "I must leave you, Señor Entwhistle. I have certain duties at home that must be attended to."

"Then may I be permitted to escort you? I feel that since you know my sister, we are not entirely strangers."

She pointed. "You see the bluff there? My horse is just

beyond it. The currents are very strong here, and when I bathe, as I often do in the evenings, I let the tide carry me where it will rather than fight it . . ."

"A philosophy," he murmured, "that is common enough."

". . . and then walk back when I have finished. I would be happy to walk with you as far as the rocks."

They strolled along the beach together toward the distant headland and talked about the island and its people, and about England and the work he had done there. And when he spoke of the Jamaican slaves, he was conscious of a very bitter anger in her. "No," she said, "they are not free, and it is not to be forgiven."

She was walking barefoot, and when they found the horse at last, he looked around and said: "But your saddle, *señorita*, I do not see it . . ."

She laughed. She gathered her long skirt and pulled it between her legs, tucking it into the waist as he stared at her in shocked surprise. "But surely," he said, "you don't ride . . . bareback?"

Again she did not answer him. Instead, she tossed the reins into place and said: "Your hands, please?"

Overcome with a kind of confusion, he cupped his hands for her and she stepped into them and threw her leg over the horse's back, just like a man, straddling it easily as it began prancing. He said desperately: "Shall I see you again, *señorita*?"

She swung the horse around. "I am sure of it, *señor!*" She dug in her heels and raced off, and he stared after her in acute astonishment.

The brief encounter left him with a very strange feeling, one of elation mixed with a certain curiosity about her. For no reason that seemed sensible at all to him, he kept his thoughts to himself for a few days; but at last, over dinner one night, he told Susan of their meeting.

He said: "Not only does she ride bareback and without a

saddle, but . . . well, *straddling* the animal! I found it quite extraordinary."

Susan's eyebrows were raised. "Extraordinary indeed! She's no lady, obviously."

"Oh, but she is! Her speech alone is enough to proclaim that, pure Castilian Spanish, the most beautiful language, very euphonic. Really, she made me feel like an oaf. I *must* polish up my pronunciation. And what was your day like?"

He was carving the roast as Arthur held his plate out, and he said: "And you, young man, ought to be in bed."

Arthur laughed. "Father! I'm not a baby anymore! In Jamaica, no one over five years goes to bed before midnight."

"And put your plate down. Your aunt will pass it to me."

"Yes, sir."

He was a strapping, robust child, very strong and solidly built, with a look in his eyes that reminded his father—so much and so often—of Dorothy. They were an odd color, not the Entwhistle blue nor Dorothy's hazel, but a strange kind of gray that seemed to deepen when he was angry, though that was not very often. He was an easygoing boy, accepting rebuke or praise very readily, sometimes a little mocking, as though, even at this age, he found the world a very strange place to live in; he was far, far older than his years. He had the habit of holding the look of someone who spoke to him and saying absolutely nothing, just *thinking*; it was a characteristic of his Aunt Hilda, now God alone knew how many thousands of miles away on the other side of the world.

Susan said: "My day? Well, it was all right, I suppose, I saw quite a number of patients. There's a lot of jungle fever here, you know. I wish we could find out what causes it."

But something else was troubling her. Peter knew it, and when she saw the look in his eyes, she grimaced. "I had an upset today with Amos Crenshaw, nothing serious, but . . . well, he wondered why I should spend so much time among the blacks."

"And . . . ?"

"I told him, simply enough, that I was merely trying to cure their diseases where I could, and he said something like: 'And your brother, what is *he* trying to cure them of?' I'm afraid it made me quite angry, and I told him it was no concern of his at all. He just laughed, and I asked myself later on if I'd been perhaps too harsh with him. He's really a nice young man."

She sighed: "But the more I thought about it, the more I realized how very long it is since anyone has visited us the way they did when we first came here. Not even Madame Phyllis calls anymore. And I wondered . . ." She held her brother's look. "That's all part of the same problem, isn't it? They don't approve of what we're doing here. Is that it?"

"That's it exactly," Peter said calmly. "I've been aware of it for a long time now. And does it worry you, my sweet?"

"No," Susan said firmly, "it does not."

"Good. We mustn't let it, ever."

She brightened suddenly: "And more cheerful news . . . I think I've found a tutor for Arthur at last."

"Ah, good."

"A man named Elliot, Martin Elliot, he's a retired schoolmaster from Coventry who came here some years ago for his health after a severe bout of influenza. He's not terribly old, and very erudite indeed. You'll meet him, of course, before we make it definite, but I think you'll like him. He will call on us soon. I invited him for tea. And if you agree that he is the right man, then we should pay him quite well. I gathered that he is living on rather meager savings."

Arthur scuttled off to bed at ten o'clock (eight had been the mandatory bedtime hour in London), and Peter set out the chess set for the customary evening play. This was always a good time for him, a quiet hour or two alone with his sister, with a warm nighttime breeze coming through the open windows, and the soothing sound of the surf.

They were closely matched, but he was playing badly to-night, and when at last he tipped his king over, he glowered at the board and said: "Damn! I should have seen what you were up to . . ."

"Your mind's not on the game," Susan said. "And I suspect it might be on your Isabella."

He laughed. "My Isabella? Susan! I hardly know her. I met her only once!"

"But she seems to have impressed you." She moved to pour her brother a small glass of brandy. "So tell me more about her. Is she pretty?"

He leaned back in his chair and stretched out his legs. "Pretty? She's gorgeous."

"Young?"

"Uh-huh. The strange thing about her is . . . well, after just one very short meeting she made me feel almost like an old friend. I'm sure that's an admirable quality."

"And she straddles a horse, bareback "

"Susan!"

"I just wondered . . ."

"On the beach in Jamaica! We're a long way here from St. James' Park!"

"Of course. Will you see her again?"

"Perhaps. I can't call on her. I don't even know where she lives."

Nonetheless, for the next few nights he found himself wandering along the beach at the bluffs where he had first met her, persuading himself that all he was doing was taking the air. And once, indeed, he saw her . . .

He was moving away from the beach to return to the house when he heard the sound of the hooves and turned. She was below him at the water's edge, galloping very fast, the horse's mane and her own hair streaming behind them in the moonlight; they made a picture of exquisite beauty. She was holding herself straight and proudly and giving the mount free rein as it thundered along the surf. He shouted her name and waved, and he was sure she must have heard him, but she did not stop or look back; and then she was gone.

Again, he spent night after night on the beach, but he did not see her.

But quite by happenstance, it seemed, Susan did.

It was more than a week later, and the dispensary was filled with some thirty local people who had come for their varied sicknesses to be cured without the expenditure of money they simply did not have. And among them, Susan was startled to see a white-skinned woman of exceptional loveliness, dressed in a very elegant and fashionable gown, with the long white gloves that only the upper echelons of Spanish society affected here. A young black man was with her, glowering.

Susan went to her and said hesitantly: "*Señorita?* I do not speak Spanish, I fear, but . . . if I can help you?"

Her English was far from perfect, but it was adequate. She said, her manner very gracious: "It is not for me, Doña Susana, but for my coachman here. I think perhaps he has jungle fever, and the doctors in Spanish Town, they are not good."

"And your name, *señorita?*"

"I am Isabella d'Alonzo, Doña Susana, and my man's name is Morisco."

He was coal-black, a brawny young man hardly out of his teens, with bulging muscles and a permanent scowl on his face. Susan felt a strange kind of premonition that something was wrong, very wrong, but she examined him carefully, feeling the strong pulse and heartbeat, with no touch of heat at the back of her hand on his forehead. She probed the wrists and ankles for the telltale swelling but could find none. She asked: "Does he speak English, *señorita?*"

"He does not speak English. Only his own language and Spanish."

"Then I must tell you: He is not sick at all. In truth, I have seldom seen a healthier man."

"No jungle fever?"

"No, *señorita*, none."

"Then I thank you for your time." She fumbled with the purse at her waist and produced a gold coin and laid it on the bench and said: "It is good that time must be paid for."

Susan said, masking a certain distaste for which she could not account: "And it is good that those who can pay, should. Your money, *señorita*, will go to buy medicines for those who need them and cannot afford them."

"Again, thank you. *Buenos días*, Doña Susana."

"Doña Isabella . . ."

When she had gone, Susan sat down and wondered what might be the reason for the unease that was on her. And at supper that night, she told Peter of the encounter. He had been out all day on one of his favorite occupations, wandering around a sugar plantation, unannounced and scarcely observed, watching the slaves at work; the slave-masters still carried their whips.

"You were right, Peter," she said, "she really is quite gorgeous. But her coachman worried me a little."

"Oh, really? And why was that?"

She sighed. "I don't know. There was a . . . crafty look in his eyes all the time, a *designing* look. I was even frightened for a moment."

Arthur, wolfing down his food, a child who was permanently hungry, said happily: "Auntie Susan . . . *never* try to understand a Jamaican. They are not like us at all."

"Kindly do not interrupt," Peter said, "when your elders are talking. Eat your supper."

"Yes, sir."

Susan went on: "His name is Morisco, and he is really quite . . . well, *surly*."

"Oh, come now! A lot of them are, you know. Tell me instead what you thought of *her*."

Susan did not answer him at once, and he waited. She said at last, frowning: "She's undoubtedly very, very beautiful, there's no denying it. And . . . enticing too, the exact word, *enticing*. But I found myself hoping you're not seriously in love with her."

Why was he so defensive? "Susan!" he said. "I met her only once!"

"And still you prowl the beach every night looking for her."

He would not answer her. He looked at his son and found a strange kind of amusement in those bright, mischievous eyes. In this summer of the year 1836, Arthur was nine years old, and almost a man already. Peter said brusquely: "Go to bed, Arthur, it's past your bedtime."

"Yes, sir." Arthur leaped to his feet, kissed his aunt, and said gravely: "All my friends here tell me, sir, that if a man is to be happy, he has to have a woman at his beck and call."

Peter said sternly: "There is nothing in the world more distasteful, son, than a precocious child. Good night."

"Yes, sir. Good night, sir."

He scuttled off.

Chapter Fifteen

It was not until two weeks later that he found her again.

He was seated on the same little mound under the bull-thatch palms, thinking of Amanda, of Susan, of James, of Arthur, and of poor Hilda in distant India; most of all, his thoughts were for Dorothy, whom he had loved so dearly. He was deep into that pressing nostalgia of *family*, and yet he could not drive from his mind the vision of Isabella; and he knew that he was in love with a woman he had met only once.

And there she was suddenly, riding at full gallop again along the beach to the bluff, the sand spurting up under her horse's hooves. He sat there for perhaps half an hour and then rose and walked to the water's edge and waited for her.

She came to him out of the surf, her arms outstretched, and the sight of her wet dress clinging to her body excited him beyond endurance. As though it were the most natural thing in the world, he reached out for her and held her tightly. There was a fierce excitement in him, and he whispered: "It's been so long . . ."

"Yes, I know." Her eyes were wide and solemn, her face upturned to him, and he kissed her on the lips. "Night after night," he said, "I've been watching for you."

She smiled. "I saw you many times."

"You did?" He could only wonder. "But . . . if you knew I was looking for you?"

"I wanted to be sure, Peter."

"And now you are? I do hope so."

"Yes. Now I am sure."

"I want you, Isabella. I need you, need you, *need* you!"

She reached behind her and took his hands and gently brought them around and placed them on her breasts, breasts that were full and very firm, upstanding under the thin wet cloth, the nipples small and hard. He clutched at them fervently, trying to control his trembling. In a few moments he picked her up bodily, dropped to his knees, placed her just so at the edge of the surf, and made love with her.

She was as emotional as he was, and she held him closely and murmured: "My love, my love for always . . ."

For a month they met clandestinely on the same beach, two or three times a week, and Peter found himself caught up in a delirium of happiness. And he said to Susan one night, after Arthur had gone to bed and they were playing their habitual game of chess: "I am in love with her, Susan, there's no doubt about it."

The candles were flickering in a breeze that stirred the curtains of this pleasant, friendly room, and three of them went out. Susan took the taper, relit them, and asked quietly: "In love? Or infatuated?"

He said wryly: "It's a fine distinction, but I would have to answer . . . both."

"She is your mistress now, I take it?"

"Yes. I want her to be more than that. I want to marry her."

She bit her lip. "Tell me why, Peter?"

"Why?" The question startled him. "How can I say why? I love her, as she loves me!"

Susan said with calculated bluntness: "Does she replace Dorothy in your affections?"

He caught his breath and said: "If any woman ever could . . . perhaps, yes."

"Was she a virgin when you first took her?"

"Susan! That's a perfectly dreadful question!"

"I know it. Was she?"

He fidgeted. "No. I think not. It means nothing."

"It might mean a great deal."

"Susan! I will not discuss her in such clinical terms!"

"So be it then. If you do marry her, Peter, I will welcome her into the family, as is my duty."

"Your *duty*? No more than that?"

Susan was trying very hard not to show her distress, but she said quietly: "Peter, there is something dreadfully wrong. And I don't know what it is."

Peter could not find the words to answer her.

He was walking with Isabella hand-in-hand at the edge of the fragrant forest one night in a postcoital stroll, and he said to her somberly: "I know you so well, Isabella. And yet . . . I know nothing about you. Will you tell me who you are?"

She laughed, a comforting sound. "And who are *you*, Peter Entwhistle?"

"Who am I? I'm a simple man, in love."

"And I'm just a simple woman in love too."

"Family? Father, mother, brothers, sisters?"

The moon was hanging over the silhouette of the mountain range, very full but about to set and let the darkness take over.

"My father?" she echoed. "A Spanish grandee and a recluse, the last of an ancient and very honorable family. My mother is . . . his *condesa*. Brothers and sisters—none. I am an only child."

"You've never told me where you live. With your parents?"

"Why, yes, of course! There is a great deal of mixed blood on the island, unfortunately, but for the true Spaniards, family is very important."

"Ah, yes! It's a concept my own mother instilled in me almost from the day I was born." He hesitated, though he was not quite sure why, and said slowly: "I feel that I should call on your father and pay my respects."

They had come to the edge of a small cliff and they sat together in the massed and fragrant honeysuckle there and looked out onto the shimmering sea.

Isabella said quietly: "The time for that will soon come. You must remember that between the Spaniards and the British here there is a kind of . . . a kind of suspicious enmity which almost equals the hostility between the blacks and the whites."

The moon had sunk till it reached the distant horizon, casting a glittering, golden path across the water, and Isabella whispered: "They say here that when the moon is down, then love dies too . . ."

"It is not true, my darling." He eased her onto her back and loved her again in a fury of passion. And when she had gone, murmuring her usual protest—"No, I will find my own way home"—he wondered about the mystery of her and still did not know who she was.

He did not see her again for a very long time, and then, quite late one evening, Nesta the maid was called to the front door by a loud and insistent knocking. Susan, a little disturbed, was aware of any argument going on there, and she went to see what it was all about; Nesta was patently frightened. Susan said, controlling a sudden apprehension: "Mr. Morisco, is it not? I am afraid the dispensary is closed for the night."

He brushed past her and entered the house as though it might have been his own. "It is not with you that I want to speak," he said rudely, "but with your brother."

She said weakly: "Peter . . . ?"

Peter strode to the door. The discourtesy troubled him, and so did the young man's aspect; Morisco was *swaggering*, looking the place over as though his approval or disapproval of it might be of consequence. "Nice place," he said, "very nice place. I like it."

"*He does not speak English*," Isabella had said. "*Only his own language and Spanish.*"

Peter stared as the visitor walked across the room and sat down in one of the chairs, and he said stiffly: "This is a private house, young man, not the dispensary, which is open only during daylight hours. Your name, sir, is . . . ?"

Susan said: "Mr. Morisco. He is Doña Isabella's coachman. He was here recently for treatment."

"Well, in that case," Peter said, "if you would care to return tomorrow?"

Morisco was laughing, and it was a very unpleasant laugh. He leaned back in the chair and stretched out his legs, making himself absolutely at home. He wore only white canvas breeches and a brown woolen cloak thrown carelessly over his shoulders; there was a very short machete in a scabbard at his belt, the kind some of the workers on the sugar plantations favored, and he said roughly: "No, I don't come back tomorrow. But you not worry, I ask one question, I go. No, two question."

"Then ask your questions, Mr. Morisco," Peter said, "and be on your way."

Morisco raised a finger. "First, you loving my sister, or not? I don't mean loving her on the beach the way you do, I mean . . . up here." He tapped his head and said again: "Loving her up here."

Peter said tartly: "I have no idea what you are talking about. I fear that you are under a misapprehension of some sort, Mr. Morisco. Your sister? I do not know, intimately, a single black lady on this island. I suggest, sir, that you are confusing me with somebody else."

"No, I don' think so. Second question is, if you marry her. In Jamaica, you make love to woman, you marry her pretty soon, before bastard get born. And you don' marry her, Mr. Entwhistle, I come looking for you. My whole village come looking for you."

"I repeat, Mr. Morisco, you have the wrong man."

Morisco leaped to his feet with a strangely impulsive movement and began striding around the room like a caged animal.

Peter said carefully: "I can understand your concern if someone is . . . well, carrying on an affair with your sister. But I can assure you, with the clearest of consciences, that that *someone* is not I. We have made very few black friends here as yet, and I cannot number among them a single lady with whom I would presume the slightest indelicacy."

Morisco said: "Isabella."

Peter stared, and he heard Susan gasp. "But . . . but . . . but . . ."

"*But?* I am black man, Isabella is white like a white woman. This is Jamaica, Mr. Entwhistle. I am *mestizo*, Isabella is *mestiza*, half-caste like me. Only she lucky, her skin white. Me, not so lucky. You marry her?"

Susan said, "Oh, God . . . !" Morisco went on, glaring: "You don' marry her soon, you got plenty trouble, I promise you!"

It seemed that the whole world was falling apart. Peter contained his anger and said coldly: "I don't think I like the idea of blackmail, Morisco . . ."

It turned him into a raging animal. He reached out and

grabbed at Peter's lapels and screamed: "You don' believe you got trouble? Maybe I teach you . . ."

He drew back his fist and struck Peter a furious blow to the face, knocking him to the floor. Susan screamed and dropped beside him as Morisco strode to the door and opened it. He looked back, and he was laughing now, mocking, and he said: "Soon I call you brother, *Massa* Entwhistle, you see."

He was gone.

Peter climbed to his feet and dabbed at a cut lip with his handkerchief. He embraced his sister briefly and said: "Don't worry, it could have been a lot worse. And, my God, if I ever needed a drink . . ."

Susan went quickly to the buffet and poured him one, then busied herself with a bowl of water and some permanganate of potash for the wound. She said angrily: "He could have killed you!"

"But he didn't."

"He . . . he *struck* you!"

It seemed that the indignity was more important to her than the physical hurt. She took his head in her hands and twisted it up, the better to examine the wound. She clicked her tongue and said: "I'll have to put a few stitches in that . . ."

"What?" Peter scowled. "Over my dead body. Don't even think of it."

He could not believe what had happened; worse, he could not believe the reason for it, and he said, glowering: "I should have hit him back. A muscled *animal*, I could still have given him a very bad time."

"But you didn't, and I'm glad."

He looked at her curiously. "I wondered," he said, "about your obvious dislike of Isabella. Did you always suspect something like this?"

She shook her head. "It was *distrust* more than dislike. I

only met her once, remember, but I sensed immediately that something was dreadfully wrong. Will you hold still?"

He let her paint his lip purple with the rag, and she fingered the cut delicately. He said brooding: "He must have frightened you very badly. I'm sorry."

The anxiety in her eyes worried him. She asked: "Will he be back, do you think?"

"Almost certainly."

"And what do you propose doing about it?"

"The first thing in the morning," he said, "I'm going to see Arnold Dawson down on the docks."

"Oh? For what?"

"He's got a gun for sale," Peter said grimly. "If that young savage does come back . . . he's going to learn what trouble really means."

Susan sighed. "Well," she said, "why don't we play some chess?"

It was her habitual palliative for all discomfitures, and they played three games in a row, not putting the set away till the early hours of the morning.

When Susan had gone to her bed, he sat up for a while and wrote a few notes in his journal:

> A personal and very unhappy confrontation today with a black Jamaican, a slave, has taught me more than anything else that years of deprivation have left in these unfortunate people an almost instinctive hatred for anything that is not part of their own culture. . . .

He blotted the page carefully and put the book away, and when he slept fitfully for the rest of the night, Isabella was no part of his dreams at all. It was almost as though she had never existed. Instead he dreamed of Dorothy, and the dreams were vivid and filled with emotion, so clear and detailed that the image of them remained with him long after he awoke, flitting in and out of his awareness, as dreams will.

He dressed and shaved and went down to the solitary breakfast; there was a note from Susan on the table for him:

I have gone into Kingston, a ship has just arrived with some medicines from Spain, and I want to procure some before the merchants get their hands on them and rob us. I found some marvelous lamb kidneys for your breakfast. The cook has her instructions. Mr. Elliot is coming for Arthur at nine o'clock, it's algebra, geometry, and geography today. Perhaps you'd like to look in on the lessons if you have time. Back some time in the early afternoon. And please, please? Don't worry about last night.

He ate the grilled kidneys which were brought to him and had some toast and English marmalade and three cups of strong tea and went to see how Arthur was faring.

His son was studying intently with the tutor, and Peter said amiably: "Well, and how are the lessons coming along?"

Mr. Elliot rose courteously and said: "Excellently, Mr. Entwhistle. I'm very satisfied with his progress." He turned to Arthur and said: "Let us see if you remember the Alexandrian Apollonius of Perga."

"Yes, sir," Arthur said promptly. " 'In any triangle, the square on one side is equal to the sum of the squares on the other two sides, together with twice the rectangle contained by one of those sides and the projection of the other side upon it.' "

"Well, that's really quite excellent, son," Peter said. He turned back to Elliot. "Trigonometry?"

"In about a month."

"Euclid?"

"In three. We mustn't rush him into Euclid. But he's learning very fast. He has the capacity for learning."

"And that is all I ask, Mr. Elliot." He turned back at the door and said mildly: "Who was the first of the Tudor kings, Arthur?"

"Henry the Seventh, sir," Arthur said at once; "1485 to 1509."

"The name of the island that lies to the south of Corsica?"

"Sardinia, sir."

"The capital of the Babylonian Empire?"

"Why, sir," Arthur said, grinning, "Babylon, of course! On the banks of the Euphrates River!"

Peter laughed. "My respects, Mr. Elliot," he said. "The boy's coming along very well indeed."

He went over to Kingston and found Arnold Dawson in the chandler's store and said: "You told me of a gun for sale, Mr Dawson. I have an uncomfortable feeling that I may need one now."

Dawson laughed, a cheerful, plump man with all the aura of commercial success on him. "Morisco, I take it," he said.

Peter stared. "You know about that?"

"This is a very small and provincial island, Mr. Entwhistle! All of the British expatriates know everything that happens to one of their numbers within moments of its happening. Yes, we know the reason for your swollen lip, and it happened only last night."

"So you know this violent young man Morisco?"

"Oh, yes. A troublemaker."

"You know his sister Isabella too?"

Dawson reached under the counter and found a bottle of brandy. He waved it and said: "You'll join me, I'm sure?"

"Well, that's very kind of you."

"His sister Isabella?" Dawson said. "Yes, I seem to recall that I met her once. Don't mention it to my wife."

"A very beautiful woman. She foists her brother Morisco off as her servant, a deception that does not please him greatly. She passes for white here. Well, for Spanish, which is the next best thing. And a number of us know her well, Mr. Entwhistle, such physical perfection . . . may not be denied. But the gun . . ."

He unlocked a cupboard and produced a revolver wrapped in heavily oiled rags. "Single-action," he said, "a Colt, one of the finest guns ever produced. Cock the hammer and it turns the cylinder. . . . You know how to use it? Just cock it, pull on the trigger, and there's a hole in your enemy large enough to drive a coach-and-four through. Stops him in his tracks, I'll tell you! Would ten shillings be a fair price?"

Peter paid the money, and Dawson said: "There is, of course, another precaution you can take. I'm told that you have an elderly gardener, a houseman who is even older, and two or three women servants. But no . . . bodyguard."

"A bodyguard?" Peter echoed, startled. "No. The idea never occurred to me."

"Then let me suggest something to you, if I may," Dawson said. "We all have bodyguards here, because we need them. I've been living on this beautiful and accursed island for longer than I care to remember, and there's one thing I'm convinced of: A white man here *must* have at least one manservant who is physically strong, emotionally on our side, devoted to his master, and as fearsome as a trained mastiff."

"I don't think I want to equate my servants with dogs," Peter said unemotionally, and Dawson laughed. "The man I have in mind is indeed a mastiff, by name Bidasso. He's a cousin of one of my own servants who's looking for work with an English family. He adores the British. He thinks the sun probably shines from the rectum of an English gentleman. And do you know? He may be right."

Dawson's pleasingly plump young wife, Zelda, joined them, blond-haired, bright-eyed, and vacuous, a young girl who could not say a single word without fussing with her hair, patting it into place this way and that. She whispered: "Bidasso? Yes, he will be very necessary now. He's so strong . . ."

Dawson glared at her and said angrily: "Be quiet, woman!"

"Yes. Yes, of course, Arnold dear."

"I commend him to you, Mr. Entwhistle," Dawson said. "If that young madman Morisco should ever attempt to carry out his threats . . . I promise you, Bidasso will break him in two and think nothing of it, however many of his villagers he may bring with him."

When Peter returned home, he had acquired the services of a new houseman, black, large, powerful, and very angry-looking, with a soft and melodious voice that was quite out of keeping with his rough appearance. Peter told him the whole miserable story of Morisco, save for the reasons behind that angry young man's fury, and Bidasso heard him out patiently and in silence. He said at last, very gently: "Then, with your permission, sir, I will consider the protection of your house the first of my duties."

From this day on, there was a strange new ambience in the Entwhistle home. Bidasso took it upon himself to move a cot from the servants' quarters outside into the kitchen, and sometimes Peter would find him prowling the grounds at night with a naked machete in his hand, disturbed, perhaps, by the slight sound of a deer rustling the shrubbery; he moved like an animal himself in the darkness.

Bidasso knew of Susan's work among the slaves—indeed, who on the provincial little island did not?—and he worshiped her. He became very friendly with Arthur and quickly established himself as an essential part of the household.

From Morisco, there was no further news at all. Peter never left the house at night, his wanderings along the beach relegated to past history. He could not entirely forget Isabella, and when Susan mentioned her to him one night, he said heavily: "No, the memories are still there, but they're only physical now. I can't help wondering whether she knew of her brother's visit, whether perhaps . . . she even *planned* it. I suppose we'll never know, will we?"

But he was to find out, and ease his conscience very considerably, when Arada Arudu came calling again.

It was around midday, and the old man said: "When we last met, Mr. Entwhistle, I invited you to my home, an invitation you were gracious enough to accept. Unhappily, for a while I have been forced into hiding. My humble house is being watched by the association, and I will not force this indignity on you. But would you, instead, contemplate attending a meeting that is being held tonight in the forest, not far from here? The intention remains the same, that you see for yourself how the slaves are living, and then perhaps raise your voice to join ours in protest."

"You spoke of a revolt, Mr. Arudu," Peter said, "and I repeat, I will take no part in violence, whatever the cause." The gun he had bought from Arnold Dawson, well hidden, was a reproach to him.

"There will be none tonight, sir, you have my promise."

"Then I accept your offer."

"Good. May I call for you as soon as the moon has set? That will be about nine o'clock tonight."

"I will be ready."

But he was worried. He said slowly: "The first time I will have been out of the house at night since we had a very unfortunate confrontation with a young man here. He made certain threats . . ."

"Morisco?" There was a thin smile on Arudu's face.

Peter would not be surprised. "You know?"

"Of course, Mr. Entwhistle. But you need have no further fear of Morisco. He is in prison. Only a few nights after he visited you, he was stopped on the street by a patrol of three association volunteers, a routine questioning. But Morisco is not a man who can be easily . . . questioned. He fought back when they beat him. He killed one of them, and he is now languishing in Kingston jail awaiting charges of murder."

The smile had not left that ravaged old face. "He was on his way to meet with a dozen of his villagers for an attack on your house. It is possible that—Bidasso or no Bidasso—you, Doña Susana, and your son would have been killed."

"Oh, God . . ."

"So now you may leave the house, if you will, with no fears for your family's safety."

"At nine o'clock then . . ."

Peter spent the rest of the day digging vigorously in the garden that surrounded the house, and planting corn. He remembered that this was the "miracle food" his late friend William Cobbett had been importing into England, hoping to feed the impoverished industrial North with it, only to see it finish up as food for the pigs.

And when the sun was low in the sky, Susan came back from her rounds of her patients in the village, and he told her of his plans to go with Arudu to the forest for a meeting that he thought would be quite illuminating; she did not seem to be overly excited about it, and he said, a little testily perhaps: "I really must find out, at first hand, what their problems are."

"Yes, of course, I understand perfectly. Did you check on Arthur's lessons today? I've been out since early morning and just haven't had a chance to."

"Yes, I did, and he's really doing very well indeed. I am delighted with the way he's picking up Spanish now. He is quite fluent."

"It comes easily to children. I find it extraordinarily hard to learn. I'm trying, though."

"Yes, and you're doing splendidly."

"Where is he now?"

"Arthur? He's up on the hill, climbing trees. There's a giant yew tree there that seems to offer some sort of challenge to the neighborhood children."

A challenge it was.

The tree was very large, nearly twenty-five feet around its trunk and fifty feet high; and in the late afternoons some of the young people would gather there for their games, one of which was trying to reach the very top. No one had ever done this; the last ten feet seemed to be quite unclimbable.

Arthur was up there now, and five of his friends were gathered below, two Spaniards, two mestizo Jamaicans, and the ten-year-old son of a Frenchman who owned a coffee plantation higher up in the hills. They were staring up at him, their mouths open, as he forced his way higher and higher, not at all sure of himself but knowing that he had to impress them. It was a point of honor that to overcome the challenge the climber's head had to be above the highest point of the tree, which meant standing on the only tip branch that seemed strong enough to bear even the fragile weight of a young boy; and it was well out of anyone's grasp.

But Arthur was determined to reach it. He threw his arms and legs around the trunk and scrambled slowly up it till he reached the critical branch, old and dead and stripped of its bark so that it was very smooth and shiny. He hauled himself up onto it; it was a stub, no more, but long enough for his purpose. Balancing his body with great care, he raised himself up to his full height and found that the tree's topmost twigs came just above his waist. There was nothing firm to hold onto here, and he held himself erect and put his arms out as counterbalances, like a tightrope walker, and he shouted at the top of his voice: "I did it, I did it! Look at me! I did it!"

He stared down at their distant, upturned faces and saw that they were all laughing, jumping up and down wildly, because the great tree had been defeated by one of their number and could no longer lord it over them. He too was laughing, and he shouted again: "I did it! Arthur Entwhistle's enemy defeated!"

And then . . . the stub of the branch broke.

He was fifty feet above the ground, but he fell onto an upper branch, landing badly on it, on his back, his head lower than his feet. In a moment of panic he felt himself toppling over and grabbed at whatever he could find, gashing his hand badly on the hard bark. He fell again and bounced into another branch, the breath knocked out of his body, and hung suspended by his jacket for a moment. He tried to reach up for the branch he was hanging from, but there was a sudden ripping sound and he fell to the ground twenty feet below him. Even in that sudden moment of fright he knew what he had to do, and he twisted his body violently around and threw up his arms so that at least he would land feet first. He saw the ground coming up at him and crashed into it. He lay still on his back, staring up into the frightened faces of his friends as they gathered around him. There was blood in his mouth where his teeth had gone almost through his tongue, and the pain in his back was appalling; but it was his ankles that hurt him the most. He rolled over onto his hands and knees and vomited and tried to get to his feet but could not.

One of the Jamaican boys said fiercely: "*Agua fria,* cold water, over here . . ." They helped him hobble to the stream that ran nearby and took off his boots and sat him there with his feet in the water, watching the process of the swelling; the ankles were turning a deep pink now.

He sat there and bit his lip to drive the pain away, and for more than an hour they squatted on the grass at his side and watched him. Arthur looked at his torn jacket and said gloomily: "My best coat, my aunt is going to be furious . . ."

The time came to go home, and he put his boots on again, a slow and very difficult process; they just did not fit anymore.

He stood up, a little unsteadily, and the French boy said: "*Eh alors* . . . now we will have to carry you home."

Arthur said clearly: "Thank you, no. I will go home on my own two feet." The pain in his ankles was almost unbearable.

He would not let them help him as they went slowly down the hill to the village, and at the gate to the property they left him to his own devices, sure somehow, with the insouciance of their years, that he would be in dreadful trouble now and not wanting to be any part of it.

Arthur walked steadily but very slowly up the long driveway to the front door and opened it, and he saw that both his father and his aunt were there, turning to look at him, the welcoming pleasure on their faces changing—in his father's case to surprise, and to absolute shock in his aunt's.

Arthur said: "I'm afraid I tore my best jacket, Aunt Susan. I fell out of a tree, a very foolish thing to do."

And then he fell to the ground, unconscious.

Susan shrieked: "Oh, my baby . . . !" and ran to him, but Peter was there first, picking him up bodily and cradling him in his arms. He said: "The bedroom . . ."

They went upstairs to Arthur's room and laid him down on the bed, and Peter stripped off all his son's clothes and stood back while Susan examined him from head to foot. Arthur was slowly coming around, and when he discovered his nakedness, he said, acutely embarrassed: "I'm all right, Aunt Susan, really I am. I just fell out of that bloody tree."

"Don't swear, please," Peter said, and Arthur grimaced. "No, sir, I'm sorry, sir. But couldn't I have a towel or something?"

"Of course."

Peter took a towel from the washstand and covered his son's loins with it, and Susan said: "That is positively the

most ridiculous thing I ever saw in my life. I am a trained
nurse, and he is my nephew! For heaven's sake!"

"Well, what's the verdict, Susan?" He caught Arthur's
eye and winked. "Will he live, do you think?"

"Peter!" She pulled the covers up over him and said:
"There's a lump on his head the size of a lemon, it's a wonder
his skull wasn't split wide open, but it doesn't seem to be. His
back . . . I can't tell, a question of time, we'll find out. His legs
. . . both his ankles are broken, Peter."

"*Broken?*"

"I can set them." She turned to Arthur: "I'm afraid it will
be quite painful. Will you be able to stand it?"

He bit his lip. "Yes."

But Peter said curiously: "But . . . with two broken ankles, how did you get home? Did your friends carry you? I
must thank them for their help."

"No, sir," Arthur said. "I walked."

There was the smallest silence, and then Peter got to his
feet and said: "Susan, over your undoubted objections, I am
going to give my son a glass of brandy, if only to take away the
pain."

"I have no objections," Susan said. "Brandy is the only
analgesic we have, and it is a very good one indeed. Please tell
Nesta I will need a bread poultice."

He went below and poured two large glasses of brandy,
then went into the kitchen and found the cook, and he said in
Spanish: "Nesta, Doña Susana would like you to make a poultice, with bread."

"*Sí, señor, un emplasto de pan, enseguida . . .*"

He took the drinks upstairs, handed one to Arthur, and
said gently: "Gulp it down, boy. At your age, it's not meant to
be enjoyed."

Arthur sipped it and said: "I like it, sir. It burns the
palate very acceptably."

"Gulp it, boy."

"Yes, sir."

He drank it down and lay back on the bed, and in a moment his eyes were rolling wildly as Susan manipulated the bones back into place, but he would not scream. Nesta came in with a large tin bowl filled with steaming bread paste and some lengths of rag and spooned the poultice onto the cotton for Susan. Arthur shrieked once when she applied it and seared the skin off his ankles, and then he fell silent. She bound the poultice into place, took her nephew's hand, and whispered: "Now, dear Arthur, a week or two in bed, three at the most, and you will be well again. You must not leave your bed now. When you have to . . . well, when you have to go, you will call me, or your father, or Bidasso if we are not here. We don't have any bed pans, so you will be carried."

"Aunt S . . . Susan . . ." His speech was dreadfully slurred. "That is . . . is an indignity I will not . . . will not tolerate. If I . . . I have to go . . ."

He was asleep. They tiptoed (quite unnecessarily) from the room and went downstairs to worry about him. And shortly after nine o'clock, Arudu was there. Peter embraced his sister and said: "I'll be back, I hope, by midnight or soon after. Will you be all right?"

"Yes, of course. Bidasso is here."

"And Arthur? Is he in pain, do you think?"

"Yes, I'm sure of it. But he's strong, Peter. He's an Entwhistle."

"Then I will leave you now."

He held Susan tightly for a moment and then left with Arudu for the long trek up to the mountain forest.

He said, plodding through the humus of the jungle floor: "My son, Mr. Arudu, this afternoon he fell from a tree that must be fifty feet tall. Broke both his ankles, shattered them. And can you believe it, he *walked* home? Three miles and more! How can a child do that? It's impossible, but he did it!"

"There is a strain in the blood, Mr. Entwhistle," Arudu said. "It is of immense importance. And with Doña Susana, your son is in the best of hands."

In the oppressive darkness of the night, they cut their way through the forest.

Chapter Sixteen

The forest was dark and menacing about them; there was no moon at all, only an absolute blackness in which Peter stumbled over fallen tree trunks as they made their way up, always up, over nonexistent trails that Arudu seemed to know intimately. The trailing thorns reached out for him with almost human awareness to find his clothes, his hands, his face as he staggered after a man of great physical competence who was old enough to be his father and who was perfectly at home here in this hostile jungle.

Arudu said, slicing at a vine with his machete: "Would it shock you, Mr. Entwhistle, to learn that I know, as all of Jamaica does, of your affair with Morisco's sister Isabella? Would it offend you if I were to comment on it? With your own well-being in mind, of course. It is a personal observation and therefore perhaps remiss of me."

There was a clutching at Peter's heart as he thought of her, rising up out of the surf like a Naiad on that awful night when he had first loved her. He did not really want to talk about her, but he said: "No, sir. It would neither shock me nor offend me."

The old man's voice was very low, punctuated by the

sharp, incisive sounds of the chopping knife as he blazed a trail up the mountainside. "It is easy to understand," he murmured, "that so beautiful a woman might affect you deeply."

"She is known to you?"

"Oh, yes, indeed. And your English friends, many of whom also know her well . . . they never told you anything about her?"

"Our English friends stopped calling on us a long time ago, I'm afraid."

"Ah, yes. I fear that it is because of *us*, Mr. Entwhistle."

Peter grunted. "A cross I find I can bear with equanimity. What should they have told me about her?"

For a little while, Arudu did not answer him. He used his machete with easy, offhand skill and said: "We must cut our way through a diversion now, to hide our tracks better. By this means, if the volunteers of the association should be following us, we will lose them."

Peter frowned. "The volunteers?"

"They watch every move I make. But we are safe from them here. They need a moon to move under. They do not understand the darkness as I do."

"But you were about to tell me something of Isabella, I believe."

"As a friend, yes. Do you still love her? If the question is offensive, I withdraw it."

Peter pushed an intrusive thorn branch away from his face; it had already drawn blood. He said slowly: "Love is a word that has many meanings, Mr. Arudu, all of them very hard to define. I was moved by her, deeply moved. I think that I am no longer. I am not sure."

"Then would it help if I were to tell you who she really is?"

"Yes. It is a question I often asked myself."

"And perhaps you are the only man on Jamaica who does not know the answer to that vexing problem. Perhaps it is an impertinence that I interest myself so much in your personal affairs, but you *must* be disillusioned. And if your expatriate friends will not do this . . . then I will."

He stopped and turned and put a hand on Peter's shoulder. "Your Isabella, Mr. Entwhistle," he said quietly, "is a very famous prostitute."

"*What?*" Peter felt the blood draining from his face.

"She is a notorious whore, working out of a small and exclusive house in Kingston. Her skin is white, she passes for Spanish, and she is therefore greatly in demand."

"Oh, my God . . . !"

"Oh, my God indeed. She was born in Spanish Town twenty-four years ago, of mixed African and Spanish blood. At the age of eleven or so, she was first seduced by her brother Morisco. At the age of fourteen, she went to work on the streets. When she was nineteen years old, she found employment with Madame Françoise on Kingston's Bay Street, a very reputable house but a brothel nonetheless. For a long time now she has been looking for a white husband, preferably a rich one. So you see, dear friend, you are lucky to have escaped her blandishments."

Peter said nothing as they moved on again. It was as though an oppressive shadow of guilt had fallen from his shoulders.

They dropped down into a deep valley, slithering down rain-washed stones and viscous mud, and far below them there were forty or fifty flares burning in a little hollow. Arudu called a halt, and they squatted together on the edge of the bluff, and the old man whispered: "We wait now till they tell us we may continue."

"They?"

"A handful of our own people have been behind us ever since we came over the top of the hill. You did not hear them?"

"No, I heard nothing . . ."

Arudu chuckled. "*Neither* of us was meant to hear them. But I am very skilled in these things. They know that I bring you here, but they are still suspicious."

They waited in the heavy, dark silence of the jungle.

Peter was staring down at the flares and wondering what might happen now, wondering, too, about Isabella; he shuddered when he thought that he was contemplating marrying her, and he even laughed softly to himself. He saw Arudu's puzzled look in the darkness and whispered: "If Morisco had not come to the house and knocked me down and cut my lip in two and threatened my family . . ."

"Yes, I know. *Shhh*, they are here now."

He turned as three men came creeping out of the forest to join them; they were obviously very frightened. They all carried machetes as they crouched down and whispered with Arudu in Creole, and Arudu said at last: "Come. We go now. They are waiting for us."

They fought their way down through the forest to the hollow, and there were more than two hundred slaves gathered there, squatting on the sandy forest floor. As they approached, one of them rose to his feet and held out his arms in an imperative gesture and shouted in a kind of English: "Mista Entwoosle! He telling us what we do now!"

Peter examined their weary faces. There was a light in their eyes that cut him to the quick. He looked at Arudu in desperation and said: "Tell them what to do? Arudu, I am not competent to do that!"

The slave leader said calmly: "You will make a speech now, Mr. Entwhistle, telling them that their aspirations are not entirely without hope. I will translate for you. They have no English and very little Spanish."

"But what can I tell them?" Peter was frantic.

Arudu said: "They need the words and sympathy of a white man who is on their side. They need *hope*, Mr. Entwhistle."

To his acute embarrassment, they had risen to their feet and were clapping, rhythmically and in unison, the women among them shrieking out a sound all their own, a strange kind of ululation.

"Very well."

Peter raised his arms for silence, and when the clapping stopped, he shouted: "I have come here, my friends, to find out why it is that the slaves, freed by Earl Grey's act of Parliament, which was passed three years ago . . . are still in servitude. It is my intention to listen to what I believe to be your justifiable complaints and to take them to the governor of this island, Lord Percy Dorcas. It may be that whereas he has not listened to you . . . he will listen to me . . . !"

Beside him, Arudu was translating his words, and Peter saw that they were all hanging onto them, some of them moving closer to him as he spoke.

He said quietly: "I believe in the power of persuasion, of the spoken word. I believe that when injustices are brought to the notice of the authorities, they can sometimes be remedied."

They began clapping again, and Arudu looked to one side and raised a hand, a signal. He had carefully orchestrated this meeting to ensure that his newfound ally would be sufficiently aroused; and a file of men and women came out of the darkness into the light of the flares, ten or twelve of them, all dressed in rags and with blankets thrown over their shoulders. One by one, they stopped in front of him, and in silence lowered their cloaks and turned their backs on him, and Arudu said gently: "The scars of whipping, Mr. Entwhistle."

A huge barrel-chested man was the last of them, and as he turned with the blanket draped over his elbows, the blood was still wet on wounds that had been opened up down to the bone; the bone was glistening, and the blood was staining the improvised cloak.

Arudu said: "Carlos Kurati, a slave at the Crenshaw plantation. He hid a young girl one of the slave-masters wanted, and he was given forty lashes for his pains, only a few hours ago."

And then, very close behind him, a volley of musketfire rang out from the forest. He saw a woman, immediately in front of him, fall to the ground, her leg shattered by a bullet.

He turned in shock and saw an extended line of a dozen troopers and civilians moving in on them. They were all armed, and at their head was a lieutenant of the Auxiliaries. Four or five of them were firing into the crowd as they advanced, and the slaves were screaming, dropping their flares, and racing for the safety of the forest. In a very few moments only he and Arudu were left, with a dozen dead or wounded bodies lying close by.

The raiders gathered around them in a half circle, sour, angry-looking men, sweaty and excited; some of them wore the black-and-green armband that proclaimed them to be members of the Planters' Association.

One of them raised his musket, quite slowly, and pointed it at Arudu's head. As Peter stared in horrified shock, he pulled the trigger and blew Arudu's skull wide open. Peter screamed out his rage and seized the musket by its barrel, struggling with a sudden almost superhuman strength. He saw the bronze hilt of a sword come down and took the blow squarely between the eyes. A thousand lights exploded, and he lost consciousness.

The silence was absolute when he came to his senses again, and the moon was casting eerie shadows over the glade, filtering through the treetops and dappling the ground. He could not immediately remember where he was nor what had happened; and when the memory suddenly returned it was a shock that sickened him. The face of the lieutenant was vivid in his mind, a young, boyish face suffused with both anger and fear; he saw again the raised rifles, heard the shots and the screaming, relived for a terrible moment the panic and the mayhem, the sound of the terror still ringing in his ears.

He could see no corpses, nor was there any sign of life, and he called out: "Hola there! Is anyone there . . .?" But there was no answer. He crossed and crisscrossed the hollow, and all he could find was a bloodied piece of rag to bolster the dreadful image, not even a sign of any wounded, the living and dead bodies dragged away into deeper forest, hiding, like animals searching for safer lairs from the hunter.

He stared morosely at the surrounding hills, trying to remember which one he had to climb to find his way home. He could not be sure, so he skirted the meetingground slowly and found at last a deep slash in a tree trunk, a blaze that Arudu had cut, with others beyond it where the machete had forced a way through. He followed them, clambering painfully up the steep and slippery slope.

He came upon a stream at last and washed the caked blood from his face and sat for a while at the top of the rise, staring down onto the coastline below, a scene of incomparable beauty in the moonlight but in which he found no pleasure.

He thought about the night's events, and the term *privilege* was utmost in his mind, the kind of privilege he had spent half a lifetime trying to escape; it was why he had not been killed, he was sure of it. That good and honest man Arudu, and God alone knew how many others, had been wantonly murdered.

But he thought, too, of Susan and Arthur as he hurried down through the forest, the sky above it lit now with the reds and golds of the dawn; Susan would have been waiting for him all night, and worrying about him, as always.

It was broad daylight when he came to the beach, and there was Commander Crenshaw cantering along the sand on his mare, a shrimping net over his shoulder. He pulled up short when he saw Peter, and said, astonished: "By God, Entwhistle! Is it you, or a ghost? I was sure you were dead!"

"Dead? No, Commander . . ." The pain was shooting up to the top of his head, and he wondered incongruously what he must look like, disheveled and bloodied, and he said: "If you would tell me why?"

Crenshaw slipped lithely off his horse and drove the shaft of his net into the sand. He said: "I just came from the barracks. There's talk there of a slave revolt in the mountains, nipped in the bud, I'm glad to say. More than a thousand of them, armed to the teeth and looking for trouble. They said you were with them, said you were killed in the fire fight when a dozen of our troopers came upon them."

"A thousand? A story, Commander, much distorted in the telling." He said angrily: "There were less than two hundred of them, and they were not armed to the teeth! Some of them carried machetes, of course, they're cane cutters, but *armed* is not the word. And many of them were simply murdered."

Crenshaw turned away and found something to do, fiddling with his mare's harness. He said, mumbling: "But it *was* at least the beginnings of a revolt, was it not?"

"No, sir, I think not. They were searching for answers. They had not found them."

Crenshaw turned back and held his eyes. "I am told that their leader, one Arada Arudu, opened fire on the troopers, and in self-defense, they shot him dead. That, surely, is true, is it not?"

"No sir. Arudu, whom I counted as a friend, was unarmed. A trooper placed a musket at his temple and blew his brains out. I saw it."

The commander's eyes were very hard. "You swear this?" he said. "That he was unarmed?"

"No," Peter said coldly. "I merely *tell* you . . ."

He moved away, and Crenshaw said urgently: "Wait, sir!"

Peter turned back, and the commander said quietly: "You return to your house now, without a doubt?"

"Yes, I do. My sister will be worried. So if you will excuse me . . .?"

"Take my horse, Entwhistle," he said. "She's fast. You'll be home in no time at all."

He was about to refuse, but those hard eyes were also tired and very old, and Peter relented and said: "You are very kind, sir."

"When you arrive, slap her haunch, and she'll find me." He hesitated. Then: "And may I call on you again, sir, as I used to?"

Peter sprang to the saddle and gathered up the reins. "You will be most welcome, Commander," he said. But there was something he had to be sure of. "They thought that I was dead?"

The commander nodded. "Killed in the fighting, they told me."

Peter laughed shortly. "Can you believe it's a consolation to me? I thought they had spared my life for . . . for other reasons, which would have angered me more. I thank you for your horse . . ."

He wheeled his mount and raced off along the sand; and five minutes later Susan was running down the gravel path to meet him, in anguish over the fearful wound on his forehead and throwing her arms around him. "Peter, Peter," she whispered. "Dear God, I was so worried when you didn't come home. What happened?"

He kissed her on the cheek and hugged her tightly and said: "So much to tell you . . ." He slapped the little mare as Crenshaw had told him to do and watched it canter off, then turned back to her. "I'm sorry, Susan, you must have been terribly worried. But it's all over now—"

"It is *not* all over," she said, interrupting him. "Let me

take care of that ghastly wound before we do anything else. Oh, heavens, it might have killed you! What was it, a cudgel? I don't suppose for one moment that you walked into an overhanging branch . . ."

"It was the hilt of a trooper's sword."

"Oh, no! *The troopers?*"

"And Arudu is dead. They murdered him." He told her the circumstances of Arudu's death, and her face was white as she listened.

She pulled herself together at last, very tight-lipped and said: "I seem to spend half my life patching you up, Peter!"

She called for Nesta and said: "Hot water at once, some bandages from the dispensary, and some brimstone too. Tell Bidasso to prepare a tub with mustard seed in it."

She sat on the three-legged stood by the tub as Nesta scrubbed at his back, and Bidasso was standing there, supervising the operation as was his right, as Peter told more of the night's calamities. At the mention of Arudu's name, the houseman threw a startled look at him and said: "It is not my place, Mr. Peter, to intrude upon your conversation. But do you say that our leader Arada Arudu is dead?"

"Murdered," Peter said. "Yes, he is dead."

It was still his habit to find release in his pen when he was enraged; and when he had recovered his calm a little he sat down and composed a letter to Jamaica's governor, Lord Percy Dorcas. He wrote:

Excellency.

Permit me to present myself. I am Peter Entwhistle Esquire, son of the late Major John Hayes Entwhistle of the Indian Army, whose name, I am convinced, will be known to Your Excellency. . . .

When he had finished, he called for wax and sealed the letter and told Bidasso to ride with it at once to the governor's residence. "I count on you, Bidasso," he said, "to ensure that it reaches Governor Dorcas himself. Doña Susana will give you money for whatever palms must be greased . . . And bring me back an answer."

"*Sí, Señor Pedro . . .*"

Bidasso rode like a maniac, thinking of his beloved leader Arudu, and paid out money and made threats where they were needed. He would not leave the governor's residence once the letter was delivered, but sat and slept among the bushes behind the kitchen till an answer was forthcoming. And within three days he was back with Dorcas' reply: "*His Excellency will be pleased to meet with Mr. Entwhistle at his convenience . . .*"

It was a major step forward: The governor was ex-Indian Army, and he knew the family name well. Peter flogged his horse almost to its death, and on that summer evening of the year 1837, he was esconced with Lord Percy in one of the anterooms of the governor's residence.

Lord Percy Dorcas was benevolent, though perhaps not very bright. Approaching his sixties now, he had nearly forty years of government service behind him. A big, unruly kind of man, he had been well seasoned by twelve years of fighting in Madras State—indeed, three of those years had been spent in Vellore, where he had been wounded no less than five times. He was handsome in a rugged kind of way, with a very bushy moustache and gray, thoughtful eyes, always a little perplexed, as though he did not fully comprehend how the world was changing around him.

The room he had selected for their meeting was carefully chosen, neither official nor personal, but somewhere in between, as was befitting. The report he had read was ambiguous and very disturbing:

Entwhistle, Peter, son of Major John Entwhistle of Vellore, Madras State, India . . . He is known not to have followed the family tradition of military service. . . . Sharing a house with his sister Susan, a nurse . . . her medical

*attentions seem to be directed solely toward the slaves,
which would provide subject with excuses for any activities
he may devise against established rule and order. . . .*

There was a great deal more about Peter's activities, and
Lord Percy scowled at the pages as he read them. He did not
much like this dependence upon covert intelligence, even
though he admitted the need for it.

He said now, uncorking the brandy bottle—another in-
dication that this talk was unofficial—"The sun's over the
yardarm, Entwhistle. You'll join me in a drink, I'm sure . . . ?"

"You are most kind, Excellency," Peter said. "I will
indeed."

"Good. It's so much easier to discuss these pressing problems in a congenial atmosphere. You told my aide-de-camp
that you were concerned about the justifiable killing of one
Arada Arudu, a slave agitator."

"It was *not* justifiable," Peter said hotly. "He was murdered!"

The governor picked up a paper and read aloud: ". . .
*whereupon the slave agitator Arudu pulled a pistol from his belt and
aimed it at the lieutenant in charge of the patrol. Trooper Wilson
then shot Arudu dead, in defense of his commanding officer's
life . . .*"

He tossed the paper back onto his desk, and said: "It
really leaves very little room for discussion, does it not?"

"Arudu had no pistol," Peter said steadily. "He was not
armed. I was there."

Dorcas sipped his brandy. "The man who wrote this report was there, too, Entwhistle, and it's hardly the kind of
matter over which a mistake could have been made. I take it,
therefore, that you are suggesting he may have lied."

"Not suggesting, sir," Peter said, "but stating it flatly. It is
a lie, to conceal a murder."

"Y-e-s . . ."

Dorcas sipped his brandy again. "And yet, if I were to accuse him of lying, would he not make much the same kind of accusation against you? What do you think? Would he not say that *you* were lying to further your own causes? Causes that are sometimes, if you'll allow me to make the point, not always conducive to the smooth and benevolent governing of an island that is very often in turmoil."

Peter began to answer him, not trying to mask the heavy sarcasm: "Whether the government of this island is benevolent or not . . ."

But Dorcas interrupted him with a curt gesture. "I am talking, Entwhistle," he said testily, "and you will do me the courtesy of allowing me to continue."

"Yes, Governor. Your pardon, sir."

Dorcas was striding up and down, frowning darkly, and he said, exasperated: "Please believe me, Entwhistle, when I say that I am *not* your enemy. It is simply that . . . well, with your family name and its most estimable heritage, I could wish that you were on our side. We *need* men of your breeding here, if only to raise the caliber of those who are trying to govern the ungovernable. The matter of your friend Arada Arudu . . ." He gulped his drink and said: "I am not a fool, Entwhistle . . ."

"No, sir. I never believed that for one minute."

"Will you stop interrupting me!"

"Your pardon, sir."

"I am not a fool, and I know damn well that Arudu was deliberately murdered, by men who were frightened of him. And if word of that confession ever leaves this room, by God, I'll have you deported! And I will make sure that the moment you arrive in England, Prime Minister Melbourne, damned Whig though he may be, will have you thrown into Newgate Gaol for the rest of your natural life! Do I make myself clear, Entwhistle?"

"You do, sir."

"Good. Then we are agreed, are we not? Arada Arudu was justifiably killed in a slave revolt. Drink your brandy, sir, and have another."

Peter set down his untouched glass. He said calmly: "It may be, Governor Dorcas, that Arudu's untimely death will have served a purpose after all. I discovered many years ago that any cause can profit from its martyrs. I thank you for your courtesy in seeing me. Good day, sir."

He slammed the door behind him, and Dorcas was in a fury. It might have been the first time in his long service that he had lost control of a meeting.

Peter rode home, and when he arrived at the little house on the beach, his first question was for the welfare of his son. Arthur, it seemed, was well, and fast asleep in his bed. He told Susan what had happened with Lord Percy, and said, worrying: "I could wish that we had something like the *Political Register* here. But there's nowhere to air our grievances, is there?"

Susan held her peace. She remembered the days in London when Peter, moved as he was now, would sit down and write furiously, finding relief in the outpouring of angry words that sooner or later were read by people who could, albeit slowly, change the course of history.

He said: "By God, there's only one thing for me to do."

"And that is?"

"A letter to Queen Victoria herself."

Susan said calmly: "Yes, I think that's a very good idea. Whether it will bear fruit or not . . . that is entirely a different matter."

He felt his passion rising, and he thumped on the table and said: "A letter to the Queen! Our name alone will ensure that she reads it!"

Susan's eyes were shining, and he was very conscious of their closeness. She was older, still heavy, still ungainly; but to him, she was utterly delightful.

Was she truly *forty-six* now? How had the years gone by so fast?

He went out late at night for his habitual stroll along the beach, listening to the surf and thinking, as always, of Amanda, of Dorothy, and of Susan, the three women in his life whose importance to him was overriding. The once-strong memory of Isabella almost never entered his mind now; and when it did, he could only wonder why he had allowed her physical perfection to blind him so completely.

But he thought now of another woman too, a young girl of nineteen years who had recently mounted the throne of the most powerful country the modern world had ever known— the young Queen Victoria. In his mind, he went over the words he would use, correcting them time and time again; and he hurried home to write her a long and very earnest letter.

Chapter Seventeen

It would take more than a year for Peter's letter to reach the eyes of its intended recipient. It arrived in London within six months, lay on one minor bureaucrat's desk after another for an interminable time, and came at last into the hands of Reginald Bowers-Wright, who fell into a spell of rumination about the strange turn of fate that had brought Peter's name to him again.

Bowers-Wright was very old now and had arrogated to himself certain privileges he had not enjoyed in the past. He said to Lord Melbourne: "A letter, Prime Minister, from one Peter Entwhistle, in Jamaica. I don't know if you know the name."

Melbourne peered at him. "I know the family name, of course. What's it about?"

"The slaves in the colonies, specifically in Jamaica. Their condition does not seem to be improving fast enough to satisfy him."

"Oh. Those damned slaves!" he said peevishly. "In God's name, they've been freed, have they not? More or less? There's precious little else that we can do for them!"

"Yes, of course, and I would not have bothered you. But his letter sheds light on certain unhappy aspects of our administration there on which I feel we should be better informed."

"Very well," the P.M. said, grumbling, "leave it with me, I'll have a look at it as soon as I can. I do have more pressing problems to worry about, y'know."

"Of course." Bowers-Wright hesitated. "And would you consider, Prime Minister, showing it to Her Majesty?"

"I certainly would not . . ."

"It is, after all, addressed to her . . ."

Melbourne exploded. "Addressed to the Queen herself? What arrogance!"

He took the letter nonetheless and began to skim through its first pages. His frown darkened as he read, and he looked up at Bowers-Wright and said sharply: ". . . *applied terror an instrument of government* . . . ? Good God, Reggie, is the man a maniac?"

"No, Prime Minister, he is not. I will personally vouch for his integrity."

Melbourne read on, all his other pressing problems seemingly put aside. In a little while he said slowly: "I think I'll talk with Palmerston about this, and yes, perhaps Victoria should see it too."

When Bowers-Wright had gone, the Prime Minister sat back at his desk and put his feet up and sank his chin into his neck and was very deeply disturbed by what he read. When he had finished, he rubbed a hand over his tired eyes and wondered why the devil his office was constantly plagued with nothing but bad news.

On the drive home that night, his coachman, trying to pass another carriage on too confined a street, locked wheels and broke his axle. Melbourne got down to inspect the damage and said: "Jenks, if you were a slave in Jamaica, do you know what I'd do to you for that?"

He was an old man, bent and twisted with arthritis, and he had served the family for more than fifty years. Startled, he said: "A *slave*, sir?"

"I'd have you whipped till your bones were showing through. You're lucky you weren't born in Jamaica, Jenks."

"Yes, sir." He had no idea what his master, the Prime Minister of England, was talking about.

The most pressing of the problems Melbourne had spoken of concerned Russian ambitions on the northwestern frontier of India, with their attendant mischief in Afghanistan.

They had been brought to climax with the murder, by Afghan mobs, of England's two envoys, followed by one of the most disastrous humiliations in British military history—the retreat from Kabul, in which the entire British force of sixteen thousand troops was slaughtered, with the exception of a single survivor; Russian intrigue there was very busy.

"The whole frontier can collapse," the Prime Minister said heavily. "And if it does—it means the end of India."

He sat in his oak-paneled office with his brother-in-law, Foreign Secretary Palmerston, and sipped his tea. He said, brooding: "And faced with this sort of danger, there's really only one man we can trust, isn't there?"

Palmerston raised his eyebrows. "Ambala?" He answered his own question and nodded. "Yes, Ambala. The late maharajah was one of the staunchest friends England ever had, and his son, Ranjet Singh, has shown the same colors. A good man, educated here. Harrow and Oxford."

"Then what do you say, Henry? I think we should persuade Victoria to invite him over here. We can find out just how the Punjab feels."

"He'll side with us," Palmerston said emphatically. "It's in his interest to do so as much as ours. But it's a splendid idea to introduce him at court. A colonial conference, perhaps. A ball at Windsor might be the best way. And your tea, Willie, is *cold*. Can't think why I can never get a hot cup of tea in your office."

He was a handsome man, Palmerston, with bushy muttonchops streaked with gray against a florid complexion, and he said: "That damned Khyber Pass! The worst mistake God ever made, and the Devil knows, he's made plenty, was when he created the Khyber Pass."

Melbourne grunted. "Yes. And then . . . wished it on *us*. The anomaly is, the Russians want Afghanistan, but in God's name, what do they think they can do with it? Yes, we'd better talk to Ambala about strengthening the Punjab."

And so it had come about that His Highness Maharajah Ranjet, absolute ruler of Ambala, and his maharanee, together with a retinue of fourteen servants, were installed in a house on Half Moon Street, only a few hundred yards around the corner from the Entwhistle house on Curzon Street, long empty now and somewhat neglected.

Within ten days of their arrival (by the same flagship, the *Bilgee*, which had taken them to India thirteen years ago), there was the climactic meeting with the young Queen Victoria, a schoolgirl quickly finding her feet as she emerged from the cocoon of her previously sheltered past.

The reception was held in one of the private rooms in the middle ward of the castle, hard by the round tower, where the royal standard was flying to show that the sovereign was in residence. It was one of the smaller rooms, a choice meant to indicate a certain close intimacy, since there were not many more than three or four hundred guests. And it was that unaccustomed intimacy that gave the reception its quality.

All the French designers who were now flooding London had been working day and night to create the gowns for the ladies, bringing to London the opulent splendor of Paris for this occasion, with enormous quantities of horsehair, cotton, and linen for the crinolines, which were embellished everywhere with flounces and garlands without number. Hoops were very popular; and deep décolleté, which left the upper part of the breasts, and the shoulders and arms, fully exposed, was the fashion. Silks, taffetas, satins, crepes, brocades, tulles and muslins, and most of all the new French watered silk, which was called *moiré*, were to be seen in great abundance; and there was not one lady who entered the Small Hall who was not convinced that she herself was the best dressed of all the ladies present.

The gentlemen were mostly in uniform, with their dress blues and their dress swords in shimmering scabbards. Even the soles of their Wellington boots had been polished by earnest soldier-servants anxious to impress their officers with their efficiency (and sure of replacement if the soles were *not* smooth and shining).

For more than an hour the guests mingled and met each other, drinking champagne and nibbling on canapés, and then there was a sudden break in the orchestra's playing . . .

There was a brief roll on the kettledrum that segued into the national anthem, and everyone stood rigidly at attention as Queen Victoria entered, her schoolgirl face flushed with pleasure. Palmerston was on her left arm, and Melbourne (he seldom left her side now) was on her right.

The guests, well drilled in the demands of protocol, had taken their positions in the reception line, and Melbourne murmured, passing from one to another of them: "Lord Michael Crane and the Lady Diana . . . the Marquess of Hastings . . . the Duke of Horley and the Duchess Edna . . . General Lord John Rye-West and Mistress Janet Jones . . . Minister Ako Fusans of Zululand and, ah, the Madame Fusans. And our guest of honor, Your Majesty, His Royal Highness the Maharajah Ranjet Singh of Ambala, and Her Royal Highness the Maharanee Hilda, of Ambala, the state of Punjab, India."

Ranjet dropped to one knee, and at his side and a little behind him, Hilda curtseyed deeply. The Queen said: "Your Highness, Your Highness, you do us great honor. We welcome you to Windsor Castle, the home of our ancestors since the eleventh century."

"The honor is mine, Your Majesty," Ranjet murmured.

"Please rise."

"Your Majesty is most gracious."

He was dressed in his most sumptuous robes, of saffron silk heavily threaded with spun gold wire; he was dark, swarthy, black-bearded, and very impressive. But it was the maharanee who held the Queen's attention, and she thought that she had never seen anyone of such startling beauty.

She saw a woman of well-preserved middle age, tall and slender, with almond-colored skin that seemed to glow with a most attractive sheen. There was a tiny mark in the center of her forehead, and her eyes were grave and understanding and very large. She wore a long gown of shimmering gold, and there were rings on her fingers set with rubies and diamonds matched by a necklace of the same combination. She had a most regal quality, and the young Queen was in awe of her.

As she moved among the other guests, Queen Victoria whispered: "My Lord Melbourne, did you ever see a more beautiful creature?" Victoria was breaking out at last into London's sophisticated society, where everything, to one so young and impressionable, was glorious, rich, and exciting.

Melbourne was alone with her for the moment, and when there was not the press of the crowd about them, his attitude was always quite different. He thought of this young girl almost as if she were his daughter, a child he wanted so desperately to guide into her future as England's Queen and India's Empress.

There was no one within earshot of them, and he said quietly: "She's *chi-chi,* Victoria. Her mother was English. The mixing of the races often produces very beautiful women. But what is important for us is that her naturally pro-British attitudes can guide her husband, whose help we need now."

Victoria said: "Oh, calamity! A *chi-chi?*"

"Yes, I fear so. But it's good for us. What England wants, she wants. And her husband worships her. It means a great deal to our aspirations." He was smiling gently. "The Russians' devious efforts in Afghanistan can be stopped in their tracks by a strong Ranjet Singh in Ambala. It is the reason for his presence here tonight."

She was a child in everything but intelligence. She said quietly: "You are a very devious man yourself, Henry, are you not?"

"Yes, I am!" He was very emphatic about it. "England can thank God for my deviousness!"

Her eyes held his. "And you want something from me too now, I believe."

"Yes. I want a free hand to ensure that if the Russians and their present allies, the Afghanis, come pouring through the Khyber Pass . . . then Ambala under Ranjet Singh will fight them. England needs his help now, Victoria."

"So be it, then."

In a little while, she found Ranjet alone at the buffet table while Hilda was dancing, to the strains of one of Mr. Chopin's waltzes, with Lord Alfred Masset, and she said to Ranjet, making small talk: "I understand, Your Highness, that you know our London well?"

"Indeed, Your Majesty," Ranjet Singh said, "my recollections of the city are among the most gratifying of my whole life. My father, Maharajah Ranjarah Singh, as will be known to Your Majesty, was one of England's most devoted friends. He insisted, and I am grateful for his insistence, that I be brought up, at least during the formative years of my life, in England."

"And where did you live, sir, while you were here? In London itself?"

Ranjet smiled. He was an agreeable and very handsome man with courtly grace to turn the heart of any young girl. He said delightedly: "Within a stone's throw of the house on Half Moon Street where you have been gracious enough to accommodate me, the Entwhistle house on Curzon Street was almost my second home. Peter Entwhistle, son of the famous Major John Entwhistle of Madras State, was one of my closest friends."

He wanted so much to say: "*And my maharanee is his half sister.*" But he did not.

It had been the subject of serious discussion between them when they had first received the invitation from Lord Melbourne, whether or not to disclose the circumstances of Hilda's birth, insofar as they were known or could be guessed at. And there was complete agreement between them from the first moment.

"A matter of some delicacy," Ranjet had said. "There is still, in England, a degree of opprobrium attached to the idea of miscegenation. In our case, there will of course never be the slightest sign of it, and yet it will be *there,* if only subconsciously. And it will fall on you. I will not allow it."

"It may help your objectives, husband," Hilda said, "if it is known that I am half English."

She sounded unsure, even a little worried, and he answered her, laughing now: "My objectives? My dear Hilda, the intent of this meeting is more to England's benefit than to mine! No, Melbourne wants to know, without a doubt, what Ambala feels about the Russian presence in Afghanistan and how it can best be countered. I cannot have it said in England that I am on England's side because my wife is half English. And there is another compelling reason."

"Yes," Hilda said. "Amanda."

"Precisely. Amanda's memory and her honor are as important to me as they are to you."

Only once more was the question raised. As they sailed

from the little seaport of Karachi, Ranjet took her in his arms and said quietly: "It is decided then? There will be no mention of your English heritage?"

"I will be more Indian than the Indians, as I have always wanted to be."

He thought of their decision now and knew that it was wise.

But Victoria was frowning, trying to remember, and she turned to Melbourne and said: "*Entwhistle,* I know the family name of course. But more specifically . . . where have I heard the name *Peter* Entwhistle? Quite recently I think?"

Hilda had drifted to them and taken her husband's arm; he could feel her sudden trembling. Melbourne said: "The letter, Marm, the letter from Jamaica which I showed you. Peter Entwhistle was its author."

"Ah, yes, those unhappy slaves. *Ex*-slaves now, are they not?"

"Yes, most of them. Some still serving out their apprenticeship."

"Mr. Entwhistle wrote . . . very *harshly* about their condition," the Queen said. "What did we decide to do about that?"

"I gave the letter to Palmerston," Melbourne said. "It's in his province rather than mine. He will take whatever action might be necessary."

The orchestra up in the gallery was striking up again, a polka, and the couples were moving back onto the floor, turning it into a place of startling color and gaiety: *one-two-three-hop, one-two-three-hop* the dance went on, with crinolines twirling furiously and the sound of the music echoing back over the timbered walls.

Melbourne turned to Ranjet and said: "Would Your Highness consent to join Palmerston and myself after dinner in a very informal chat? On matters of some importance to us both."

"You have reference, no doubt, to Afghanistan?"

"Afghanistan, Russia, and the Khyber Pass."

"I will be delighted to do so," Ranjet said. "And I venture to suggest that my views on that powder keg are very similar to your own, Prime Minister."

"Splendid!"

As they moved away, Hilda found there was a catch in her voice. She said quietly to Ranjet: "Do you realize it has been nearly twenty years since we saw Peter?"

He held her gently. "Ah, yes, the years fly past us at great speed, don't they? But in that time, we haven't changed very much, you and I." He smiled. "It's only Ambala that's changed, and it's all your doing. I sometimes feel that you've brought us out of a past that was often catastrophic . . . into the enlightened nineteenth century."

"Very little of it was my doing, husband . . ."

"No, that's not true, it was almost *all* your doing. Your work among the villagers has brought them a kind of hope they never really had before. And they worship you. You know that, don't you?"

"Yes, they've showed me in so many ways." She laughed suddenly. "Ambala's my home now, I have no other. And yet . . . when your flagship brought us up the Thames, I felt that I was coming . . . *home.* London is still very dear to me, even after all these years."

"Well then," Ranjet said happily, "shall we go for a walk in the park tomorrow, as we used to?"

She could not contain her excitement. "I'd like that so very much! I believe the rhododendrons are out now. And we haven't yet looked at the old house. It's so close to us . . ."

"Then we will do that tomorrow too."

For Hilda it was to be an experience she would never forget. Responsibilities of state had not robbed Ranjet Singh of his old impetuous ardor, a certain *élan* that was an essential part of his character. He rose very early in the morning and went to the Curzon Street house alone and found it locked and looking forlorn. But there was a watchman camped in the shed at the back; he had been living there, he said, for the past seven years, replacing the last watchman, who had died of old age.

He was a cheerful rogue of a fellow, and they went into the house together, to long-past memories that were shrouded now with white sheets over all the furniture, as though a war on encroaching dust could hold back the passage of time.

Ranjet gave the old man a great deal of money and made certain requests. He said: "How long will it take you, do you think? The hall and this room only."

"Well, sir," the watchman said, "I'll get me missus to go over it with a broom, take off all them covers, set the place to rights. . . . It should be ready for what you have in mind by the early evening."

"A fire too. There must be a fire."

"That's easy enough, sir. And would a bottle of wine be fitting, sir?"

"Yes, I think it would. And your wife, is she accustomed to domestic service?"

"Oh, yes, indeed, sir, all her life! She's old now, but she still gets around."

"And her name?"

"Annie, sir."

"Good, then have her here to wait on us. You will not find me ungrateful, I promise you."

The old man was grinning broadly. "You've already made me a rich man, sir. I'll not ask for more."

Ranjet returned to Half Moon Street and told Hilda a little white lie, giving her the splendid roses he had bought for her in Shepherd Market, and when she asked: "Shall we go first to Curzon Street?" he said happily: "No. First, the park.

The band of the Third Dragoons is playing there this afternoon, and I'm sure you'd like to hear them . . ."

"Ah, good, yes."

"Then we will stroll down the Mall for a while, arm in
arm, while I show you off as I used to. We'll watch the riders
there. And, toward early evening, we'll go to Curzon Street
and perhaps stand outside the house, empty and unattended
now, and just . . . stare at it like the sentimental fools we both
are."

"And I wonder . . . do you think we might even go inside?"

"I'll see. It might not be easy. We can hardly break in,
can we?"

It was five o'clock in the afternoon when they finished
their ramblings in the park and the Mall, and it was just as it
had been in the old days: People turned to stare at Hilda as she
passed by, startled by her beauty and forgetting their manners
altogether. And when they arrived at the Curzon Street house,
Ranjet took her arm and led her past the little iron gate and
up to the front door; and to her considerable surprise, he
opened it even without a key and picked her up and carried
her over its threshold. He strode with her through the hall,
clean and neat and tidy and just as it used to be, and took her
into the Small Library, which had always been their favorite
room.

Here, too, there was not a speck of dust to be seen, there
were no sheets over the furniture, the dresser and tables and
shelves were polished and shining nicely, and there was a log
fire burning in the hearth.

He set his bride down on one of the sofas, conscious that
her fingertips were at her cheeks, brushing away the tears. He
went to a bookshelf and put his hand at once on the bound
portfolio he wanted. And when he turned back he said: "But
something is wrong! You must sit on the floor, as you used
to . . ."

Hilda slid down to the carpet expectantly and drew her knees up to her chin, her arms around them, and Ranjet sat beside her and opened up the book and said: "Now, where shall we begin? Let me see . . ."

The maid came in, an elderly woman dressed in a stiff black uniform with a well-starched white apron, and she said: "Will you take your wine now, sir?"

Hilda was almost in shock. Ranjet said casually: "Thank you, Annie. Yes, you may pour it now."

"Very good, sir."

She poured the wine into two gleaming goblets for them, set them down close at hand, and went out about her business; and Ranjet took the book and began to read his poems to her . . .

Hilda could contain herself no longer. She moved to Ranjet and held him tightly and wept. They kissed, and she knew that in all of her happy life she had never been happier than she was at this moment.

They were children again, and the house on Curzon Street was their shelter.

They sat together with their thoughts, in the kind of silence that means so much to lovers. And it was not until the very late hours of the night that Ranjet's little game was over and they went back together, hand in hand, to their new quarters on Half Moon Street.

A gentle September rain was falling.

Chapter Eighteen

Almost a year slipped by, and 1837 was entering time's relentless orbit before Peter's letter to the Queen was answered, and the answer came, not from Victoria herself—as he had half hoped it might—but from an obscure fourth secretary in Lord Palmerston's Foreign Ministry. Moreover, it merely suggested, in somewhat cool terms, that he refer his complaint back to Her Majesty's governor-general of the islands, Lord Percy Dorcas, in whom Her Majesty enjoyed the greatest confidence . . .

Under other circumstances, or in other times, he might have been angry. But there were other questions on his mind now, questions that loomed very large on his own personal horizons, and he shrugged off the letter as though it were of no consequence.

There was excitement and even exuberance in his voice, and he said to Susan, abruptly: "Come, let's go for a walk on the beach. It's a splendid evening."

"All right." She was surprised; it was so long since they'd done this together.

They plowed through the sand down to the water's edge. Peter took off his boots and hung them by their laces around his neck and stuffed his socks into his pocket and rolled up the legs of his trews. He even persuaded Susan to remove her high-buttoned boots, and her cotton stockings too, and hold up her skirt delicately as she let the surf play over her feet. She squealed as it came racing up to cover her ankles, and she muttered: "I'm not at all sure that *paddling* in the sea is compatible either with my age or with my position here as an English spinster of natural and inherent dignity. It's probably not even *safe*! Are there sharks here?"

"Susan! Arthur goes swimming here every day, as you must know, and in twenty-one years he's never yet been eaten alive by sharks, as you must also know. You really do postulate the most ridiculous arguments sometimes, don't you?"

"Well . . ." She wasn't in the least reassured. "And now? Will you talk with Lord Dorcas again?"

"No."

He scowled. "Dorcas is an idiot, and I'd have nothing to talk to him about. The slaves are free now, scurrying by their thousands up into the mountains to search out homesteads for themselves. Good luck to them."

"Then what was it you wanted to tell me about? There was that kind of look on your face . . ."

"I spent most of that day," Peter said, "covering Amos Crenshaw's estate from border to border. He has a wonderful property, and he wants to sell it."

She could feel a sudden tightening in her stomach. "And so?"

"I think we should buy it. We've cut the umbilical cord to London, almost completely. Almost, but not quite: Our money is still there." He took a long, deep breath. "With your approval, of course, I want to take all our money from Child's Bank in London, transfer it out here, and buy the Crenshaw estate. There's just enough left for us to cover the purchase price."

That tightening at her stomach was acute now. She whispered: "*All* of it?"

"Only with your consent."

"Peter, Madame Phyllis tells me that Amos Crenshaw's estate is losing money so fast that he's on the verge of bankruptcy!"

"Through inept management," Peter said, "nothing more than that! His whole operation is predicated on the use of unpaid labor. I believe that we can pay the workers and still make a good living."

Carried away with his own argument, he said didactically: "We are *landed gentry*, you and I, and Arthur too! But we have no land! We simply rent our present housing, and this is a situation that cries out for rectification. If we do this, it will ensure your future and mine. More importantly, it will ensure Arthur's future. What do you think?"

Susan did not like to dispute him, perhaps because most of the time he was right. But she said hesitantly: "Is it perhaps a little naïve to think that you can make a living from the Amos Crenshaw estate when he cannot?"

He was quite angry. "Naïve? *Naïve*, you say? Naïveté is not one of my weaknesses, Susan dear."

"Ha!"

Nevertheless, she fell silent; she could never argue successfully with a brother whom she worshiped.

It was the worst mistake she had ever made; and she went to her room that night and wept.

Nor did she once, during the days of discussion that followed, even once raise her voice in protest; Peter was the patriarch, the head of the family, and always knew what was best for all of them. She blamed her misgivings on herself and just desperately hoped that in spite of them, everything would turn out well.

And so, some four months later, the transferred funds arrived in Jamaica, and the family had embarked on the first step of their new adventure. By the end of the year, Peter, Susan, and Arthur were officially enrolled as the new owners of Amos Crenshaw's estate. It had cost them almost every penny they had, but rundown or not, it was a property that enthralled Susan at the very first intimate sight, and as she walked with her brother over the vast acreage, all her previous doubts seemed to disappear completely.

"I've seen it before," she whispered, "but until this moment I never quite realized how very beautiful it is . . ."

The plantation lay on a spit of red land that fingered its way out into the aquamarine sea, so that there were always cool breezes to temper the heat of the broiling sun. There were sandstone bluffs washed by the waves, and surf-swept rocks where lobsters lurked in their holes, their antennae waving in search of their constant enemies, the morays. Yellow and purple lantanas grew in crevices almost down to the shore, and sometimes a solitary and unexpected pine had taken root on an offshore slab of rock, struggling mightily against the seawater.

On the landward side, there were scarlet-flowered trees growing, around which hundreds of tiny hummingbirds fluttered, searching out nourishment in sudden darting forays, the brilliant sunlight striking against the luminescent greens at their throats.

The promontory struck due south into the blue water, and it was a child of the hot sun that rose on one side and went down on the other, urging all the plants there in its passing on to more and still more fruition.

There was a splendid old house that was large, airy, and very solidly built. There were sheds for the labor to call their homes, a good stream running nearby with masses of herbs growing on its borders; basil, coriander, wild thyme and tarragon, sage and oregano, and lavender in great abundance. There was a sufficiency of machinery, and almost everything else that was needed.

Peter called in a contractor to rebuild the workers' housing—he had no labor yet—and sent out runners into the hills

to find the ex-slaves to tell them: *There is work, well paid. . . .*
He was offering a wage greatly over the government-stipulated
minimum.

The contractors finished their work in only a few weeks
over the expected three months, and Peter inspected it carefully, well satisfied with what had been done. He showed
Susan and Arthur over the remodeled house, still smelling
strongly of fresh paint, and was delighted by their obvious
pleasure in it.

He said to Susan, smiling: "You had certain misgivings,
didn't you?"

She nodded. "But only for a little while. Now I'm sure
it's going to be all simply marvelous."

He turned to his son. "And you too, Arthur? Did you
share your aunt's apprehensions? I never really knew."

"No, sir. I was aware of them, but I never shared them."
He grinned suddenly. "I've known you all my life, Father,
haven't I? I never yet knew you to make a wrong decision."

"Well, that's very flattering," Peter said dryly. "I only
wish it were true."

A new name was required for the estate, and Susan said:
"Those beautiful trees the hummingbirds are so fond of . . .
what are they called?"

They were tall and splendid trees, with lush and deep-
green foliage and small red blossoms on which, indeed, the
hummingbirds feasted constantly, buzzing around them in
enormous agitation, filling their tiny bellies with a kind of
honey.

"*Coratoe,*" Arthur said "A splendid name for a plantation!"

But as soon as the work began, the trouble began with
it . . .

Peter returned one night from the fields and went straight
to the stables to ensure that his horse was properly fed; and he
saw that the groom was patently frightened. But the houseman

was waiting for him too, the formidable Bidasso, grown older now but no less angry, and there were two Jamaicans of mixed blood with him, big, burly men who just seemed to be hanging around, squatting on the straw and just . . . waiting.

He said, puzzled: "What's wrong, Bidasso?"

"Trouble, Mr. Peter," Bidasso said. "Two gentlemen to see you. They are in the living room with Doña Susana. They come from the Planters' Association."

"Well, that doesn't necessarily mean trouble, does it? Let's find out what they want."

"Yes, sir."

"Arthur?"

"Mr. Arthur took the cart into Spanish Town to buy new harness. He's not back yet."

"Ah, yes, I forgot." He threw a look at the two Jamaicans. "And these people?"

"My friends, Mr. Peter. Just in case there *is* trouble."

Peter went into the house and found Susan serving tea to the two visitors. One of them was elderly, studious-looking, and quite bald, and the other was a much younger man, in his early twenties, perhaps, with a round and boyish face that had a very sullen look to it. There was a blackthorn cudgel in his belt. Peter kissed Susan quickly and turned to the two men. "Good evening, gentlemen," he said courteously. "I'm Peter Entwhistle. What can I do for you?"

The older of them had risen, holding out his hand. Peter took it, and the old man said, smiling: "And I am Red Barstow, Mr. Entwhistle, and your servant. This is my son Gavin, and we are representatives of the Planters' Association, an illustrious organization which seeks the pleasure of your membership now that you are, *de facto,* so to speak, one of us. Our fees are minimal, the advantages great. And I am sure that you agree with me when I say that unless we planters stick together more strongly than ever before, then we will all fall . . . apart. I have reference, sir, to the government-mandated minimum wage for labor, which we feel is far too high. Our aim is to establish a *maximum* wage, which will be far less than government's so-called minimum. And if we stick together, we can do it. The wages you are offering are quite unacceptable."

"Pragmatism, Mr. Barstow," Peter said evenly. "Sheer pragmatism. Because they simply won't work for less."

"Oh, but they will," Barstow said, smiling. He cracked his knuckles. "A few broken heads is all it will take, believe me. And now that you are an estate owner, it is our wish that you support us in every move we make." There was a little pause, and he did not lose the genial smile. "Wish? No, it is a demand. We will not tolerate any holdouts. And your answer, sir?"

"My answer," Peter said tightly, "is that I will never disgrace myself by wearing one of your damned armbands. I am sorry to disappoint you, Mr. Barstow, but I do not approve of the association's past history. It has been one of violence, not excluding murder. I have particular reference to the wanton killing of Arada Arudu, who was my friend. I will have nothing whatsoever to do with your association, sir. Good day to you."

The old man was chuckling. He raised a placatory hand and said: "Yes, yes, we are aware of your sympathy for those on the other side of the fence that protects *us* from *them*. But you *will* join us, Mr. Entwhistle." He gestured vaguely. "Oh, it is not a question of the fees, as I said, they are minimal, though in your own personal case the committee might wish to . . . to raise them a little to compensate for past and present mistakes in your thinking."

"I will not join you, sir. And that is an end to the matter."

Susan's eyes were wide, and she was sure that there was trouble in store. Red Barstow threw her a condescending glance and turned back to Peter. "No, sir," he said softly, "it is the *beginning* of the matter. Merely . . . the opening salvo, shall we say? The second salvo might be . . . perhaps the burning of your beautiful house? Or an assault on your person one night? An assault on your sister?"

The young man was laughing suddenly. He had not moved from his chair, and he said loudly: "As long as I don't have to do the assaulting. I'm too pernickety to mess around with fifty-year-old cows . . ."

Peter was white with fury. He strode across the room, seized the youth by the collar, yanked him to his feet, and smashed a fist into his face, knocking him down. The boy looked up at him in acute astonishment, his mouth open; blood from his broken nose was trickling into it. He said slowly: "By God, you are going to pay for that."

He began to rise to his feet, his face contorted with his anger, and Peter was ready for him. There was a considerable difference in their ages, and the younger Barstow was already hefting the murderous cudgel from his belt.

But the door from the kitchen had opened silently, and Bidasso was there; had he been listening? Beside him, his two brawny friends stood, and they carried naked machetes now.

The young man stopped and glared at them, and his father said, smiling still: "Knocked to the ground by a man of his age? Shame on you, boy! Shame on you!" It seemed he could not stop laughing. But he looked at the trio at the door, and there was no laughter in his eyes at all. He sighed and said: "Well, it seems that it behooves us to leave you now, Mr. Entwhistle." He turned to Susan and bowed. "And I thank you, ma'am, for your hospitality. Truly a most enjoyable cup of tea."

He went to the door and opened it and turned back and said, still smiling: "The membership fee I spoke of, sir, is a trifling two English pounds per annum. The entrance fee will be . . . I think one thousand pounds would be adequate. You are paying your labor far too much, and we won't allow it. Good night, sir. You will hear from us again."

They were both gone, and Bidasso turned away to move back into the kitchen with his cohorts, but Peter stopped him. He said: "Bidasso, I thank you. And do you think your two friends might care to join our staff? By God, they scare *me.*"

Bidasso nodded gravely. "These days, Mr. Peter, an estate needs guards. They have no work. They will be happy to stay."

"Do they speak Spanish? Or English?"

Bidasso grinned suddenly. "Sir, they don't really speak at all! When they do, only Creole."

"Then kindly thank them for me. Acquaint them with their duties, which will be largely to Miss Susan and to the house. See that they are paid a good wage, at your own discretion. The laborer is worthy of his hire, and I feel that tonight they have saved us both from considerable embarrassment. Make sure they know how grateful I am to you all."

"Yes, sir."

Twenty minutes later, Arthur returned. His face was swollen to twice its normal size, and there was blood dripping from it onto his shirt, but he was laughing as Susan ran to him, wailing. Her arms were around him, and she was moaning: "Oh, my baby, my baby, what happened?"

He would not stop laughing. He said, echoing her: "My *baby?* Aunt Susan! I'm a grown man now! By God, ma'am, in a few years I'll be old enough to be your father!"

"That's quite enough of that," Susan said primly. "And we really have to do something about your face . . ."

"It's a dreadful mess," Arthur said. "I'm sure it looks awful. But it's nothing, Aunt Susan. I swear. Nothing."

Peter could not believe his son's good humor. But Arthur said happily: "Could I have a drink, sir? I feel I have earned it, and with a glass of brandy in my hand I will happily recount the gory details of an encounter that has given me tremendous pleasure."

"And I need one too, boy. This house tonight has not been without its troubles."

Arthur was suddenly very serious, and as Peter poured the drinks he said sharply: "Two men? One old, one young? They were here?"

"Yes, they were here."

"Oh, God." He looked at Susan. "And . . . were you harmed?"

"No, I was not. Your father took care of them. But first . . ." She strode to the kitchen door and threw it open and called out: "Nesta! The brimstone! And I need cold water! Draw it fresh from the well, as cold as possible!" She turned back to Arthur, and there were tears in her eyes. "Oh, calamity! It's on us again, is it not?"

Arthur sat down and sipped the drink that Peter gave him and said: "They weren't just robbers then, were they?"

"No, they were not. They came from the Planters' Association to solicit my membership. A thousand-pound entry fee to wipe out my 'past mistakes.' "

"And you told them to go to hell, I hope?"

"Please don't swear in the presence of your aunt, Arthur."

"No, sir. I'm sorry, Aunt Susan."

"And that, of course, is what I did," Peter said. "I told them to go to hell. You met with them?"

"Half a mile down the road. They rode up on either side of me, and the old man asked me, smiling, if I were Arthur Entwhistle. I said yes, and I was simply not ready. Half behind me, the younger one swung a kind of cudgel at me and caught me squarely across the face, knocking me off my horse. I fell to the ground, got up again, took his foot in my hands, and threw him from the saddle. I gave his mount the benefit of my crop and sent him on his way . . . and the last I saw of him he was being dragged at a very commendable speed by one ankle caught in the stirrup."

He looked at Susan, very gravely: "But if he harmed you in any way at all, I will go back now and find him."

"No, no, there is no need."

Nesta was coming in with a basin of well water, bandages, and the bright yellow sulphur powder from the brimstone. A very knowledgeable young woman, she had a jar of treacle too, and she said: "I mix some of the *melado* too. Master Arthur eat it, make him feel well again."

Susan held his face down in the cold water for an interminable time, till he forced up his head and said, gasping: "Aunt Susan! You're drowning me!" She pushed his head down again, and when she was satisfied, she dusted the wounds with the powder and bandaged him, and Nesta held out a spoonful of brimstone and treacle for him. He looked at it with distaste and said: "If you think I'm going to *eat* that disgusting mess . . ."

"Eat it," Susan said. "It will clean your blood."

"My blood is clean."

"Eat it!"

"Yes, ma'am." He took a hesitant mouthful and found that it was very pleasant to the taste and took more and more.

It was more than three weeks before the violent scars of the cudgel blow had disappeared and Arthur was once more his normal self.

And in that time . . . In the first week, one of Bidasso's silent friends found a tiny fire of charcoal twigs in the stable, covered over with a compacted pile of horse manure; in five, six, or seven hours, the fire would have burned through its covering, by which time the arsonists would be well away and back where they came from.

Ten days later, Bidasso himself found another fire set in one of the storerooms of the house. A month later, a fire broke out in one of the empty bedrooms and was quickly stifled by Bidasso and his friends. Once, a musketball shattered the glass of the dining-room window, and Arthur ran furiously off into the darkness, the revolver that he carried constantly now strapped to his waist; but he could not find the perpetrator, and it was an exercise in futility.

But the unseen enemy was strong and would not so easily be defied.

There had been a lull in the secret fighting; for more than a month, there had been no more incipient fires, no more threats . . .

And then, one night, Peter was woken from his sleep in the darkness by the gentle touch of Bidasso's hand on his wrist. He was instantly wide awake, and the houseman said very quietly: "Now we have big trouble, Mr. Peter."

Peter was reaching for his clothes. "Tell me, Bidasso . . ."

"There are men out there, how many I don't know. Maybe twenty, thirty, maybe very many more. Riders, I cannot hear them, but I smell their horses."

"Miss Susan?" It was his first thought, and Bidasso said: "Nesta is with her now. I tell Nesta to take her to the cellar. She will not go there, I know it."

"And Mr. Arthur?"

Bidasso grinned, a man of formidable powers who would be troubled by almost nothing. "Mr. Arthur was dressing when I left him. He wants to go up on the roof with one of the muskets, a good thing to do."

"And how many are they? Twenty or thirty, you say?" He strapped on his gun belt and checked the chamber of the gun. He went to the tiny night-light and snuffed it out as Bidasso gestured. "A guess," he said. "There may be many more. We will know soon."

"Your two Jamaicans?"

"Abdara is with Miss Susan and Nesta. Grisalo is out

there now, scouting in the darkness. He will report to me soon."

"Then we go to Miss Susan now . . ."

"Yes, the best thing, I think."

They went to her room and found her fully dressed and waiting. She was clutching the heavy revolver that Peter had bought from Arnold Dawson, for other reasons, so long ago. She had carefully drawn the heavy drapes over the windows, and the room was faintly lit by a solitary candle. He could feel the tension in her, almost a tangible sensation, and he said gently: "At the first sign of trouble, you will go with Nesta and Grisalo to the cellar and bar the door."

But she shook her head and said tightly: "No, I'll stay with you."

"Until we know more about them, what they want from us . . . Well, we will see."

There were slight footsteps on the roof over their heads, an ominous sound in the night, and they listened. Bidasso whispered: "It is Mr. Arthur . . ." And then, in an uncanny animal silence, the second of the guards was there, Grisalo, and he whispered earnestly with Bidasso in Creole for a very long time. There were questions and answers, and at last Bidasso said quietly: "He counted forty-five men, but thinks there are others too. Most of them are grouped together under the clump of bamboo beyond the sheds, but they were preparing to move out."

"Mounted?"

"All of them."

"Our workers?"

"Not one of them left," Bidasso said grimly. "They have all gone, running for their lives to the dark woods, and so have the other servants. It means that there are five of us only to fight for this house, if we must."

"The horsemen are armed, of course?"

"With muskets, some with revolvers, too." He frowned, a puzzle worrying him. "And Grisalo reports the barking of many dogs, over in the fields, he thinks."

"*Dogs?*" Peter said, startled. "In God's name, do they hope to set dogs on us? How many guns do we have now?"

"Five muskets all told and two revolvers, but only five men to fire them."

"And one woman," Susan said tartly.

Peter sighed. "Very well." He turned to Bidasso: "Then the two women will stay here with me. Send your two men to the east and the south rooms to keep watch, you yourself join Arthur on the roof, and make sure every side is covered. Try to keep in touch with all of us."

Bidasso nodded and left silently with his two friends, and Peter said quietly: "The candle, now . . ."

Susan snuffed it out, and he drew back the curtains to peer out into the impenetrable darkness. It was so black out there that at first he could see nothing at all, but then he slowly became aware of a lighter sheen that was the water, a darker silhouette of the mountains. He could see nothing else; and so they waited.

There were fifty-seven of the association's men out there, all wearing the dreaded green-and-black armbands, and they were led by Red Barstow. Down by the sheds, he sat his horse quite motionless, his chin on his chest; he might almost have been asleep, but he too was waiting. In a little while, his son Gavin cantered up to him and said quietly: "We are ready."

Barstow raised his head. "The dogs?"

"Ready for the signal. All twelve of them, upwind."

"Harper's group?"

"Two hundred yards to our left. Driscoll is two hundred and fifty to the right."

"The tinders?"

"Ready." He smiled thinly. "*Everything* is ready, Father."

"Very well then."

He was the general now, well in command and on the verge of executing the plan he had fought for against the milder segments of the association's membership—"the *fearful* members," he called them scornfully, "wishy-washy creatures like the Crenshaw boys and many others . . ."

The plan was his, and he was pleased with it.

He was a deeply religious man for whom the Holy Book was almost a way of life, and he knew well the story of Samson and the foxes in the cornfields of the Philistines. He raised his musket and fired it once, the signal, and in a few moments he saw the first of the flames.

A few hundred yards downwind, the men had lit the flares they had tied to the dogs' tails, and the animals were racing, yelping out their fear, through the standing cane, much of it already cut and dry as tinder. The flames were taking hold very quickly, and in less than five minutes the men over there were charging back to the rendezvous, all need for silence gone now; they were whooping their delight and screaming out their venom. Red Barstow shouted angrily: "Order there, men! Let's have order!" He waited till they were correctly lined up in the places that had been allocated to them, their horses dancing in the vicarious excitement; and then he raised his gun and shouted: "At the full gallop: For . . . *ward!*"

Twenty men charged across the sand, quickly joined by Harper's and Driscoll's columns wheeling in to take up their positions. Barstow was at their head, riding easily, ramming a new charge down the barrel of his musket as he rode, quite expertly. In his younger days he had been a corporal of Dragoons (though he told everyone that he had held field officer's rank), and he was reliving now the exploits of his youth, justifiably secure in his own competence both as a rider and as a rifleman.

The enemy position was the house, and the column circled it three times at a fast gallop and then slackened their pace to an easy canter. In the distance, the canefields were burning furiously, and Barstow raised his gun again for the second signal. He fired the half-inch bullet into the front door, and at once the other guns answered him, a ragged and uncontrolled but still murderous volley at doors, windows, and walls.

Now the defenders answered the fire, and the first shot was Peter's. He passed the gun to Nesta for reloading and took the one she handed him, searching out a target in the darkness, a heavy body of horsemen cantering past him silhouetted against the flames. He fired again and heard a scream, heard too the shots from the other defenders.

And then suddenly the riders were gone, the sound of the horses' hooves diminishing as they swept away across the fine lawns and the flower gardens.

But the assault on Coratoe had only begun. The attackers regrouped five hundred yards from the house and collected the flares they had stacked there, three or four bundles of dry reeds coated with pitch to each man, passing the tinders from one to another to light them.

All down the line, one by one, the bundles caught fire and flamed redly. The men sat on their prancing, nervous horses for a moment, knowing that they were well out of musket range from the house, lined up like an avenging army; the flames reflected the anger in their sweating faces.

And at last, Red Barstow shouted, exulting: "Don't worry about their gunfire, boys! We'll move faster than their bullets! You know what has to be done now, so: *Charge!*"

In a long and fiery line, fifty-seven horsemen thundered across the vegetable gardens, the flower gardens, and then the herb gardens, flattening in furious charge all the plants that had been so lovingly set out; they cut up the lawns with their flailing hooves and circled the house again as the defenders opened fire. This time they hurled their flares through shattered windows, dropped them on the wooden porch, threw them against the mahogany-plank walls, almost two hundred individual fires starting in no time at all, and joining up with each other as the fine old building went up in flames.

When the last of the flares had been thrown, Red Barstow wheeled his horse and screamed: "Home, boys, home! Catch me who can . . . !"

They followed him down to the beach and along the sand as he outrode them all; and the victorious cavalry were in retreat, their work done.

All that was left of Coratoe's splendor was a flaming wreck; the house, the sheds, the outbuildings, the presses, the fields themselves—all were quickly being reduced to ashes.

For a while, as Susan wept, the men filled buckets with water and used them, but it was a hopeless and even ridiculous endeavor. And when the tip of the sun came up over the sea, gilding a scene of utter desolation with a stark and ravaged beauty, the whole of the once-flourishing estate was a charred shambles, and nothing was left of it.

Chapter Nineteen

Coratoe had fallen into ruin, and not a single one of the workers had dared to return; they had all fled to the mountains to join their brothers, to grow millet and cassava for themselves, to live off the wild guava, papaya, and mangoes that grew there till their crops might come in, only barely managing to feed their families.

But this was not the sum total of the disaster.

Peter said to Susan, very heavily: "I don't quite know how to rebuild this place, Susan," and she answered fiercely: "But we must! Your dream and mine, Peter, and if it takes every penny of the money we have left . . ."

He sighed. "Yes, that's the point exactly. There's almost *no* money left, Susan. We have a little over two hundred pounds in the bank . . ."

She was aghast and could not contain herself. "What? All the family fortune . . . ?"

"Had we been able to harvest the crop, we'd have made a small profit, perhaps." He said bitterly: "They chose just the right moment to burn us out. Yes, I'm afraid it's all been spent. I had a session with the bankers this morning, the matter of a loan. Their misgivings are far, far more severe than yours, so correctly, ever were. They just don't believe that we can make this place pay. I couldn't even raise a miserable two thousand pounds to get the place going again. We've no money, Susan! For the first time in God alone knows how many generations, the Entwhistle family is . . . down at heel."

Susan turned her mind back to her embroidery. And in a little while she said quietly: "You'll find a way, Peter. I'm sure of it."

The fields were sprouting green again, with weeds fertilized by the potash of the fire, and there was almost nowhere to live.

But Arnold Dawson had come calling, with his lovely young wife, Zelda, and it was she who had decided that neighborly help was needed now. "Arnold," she had said impatiently, "the Entwhistles are very nice people, truly they are. Why don't you ever listen to me? And we have all those tents just lying around and taking up storage space. We'll never sell them, you must know that! So let's put them to use."

In a moment of weakness, Arnold had bought six large rectangular tents of the kind known as E.P.I.P., which stood for "English Pattern, Indian Pattern." They were twelve feet wide by sixteen feet long, made of heavy white canvas lined with yellow canvas of a lighter weight and supported by two nine-foot-high poles and thirty-two guy ropes. "At the very least," she said, "it will give them a roof over their heads." For a week the family had been sleeping out in the open and suffering the tropical storms when they came.

And so there were now four tents set out on what had once been the Coratoe lawns to house the family and the servants; Bidasso, his two friends, and Nesta had decided to stay, though the others, fearing for their lives if they openly tried to help in any kind of reconstruction, had returned to their villages. Bidasso said, speaking for the four of them: "One day, Mr. Peter, you will have money again, and we will all be happy to be paid once more. But not now. I will not leave this place, it is my home. And neither will the others."

In the absence of any income, Peter and Arthur, much to Susan's horror, had found temporary work of sorts in Kingston docks as simple stevedores.

It was a matter of horror, too, for their expatriate friends who had not always stood by them before in times of difficulty. Madame Phyllis came bicycling over, wearing her bifurcated trousers and carrying a small satchel in which there were twenty gold Spanish doubloons. "Sell them, Peter," she said, urging. "And when your fortunes have righted themselves, you can repay me . . ."

Commander Crenshaw came calling too and stared around at the yellow hangings of the tent and said, harrumphing: "By God, Entwhistle, it reminds me of the days in India. A man can live very well in a good tent. Shouldn't have to do it for too long, of course, not if he's British."

He produced a bottle of wine and said, almost shame-facedly: "Been drinking all day long, dear boy, and I didn't want to stop. You'll join me?" He even brought two rag-wrapped glasses from the voluminous poacher's pocket in the tails of his frock coat and mumbled: "Your beautiful place was quite destroyed, wasn't it? Assumed that all your fine glassware was gone with it . . ."

"You're very thoughtful, sir," Peter said as the old man poured, first polishing the glassware with his handkerchief.

Old? He was a skeleton now, parchment-faced as he neared his eightieth birthday. He raised his drink and said: "Your continuing good health, sir."

"And yours too, Commander, with my thanks."

"And the Mistress Susan? Well, I hope?"

"As well as might be expected, sir." He laughed. "No, much better than that! She is almost as resilient as I am."

"Yes, of course . . ." He cleared his throat. "And the reason for this visit, unexpected as it might be . . ."

"But nonetheless very welcome, Commander."

"Ah, thank you. The reason is . . ."

He could not get to the point, and he said: "Me two boys, Amos and Gerald. I take it you know they've been longtime members of the Planters' Association?"

"Yes, sir. I know that."

"Then you should also know that they have both resigned in the aftermath of damned Barstow's quite unforgivable shenanigans. They tore their cards into pieces and sent them back with their armbands too. Just thought you'd like to know."

"I'm glad to hear it," Peter said, meaning it. "They are good men, both of them."

"Never understood, meself, why they joined up in the first place, but they were both very young then, no gumption, no gumption at all." He said earnestly: "Their mother, you know, rest her poor soul, always quoting the damned Bible at them."

"The Bible, sir?"

"The Bible," the commander said. " 'By uniting, we stand, by dividing, we fall.' Who was that? Moses, without a doubt. Foolish fellow, never realized that a man has to stand on his own two feet without a hundred others to back him up."

"Er . . . I think that was a later American, Commander," Peter said cautiously.

"Oh, really? Well . . ." He fidgeted and said again: "The reason for this visit . . ."

He took a long deep breath and went on, plunging into it: "I'm not the kind of man to listen to gossip, Entwhistle, as you must know. But they do say that you're trying to rebuild Coratoe with no access to funds at all. Hardwick, at the Kingston Bank, told me—and this is undoubtedly an indiscretion—that he's refused you credit because of the island's sinking economy. Well . . . it so happens that I have a few thousand pounds in the bank, money I could happily have spent on women if I had realized earlier that the time comes when a man just can't enjoy their charms anymore. . . . It's all yours, Entwhistle, if you can use it. You can pay me back, if I'm not yet under six feet of Jamaica's warm earth, when you get onto your feet again."

As he had done with Madame Phyllis, Peter refused him, touched as he was. He said gently: "But there is great consolation, sir, when a man realizes how very generous his friends are."

"Remember only," the commander said sternly, "that there is no shame in accepting help when it is needed."

"No, sir. And I cannot begin to express my thanks."

When the old man had gone, Peter told Susan what had transpired, and she nodded, trying to mask her unhappiness. "Of course," she said, "you were right in refusing. Somehow, Peter, we'll manage. Somehow."

The work on the docks was hard for both of them. It consisted of loading and unloading heavy crates of machinery with inefficient winches, knowing that sometimes there would not be enough money even to buy their simple necessities, though these were very few; they were growing most of their own food now, fruit, vegetables, and corn.

And then, after almost a year of this hand-to-mouth existence, a visitor arrived from New York on one of the new iron-hulled steamers, the *Helena,* an ebullient and shrewd businessman who hailed from the North of England. He was a bluff and hearty man in his forties, rough-cut, excessively fat, and even a little comic; he was accompanied by a very sweet and utterly charming young girl who was his daughter.

And it seemed that he had been drinking a little heavily. He stumbled on the gangplank and fell into the narrow stretch of water that lay between the ship's hull and the timbers of the wharf. It was a highly dangerous situation to be in, and there was much confusion on board; someone was dropping a rope down and shouting urgently: "Quick, man, grab it, or you'll be crushed!" But he had struck his head a severe blow as he fell, and even the sudden shock of the water was not sufficient to revive him. The young girl was screaming, and Arthur was the first to arrive among those running to see what the yelling was about.

He did not wait. He heard Peter's voice behind him: "Careful, Arthur!" as he jumped off the wharf and dropped down into the narrow chasm. He saw the great bulk of the hull slowly closing the gap, and he took hold of the unconscious body by the collar of its frock coat and dragged it as fast as he was able, pulling himself along the timber piles till he could find safety under the pier itself. He worked his way through to the other side and yelled, and soon there were sailors from the ship throwing down rope ladders and clambering down to help him, and one of them said: "Eh, he's heavy, ain't he?"

They raised him up to the top at last, still unconscious and bleeding from a cut at the back of his head, and the ship's doctor was hurrying there, with the purser and two of the other officers trailing behind them. The young girl was crouched over her father and sobbing hysterically, and as the doctor bent to examine her, he said to her: "It's all right, Miss Livingstone, he's not badly hurt. Thanks to the timely efforts of this young man here."

He looked up at Arthur and said: "Who is either a very brave man or a fool, it's almost certain death down there. A four-hundred-ton vessel's a mighty hammer against the anvil of a pier."

The captain was with them, a thick-set, gray-bearded man in his sixties, and he looked at Arthur curiously, his shrewd eyes taking in the cheap canvas breeches and shirt, and he said: "Yes, I will heartily endorse Dr. Grey's comments, young man. I will add that you have saved the life of one of my passengers, and I'm deeply beholden to you. I am sure that a suitable reward can be arranged if you'd care to accompany me on board."

"I thank you, sir," Arthur said politely. "It will not be necessary."

The skipper held his look, wondering. "Are you sure of that?" he said. "You richly deserve it, sir."

"I am sure, sir, though you are most kind."

The plump body was carried back on board for more careful attention by the doctor, and for Arthur and Peter the incident seemed to be closed.

But it was not.

They were sitting at supper in their tent that night and happily telling Susan of the day's excitement, and her tired eyes were shining with pleasure as she listened. There was a sound outside, and soon the flap was raised and the subject of their discussion was ushered in by Bidasso; and the young girl was with him too. He looked at the wooden trestle table and said, crestfallen: "Oh, dear, I seem to have chosen the time for my call very badly . . ."

Arthur and Peter had risen to their feet, and Peter said, smiling: "Not at all, sir. It's hungry work on the docks, and we usually eat as soon as we get home, rather earlier than civilized tastes would suggest."

"And you are Mr. Arthur Entwhistle?"

"No, sir. Arthur is my son here. I am Peter Entwhistle, and may I present my sister Susan?"

"Your servant, ma'am," the visitor said, his chins bobbling ridiculously as he nodded his head in a half bow. "And I am Henry Livingstone of Manchester, England. I present my daughter Faye."

The girl curtseyed, and the men shook hands all around; and when Livingstone took Arthur's he said gravely: "You saved my life, sir, and what words are there with which to express my gratitude? There are none."

"And none are needed, sir! I just . . . happened to be there at an opportune time."

"Nonetheless"—he hesitated—"the captain of the *Helena* tells me he offered you a reward, which was refused."

"Of course."

"I hope you will not refuse one from me, sir. Refusal is not something I'm accustomed to." His accent was as remarkable as his appearance, pure Manchester, and it came out as "soomthin' Ah'm not accoostumed ta."

Unobtrusively, his eyes were taking in the accommodations. They had told him on the docks: an English family living in the most desperate poverty, refusing help from anyone. But a *tent?*

Arthur said pleasantly: "I thank you, sir. But yes, I will refuse you, with gratitude."

Livingstone said gently: "I am not talking in terms of a trifling sum, Mr. Entwhistle. Praise the good Lord, I am a successful and therefore a wealthy man. And there are very few people to whom an extra few thousand pounds or so would not come in handy." Oh, those broad, broad vowels!

Arthur said, laughing: "I will not hide from you, sir, the fact that we are not as wealthy as once we were, and will be again when our fortunes change. But we will not change them by accepting money that I have not earned. And I am sure that my father and my aunt both agree with me."

"Of course," Peter said, and Susan was nodding. She said brightly: "And now that this little matter is closed, perhaps, Peter, you would like to offer our guests a glass of wine?" As Peter poured, she said proudly: "It is made from guava, Mr. Livingstone, a recipe that one of our neighbors gave us, an elderly lady who rides a contraption called, I believe, a velocipede. I think you will find it quite excellent."

"Quite excellent?" Peter murmured. "Well, I would prefer to say *adequate*. But we had a fire here, sir, a little over a year ago, and we lost our grapevines. They will recover, in time, and perhaps improve by adversity, as we all do. But meanwhile, our wine is . . . yes, *adequate.*"

And so began a long and endearing friendship that was to put those elusive fortunes of the Entwhistle clan back on the rails again.

Livingstone had come here, he told them, to plant indigo. "I am not a planter myself, Mr. Entwhistle," he said. "I am rather what you might call a businessman, a financier. My family has always made its living from good English cotton. And our textile scientists up in the North have recently perfected a way, that has long eluded us, for applying indigo to cotton fabric. You know what indigo is, I take it?"

"I know of it," Peter said, "only as the *woad* the ancient Britons used to paint their bodies with. A dye, I believe, extracted from certain plants?"

"Specifically from a plant called indigofera. Extraction of the dye is a long and difficult process, and I'll not bore you with the details of it. But since we've learned how to apply it successfully to cotton, its price on the world market has gone up to a point that can only be called ridiculous, and my company has decided to grow its own. Conditions in Jamaica seem to be about right, and we hope to make a success of it."

Peter said, frowning: "Your family name, sir. More years ago than I care to count, I was employed, also in Manchester, to translate foreign-language documents for a man named Abel Livingstone. Would he be a relative perhaps?"

His guest was greatly excited. "My uncle!" he said delightedly. "Passed away now, rest his soul, but Abel was my uncle! And you knew him, Mr. Entwhistle?"

"Only in the capacity of a rather junior employee," Peter said with a smile. The memories of his distant youth were flooding back, the comfort of nostalgia, and he said happily: "I recall once that he gave me three cigars, and I smoked one of them with great relish. But in those days I was not much accustomed to them, and when I tackled the second, I was dreadfully ill . . . Yes, I can say that I knew him. I thought he was a good and honest man."

"As good and honest as a textile jobber can afford to be," Livingstone said blandly. "When I was a child he used to give me a shilling every time he came visiting, a great deal of money in those days, and he'd always say: 'Put it to work for you, boy. Don't squander it on flippancies.' I always took his advice, and perhaps that's why I'm a wealthy man today."

There was a tremendous difference in their philosophies, their backgrounds, even in the way they spoke. But they chatted amiably together long into the night, and all the time the young girl, Faye, said scarcely a word. She just sat quietly with her hands in her lap, watching Arthur surreptitiously from time to time, and dropping her eyes at once when he caught her looking at him so secretively.

And Mr. Henry Livingstone went back to his quarters a very happy man. He had a strong feeling, no more than an intuition, that this chance incident might turn out very much to his advantage. He was a shrewd, straightforward, and businesslike man who liked not to waste time (which was money), nor to waste words, which were valuable.

He went to the residence of Governor-General Dorcas, still at his post and wearying of it now, and quickly found a young aide-de-camp there who was not averse to accepting a sizable bribe. He said to him: "I want to know all there is to know about this Entwhistle family—father, son, and his sister too. And when I say everything, Lieutenant, I mean just that. It shouldn't take you more than a few days to get together a dozen sheets of paper for me, and if it's detailed enough . . . then you can expect another present."

As his Uncle Abel had urged him, Henry liked to put his money to work.

But he was a kindly man too, goodhearted and generous

to a fault, and he said to his daughter: "I feel right bad about that young man, Faye. I wish there was something he'd let me do for him."

"He won't take money he hasn't earned," Faye said. "His own words, you heard them."

"Aye, I did too."

"A job in the factory, then, when it starts up?"

"That's what I've a mind to do. And for his father as well. It's a question of what *kind* of a job, and I want to be careful about that. They're stevedores, both of them, but did you notice . . . ?"

"The way they talk?"

"They both talk like gentlemen. Of course, it's clear they come from the South, from London probably, and you never can tell. But I'll know in a few days."

It was less than a week later that the young lieutenant delivered his dossier on the Entwhistle family and picked up his present.

There were eleven sheets of paper closely written, and detailed far beyond Livingstone's expectation. He read them through, his excitement rising, and then read them again and again. When Faye came in with a cup of tea for him, he waved the papers at her and said happily: "Sit down and listen to this, child! That young man is practically a *lord!* Listen . . ."

He began pacing the room and reading short extracts to her, flipping through the pages rapidly:

"A well-born family of independent means . . . which is to say they had money once . . . A house in Curzon Street . . . Curzon Street, there's not a man living there who isn't an aristocrat! Peter's father was a major in the Indian Army and became a legend during his own lifetime . . . His grandfather was Sir Richard Hayes Entwhistle, *Sir* Richard, mark you! A highly placed official at the Foreign Office in Mr. Pitt's government . . . Peter is not much liked, apparently, by the authorities here, but for very good reasons, he seems to have spent all his energies on agitating for the slaves' freedom, and I like that, you know what I've always thought of slavery. He had a great deal of money once, but put it all into a sugar plantation, *all* of it, mark you, a man with no sense of money at all, all his eggs into one basket! And they burned him out of business because of what this report calls his radical ideas!"

He laughed and said: "I'm reading between the lines, luv, and do you know what 'radical ideas' means? It means that he is a man with *feelings!*" He could not stop laughing, and he said: "It's obvious that he's not a businessman, but I am, so it doesn't really matter a great deal, does it?"

He sighed. "As you know, child, I'm a self-made man, and I'm proud of it. But I've always had a sneaking respect for the gentry."

Faye giggled. "Are you sure you don't mean jealousy, Father?"

"Aye, it could be. And I'm not ashamed of that either. It never hurt a workingman to look up to his betters. . . . Peter is sixty-three years old, and his son, Arthur, is twenty-four, and what did you think of him, Faye?"

"The father? Or the son?"

"You know what I mean."

"I liked them all."

In this bright summer of 1851, Faye was only sixteen years old, but he had great confidence in what he liked to think of as her intuition, and he said: "You think either of them would make a good manager for the indigo works?"

"Yes, I do. They'd have a lot to learn, of course."

"Learning comes easy to an educated man. I was thinking of bringing Ellenstein out from Manchester to run it for me, but . . ."

"Oh, Father, no! Not that dreadful man!"

"Well," he said defensively, "Ellenstein knows the machinery, though I'll admit I'm not too fond of him myself either. Shall we invite them all around for supper one night? What do you think?"

"Oh, yes, please! I'd love that!"

He doted on Faye, and he knew that all she really wanted was to see Arthur again. "But you'll leave the talking to me," he said severely.

She nodded. "Of course, Father. Of course."

Faye was the kind of young girl who knew precisely when to talk and when not to. She was sweet and intelligent and quite pretty, with a round and chubby sort of face and very agreeable looks, and since the death of her mother five years earlier, she had grown fast and far beyond her years.

And she loved her father as much as he loved her; they were quite inseparable.

The supper was a great success.

Henry had found himself a house of lavish proportions and had engaged eight servants to take care of him and his daughter; Jamaica was still a good place to be for a man who had enough money. And he was a genial and outgoing host.

The matter of employment was not broached till after dinner, when they were all seated out in the garden by a small pond that was filled with water lilies and hyacinths, giving a wonderful scent to the evening air; there were splendid trees around them—flame trees glowing redly in the moonlight, beautiful jacarandas, tall and stately silk cottons, and great clumps of giant bamboo. Flares had been set out among the white-painted chairs and tables, and white-gloved servants were standing by to refill their glasses.

Livingstone began the probing very casually, knowing most of the answers already: "And have you been long in Jamaica, Mr. Entwhistle?"

Peter nodded. "Yes, quite a while now." He looked at Susan. "What, fifteen years?"

"No, seventeen. Time passes very fast . . ."

"Ah, yes."

"And I gathered that your place is what? A sugar plantation?"

"It *was*, Mr. Livingstone. But I made what was perhaps a mistake in refusing to join the Planters' Association. It's a kind of union . . . I spent all of my formative years in England fighting for what eventually became unions, and yet . . . when it became mandatory for me to join one, I refused. The result was the burning of my property."

He told Livingstone in great detail about Red Barstow's attack, the pain of it only slightly mitigated by the passage of time. He sighed. "It was such a beautiful house. Please God, we'll rebuild it in the course of time. It's very important to me, a matter of honor."

Livingstone nodded. "That's almost a Mancunian point of view, Mr. Entwhistle; the harder they hit you, the faster you stand up again! But you're what, a Londoner, by your speech?"

"Yes, we come originally from London."

"It's a fine and important city. I've always had a great liking for Londoners. And if it would not be presumptuous of me, Mr. Entwhistle, to ask what your plans might be for the future? I would add that I do not ask so personal a question out of idle curiosity."

"Well," Peter said thoughtfully, "that is a problem we have been discussing at some length. The land still belongs to us, and we've thought of putting it under maize for export to England." He smiled. "I had a good friend once who grew maize here and tried to feed half of England with it, not very successfully. William Cobbett—you may have heard of him?"

"No, but I've heard of Cobbett's corn. It's a very small market."

"Yes, it is. We've been looking for ways to expand it before we plunge too deeply into such a venture." (He did not want to mention the real reason: They had been unable to raise the necessary financing. *Nobody* wanted to invest in Jamaica's future now.)

Livingstone said: "Would you contemplate selling Coratoe, Mr. Entwhistle?"

"No."

Peter looked at his sister and said, smiling: "We did talk of that once, but only very briefly. Coratoe is our home, we've put a great deal of work into it, and yes . . . a great deal of love too. It has, admittedly, fallen on hard times, but our difficulties are by no means disastrous. There are hundreds of thousands of people living up in the mountains at what *must* be called the starvation level. We have good soil, and we can at least grow our own food. We are more fortunate. And to sell our home because of problems we are all convinced are purely temporary and really not intolerable . . . well, the idea seemed to all of us to have no merit at all."

"A sentimental decision?"

"I suppose it might be called that."

"I'm glad of it. I'm a sentimental man myself." He laughed. "Oh, you Londoners think we're a hardheaded lot up North, and perhaps we are, but there's a strong streak of sentimentality in all of us. And it does my heart good to see a man sticking to something he likes just because he likes it! So will you listen to another proposition I'd like to make to you?"

"Of course."

A servant was there again, silently pouring cognac, and Livingstone went on: "I told you, I think, why I'm here. *Indigo.* My machinery is on its way, and soon after its arrival the plants will be coming in too, from India. The best strains in the world are being grown now in northern India, and I have made an arrangement with the ruler of a place called Ambala . . ."

Peter heard Susan catch her breath and felt her hand on

his. Livingstone turned to her, conscious of her sudden interest. "You know where Ambala is, Miss Entwhistle?"

She nodded. "Yes, in the Punjab. Our family has long been connected in one way or another with India, Mr. Livingstone . . ."

"Oh, really? Well, I find that very intersting."

"And we had a friend once in London, an Indian boy who . . . who came from Ambala."

"Indeed? Well, I've been in touch with the maharajah there himself, Ranjet's his name, a very progressively minded fellow. I'm buying a quarter of a million young plants from his people over the next three years, and in the next six months I've got to find somewhere to put the first of them in."

He took out a cheroot, and there was a servant there at once, well trained, to light it for him. He puffed out a cloud of blue smoke and went on: "Now, Coratoe, it seems to me, is a fine place, it's lying idle, it's close to Kingston Port, and you are in a postition to do me a fine service and help yourself along too. What I'm talking about is a partnership, Mr. Entwhistle, in which you and young Arthur would manage the plantation and the factory, and I would take care of the shipping, the selling, and the financing. We would work out a just and fair division of the profits, which would be considerable. What do you say? Does my suggestion interest you?"

Peter felt Susan's hand tightening on his, and he said: "It interests me greatly, Mr. Livingstone. There are, however, two problems that might militate against such an arrangement, and I think you should be aware of them."

"Oh? And what might they be?"

"First of all, I know nothing about indigo . . ."

"Ha! Three months ago, neither did I. Except how to apply it to cotton fabrics. But now I can talk to you at great length about *Indigofera erecta,* and about the glucoside indican which is in the leaf, about the enzymes in the plant which transform it into colorless indoxyl, and about how that indoxyl is turned by paddling into the dye we need! It took me a few weeks to find out *all* there is to know about indigo, Mr. Entwhistle. I'm sure it will take you less. And the other matter?"

Peter smiled. "The other matter may be more important. And that is, you know nothing about *me*. I may be the wrong man for you."

"Aye, it's true enough," Livingstone said glibly. "All I know about you is your name and that you're a man I feel instinctively I can rely on, and that goes for young Arthur too. Come to that, you know nothing about me either, and if you are prepared to take the risk, then I am too. Come, sir, if you say yes, then you'll make me a very happy man."

"A labor force?"

"A management detail, Mr. Entwhistle," Livingstone said. "It would all be in your hands. I've no wish to bother with it myself. An intelligent man doesn't hire a watchdog and then do his own barking."

Faye reached out and touched his hand and said, laughing—the first contribution she had made to the discussion—"Father! That was not very well put . . ."

He shrugged and said amiably: "Mr. Entwhistle is a bright man. He knows what an uneducated fellow like me means when he tries to express himself without the use of language to back him up."

He was not in the least put out. He snapped his fingers for someone to replenish their glasses and said: "It's an offer, Mr. Entwhistle. And where I come from we do business over a drink and change the history of commerce. So what do you say?"

Peter looked at Susan and saw the light in her eyes; Arthur was just sitting there, his eyes cast down; but there was a slight smile on his lips. Peter said: "Then I accept your offer, Mr. Livingstone."

"Good!" He shot out a hand and took Peter's and said: "Up North, a man's handshake is as good as his bond. We are in business, Mr. Entwhistle! And now we'll say no more about it until the first of our meetings to work out the details. Tomorrow morning?"

"Tomorrow morning it shall be."

They talked of other things for a couple of hours, and the three men had a little too much to drink to celebrate the new partnership.

And when Peter was settling down to sleep in his tent, there was a loud warning cough outside, and Susan raised the flap and came in, dressed in her night chemise and robe and carrying a candle. She had been crying, and he said, surprised: "Tears? But this is a very good day for us, Susan!"

"Yes, I know it. I still felt I needed a good cry, so I had one."

She put down the tallow and sat on the edge of the canvas cot and held his hand and said: "I was thinking of how hard the times have been for you and Arthur! Working on the docks as laborers! What is it, for more than a year now? It never seemed right to me, and I thought it was never going to end!"

"There is absolutely no reason why a man should not roll up his sleeves and do an honest day's work when he has to. I never minded it in the least, though I often found myself hoping for better things for Arthur. But he's always enjoyed it, and it was good for him."

"And the plants, Mr. Livingstone says, are coming from 'a very progressively minded' maharajah named Ranjet! Dear, dear Ranjet! I couldn't help wondering what Mr. Livingstone would have said if I had told him, quite casually: 'Oh, yes, I know Ranjet Singh, I almost married him once. . . . Our sister, Hilda, is the maharanee. . . .' "

"I can imagine the surprise on his face! I think he would promptly have tried to turn it to some sort of advantage. I'm glad you kept quiet. What do you think of him, truly?"

"I like him," Susan said at once. "I like him *very* much. A diamond in the rough, I suppose, but he's a good and kindly man."

"And his daughter?"

"She hardly spoke a word all evening! But I suspect she's a very sensible young woman indeed, with a lot of strength hidden there. Quiet, yes, but still waters do run deep. And you?"

"I think it is greatly to his credit," Peter said, "that he is willing to take me on trust. There was just that little tinge of apprehension that he was really trying to reward Arthur for saving his life."

Susan gestured: "And why shouldn't he? That is greatly to his credit too."

"Yes, I suppose it is. I have a feeling that we'll all quickly get to know each other better, beginning with our meeting tomorrow. At which . . . I will insist on one thing. '*A just and fair division of the profits,*' he said, and I intend to make sure that we don't make a penny more than is right. Arthur will agree with me, as I am sure you do."

"Yes, of course I do."

"So go back to bed and sleep and get a good night's rest. Tomorrow promises to be a very exciting day for all of us. Good night, my sweet."

"Good night, dear." She pecked him on the cheek and went back to her tent to lie half awake and remember times long gone by. And when she fell asleep at last, she dreamed only of Ranjet Singh.

The weeks and months that followed were a period of great activity. Peter set himself to clearing the fields with a small force of Hindis and ex-slaves (now beginning at last to trickle back to work), while Arthur supervised the rebuilding of the sheds that would house the machinery and the great oaken vats that were arriving from England. There was no more trouble from the Planters' Association. With the aftermath of the overt and brazen attack on Coratoe, in which two of the attackers had been killed, Lord Percy Dorcas had felt obliged to take some sort of action. Barstow was in prison and likely to remain there for a very long time, and the repressive wing of the Association had simply collapsed.

Approaching his sixty-fifth birthday, Peter was gaunt and hollow-cheeked but still fit and energetic. Susan had lost a great deal of her surplus weight now and was beginning to grow quite lovely, with that strange, weathered bloom of full maturity; a kindly, gentle woman with all of her goodness reflected in her eyes. Arthur was now almost the man of the house, though it was a position he did not really want to assume; for him, Peter was the patriarch. In spite of his great physical strength he had Susan's gentleness, and he was tolerant, easygoing, and as devoted to the concept of family as his grandmother, Amanda, had been; one of his most prized possessions was a small gold locket he always wore in which there was a picture of Amanda as she had been in her early thirties, a woman of the most surpassing loveliness.

The tents had gone from Coratoe; the beginnings, at least, of the new house had been completed. Henry and Faye were constant visitors, and Henry had insisted in their agreement that the estate would remain the Entwhistle property exclusively; and they were just as frequently visitors at Henry's fine old house, which he had decided to purchase now. They were fast becoming good friends as well as business partners; and perhaps it was all because of Arthur's delight in the company of the sweet and innocent Faye.

Chapter Twenty

It was a very warm summer's day, and the hibiscus that bordered the rose garden was blooming splendidly, in pinks and reds and yellows, opening up their urgent blossoms to face the hot sun; the morning glory, in specks of brilliant blue and white, was twining its way up the taller stalks of the hibiscus, some of them as much as twenty feet high. There was jasmine there too, sweetly scenting the air with the little yellow-white flowers, and the hummingbirds were fluttering with astounding energy around the honeysuckle. The blue jays were swooping down to attack them, and the hummingbirds swiveled around to defend themselves, driving their murderous pointed beaks for enemy eyes. . . . It was Mother Nature at her best.

Arthur found his Aunt Susan at a window, and he went to her so quietly that she did not hear him. He put his arms around her, holding her tightly. She was so small now!

He said, whispering: "What are you watching, Susan?"

"A squirrel there," she answered, "burying one of our almonds. You see the way he uses his paws? A lesson in energy for all of us."

"But your thoughts were not with a squirrel. You were . . . brooding."

She turned to him, her eyes alight with pleasure, and she was laughing. "Brooding?" she echoed. "Arthur, I am not *brooding*, I assure you! I was thinking about *you*, wondering what you are going to do with your life. With the opportunities that present themselves now."

"About *me*? And my opportunities?" He swung her around and held her at arms' length, laughing into her eyes. "And what dreadful sins have I committed to make you worry about me?"

"I am not *worrying* about you. Just . . . *thinking*."

"About me?"

"Yes. Why don't we sit down and have a heart-to-heart talk?"

"Oh, calamity!" he said, mocking her. "No, we won't sit down. Instead I will walk with you to the stables. I want you to see the new colt."

"Oh, mercy! A new colt?"

"Yes, from Felicity. And he is beautiful! Come, you simply have to see him."

They walked through the new gardens to the stables, and Susan said: "I spent twenty years of my life trying to persuade your father to take a wife. But after your mother died . . . he never would, you know. He had one quite . . . traumatic affair with a local girl named Isabella, but for one reason or another it didn't last. And for myself, I have always believed in what your grandmother always insisted on, the importance of family. But she thought in terms of what I might call the *vertical* line—that is to say, father and mother to son and daughter. I believe in horizontal lines too—husband and wife to wife and husband."

"And it is time I married. Is that what you are saying?"

"Yes."

He laughed. "And have you picked a suitable wife for me?"

"If you have not done so yourself, as I suspect you have, then yes, I will do so."

"Faye?"

"*Faye.*" They passed a stand of honeysuckle, and Susan plucked a blossom and put it between her teeth to draw out the sweetness.

"She is a wonderful woman," Arthur said, "and I will confess to being head over heels in love with her."

Susan was startled. "Then, for heaven's sake . . . ! Have you not thought of marrying her?"

"Oh, yes, constantly."

"And?"

They had reached the stables, and Susan gasped when she saw the pretty little amber-and-white colt, only a few hours old, trying to stand on its unsteady legs. She dropped to her knees and hugged it and said breathlessly: "He is beautiful!"

"I thought of naming him Khuruba. What do you think?"

"Khuruba? That's a very strange name!" A thought came to her, and she frowned. "But I've heard it before somewhere, I think."

Arthur said happily: "In Grandfather John's journal. It was the name of his favorite pony, the one he rode at Vellore."

"Ah, yes, a splendid idea!" There were tears in her eyes as she thought of her father, so long passed away now. "Yes! Khuruba it shall be!"

Hugging the hesitant animal, she looked at him. "And tell me why you have not yet married Faye."

He squatted beside her and stretched out his long legs and found a straw to suck on. He said slowly: "Why? I will admit that my reasoning is a little obscure. I love her dearly, and I fancy she is quite fond of me too . . ."

"*Fond* of you? She dotes on you! I have seen the look in her eyes!"

"Yes, perhaps. If I were to propose to her, I'm half sure she would accept. But do you realize how much Henry depends on her?" He was very serious now. "I'm very fond of Henry too, and if I were to take Faye away from him . . ." He left it hanging, and Susan said urgently: "Arthur! How very wrong you are! Henry would welcome it, I am sure."

"You really think so?"

"Yes, yes, *yes!*"

Arthur was not at all sure she was right. Frowning, he stared up at the dark rafters; a lizard was there, lying in wait for insects, and he saw its tongue flick out and catch a moth. He said slowly: "He is not a well man, you know. I don't know what it is that's wrong with him, but he is quite sick."

"Yes, I know," Susan said sadly. She had long seen the telltale signs and had worried herself half to death about them. "It's his heart, the symptoms are unmistakable. He was very ill as a child, he told me, something no one seemed able to diagnose, but I suspect it was rheumatic fever, and that, sometimes, leaves the heart in a dreadful state. He may or may not live to a ripe old age. But one thing is certain: He is a very devoted father, and that means he will want to be sure that Faye is in good hands and happily married before he passes on, whenever that may be. He is that kind of man, Arthur."

"Yes, he is. But . . . he *depends* on her every moment of the day, Susan. She seldom leaves his side. They're almost always together."

"And an assurance of her future well-being," Susan said, "would be the best possible tonic he could have! That in itself, of course, is no reason for you to marry her, but it is a reason not to *abstain* from marrying her if that is what you both want. I swear to you, Arthur, not only would it be the best thing for you . . . it would be good for Henry too."

She reached out and took his hand. "But it is *your* well-being that I am concerned with. You never knew your mother except at second hand, what we have told you about her. But

Dorothy had a kind of . . . hidden strength, and Faye has precisely that quality too. She would make you a wonderful wife."

Smiling, Arthur rose to his feet and helped her up and said: "So let us see what happens now."

And in the Livingstone house, a very similar conversation was taking place between Henry and his daughter, Faye. They were sitting together over high tea, the table loaded down with bread and ham and cheeses, with onions, and four different kinds of pickles all imported from England, with slices of roast lamb and beef, and a Lancashire pie of pastry and meat; there was even a bowl of tripe and onions, Henry's favorite dish, which Faye had taught their cook (somewhat to her consternation) how to make.

Henry said offhandedly (he was not a very subtle man): "What do you think of young Arthur, Faye?"

"Arthur? He's marvelous, Father."

"Aye, he is that. And you know he's in love with you, don't you?"

"Aye."

"Then what are you doing about it, luv?"

It was a strange thing. They had both taught themselves common educated English; but when they were alone together, their Mancunian accents seemed to become stronger and stronger as the conversation progressed, until, after an hour or two of it, a Londoner would hardly have understood a single word they were saying.

"I am waiting, Father," Faye said calmly. "Waiting for him to ask me."

"Then hurry it up, child! I've seen the light in his eyes when he looks at you, and I can't for the life of me imagine what's holding him back." He said sternly: "He's not taken you to his bed, I hope?"

She was not in the least shocked. "No, Father. He has not."

"I'm glad. It's not only that I wouldn't look kindly on a bastard in the family. There's the other matter too."

"Yes. Yes, I know."

There was a sudden discomfort in her, and Henry reached out and touched her hand and said: "Eh, come now, it's not a matter to cry over. They were very hopeful at t'hospital, very hopeful indeed."

There was a long silence, and then: "If he should ever ask you to marry him, will you tell him?"

"I don't know, Father. When, *if* the time comes, yes, I will know then. But now I do not."

"It's only right he should know! A man doesn't get married just for what he can buy in any marketplace for a few shillings. He gets married because he wants a family. He has a *right* to know."

"Yes, I know it." She was close to tears. "Let me face it when the time comes, Father."

Henry raised a didactic finger: "As it will, luv. As it will, I'm sure of it."

He was suddenly very somber. "We come from very humble stock, Faye," he said. "Never forget that, though it's nothing to be ashamed of. We've got money, which matters, aye, and to a certain extent we've overcome the class barriers because of it. But it's to a very limited extent. The Entwhistles are *aristocrats*, and you have a chance now to marry into a family of noblemen. It's not to be thought lightly of. But I won't have you marrying him just because it would give pleasure to your poor old father. It'll be only if you truly love him, as I believe you do."

"I do, Father! I love him very dearly! And what's more, I know that I'll make him a good wife."

"Then I'll arrange a wedding," Henry said. "You're probably a very spoiled young woman, but be that as it may . . . Anything you want that I can give you, I *will* give you. And that includes Arthur Entwhistle."

Faye felt that she had to protest. "Father! You can't *buy* him for me!"

"I can," Henry said gently, "but I won't. I'll just do what I can to encourage it."

As he spoke, Faye was aware that the blood had left his face, that he was sitting very still, with a look of resignation in his eyes that came to him more and more frequently now; it always frightened her. She held onto his hand and said quietly: "Is it painful?"

His voice was very low. "No. It will pass."

She put a hand over his heart and felt its irregular beat, as he just sat there, his mouth slightly open, his breath rasping, his eyes clouded; his face was the color of cold wood ash, and he did not move. But in a little while the agitation was gone and he was almost his normal self again. He embraced her and said: "Don't worry about it, child. I've no intention of dying for a long time yet. I have a good marriage to look forward to . . ."

But there was no need for Henry to make any of his devious "arrangements" at all; for the two young people, events took their own natural and desirable course, with no more prodding from the parents in either family.

Faye came visiting, alone, one early evening, and Arthur took her, very proudly, on a tour of the new factory. Their first crop of indigo was being processed, and he said happily: "It grows very quickly indeed, two months from seed and another crop two months later."

He showed her the great vats with the paddle wheel at work and said: "We'll be getting a steam injector soon. It's already on order from Sheffield."

The solidified indigo was being taken from its molds and baled row after row, and he said, laughing: "Each one of them is almost worth its weight in gold. This is becoming a very profitable operation. We have eight hundred men at work now, and come planting time next April we'll need double that number. Peter's already getting another seventy-five acres ready, and Coratoe . . . Coratoe is positively blooming!"

"Yes, I'm so happy to see it all growing so well. And so is Father."

"We all are. It does a man's heart good. Shall we wander down to the point? I have a basket out there for crayfish."

"All right."

She took his arm and they went down to the beach and strolled along to the craggy rocks of Morant Point, spotted with greenery, and climbed to the top to stare out at the brilliant aquamarine of the waters to the east of them. The evening was cool and quiet, with only the wash of the waves on the rocks below to break the silence. Behind them, the setting sun was silhouetting the high mountain, gilding the valleys where they cut through the deep gorges, and it was a picture of exquisite beauty.

They clambered together down to the rocks, the thrown spray soaking them both to the skin. Arthur hauled in his lobster trap, a wicker basket he had made himself, and found four splendid crayfish in it. "A good supper tonight," he said delightedly.

They came to a small pool and crouched down at its edge to watch the brilliantly colored fish there, each enjoying the other's company, like very young children. They found a patch of white sand and lay down on it to dry out in the last rays of the sun, and in a little while he rolled over onto his side and propped himself up on an elbow to look down at her. Her eyes, on his, were grave, and he said quietly: "You are very beautiful this evening, Faye. I have never seen you look more lovely."

She did not answer, and he began tracing the line of her cheek with his fingertips, resting it on her lips. He leaned down and kissed her and felt her shudder. He laid his hand on her breast, very small and immature, and fancied he felt the nipple hardening under his touch. He whispered: "I love you so dearly. Do you know how dearly I love you?" She still would not answer.

He laughed suddenly, a very happy young man, and he rose to his feet and pulled her up and said: "It is not fitting that you lie down to listen to what I have to ask you."

He dropped to his knees at her feet and took her hand in his; the laughter was gone now, and he was very solemn. He looked up into her eyes and said: "Will you honor me, dearest Faye, with your hand in marriage?"

She broke her silence, and there were tears in her eyes. "Oh, yes, dear Arthur, yes, *yes* . . . !"

She dropped to her knees and embraced him; he could feel the moisture on her cheek against his. He held her tightly, pulling her closer to him, knowing that there was nothing in the world he wanted more, nor more urgently, than this lovely young girl. He laid her gently down on the sand and reached into the pocket of his breeches for a tiny rosewood box and opened it to show her the ring he had caused to be made, a narrow band of gold in which were set a single diamond and two rubies. He whispered: "A Hindi made it for me. The rubies come from Ambala, where we have . . . certain interests."

"Oh, my love . . ."

"A short engagement?"

"Yes! A few months, no more."

He whispered: "A few months? No, my love, days only!"

"Arthur! That would be quite shocking!" His hands were cupping her young, immature breasts, and she trembled. "Six weeks, then."

"Not even six days!"

"My darling! That is a dreadful suggestion! What would people think?"

"They would think that for country reasons a quick marriage was necessary. But you and I know that we marry for love, not for convenience. Susan and Peter will know it, Henry will know it too. And as for the rest of the world . . . I care nothing for what they think!"

Quite deliberately, forthrightly, and honestly, he set about seducing her. She trembled when he slid the blouse down over her shoulders and kissed her naked breasts. But she could not resist him, nor could she when he moved on top of her and slowly, gently, penetrated her. She bit her lip, not with the sudden spasm of sharp pain, but because she had not, after all, told him of her secret, as she had long ago promised herself she would.

It was not the time now; it was time only for the great love she felt for him, for the utter contentment of his warmth and the closeness of his embrace. She let the tears come, knowing that he would take them for tears of pleasure, which, in part, they were.

But only in part . . .

The secret had been kept even from her until the death of her mother, some four years after her twelfth birthday. Laura Livingstone had never been a very agreeable woman, though she had always taken fairly good care of her husband, more from a sense of duty than anything else; she was intolerant and constantly bickering, and Henry felt a slight sense of shame on her passing because he could not hide from himself the overwhelming feeling of relief.

He had grown closer than ever to Faye (Laura had always distrusted the way he sometimes looked at his daughter, with absolutely no reason at all; it was merely a sign of great affection), and within a few months he had told Faye in simple and very casual terms, not only about his own sickness, but about hers too. His own he could shrug off with no qualms, but Faye's touched him more deeply . . .

"Do you remember that nice young doctor at the hospital last year?" he asked.

Faye frowned. "No, I don't think I do. The one I liked so much was Dr. Hailey."

"That's the one I mean."

She laughed. "Oh, Daddy! He's not *young!* He's an old man!"

"Well, in his thirties perhaps. I want to take you to him again, Faye. I want him to tell you exactly what the results of your illness then might be in the future. It's only right that you should know."

"In the future?" She was surprised. "But I was cured . . ."

"Yes, you were. But Dr. Hailey told me of possible—only possible, mark you—aftereffects for you later in life. Your mother always wanted to hide it from you, I never did, but I always gave way to her, you know how she used to carry on if I didn't agree with her."

"But if the doctor told you, can't *you* tell me?"

He sighed and said awkwardly: "I suppose I could, but it's a little indelicate for a man to be talking to his daughter about. It's about . . . pregnancy. When you get married."

"Daddy, you are my *father* . . . !"

"Yes, that's why I don't feel I should discuss it with you. I'd rather have you hear it from Dr. Hailey himself."

"Tell me, please?"

He was stubborn and would not. But when she went off to bed that night and he sat with her for a while, as he always did, to talk about the events of the day, she asked him again, insisting. And at last he relented.

"It was what they call Mediterranean fever," he said heavily. "And Dr. Hailey told me all about it. Its medical name is *Brucella abortus*. Sometimes, not always, it results in . . . well, great difficulty in pregnancy. Do you know what a miscarriage is?"

Her heart was in her mouth. "Oh, yes. Mrs. Leatham at the mill had one a few years ago. She told me about it."

"Well, Mrs. Leatham is a very talkative woman, and she has no right to be telling a young girl about a thing like that!

But what Dr. Hailey said was, you may not be able to have children. Every time you get pregnant, you must expect a miscarriage. You won't necessarily have it, and I hope to God you never do. But it's always a possibility."

She was a very phlegmatic young girl, the northern blood very strong in her, and though her eyes were wet, she blinked the tears away and said: "I'm glad you told me, Daddy. I wouldn't want to hear a thing like that from a stranger, even from a doctor I always liked."

"It's not an easy thing to bear, luv, but I've always taught you to take the rough with the smooth, and a young girl's life never was a bed of roses."

She was holding his hand, and the flexing of her fingers betrayed her emotion, but she smiled at him and said: "Well, that is a long way ahead of me, isn't it?"

"Aye, a number of years yet. And it may never happen."

"It will give me time to . . . well, to get used to it."

"You are a very brave girl, Faye, and I'm right proud of you, I always was." He held her tightly and kissed her.

And as the years went by and her flowering began, she grew to be, if not entirely resigned to, at least *patient* about a possibility she knew was strong.

And now she was lying on the sandy beach in the fading light, in the arms of a man she loved dearly, a man who had just taken her, a man whose child she wanted with a passion that bordered on desperation. And she still would not bring herself to tell him. *A possibility*, she said to herself, *it's not a matter of certainty at all.*

There was the greatest celebration of the good news when they returned to the house. Word was sent to Henry that his presence was required at Coratoe for a matter that could not be toasted without him, that Peter, Susan, Arthur, and Faye were waiting impatiently for his arrival.

And he knew at once!

When he reached Coratoe, bubbling over with delight, and was solemnly and officially informed of the engagement, there was a great deal of back-slapping and hugging and kissing, and he shouted happily to his daughter: "Faye, luv, you've made me the happiest man in all of Christendom! I promise you all, two months from today, an engagement not too short, not too long, we'll see the finest wedding that the island has ever witnessed!"

Arthur said amiably: "We have decided not to wait quite so long, Henry. We thought perhaps . . . the end of the week."

Henry's mouth dropped open, and he snapped it shut.

He saw Peter's look of mild surprise and glanced quickly at Faye, a silent question; her face was alight with pleasure. She held his look, and there was a faint smile at the corner of her lips, and he *knew*. He recovered his aplomb and said quickly, raising his voice to make sure everyone understood how pleased he was: "Then the end of the week it shall be, and to the devil with long engagements! Yes! The end of the week!"

He was accustomed to making himself at home here, and he went to the sideboard and poured himself a long drink of brandy to gulp down before remembering his manners. He raised the decanter high and shouted: "The bar is open, ladies and gentlemen, and the drinks are on me!"

He thought it was marvelously funny, and he roared with laughter at his own little joke.

It was a deliriously happy evening for all of them.

Even at such short notice, the wedding was indeed a splendid occasion. It was solemnized in the little Spanish Town church, with the reception that followed held in Coratoe's lovely gardens, under great flare-lit tents that Henry had caused to be set up. All their friends were there, the skeletal Crenshaw and his two sons, Madame Phyllis wearing a decent gown in honor of the occasion, Arnold and Zelda Dawson. Peter was no longer ostracized, and there were others there too; merchants, planters, shipowners, and a sprinkling of government officials. The factory foremen and the overseers from the fields had been invited, with Bidasso, elevated now to the position of majordomo, keeping his suspicious eyes on what he thought of as the lesser guests, to make sure they did not disgrace themselves, and him, by drinking too much.

The servants from both houses had joined forces, and there were great plates of lamb, beef and pork, casseroles of okra, peppers, onions, sweet potatoes, peas, and beans, with sliced mangoes, pawpaws, bananas, guavas, and half a dozen kinds of melon. There was champagne and brandy in abundance; and a small orchestra played for them all night long.

And in the weeks that followed, Coratoe was a place of great happiness.

Susan seemed ten years younger, and she delighted in Faye's presence about the house. Arthur was cutting down a little on the long hours he was accustomed to spending in the factory so he could be with his young bride. Henry spent a great deal of his time at Coratoe now, and Peter . . . Peter was anxiously awaiting signs of his first grandchild.

It was in the third month after the marriage that Faye announced she was pregnant. It was the news that all of them had been waiting for, and the celebration was quite riotous. Susan was the first to embrace her and she felt, she was sure, a tremor running through her body. She said, smiling: "Faye. Is it excitement only? Or are you frightened? There's nothing to be frightened of, I'll be with you when the baby is born. And you're fit and well, it will be an easy birth." She hugged her tightly and said: "And it will be a boy, I'm sure of it."

It was a cool night, and a fire had been lit, and the men were gathered around it, slowly and happily getting just a little drunk in celebration as the evening wore on. The women accompanied them with little sips of wine occasionally, and Susan felt a strange unease growing in her; every time she looked at Faye, it seemed, her look was met with a quiet smile and then a dropping of the eyes, and she was sure that something was wrong, terribly wrong. But she said nothing, though it puzzled her and disturbed her deeply.

And as midnight approached and the men were still congratulating each other and passing the decanter around for the eighth or ninth time, Susan rose to her feet and said abruptly: "Well, I think I'll go to bed."

The men were barely conscious of her leaving, but when she had been in bed for only a few minutes, there was a knock at her door. She had left all the tallows burning, expecting it, and she said quietly: "Come in, Faye darling."

Faye was carrying a candle of her own, standing in the doorway with a strange look in her eyes. She wore a long blue gown, and her hair was combed down over her shoulders, hanging almost to her waist. There was that elusive and very Faye-like smile on her face, and she was very lovely indeed. She whispered: "May I come in and talk to you?"

"Of course, darling."

Susan patted the bed and said: "Come and tell me what's troubling you. Is it about the baby?"

"Yes."

"Then make yourself comfortable and unburden your heart to me. But there's nothing worrisome in having a baby, you know." She made a little joke: "Almost every mother does it at some time or another."

Faye sat beside her and took a long, deep breath and came to the point at once. "I come from Lancashire," she said, "as you know. And up North . . . well, we are very direct and uncompromising. I suppose you know that too."

"Yes, Peter was in Manchester for a long time."

"So I won't beat about the bush, it's not my habit."

Unconsciously she was drifting into her father's pattern of speech, into his northern accent. "Do you know about *Brucella abortus?*"

Susan caught her breath and tried not to show her sudden fear. "Yes, of course I do, I'm a trained nurse! It's more often called Mediterranean fever."

"Yes, I know. I had it once, Susan dear, when I was twelve years old."

There was a little silence. And then: "And did they tell you about its possible aftereffects?"

"Possible? Oh, God! If you only knew how comforting that word *possible* is! Yes, I learned of them, through my father. The doctor told him, and Daddy told me at secondhand, so I have not, therefore, been able to . . . to judge how strong the possibility really is."

"You had the disease when you were twelve?"

"Yes."

"Then that was what, eight years ago?"

"Nine."

"You must tell me when your last period was."

"Three months ago."

"Pains?"

"None at all."

"And how much did your father tell you about the possible aftereffects?"

"Only that I might miscarry every time I became pregnant." The candles were flickering, casting yellow-rimmed shadows over their faces.

"The important word," Susan said, "is *might*. Nothing is certain. You will have to worry for three months. Premature ejaculation of the fetus must be feared by the sixth month. That is the crucial time. If you pass six months, then you have nothing more to worry about."

Faye searched for the words and found them only with

great difficulty. She said slowly: "It is not my own condition that I worry about, Susan dear." Susan waited, and Faye went on with a touch of nervousness now: "Ever since the Entwhistle family and my own became so close, and it happened so quickly and naturally, you remember? Ever since those very early days, I have looked on you as . . . well, as a mother."

"And I am so glad of it . . ."

"What I worry about is . . . I have not told Arthur. I should have told him, and I know it. I had made up my mind, a long time ago, that if he ever proposed to me . . . But the circumstances were such that I was overtaken by the urgency of a moment. I suggested a long engagement, and Arthur did not want that. And to make sure that he got his way . . ."

She was smiling now, remembering. "He took certain steps, Susan, to assure that the engagement would *not* be long. And I acquiesced, most willingly. And then . . . it seemed, somehow, to be too late, too late to tell him what I had determined I should and *would* tell him. Was it so wrong?"

Susan said promptly: "Yes. But under the circumstances, the omission is forgivable, I would say. Arthur is a very impulsive young man. Yes, it is forgivable."

"I must tell him soon, and I find it very hard to do. He wants a son so much!"

"Wait," Susan said, urging her. "Wait for three more months, and we will see . . . what we will see. If you pass that crucial time, then there will be no difficulty."

And so it was decided. The fourth month passed by safely, and the fifth. Arthur was the most attentive of husbands, lying awake at nights now with his hand on her stomach, feeling for that vital kicking. The sixth month came all too quickly, and Faye awoke in the night screaming, her body writhing, and she was biting her lip to stifle the screams. Arthur leaped out of bed and ran to Susan's room and shouted: "Susan! In God's name, come quickly!"

Susan ran to her and ordered Arthur out of the room. He

went to Peter and woke him and told him what was happening. Arthur asked in desperation: "For God's sake, can a six- or seven-month-old baby live? Can it?"

"Calm yourself," his father said. "Calm yourself, she's in good hands, the best hands! We will wait and see."

They were downstairs together and they waited, pacing back and forth like caged animals. And two hours later, Susan came to them, her eyes moist, and she said quietly: "I'm sorry, Arthur. A half-formed fetus, nothing more. Thank God, it is lifeless."

He was tight with a deep emotion. "And Faye?"

"Exhausted and sleeping. She will recover. Let her sleep now."

"No. I will go to her."

"Arthur . . . !"

He was already halfway up the stairs, with his aunt and her brother hard behind him. He burst into the room like a man possessed and pulled up short to look down at her; her face was pale and drawn, and he dropped to his knees beside her and cried. In a little while he rose to his feet and said: "Will she be all right?"

Susan nodded. "Yes, if you let her sleep."

"And where is it?"

"Where is what?"

"The fetus?"

Susan felt the blood draining from her face. She whispered: "In the pail there."

Arthur looked at it only briefly; it was covered over with heavily bloodied rags, and he picked up the bucket and strode out with it, not saying a word. Susan reached for her brother's comforting hand. "Peter . . . ?"

Peter drew her to him and embraced her. He said, very quietly: "There is nothing we can do, dear Susan. He must have his way now."

They sat with Faye for a while, listening to her breathing,

and when they went downstairs Peter stood at the window and watched his son out there in the garden, wielding his shovel.

He was digging a hole under the tamarind trees, and Bidasso was with him, anxious and even frightened, and Arthur said to him very calmly: "Our prayer book, Bidasso. You will find it on the shelf in the study."

"Yes, Mr. Arthur, at once . . ." He scuttled off, and when he came back with it, Nesta was with him, but following him at a discreet distance, almost *creeping* behind him, as though her presence might disturb the awful solemnity of the occasion. They stayed in the shadows and watched as Arthur took the prayer book, opened it, found the page he was looking for, and read, raising his voice and addressing a crowd of mourners that was not there:

> *Man that is born of a woman hath but a short time to live, and is full of misery. . . . He cometh up and is cut down like a flower, he fleeth as it were a shadow, and never continueth in one stay. . . . In the midst of life we are in death; of whom may we seek succor but Thee, O Lord, who for our sins art justly displeased? Yet, O Lord God most Holy . . .*

His voice was faltering, and he caught his breath and went on: " 'O Lord most mighty, O holy and most merciful savior . . .' "

He could not continue, and he looked up at the sky and shook his fist and screamed in a sudden paroxysm of fury: "For what sins have you taken him? *Damn you!* Damn you to hell for what you have done . . . !"

Nesta and Bidasso, watching in terror, crossed themselves as he emptied the bloodied pail into the hole he had made and began shoveling in earth. He went to the stables and found timber and a machete and fashioned a cross and took it back and placed it over the grave he had made and went into the house to find his father and his aunt still waiting there for him. Their eyes were anxious as they looked at him, and they did not speak.

He went to the sideboard and poured himself a glass of brandy and said very calmly: "With your leave, Father, I will now search for oblivion. Will you join me?"

Peter shook his head. "No, son, I think not."

"Aunt Susan?"

"Yes?" It was so long since he had called her *Aunt* Susan.

"You swear to me that Faye will recover?"

"I swear it. It was not her fault, Arthur, you must not blame her for it."

"I do not. Why should I?"

His voice was very controlled, but he turned away quickly to hide the sudden emotion that overcame him. He said, his voice choked: "I love her so dearly. . . . Will she sleep to-night?"

"Till morning. I gave her medicines."

"Then in the morning I will go to her, when I have quite recovered from . . . when I have recovered. Good night, Aunt Susan, Father."

"Good night, Arthur. Good night. There is nothing more to be said, is there?"

"No. There is nothing."

Peter took his sister's hand, and they left him alone with his sorrow. Arthur finished his drink quickly and poured himself another, and then another and another . . .

During the night, Faye awoke to find Susan fast asleep in the chair beside her bed. She murmured weakly: "Ar-thur . . . ?"

Faye arose very slowly and put on a robe and went unsteadily downstairs and found her husband sprawled out on the floor by the dead embers of the fireplace. She was still bleeding, but she dragged him laboriously up the stairs, step by step, stopping every minute or two to catch her breath, biting her lip to drive away the awful pain. She could not lift him onto the bed, so she laid him down beside it and took a blanket for a covering and lay down close to him with her arm about him and slept.

The bright sun was striking through the jalousies of the windows when they awoke, and Susan was there still, but wide awake now and bringing tea. She said cheerfully: "Now, into bed with you both. You've a lot to recover from."

She left them to sleep, and toward midday Arthur propped himself up and looked at his wife and said quietly: "It was a search for oblivion, my beloved. Will you forgive me? And are you well?"

"Yes and yes, my dearest. And the time has come for me to tell you what you should have known long ago, had I not feared . . . feared that it might have destroyed your love for me."

She told him in great detail all that she knew of her sickness, and all he would say, very gravely, was: "Does it mean I must no longer make love with you?"

"No, no, *no* . . . ! You must never cease making love to me! I would die without your love!"

One year later, almost to the day, Faye had another miscarriage, at the sixth month of her pregnancy. And Arthur was in the depths of despair.

Chapter
Twenty-One

Coratoe, rebuilt with the infusion of Henry's considerable money, was flourishing splendidly, and the new house—for reasons of pure sentiment—was almost an exact copy of the old one. Peter and Arthur had added another hundred and forty acres to the plantation, and the quality of the Coratoe indigo, produced under conditions of the most meticulous control, was high enough to be in worldwide demand. More than two thousand men were working the fields and the factory now and being paid good wages for their work; many of them were men who, twenty years ago, had been slaves.

Once every week it had become the custom for Peter and Henry, the senior partners, to ride completely around the estate, ostensibly to check on the fences but in fact to enjoy the sweeping, rolling beauty of the scenery and talk over the week's events together.

Henry was an abominable horseman, never quite comfortable in the saddle, but this was part of the new life he had chosen for himself, and it gave him the feeling of being a "country gentleman."

They came to a spot of which he was particularly fond, a

stand of the great coratoe trees that had given the plantation its name, and he reined in and said: "Why don't we sit here for a while and admire the view, Peter?"

It was the point at which the stream which ran through the property dropped down from the foothills in a pleasing weir, very broad and bubbling over shining pebbles; there were always freshwater fish there that could easily be caught for supper by the simple process of tickling.

Henry slipped off his mount with a sigh of relief, patted his stomach, and said: "It's not that *I'm* tired, mark you. It's just that I've a feeling my horse might be. He has a great deal more weight to carry than yours."

"That is absolutely correct," Peter said. "And you really ought to get rid of some of it, Henry. Susan tells me that excess weight is bad for the heart. Did you know that?"

"Well," Henry said scornfully, "you know how much I love dear Susan, but with due respect to her and to her medical training, that must be the most ridiculous idea I've heard for months."

"Yes, perhaps. It's just one of the new theories the doctors have taken hold of. It might be true."

"If a man eats as well as I do," Henry said tartly, "he's naturally going to have a paunch on him! It's all that good tripe and onions."

He had begun carrying a slim silver flask of brandy around with him ("For when my heart starts playing up," he would say), and he took it from the pocket of his redingote, immaculately cut in the new French fashion, and offered it to Peter as they sat on the grassy knoll and looked down on the distant house. From this point of view, white-painted, covered with green creepers, surrounded by well-kept lawns and gardens, it was a jewel in the evening sunlight.

Never a man to waste too much time, Henry said very casually: "Did I ever tell you of a man named Ellenstein?"

Peter shook his head, sipping. "No, I don't think you ever did."

"He is a Mancunian, the same as I am. But without my . . . can I call it *geniality*?"

"A well-chosen word, Henry."

"And without your sophistication too. I don't think he ever left Manchester in all his born days. But he is a good man with indigo. When Faye and I first came here, Ellenstein was the man I had standing by in England to come out here to run the operation that you and Arthur took over instead. And I'm mighty glad that I changed my mind. But that's what I want to do now, Peter. He's sitting there in Manchester on the wrong end of the business, in a job that any five-shilling-a-week clerk could handle. I'd like him to come out here and manage Coratoe. Both the fields and the factory. He'd make a first-rate job of it."

Peter was frowning, worried about the implications. He said, puzzled: "I don't think I understand you, Henry . . ."

"Mind you, I'll not make a move without your consent! We're partners, share and share alike, and it's brought us nothing but satisfaction—for me, for you and Susan, and for Arthur and Faye. But . . ." He hesitated, and said suspiciously: "You'll not laugh at me if I tell you what's on my mind?"

"No, of course not."

"A great number of people have laughed at me in my time, for one reason or another, and it's never worried me in the least . . ."

"I can't think why they should do that."

"Eh, a self-made man! And a man who isn't just that would never understand it, so I won't even try to explain it to a man of your education. The way I *talk*, I never lost my Lancashire accent . . ."

"And why should you?"

"Though, thank God, Faye had the knack for it. The way

I look, too, they say it's quicker to jump over me than walk around me . . . the way I've chased the great God of Manchester all my life, a God who goes by the name of Profit! Eh, they laugh at me, but I'd not like it coming from you."

"Henry, you're becoming maudlin. I won't have it."

Poor Henry Livingstone brightened at once. "And one of my own kind," he said, laughing, "would have slapped me on the back and said: 'Henry, you are talking about your *virtues* . . .'" He was suddenly very serious. "Peter, I want to found a *dynasty*. Does that seem foolish to you?"

"No, it does not! It sounds like a very worthy endeavor."

"I love Coratoe as much as you do, perhaps even more, because it's been the source of Faye's happiness and security. I want to expand it. Not by another few hundred acres. By a few thousand."

"A few *thousand*? Well, we're being hemmed in here now by the marshes. We would have to look for new ground and build . . . Coratoe Two."

"Coratoe Two? Eh, that's a marvelous name. I like it, exactly what I have in mind . . . !"

"We would have to look to the west, or perhaps to the north side of the island. There are dozens of the old sugar plantations we could buy. And we've already proved that indigo grows well on land that once was under sugarcane."

"Not the north side of the island," Henry said gently. "But Mexico."

"*Mexico?*"

"Yes, Mexico. And let me tell you why, from the point of view of a right businessman." He said earnestly: "There are cotton mills springing up all over the United States of America now, and we should start forging a link to a country that in the course of time will become the center of our civilization. Believe me, Peter! Not in your lifetime, nor mine, but perhaps in Faye's and Arthur's . . . North America will be the hub of the universe. We should start thinking of markets there *now*.

What we call in Manchester 'getting in on the ground floor.' "
He was being carried away with his excitement, and Peter was
listening carefully.

"Most of those mills," he said, "are in the Mississippi
Delta. That's a long way from civilization, but it's farther still
from Jamaica. They are buying their indigo, still a very fashionable dye, from England, and for the most part it's *our* indigo. Now, if we had a plant somewhere near Vera Cruz, we
could ship our product straight across the Gulf of Mexico to
New Orleans and save seventy percent in both time and sea
miles. Seventy percent, Peter! To a pragmatic Northerner like
me, seventy percent is a figure that has magic in it! So, with
your permission and your help, I want to found Coratoe Two
in Mexico."

"Henry, Mexico is at war with itself now. There is a civil
war being fought there!"

"I know it," Henry said imperturbably. "I've been in
touch with President Juárez. He tells me that the Vera Cruz
area is safe and that we can buy up to eighty thousand acres of
good land there . . ."

"*Eighty thousand?* Henry! It boggles the imagination!"

"There's a saying we have in Manchester," Henry said
blandly. " 'Pennies and shillings are good, but pounds are better.' It's a matter of common sense, Peter. The whole hog is
better than a cut off the shoulder." He went on: "I've also
been in touch with Ambala, in India."

"Ambala?"

"Yes, where we bought the first plants that established us
here, starting Coratoe on the road to prosperity. It just might
be that the Jamaican strain has become too accustomed to the
soil and the climatic conditions here, so I thought it better to
start the beginning with new plants."

Peter said gently: "And when did you first put this
harebrained scheme in motion, Henry? You seem to have done
a great deal of planning already."

"A little over a year ago. I didn't want to talk to you about it till I was sure it was feasible, as I am now. And it's not harebrained, either, as you'll find out for yourself when you've studied the figures I've prepared for you."

"Harebrained! Coratoe in Jamaica is making enough money to ensure a fine future for us, not only for you and me, but for Arthur and Faye as well. And their children and their grandchildren."

"Aye, that's true enough." But there was a faraway look in his eyes now, and Peter fell silent. Henry said at last, very quietly: "Their children . . . it's a sad, sad thing. Poor Faye is pregnant again, isn't she?"

"Yes, I believe so. Susan tells me she's into her third month, though Faye herself has said nothing about it."

"That's understandable too. It's like tempting the Devil to talk about it. And Arthur?"

"Devoted to her."

"Eh, I know that. But how does he feel?"

Peter said slowly: "I think they've made . . . some kind of a *pact* between them. They've decided to keep on trying."

Suddenly Henry recovered his habitual good humor, and he was chuckling: "Eh, that's my daughter Faye! She's a woman of great quality, Peter."

"Yes, she is. We all know that."

"Will you talk to them about Mexico? I don't want any hasty decisions made between the two of us."

"Of course. I'll discuss it with them tonight." He thought about it for a while and then said, musing: "Eighty *thousand* acres? It's a thought not lightly to be dismissed. By God, perhaps it's not so harebrained after all. You are a man of vision, Henry."

"Aye," Henry said, very pleased with the comment. "Because I'm a Mancunian." He began waving his arms. "Look what we did in Manchester! We can't grow cotton, but we bought it from India and from Egypt, and we learned how to make it into the finest cloth the world has ever known! To a great extent it was because of our weather, the best cotton is loomed where it's constantly damp . . . but most of it was, yes, the *vision* of the Mancunians! So you'll talk to Susan and Arthur about it? About Mexico?"

"Yes, I will," Peter said at once. "Tonight. And I'm sure they'll agree to it."

"And you will too?"

"Unless Susan does not want to leave Jamaica, which might well be the case. She's never said a word to me on the matter, but I suspect that she likes it here . . . Yes, I will agree." Peter was smiling now. He said, musing: "And shall I tell you something that might interest you about our source of supply? About Ambala?"

Henry raised his eyebrows and Peter went on, laughing now: "I never wanted to tell you before, for reasons that I find in my old age to have been quite foolish. But your Maharajah Ranjet Singh . . . he is an old and very dear friend of the Entwhistle family, Henry."

"*What?*"

"Yes. And there is more. His maharanee is my sister."

Henry could only stare. "Your . . . your *sister?*"

"Yes. Ranjet married an English girl."

Their friendship was very close, but he still could not say "She is half Indian." There was always Amanda to think of.

"And in all these years I've been dealing with them . . . you never told me?"

"No. It was very remiss of me, was it not?"

"Eh, I could have turned it to such advantage!"

Peter laughed. "Yes, I'm sure of it. And that was what I was afraid of. I did not want to turn family relationships into financial profit."

"A Londoner! A good Mancunian would never think like that!" He sighed. "Well, perhaps to your way of thinking, you were right. Your sister, the *maharanee?*"

"Yes, an English girl."

"Well I'll be damned! But now that the secret is out, you won't object if I mention it?"

"I will write to them myself."

"And you'll talk to the family tonight?"

"Yes, I will."

"And let me know at once?"

"Of course."

"It's not too late to cancel all the arrangements I've made, Peter. And we'll not move house unless every one of them agrees."

"I have a feeling they will. Arthur and Faye . . . yes, they will agree at once. Susan . . . ?"

He worried about her. "Susan is quite old now, and . . . well, she's older than her years. It will be hard for her to leave Jamaica. But the future well-being of the youngsters is all she lives for. I don't think she will raise much of an objection."

"Any objection at all, Peter," Henry said earnestly, "and we'll do what you suggested, open up Coratoe Two on the north side of the island and let Ellenstein manage it. The rest of us . . . we'll stay here."

He got to his feet heavily and glowered at his horse. He said: "When the good Lord designed the horse, he designed it as a beast of burden. But he never had in mind, I'm convinced of it, the fact that one day civilized man would take it upon himself to sit on the damned animal."

That night, Peter called one of his family meetings.

He told them at great length of Henry's plan and showed them the facts and figures Henry had briefed him with. Arthur said at last: "Coratoe Two in Mexico, Coratoe Three in North America itself . . . it's a marvelous idea, Father!"

Faye was holding onto his hand and nodding eagerly, and Peter looked at Susan and said gently: "Susan, my dear . . . if you have any reservations at all . . . I know how dear to you this place is."

He was startled both by her answer and its vehemence. Perhaps for the first time in her life, Susan was close to losing control of herself, she was almost in tears. She said, as though her brother were suddenly her enemy: "You've never *understood*, have you, Peter?"

He was staring at her in shock, and she went on: "I *hate* this island! When we first came here, we had friends, until they discovered what you and I were both doing, caring about and *for* the unfortunates. And they ostracized us . . . !"

He had to interrupt her: "Susan! That was a very long time ago! When we fell on hard times, they rallied around us, Dawson and Commander Crenshaw and even Madame Phyllis! They wanted to help us!"

"Because you were no longer fighting for the people they thought of as their enemies! Fair-weather friends, no more than that!"

He was stunned by her outburst, and she went on, the tears streaming unheeded down her wrinkled cheeks: "You never *understood*, did you?" There was a handkerchief in her hand, wiping at her eyes, and she recovered her composure and said: "There . . . at last you know how I feel."

She had wounded him, she knew, and she reached out and took his hand. She said quietly: "You have devoted a lifetime to me, and I am grateful, grateful, *grateful*! A widower still, when you should have married again years ago! And I know why. A remarriage would have meant leaving me. I know it!"

Her hand was molding his. "Forgive me, Peter, forgive me all of you. I know very little of Mexico, though perhaps more than I knew of Jamaica when we first came here. But I am told that the people there are gentle and kind, which they are not here. I have prayed so often and so desperately: 'Dear God, let

Peter take me away from this *damned* island! I want no more of
it . . .' "

Peter found it hard to control himself. He whispered:
"And you never told me . . ."

"You were so happy here."

"But I cannot and will not buy my happiness at the expense of yours!"

"And the children too . . ."

"The children?" He could not help smiling; Arthur was
thirty-two years old now. He said gently: "Will you forgive
me? I never knew."

"And it was foolish of me, perhaps, but . . . well, Coratoe
has become so important to all of us, not only to you, but to
me as well. And yes, I would be glad if we could move it, lock,
stock, and barrel, to another country. If it means starting
again, as we started here, I will welcome it. As long as we are
all together."

"We will be. Is it decided then?"

"Coratoe Two," Arthur said happily. "It has a good ring
to it."

Faye smiled and said: "And then . . . Coratoe Three, Four,
Five. Who knows? We might one day build an empire."

"Then I will tell Henry that we are all agreed," Peter said.
"Ellenstein can be brought here at once. We'll need a month
or two to hand it over to him, and he'll have enough time to
settle down before the new planting begins. And the servants?
They have been with us a long time."

"Then ask them, Peter."

He called for Bidasso and told him of their plans and was
delighted to find out that he and Nesta wanted nothing more
than to stay with the family wherever it might choose to settle.

And on the seventh day of April in the year 1859, the
Entwhistle family, together with Henry Livingstone and their
servants, sailed west through Yucatán Channel on the good
ship *Aurora* and on to Vera Cruz.

* * *

It was the time in which the President of the United States, James Buchanan, recognized once and for all the Zapotec Indian Benito Juárez as Mexico's legitimate ruler.

It meant, for this remarkable man, arms and volunteer soldiers with which to continue the fighting. Juárez, thus encouraged, seized the property of the Church—amounting to some hundred-twenty-five million dollars—and suspended payment on all foreign debts. These amounted to almost as much and were mostly to Spain, England, and France, stemming from past contracts that were generally recognized as fraudulent, or usurious, or both. All three European countries promptly broke off diplomatic relations with Mexico, and the French Emperor, Louis Napoleon, at once proceeded with a plan that had long occupied his mind. . . .

It was nothing less than the conquest of Mexico, and it was to have far-reaching effects on the fortunes of the family. Louis Napoleon called on Spain and England to help in his endeavor, and within a very few months there were patrols of foreign armies roaming everywhere, not always sure who the enemy really was. There was little effect on civilian life in general; the nebulous war was being fought almost exclusively by soldiers, though the troops themselves were never too sure about this, since the Mexicans were at war with each other too.

But Coratoe Two, lying in its vast green valley, was safe, and the only close knowledge of the fighting that reached them was occasional firing in the hills, and the sight, once in a while, of wounded men being carried by mulecart into the town for treatment.

The new plantation, spread over vast acreage in a very pretty valley, prospered from its beginnings. Both the machinery from England and the new plants from Ambala arrived almost precisely when they were supposed to arrive; the soil was good, the labor plentiful and hardworking, and conditions could not have been better. And their contentment was so great that it could not possibly last.

Only three months after their arrival in Mexico, Henry came home one evening from the shipping office at the docks, and though he was smiling, his face was ashen. He was well aware of his condition, and he stood in the doorway with his feet widespread, as though he needed support and did not wish to clutch at the doorjamb. They were all there, and they stared at him for a moment, and Faye's hand was at her throat.

Peter said, acutely alarmed: "For God's sake, Henry . . ."

But Susan was brushing quickly past him to take his arm. She said brusquely: "Come along, Henry, you must lie down. I'll take you to your bed, the only place for you . . ."

He was almost chuckling. He said quietly: "No, I just came for a word with Faye. Can I take her away from you for a moment?"

She went to him and took his hand, and Susan said urgently: "Henry, it's a good nurse you need now, or a doctor . . ."

"No."

He was very determined, a man who knew with certainty what was in store for him now and was even resigned to it. He said, and his voice was very steady: "I need only my daughter now. I would like to be alone with her for a little while. I will not keep her from you too long, I promise you."

Faye threw Susan an anguished glance and went with her father to the pleasant little bungalow close by the main house where he was living, and the others waited, knowing that something dreadful was happening now and fearful that there was nothing they could do to ward it off.

It was seven o'clock in the evening, and the supper waiting for them was untouched. There was a great deal of pacing back and forth and of looking at the clock on the mantelshelf. Once, Peter muttered: "We should go to him . . ."

"No," Susan said, "we must respect his wishes. Alone with Faye, he said . . ."

But by ten o'clock, she could wait no longer. She went to the bungalow and found Henry sleeping peacefully, with Faye, very calm and patient, sitting beside him on the edge of the bed and holding his hand.

Susan said quietly: "Let me feel his heart." She was shocked by the erratic force of it, and she said, her senses quite numbed: "There is nothing that can be done, Faye. Not even the doctor can help him now."

"Yes, I know. I wanted to send for him, but . . . Father said no. He wants . . . wants to go quietly. For the past few weeks he has been in great pain."

"I suspected it. Shall I stay with you?"

"Yes, I think he would like that." She said miserably: "He gave me a letter, a letter for all of us, and I want so much to open it . . . but he said not to do that until he was gone."

"Then we will not."

It was on the dresser, a single sheet of paper folded over and sealed with red wax.

And at two o'clock in the morning, Henry Livingstone died peacefully in his sleep.

There was a dreadful feeling of loneliness in the house, and a great wash of tears from the women in spite of his instructions to the contrary. He had written:

To my beloved daughter Faye, and to my dear friends, Susan and Peter and Arthur . . . Forgive me that I do not say good night to you all; I will not have you share the knowledge that I am dying until I am indeed dead, and gone to whatever corner of heaven it may be that the good Lord has set aside for the lucky ones among us who come from grimy, overcrowded, and beloved Manchester. I go there quietly and in peace, and my only regret lies in leaving you. It is my hope that the reading of this letter will not be marred for too long by tears. I am, as you well know, a very sensible man, and the idea of death has never disturbed me greatly, since I have always regarded it as inevitable even for the best of us; even Mancunians must pass on to better factories sooner or later. You know, too, of the great love I have for you all, and I will say that the happiest day of my life, bar none, was that on which the daughter I have always adored married into a family I so quickly learned to love and respect. I say to you, Arthur: God bless you for bringing her the happiness which I know is hers. My will is a separate document, duly attested to by a notary, with copies deposited with the National Bank of Vera Cruz, and with my lawyer, Señor Valdez. And of it, I will say only briefly that on my death it is my wish that all of my property, here and overseas, including all shares in our partnership, now pass to you jointly, to Faye and dear Susan, to Peter and Arthur, to be held or disposed of as you see fit. About the plantation, our Coratoe, I will make a suggestion, and that is: The time has come for you to get out of the indigo business. I learn from my friends in England that the Royal College of Chemistry in your London Town has succeeded in making an artificial dye—from coal tar, if you please! I would not be so alarmed if it were green or yellow or even red, but it is purple, and very close to indigo. It means that we are on the verge of a period in which all dyes will be made by chemistry and it is, therefore, the time for all good businessmen (which you are not, Peter) to forget about natural dyes and find other interests; it never hurt a man to think of the other Great God whose name is Common Sense. Together with my will, there is a personal letter for my Faye. It concerns only her, but I will tell you what it is; it

*is nothing more than a love letter from a father who has
been kept alive far beyond his time by her devotion. Good-
bye, my dearest ones. God bless you all. Do not weep for
me too long, a very few tears will suffice.*

> *With great affection,*
> *Henry Livingstone.*

The will, when they read it, called for a quiet funeral
"without any fuss" and with none save the family in attendance.

Henry was buried in the graveyard of the little Protestant
church in Vera Cruz, and for a very long time, a somber pall
lay over the house.

Peter wrote to Ellenstein in Jamaica to inform him of
Henry's death and also of the suggestion concerning the future
of the indigo business.

In time the reply came back, and it seemed that Mr.
Ellenstein knew *all* about the threat posed by the chemical
advances in England and was very concerned about it. A
young English scientist named W. H. Perkin, he wrote, was
responsible for the breakthrough and was presently manufacturing his new artificial dye at a plant he had set up in Green-
ford Green, very cheaply indeed, calling the stuff *mauve*, after
the Latin name for the field mallow, the flowers of which its
color resembled. He himself was desirous of returning to England, and what should he do about Coratoe One?

Peter called a family meeting and said: "The loss of both
Coratoe One and Coratoe Two would seem to me a small
thing now, after the loss of the man who made them both
possible. The immediate question is Jamaica. What shall we
do about Ellenstein? Arthur?"

Arthur said promptly: "I think he should be instructed
to sell the estate. He should be paid handsomely for the
work he's done, and the rest of the money should go to the
workers."

"Arthur, you are a man after my own heart. Susan? Faye?"

Susan nodded, and Faye said: "Father would have been so pleased to hear you say that . . ."

"Can we safely leave it to Ellenstein?"

"I'm sure of it," Susan said. "A very rough-and-ready sort of man, even . . . uncouth. But I know that he is honest. He's cast in Henry's mold, though a very much smaller one."

And so it was decided.

Peter wrote him a long letter, telling him to put Coratoe One on the market. *"I leave this to your own discretion, Mr. Ellenstein,"* he wrote. *"Please accept, with our best wishes, one tenth of the selling price for yourself, a just reward for your good services. The remaining nine tenths are to be divided, as equitably as you can arrange, among the plantation workers, a reward for them which is even more just . . ."*

Henry's will, in accordance with the reciprocal laws of the two countries involved, was sent to Somerset House in London for formal registry and probate; it was not a fast procedure, and they knew that it would take a very long time, perhaps as much as two years.

But the family's gravest concern now was with Faye. The dreaded sixth month, marked by the gravestone of *Brucella abortus*, had come and gone without incident.

Susan almost never left her side, Arthur was always within call, and Peter, knowing that here was an injustice against which protest would be futile, seemed to find one excuse after another not to leave the house.

As the beginning of the eighth month approached there was dreadful tension among them, and Susan took Arthur aside and said to him: "I want you to come with me into town, Arthur. There is a doctor there I want to talk to, and I cannot talk to him without you. I want Faye *not* to be with us, not even Peter. You and I only."

He readily agreed, and they sat together in the sparsely

furnished office of one Dr. Jean-Claude Moulins, an elderly, benign, and somewhat pedantic Frenchman who was well known to her as a physician of very considerable technical knowledge. She said: "I want to talk to you, Dr. Moulins, about Cesarean section. As you know, I am a qualified nurse . . ."

"Yes, I know indeed," he said, pushing his spectacles down to the end of his nose. "Doña Susana la Buena, they call you, and may I say that it is a title worthy of the greatest respect? So how may I help you?"

"A case of *Brucella abortus.*"

"*Brucella?*" He was already alarmed. "It is an area of great difficulty," he said. "And of very little knowledge."

Arthur was silent, knowing he was a listener now and nothing else, and Susan went on: "My niece had Mediterranean fever as a twelve-year-old child. The first time she became pregnant, she had a miscarriage . . ."

"At what month. I must know that."

"At the sixth."

"Ah, yes, *Brucella* indeed. Please continue."

"She is now in her ninth month. Though my knowledge on the subject is less than I would like it to be, I believe that Cesarean section would improve the baby's chances of survival."

"Her time *now* . . . can you be more precise?"

"Not with certainty, but I would say the thirty-third week."

The doctor worried about it for a while. He said at last, very heavily: "Do you know the meaning of the word *craniotomy?*"

Susan nodded. "Of course." She looked at Arthur and said gently: "Craniotomy, I'm afraid, entails the destruction of the fetus in order to save the life of the mother," and the doctor sighed.

"Precisely. We may be faced with this decision."

Arthur was trembling, and the doctor went on: "You, sir, are the husband, I take it?"

"I am, Dr. Moulins."

"Then the decision must be yours. It may well be that we are dealing with a question of *either/or*. Either the mother, or the child."

Arthur tried to control the terrible fear. He whispered: "I must make it in favor of the mother, sir."

The doctor nodded. "But you must understand that our knowledge in this area is very limited. I can offer you neither the prospect of distress, nor of hope." He said, frowning: "Medical science has progressed far beyond the teachings of the Holy Book, but in this case . . . the final arbiter is God himself. I *fear Brucella*."

"But will you operate if need be?"

"*Only* if need be. To save her life, or that of the child, or—please God—both of them. You must bring her to me before I commit myself."

"I will do so."

He brought her the next morning for an examination. And six days later, Faye lay in the little surgery while Dr. Moulins performed a Cesarean section on her. Arthur, half out of his mind with anxiety, waited in the anteroom with Susan and Peter.

The child was delivered, a perfectly formed baby of eight and a half months, and it was still living.

Thirty minutes later, it died.

This time there were no histrionics. They waited overnight, sleepless, till Faye was well enough to be taken home again. And Arthur lay beside her in their bed that night and whispered: "My love, my love . . . I will never touch you again, and I will still love you, till death us do part . . ."

Her face was white, and she was still in pain. Her voice was almost inaudible. "No, do not say that! In a little while, I cannot now say how long . . . I *will* give you a child, dear

Arthur. It will be a son, and we will name him after your great-grandfather, Sir Richard. I give you my solemn promise, a *son*."

There was no change at all in the tone of her voice, and she said: "And love me now, Arthur, please?"

He could only stare at her. In the light of the candles a strange luminosity was on her features, a line of yellow light tracing its way down her profile, *gilding* her beauty with an ethereal splendor; she was an angel from heaven. He whispered: "Are you mad? Two weeks, three or even four, the doctor said."

"*Now*, my beloved."

He was almost wailing: "No, no, no, I will not!"

She reached for him and found him strong and whispered: "I want your seed inside me always . . . *always*. Not a single day to pass without it! Do you understand what I am saying? I had a sickness once, a long, long time ago! And I will not submit to its indignities!"

There was a strength in her genes which came from an ancient Celtic heritage of which, perhaps, she was not even aware, from the days in which her family's native Manchester was known, more than a thousand years ago, as Mancenion, "the place of tents"; the Romans who drove out the local Celts had left their strong blood there too.

She was moving toward him, and she was close to hysteria. But he said urgently: "No! Lie still, lie still, my love . . ."

Soon she slept; and lying awake beside her, Arthur could not begin to comprehend the look of utter peace that was on her face.

Chapter Twenty-Two

History was overtaking the family.

France was pouring troops into Mexico, and the country was in chaos. The Spanish contingent was very dubious of France's intentions, and the token British force—numbering only seven hundred men and soon to be withdrawn—regarded almost everyone in sight as a natural enemy.

But still the fighting was, for the most part, confined to soldiers of one persuasion or another, and the war had not yet touched the estate.

And on an early May morning in the year 1862, Arthur and Peter were out riding, hunting for quail in the hills around Vera Cruz.

It was a splendid day, fresh and crisp, the sun rising to warm the night-cold earth in a blue sky that was dotted with white cotton puffs of cloud. They carried their ponchos over their shoulders, with sombreros at their backs as they rode at a steady canter through a gorge known as La Barranca de Desastre, and the sound of the ponies' brass tinkled pleasantly as they rode.

But then there was a sudden burst of musket fire from the nearby cliff, and to their acute astonishment, a lead ball chewed up the sand at their feet. They reined in sharply and Arthur said: "My God, are they firing at *us?*"

They turned to look, and on the bluff above them they saw a group of six horsemen no more than a hundred and fifty paces away from them. They seemed to be reloading their muskets, and Peter said, quite unconcerned: "Indeed, I do believe they are. But by their uniforms . . . are they not English?"

"Yes, they are. English marines. And what the devil are they doing here? Perhaps it behooves us to leave this place at once."

"Why should we?" Peter asked. He laughed shortly. "We have more right to be here than they have . . ."

They spurred their horses, and to their consternation there was another volley fired after them. It did no harm at all, but as they looked back they saw the six men riding down after them, and Peter shouted: "Do we stop and tell them who we are?"

"No! We outrun them! They seem not to be in the mood for sensible discussion. *Hi-ya!*"

He whipped his mount savagely, and Peter followed him, riding easily and with great competence. He was seventy-four years old now, skeletal, and worn to a shadow; but he was still physically and mentally alert, and still—with deference to Arthur—very much the family patriarch. Peter's body was light and slender and fragile, but he sat on his horse as though he were born in the saddle.

A lead ball caught him in the hip, turned on the bone, and went on to bury itself into his horse's neck. They fell together, and a hundred yards ahead Arthur swung his horse around and galloped back. He dropped quickly to the ground and knelt beside his father and said: "Father, Father . . . lie still, do not move now, I will deal with them . . ."

Peter was gasping out his pain and could not speak, and the troopers were riding up on them fast, a sergeant and five men. Three of them slipped out of their saddles as the others sat their prancing horses and waited, and one of them raised his musket high, an expression of uncontrollable fury on his face. There was a bayonet attached to the musket, and in shock Arthur saw the sunlight glinting on it as the sergeant drove it down into Peter's chest, pinning him to the ground. He saw his father's eyes roll up in startled death, and he threw himself forward with a savage scream and wrestled the musket away from him . . . and a blow at the neck knocked him unconscious.

He could not know how much time had passed before he came to his senses. He was lying on a flagstone floor, and his hands were tightly bound behind his back. There was a trooper leaning over him and saying in an atrocious accent of the London slums: "Wake up, matey, the colonel wants to see yer . . ."

He could think only of Peter, lying there in the sand with a bayonet through his chest, a dream destroyed, and why, why, *why* . . . ? In God's name, *why?* It was a nightmare, something that could not have happened, and when he awoke from it and returned to sanity . . . he stumbled off, uncomprehending, with the trooper, and was taken to the commandant's office.

He was Colonel Edward Giles Annery Matthews, ex-Khyber Rifles, an Indian Army Officer who had been temporarily assigned to the British Expeditionary Force to Mexico, an elderly man plagued with problems he was not capable of overcoming; he was a little drunk, though it was only seven o'clock in the evening.

He said to the trooper, very testily: "He does not need to be bound, soldier."

"No, sir." The trooper produced his issue jackknife and sawed through the ropes; the knife was very blunt and it took an intolerably long time, but at last the colonel said: "Sit down, Mr. Entwhistle."

Arthur said tightly: "You know my name?"

"There was a letter in your pocket, from the maharanee of Ambala. I am ex-Indian Army, sir. And it is my ardent wish that you tell me now . . . that you are *not* related to Major John Entwhistle of Vellore."

"My grandfather, sir."

The colonel sank his head into his hands. "Oh, Jesus Christ! And the man who was killed?"

"My father. The major's son."

"Oh, God above . . . !"

There was a half-empty bottle of brandy on the desk beside him, and a glass; the colonel filled the glass and drank deeply from it and said mechanically: "Will you join me, Mr. Entwhistle?"

"I will not."

"No, I thought as much. And what can I say? My troopers thought you were Mexicans, you wore Mexican ponchos, both of you. And all Mexicans are our enemies, or potential enemies. May I know your father's name?"

"My *late* father, murdered by your troopers."

"If I may know his name, sir?"

"It was Peter Entwhistle. He spent his whole life fighting against . . ."

He could hardly control his emotion, and he shouted: "What in God's holy name are you doing here? Is this a reprise of *empire*? Are you adding Mexico to India, to Africa, to half the poor benighted world? Is that it? You wish to make Mexico too part of the far-flung and abominable British Empire? Is that your dream?"

Colonel Matthews was shaking. He said, drinking again: "Last night . . . an anniversary of some sort, and for . . . for the life of me I cannot remember what it was. We toasted . . . toasted the health of Major John Entwhistle, your illustrious grandfather. No. Mexico, sir, is not part . . . no . . . not part, nor ever will be, of the British Empire. The British contingent is a token . . . token force, no more. We have been ordered to withdraw. In a few weeks, a few . . . a few days perhaps, we will be returning to England. Her Majesty's . . . Majesty's government has seen fit to . . . to . . . to recall us."

"A few weeks? A few days? And in that time you contrive to kill an English gentleman of such . . . such *nobility*? God damn you to hell, sir!"

"They thought . . . you wore Mexican ponchos."

"Damn you to hell, Colonel!" Arthur was beside himself. He shouted: "You murdered my father in the name of . . . of what stupidity? Are you deaf to the entreaties of simple humanity? Have you no eyes for the common decencies? Can you not even *smell* the stench of your own evil?"

He could not dismiss the image of that beloved body lying there, an upended musket over it like a flag demanding recognition. He knew that the real force of the shock would come later, and his vehemence was draining away.

He said bitterly: "My father spent all his life fighting the abuse of authority, and it is that which killed him! An Englishman fighting against England's abuse of power. I did not always agree with him, but now, because of his convictions, he has been callously . . . murdered."

"Not because of them, sir. By accident."

The passion was flaring again, and Peter shouted: "He was seventy-four years old, and a good man! What possible harm could he have done you?" He said quietly: "I have nothing but contempt for you, Colonel, and for all your kind. Contempt! I have only one wish—that you and all your ilk rot in hell! You have murdered a good man . . ."

"I admit it."

"And if I could destroy you . . . but I cannot, can I?"

The colonel did an extraordinary thing: He unholstered his Army revolver and offered it to Arthur, butt first. He said, his voice tight with emotion: "You are free to use it, sir. Your grandfather, John Entwhistle . . . he was the stuff legends are made of, an inspiration to any honest English gentleman. Take my revolver, sir. Use it on me, and silence my guilt forever."

Arthur looked at the gun and said coldly; "Am I free to go now?"

The colonel said, trembling, urging him: "Use my gun, sir! For reasons with which I will not bore you, my life has long seemed quite valueless. Take it from me. I lack the courage to do so myself."

"Barbarian that you are, I will not do you that courtesy."

The colonel laid down the revolver and picked up his drink. He said very casually: "Then you are free to go, sir."

Arthur turned on his heel and stalked out of the room. The colonel watched him go and took another drink. He called his sergeant and said: "Do you know, Sergeant, who it was your men killed out there?"

"No, sir."

"It was John Entwhistle's son."

"Who, sir?"

"Major John Entwhistle of Vellore."

"I'm sorry, sir. I don't think I know him."

"That's all, Sergeant."

"Yes, sir."

"I don't think I know him." Was the legendary Entwhistle family becoming . . . just ordinary people?

That night, Colonel Edward Giles Annery Matthews, late of the Indian Army, went to his unhappy married quarters and sat on the edge of the cot in his room, thinking about a wife he did not like very much and who despised him, thinking of the gambling debts he could never hope to pay, thinking of the name *Entwhistle* . . .

And when he heard that harsh and angry voice calling from the bottom of the staircase: "Edward! Are you coming?

Dinner's on the table and getting cold!" he put his service revolver to his temple and blew his brains out.

Arthur did not know how to *begin* to tell her.

He took Susan in his arms and said, as gently as he could: "There are no words, dear Susan, which might soften the blow. Peter is dead."

The sound that came to her throat cut him to the quick. She fainted and was hanging on his arms, a frail and shrunken woman, now seventy years old and no longer blessed with that great self-assurance that had always been part of her character.

He called Faye, and together they took Susan to her bed and laid her down there. Arthur looked into her eyes; they were glazed over and distant, and all she could say, murmuring, was: "Ranjet? Ranjet Singh? Where are you now that Peter needs you?"

She slept, and woke up again in the night and found them both there still, their anxious faces silhouetted in the light of the tallows. She reached out and found Arthur's hand and clutched at it and said very earnestly: "Arthur, there is something you must do now."

"Yes, of course, Susan. Tell me what it is."

"There's a man named Frank Watson, Dorothy's father. He's in Manchester, or perhaps in Newgate Gaol. . . . Bring him here, Arthur. If Peter has to die now, he'd like Frank to be by his side, I'm sure of it." She was suddenly very excited. "And William Cobbett, you remember William Cobbett, a firebrand if ever there was one. . . . You'll find him at the offices of the *Porcupine Gazette*, no, it's not called that anymore, it's the *Political Register* now. Tell him, too, that Peter needs him. Will you do that for me?"

"Of course," Arthur whispered. "Sleep now, Susan. You must sleep . . ."

"Yes. And how good it is to know that you are beside me. And Dorothy . . . ?"

"Here beside you," Faye said. "Sleep, Aunt Susan. Sleep."

"Yes. I think I will do that now. I am very tired."

She slept, and they sat beside her all through the night. And when she awoke in the morning, it was apparent to both of them that Susan's mind had lost a great deal of its customary clarity. They feared, at first, total madness, but it was not that; it was simply a semiconstant state of aberration that manifested itself in little things.

She took to wandering about the house for half the morning before she properly dressed herself, something she had never done before. All her life she had been careless in her dress, but now that carelessness was growing beyond the bounds of reason. And yet, when Faye said to her gently, as she often would: "Why don't you go and dress, Susan, you'll feel better for it, I'm sure," Susan would answer—sometimes quite brightly, as though a happy thought had just been given her—"Yes, I should do that, shouldn't I?" She would then disappear to her room and dress with more attention to the petty details than she had ever given before, sometimes even pinning up her hair with the most meticulous precision.

And yet, most of the time she was almost perfectly rational. Though Faye had taken over the management of the house, Susan would often call the elderly Bidasso in and tell him in great detail what was to be done that day; he would answer solemnly: "Of course, Doña Susana," even though half the things she wanted done had usually already been attended to.

She still sat in on the family meetings, though sometimes she seemed to fall into a kind of distant dreamland and just stare vaguely out at nothing till someone addressed her personally and brought her out of it.

And on one such occasion, they were discussing what to do about Coratoe Two; as Henry had predicted, the market for indigo had collapsed completely, and the estate was losing money very fast indeed, with four thousand workers whom

Arthur simply refused to dismiss to be paid weekly, and un-counted thousands of bales piling up on the wharf, awaiting buyers and incurring demurrage at a fearsome rate even as, exposed for far too long to the elements, it began to lose its quality.

Out of the blue, Susan said clearly: "America, *North* America. Florida, perhaps. I've always wanted to go to Florida, such a pretty name . . ."

"We were wondering about the plantation, Susan," Arthur said gently.

She shrugged and said, "We'll have to sell it, won't we? Peter told me how much money we're losing now, and hon-estly, it can't go on forever." She was talking with perfect lucidity, but she brightened suddenly and looked around the table and said: "But where *is* Peter? Shouldn't he be here? After all, it's really his decision . . ."

Faye wanted to weep, but Susan went on, prattling hap-pily: "Of course, there's a war going on there now, isn't there—the War Between the States? But then, there's a war here too, it's a condition we've become accustomed to! Yes. Let's all go to Florida."

She laughed suddenly, and she looked at Arthur and said, as though it would settle the matter once and for all: "What-ever you want, Peter. You know how much I've always counted on you to do the best thing." Her smile was infec-tious, and she said, excited: "Yes, we'll all go to Florida, the whole family, each and every one of us. James doesn't really *have* to go up to Sandhurst, does he? And Amanda . . . well, Amanda might not want to leave London, she's so happy here. But I'm sure that if we all try very hard we can persuade her what an excellent idea it is . . ."

She would not stop talking, and all they could do was listen and weep for her.

* * *

The seed was planted now, and growing; and in bed that night, after they had commiserated long with each other over Susan's sporadic delusions, Faye raised the subject again.

They were lying side by side with their arms about each other, and she said, musing: "I was thinking about poor Susan's comment. About America, I mean. It would be wonderful if our son could be born there, would it not?"

The idea of a son was never far from her mind, as though her kind of North country obstinacy, a refusal to accept defeat, might in itself turn that defeat into victory. And some of her resolve had brushed off onto Arthur; only a year ago he had been certain that he would never have a child, boy or girl, and now he was equally certain that he would. Twice he had been to see Dr. Moulins, unknown to Faye, and twice he had been at least partly encouraged.

"I have the impression," the doctor had said, "that your wife is a lady of very determined character. Am I right?"

"Yes, indeed. I am beginning to think that her will is . . . quite unconquerable. I sometimes think that she is almost *willing* herself to have a child. Does that seem fanciful?"

"No, it does not, not by any means. And this may well be a matter of the greatest importance."

He hesitated, toying with a quill. "In the medical profession we are apt to discount what is loosely known as *faith healing*, because it sometimes smacks of conjuration. But I myself have always believed that it should not be lightly dismissed merely because we do not understand it. And in this case . . . how shall I put it? It may well be that subjugating the medical *aftereffects* of physical ailments lie more in the province of the mind than in that of the body. And now *I* am being fanciful, perhaps. But I am convinced that a woman who has made up her mind to overcome those aftereffects is far more liable to do so than one who has not."

Arthur said now, delighting in the warmth of her body so

close to his: "If you want our son to be born in America, my darling, then that is where he *will* be born."

She leaned over and kissed him. "Then we should not wait too long, my love."

His hand slid from her breast to her stomach, and his heart was beating very fast. "Again?"

"Yes. And this time I will present you with a fine, strong boy, I know it!"

He raised the question with Susan the next morning at breakfast, saying happily: "Faye and I talked about your idea last night, dear Susan, and we both think that it's a splendid idea."

She turned to him, smiling. "Oh? My idea? What idea was that, Arthur?"

"Why, that we go to America, of course."

"*America?*" Her pale eyes were wide with surprise. "What an extraordinary notion! I am quite sure that I never mentioned it. Good heavens, they are all fighting each other there—the War Between the States! But I don't suppose that would affect us very much, would it? And now that you mention it . . . yes, I think I would rather like that."

He searched out a certain Señor Jorge Carrera, a local shipowner who was interested in buying Coratoe, merely for its land. Carrera said disparagingly: "Of course, all that expensive machinery is quite worthless to me. I'm not interested in indigo. I thought of putting the acreage under hemp. It's a slow market, but in time, perhaps . . . ?"

The offer was disappointingly small, a mere fraction of what he had hoped for, and Arthur hesitated. He said, crestfallen: "I must, of course, discuss it with my family."

"Of course, Mr. Entwhistle, of course."

"And if we decide indeed to sell, you would want to take possession . . . when?"

"In three months' time, if that should be convenient for you."

"Very well. If I may come to your office in a day or two and give you my answer?"

"You will always be most welcome, whatever your decision." Carrera was a crafty old man, and he added: "Remember only that you are selling a commodity of which Mexico has a great deal. You are selling *land*. And nothing else."

There was yet another family meeting, at which it was decided to accept the paltry offer, the quickest way to further their dreams.

And then the blow fell.

Neither Arthur nor Faye knew it, but Susan had taken to wandering the grounds in the very early hours of the morning. She would rise from her bed and go, barefoot and wearing only her night chemise, into the gardens to call, in a soft and broken voice, for her brother Peter. Not finding him, she would return to her bed and sleep peacefully till Bidasso came in, precisely at eight o'clock every morning, with her all-important pot of tea. She sometimes wondered, in moments of clarity, why there were so often grains of sand in her bed, and once she spoke to Bidasso about it, saying to him quite severely: "I cannot understand, Bidasso, why the sheets on my bed are never as clean as they should be. Are they not being washed often enough?"

"I will see to it, Doña Susana," he said, and he sought out Arthur to tell him: "I think Doña Susana sometimes goes out into the grounds in the night, Mr. Arthur. I would not mention it, but . . . this is not good."

For four nights in a row, Arthur sat up all night, waiting for this unaccountable occurrence; but nothing happened.

But one morning, when Bidasso brought her the silver tray with the tea, together with two of the biscuits that Faye liked to bake, he found her bed empty. He hurried at once to Arthur and told him, deeply alarmed. Arthur, Faye, Bidasso, Nesta, and some of the early arrivals at the factory all began a search of the grounds. And it was Arthur who found her.

Susan, in one of her demented spasms, had fallen into the well.

Arthur, in anguish, dropped down on the end of the rope as Bidasso toiled at the winch. By the grace of God, there was less than two feet of water in it, and Susan was doubled up there, quite unconscious but with her head above water, and she was still breathing, albeit heavily. He tried to move her and found a strange articulation to her body that terrified him. He stood in the bottom of the well and shouted: "The doctor! I dare not move her! Get Dr. Moulins, quickly!"

Faye, still in her nightclothes, drove the carriage, scorning the services of the coachman, driving like a maniac as Peter, so many long years ago, had driven another coach to be by the dying Amanda's bedside. Faye came back less than forty minutes later with Dr. Moulins, and he, too—an old man and worried about his own safety—gritted his teeth and took the fearsome ride on the winch to the bottom of the well, more than thirty feet down. Susan had recovered consciousness and was in great pain, her eyes clouded. She was groping for Arthur and whispering: "What a foolish thing to do . . ."

Dr. Moulins said: "I may not move her, and yet . . . I *must*. Her neck is broken. Can you have a sling fashioned?"

"I will do that."

Arthur shouted up his instruction to Bidasso, and Faye was lithely dropping down the rope, not using the winch. The three of them waited there in knee-deep water and ankle-deep wet sand, comforting Susan as best they could. She was passing in and out of consciousness, and when at last the sling came down, quickly fashioned from a fishing net, she showed no sign of life.

Arthur carried her to her room as the doctor carefully held her head in the correct position, and Arthur's heart was breaking.

Susan was very still and her face was white, but she was conscious again. She reached out and took Faye's hand and whispered with perfect clarity: "When Amanda died, she wanted no tears, and I remember too that your dear, dear father, Henry, said just the same thing. Well, I'll be going soon, and I want no tears either. I've had a good, good life . . ."

As Faye took her hand and kissed it, Arthur sank to his knees by the bed and rested his head on the sheet close by Susan's cheek. Her other hand found his and held it, and he bit his lip till the blood came. "We both love you so dearly, Susan . . ."

"Yes, I know. I am so glad of it, my darlings . . ."

There was a long, long silence. Susan's blue eyes, the pale blue of the Entwhistle family, were lighter than they had ever been, and they were staring out at imaginings that had gone forever. Stifling a sob, Arthur gently closed them with his fingertips.

At the age of seventy-one, Susan Entwhistle was dead.

Chapter Twenty-Three

The sadness that hung over the house was unbearable, the loneliness heartwrenching. In the space of three years, an entire generation had died—Henry, Peter, and now Susan.

The fact of time's inexorable compulsion was not a consolation; Arthur was the last surviving male of the Entwhistle line now.

Faye was constantly at his side, and she would whisper to him: "I loved her just as much, Arthur . . ."

"Yes, I know it. There was never anyone quite like dear Susan. Something of me died with her, with Peter, and yes, with Henry too."

They were strolling hand in hand through the fragrant gardens in the cool of the evening, a slight breeze coming to them across the water. The broad sweep of Faye's crinoline, fashioned from tulle and muslin in a pleasing shade of light blue, brushed against the yellow daisies that bordered the lawn. "A new life, then," she said, "in America, as Susan and Henry both wanted. And if we go soon—our son will be born there."

Arthur nodded. "We'll be free to leave very soon now. I'm afraid the purchase price for the estate was not a good one. We'll have very little ready money."

Faye shrugged. "Surely it will not be much longer before Henry's will is probated."

They sat together on a white-painted bench under a glorious arbor covered over with a scarlet trumpet vine, to watch the setting sun across the sea. A small fountain was playing close by, a marble statue of Ceres pouring water from an urn on her shoulder.

"Of course," she went on, "I never knew nor cared about the extent of his fortune. I know only that it was immense."

And in the course of time, the long-awaited letter arrived from Mr. Godfrey Dallas Chandler, from the firm of Chandler, Brent, Weybury, and Lawson, solicitors at law, in Manchester, England. It was a gentle and even benign letter, rather rambling and verbose; and it was a shock to both of them.

Arthur read it aloud to Faye as she sat expectantly by the big bay windows of the parlor, framed in the old-rose velvet curtains with the brilliant greens of the magnolia, acacia, and mimosa trees beyond.

Mr. Chandler had written, in part (and they could sense his sympathy):

> . . . *the Probate of Mr. Henry Livingstone's Will has been put in the hands of the Lancashire County registrar, who has requested that I communicate with you on the matter, since my partners and I have long represented Mr. Livingstone in his financial dealings . . . It is greatly to be regretted that some four years ago, when the Confederate States of America were formed, our client made certain arrangements with Mr. G. G. Memminger of South Carolina, then Secretary of Treasury of the seceding states, since which time, greatly to our dismay and against my*

*own advice as his financial representative, more than five
hundred and twelve thousand pounds, the entire extent of
Mr. Livingstone's fortune . . .*

Arthur broke off. He read on in silence for a while as
Faye, her heart beating fast, watched him and waited; he was
frowning darkly.

He tossed down the letter at last and went to her and
held her hand and said quietly: "Dear Henry, it seems, owned
nothing but Confederate bonds, his whole fortune . . ."

Her eyes were wide. "And that means . . . ?"

"They are not worth the paper they are printed on."

"Oh, God . . ."

He sat beside her and said: "It's apparent that from the
very beginning of the War Between the States, Henry started
putting his money in the future of the South, hoping to double it, perhaps multiply it tenfold. And when he passed away,
with no instructions to the contrary, Mr. Chandler's company
simply went on buying . . ." He sighed. "It's understandable, I
suppose. England has always believed in ultimate victory for
the South. Though, had he lived only a little longer, I'm sure
Henry would have begun to realize it was all just . . . a dream."
He rubbed a tired hand over his face. "Well, the war's winding
down there now, to all intents and purposes it's over. America
will be a good place to live now."

"And we go there *completely* penniless?"

He waved the letter at her. "Not even enough left to pay
the legal expenses for probate. It means that we start our new
life in debt."

Her eyes were holding his. "And is that as alarming as it
sounds, dear Arthur?"

"No," he said emphatically, "it is not. Peter, and Susan
and I were heavily in debt once before, and we paid them all
off, honorably, with the paltry wages of stevedores."

He got to his feet abruptly and began striding around,

carried away by his enthusiasm. "Peter spent his whole life," he said emotionally, "fighting what he thought of as injustice. There was a war going on in England, all the more dreadful because it was merely a *class* war. In Jamaica we found a different kind of war that ended in chaos, and when we came to Mexico we found yet another, more savage than ever, because it reached out and touched us personally. But in America they're moving now into a period in which all that matters is *rebuilding*."

He turned to her and made a dramatic little gesture, holding out his arms and his spread hands for her to see. "I'm strong," he said gently. "I want to be part of that rebuilding. I want our son to be part of it too."

She ran to him and hugged him as he kissed her, and she whispered: "And we have each other, dearest. It's all that really matters."

The awful interim period of waiting was fraught with danger for them now, and on one sultry evening, forty or fifty heavily armed troops rode in from the hills and attacked Coratoe.

As Arthur whittled away at a baby's rattle he was fashioning from a dried crookneck gourd, Faye sat close by him and read the latest entry he had made in his journal:

The British and Spanish withdrawal from Mexico was greatly to be desired. But an unexpected result has been that the field is now open to the devious machinations of the French. Louis Napoleon's personal choice as ruler of his new Mexican Empire is the Austrian Archduke Maximilian, by all reports a kindly and gentle man. But he has made a terrible mistake in declaring the legitimate government of Pablo Juárez to be rebels. The whole country is now being ravaged by roving bands of angry Mexican soldiers, seeking out Frenchmen on whom to vent their

*quite justifiable anger. I fear that even Coratoe is not safe
now. . . .*

His writing was prophetic, and it was a swift and terrify-
ing assault.

Within the house itself, there was almost no one who
could have offered them any resistance at all, save Arthur and
the elderly Bidasso; they armed themselves and took refuge in
one of the upper rooms, and Faye was desperately trying to
hide her fears as they watched at an open window. The Mexicans, all expert riders, were circling the house on their fiery
ponies in what was almost a reprise of that other assault, in
Jamaica, firing their rifles into the air almost as if they did not
want the attack itself to begin until the occupants were driven
into a kind of desperation.

Bidasso said urgently, readying his musket: "Their leader,
Mr. Arthur, a quick bullet through his skull, and it is possible
that the others may withdraw. . . . I know these people. They
are cowards."

Arthur shook his head. "No. You do not know them well
enough, Bidasso. They are *not* cowards, but very brave men."
He said moodily: "And they are driven against us now by a
kind of anger that I can well understand, even though it is
misdirected."

Out in the fields, the laborers had long since withdrawn,
prudently, torn between their desire to help the English family
they had come to love, and the awful danger of taking up
whatever arms they could find against their own people; one
of their empty barracks was burning now.

In the kitchen, Nesta had fled too, at Bidasso's urging.
"Go," he had said, "go to the village, where you will be safe.
The master and I will fight off this attack alone. Go through
the stables and the machine sheds, and God be with you."

For almost an hour the raiders circled the house, and in

the upstairs room Bidasso said unhappily: "They wait for the darkness, Mr. Arthur."

Arthur nodded. "Yes, I think so."

And it was true. As soon as twilight came, flares were lit out there, and then at last the charge came. They thundered onto the house, and some of them dismounted and burst open the locked doors; some of them rode into the rooms, their horses prancing wildly, and they carried the smell of death with them. Some of them ran up the stairs and broke into the room where the lone defenders were, and they pulled up short at the sight of Arthur's gun . . .

But their officer was grinning broadly, quite without humor, a heavily built man in ill-fitting military uniform, with a thick beard and a very excitable appearance.

He looked at Arthur and said scornfully: "One gun against so many? No, two? I think I kill you now."

He turned those dark eyes on Faye and said: "Only maybe first I take your woman, you like that? What you say, Frenchman? You tell me . . ."

Arthur's musket would fire only one shot, and the labor required for reloading was interminable; it was not a time, against such odds, for precipitous action. He was aware of more than half a dozen assorted arms leveled at him, aware of six or seven grinning faces, and he said harshly: "First you will have to kill me."

He had swung the musket around slightly, and it was aimed now not at them, but at Faye; he dared not take his eyes off them, but he was aware of the catch in her breath as she saw the movement, and he heard her whisper: "Yes, yes, Arthur my love . . ."

His eyes still on the leader, he said coldly: "We are not French but English, as you should know. We are your friends."

"Friends, friends! We have no friends!"

"And we have no quarrel with the Mexican people, nor have you any cause for quarrel with us."

His gun was very steady, and he was conscious that Faye was moving slowly to him; she took the barrel of his musket in her hand and held it at her breast, turning herself a little toward it, and she whispered: "I am ready, my darling. Remember only how much I have always loved you."

For a moment, no one moved. The Mexican officer, awed by the look in Faye's eyes and her determination, stared at both of them and he said harshly: "If I raise my hand . . ."

Arthur said scornfully: "What, raise your hand? To order the execution of those who have never been your enemies? Is this the way Mexicans fight? Is this your sense of honor? If it be so, it appalls me."

"English, you say . . . ?"

"As you should know . . ."

"Your name, you tell me your name!"

"I am Arthur Entwhistle, the late owner of this property."

"Exploiting Mexican labor for profit."

"I do not think we have ever exploited them. They have worked for us, yes, and shared in our profit. And now we have disposed of the plantation at great loss to ourselves, to a Mexican who will work it for Mexico's advantage."

"But the English came here with the French, to oppress us."

"And when the oppression became apparent, the English troops were withdrawn. My people would have no part of it."

"They were here long enough . . ."

"Long enough to murder my father, who was also Mexico's friend."

"To do *what?*" The officer scowled.

"Talk to the people in the village," Arthur said tightly. "They will tell you."

"The English troops can kill one of their own kind? No, *you* tell me your lies."

"We were out riding. The British troops thought we were Mexicans because we wore ponchos. They opened fire on us, and my father was killed. Talk to the villagers," he said furiously. "They know."

The officer's eyes found Bidasso, silent and waiting for the outcome of this confrontation. He said: "A black man—you are not a Mexican."

"I am from Jamaica, Señor Coronel. A servant."

"And what your master says is a lie? He lies to save his miserable skin?"

"No, he does not. What he says is the truth."

"And as a friend of Mexico," Arthur said clearly, "I ask you to leave my house. Take your damned rabble and get *out!*"

"Rabble? *Rabble,* you say? No! We are soldiers!"

"And without honor! You dare to threaten me—I accept! That you dare to threaten my wife—that I will *not* accept! And will you tell me your name, if you are not ashamed to do so?"

His eyes were on fire. "I am Colonel Alfonso Espartero Philippe de Serrano, serving His Excellency Benito Juárez, our legitimate ruler."

"His *Excellency!*" Arthur said sarcastically. "And does *His Excellency* condone this savage behavior? 'First I take your woman,' you said! Is this the new Mexican Army? The idiot Maximilian has declared you to be rebels, *bandidos,* and his declaration has, until this moment, pained me." His voice was like ice. "Now I am beginning to believe that there may be a certain validity to his argument."

For a long time, Colonel Espartero held his look, and there was a terrible anger in him. And then he turned on his heel and stalked to the door and flung it open, and he shouted furiously: "Out, out, all of you, out!"

They were *scuttling* out, not understanding too clearly

what had happened, knowing only that this mad foreigner had dared to face down their colonel, whom they knew to be a violent and very dangerous man, as was befitting an officer in Juárez' army.

Faye was trembling violently, and Arthur took her hand and led her to the window and said urgently: "They have gone, my love, they have gone . . ."

They saw the rest of the commandos down there, prancing their horses on the lawn, and men were running out of the house, carrying filled saddlebags. They heard the colonel's furious shout: "No! No! We take nothing! Are we thieves? Or honorable soldiers?"

The saddlebags were being emptied onto the grass, the bottles of wine from the cellar tumbling, a silver tea service falling under the excited horses' hooves, a fine marble clock shattering as it hit the ground. And then, they were leaping with extraordinary agility onto the saddles and racing off, screaming out their war cry: "Pablo! Pablo! Pablo!"

Arthur saw the shock in Faye's eyes and feared for her. He led her to the bed and made her lie down, then turned to Bidasso and said: "Good Bidasso . . . dear friend, I thank you for your help. The danger is passed now. You were at my side, as always. I cannot begin to express my gratitude to you. So many years now . . ."

Bidasso went to the door and turned back. His eyes were wide, and he was shaking his head slowly from side to side. "Mr. Arthur," he said, "I cannot easily believe what I saw. We were dead, and yet . . . we are still alive. When you leave Mexico . . . my heart will break."

"Then come with us, Bidasso!" Arthur said, filled with a sudden exuberance. "We leave penniless. But if you will share our fortunes with us . . . ?"

The old man's weathered face broke out into a broad, broad grin, and his eyes were shining brightly. He bowed, then closed the door behind him. As he moved off down the long corridor and was alone again, he was doing a little jig and singing to himself in that strange, persuasive Jamaican rhythm: "*Am-eri-ca, Am-eri-ca, Am-eri-ca, Am-eri-ca* . . . !"

Arthur was on his knees beside the bed, his hand at his wife's forehead. He whispered again, feeling her pain: "Gone, my love, they have all gone now."

"Yes. And I am a weak, weak woman."

"Not weak. Justifiably alarmed."

"*Weak* . . ."

"No." He moved his hand to her swollen stomach and said quietly: "He is strong. How soon now?"

"A month, no longer. And shall we leave this dreadful country soon?"

"In two weeks. There is a ship sailing from Vera Cruz for Florida, a port called Tampa. A strange name, and I am told it is a strange place too . . . but it is quite old, there will be traditions there."

"And the ship?"

"A schooner called the *Victory*. And we shall have passage on her, the two of us, I promise you."

"The two of us . . . and Bidasso."

"Yes."

He was laughing suddenly and embracing her. "Even though we arrive in America with no money, we cannot arrive without at least one good servant. It would not be fitting."

"But not only a servant. A friend, too."

"A new concept, but I am sure it is a good one."

"Will you come to bed now? I want to know that you are beside me."

"Beside you, always . . ."

He stripped off her clothes and then his own, and they lay together in each other's arms, like the lovers they were.

Thirteen days later, they were aboard the schooner *Victory*.

She was a fine ship, commanded by a captain named Allen MacCrimmon, a Scot who hailed from the island of Skye, where his family had been hereditary pipers since the ninth century, attached to the Macleods of Macleod, who lived on Dunvegan.

He took one look at Faye; no number of horsehair-and-linen crinolines, nor even her seven petticoats, could hide her condition now, and he said, not seeking to mask his anxiety: "Y'r lady seems to be very near her time, Mr. Entwhistle. I'd have ye know that should there by any complications, there's no doctor aboard my ship."

"A doctor will not be needed, Captain MacCrimmon," Arthur said. "We will be in America before the child is due, and my wife is in the best of health." He smiled. "Indeed, it is her most ardent wish, and mine too, that our son be born on American soil."

The topsails were snapping under a captured wind, and the sheets were giving out that strange creaking sound that meant maximum capacity; the timbers groaned as the ship heeled over a few more degrees, and the captain said: "If ye'll excuse me, sir, there's work that demands my attention. We'll be sailing within the hour."

The journey was smooth and very pleasant, with calm seas broken by the curved backs of porpoise and pitted with the sudden excursions of flying fish; the sky was a deep and heated blue, dotted with little puffs of white cloud that never seemed to move.

Faye would not stay lying on her bunk, as Arthur wanted her to, but insisted on taking his arm every day and wandering with him over the schooner's decks, hiding her anxiety from him; she was sure she was in the thirty-third week of her pregnancy, perhaps even the thirty-fourth, and there had as yet been no signs of even the slightest difficulty. As the ship plowed through the serene waters of the Gulf of Mexico, each day brought more and yet more hope . . . but her misgivings were still formidable.

On the fifth day of the journey, they came within distant sight of the low-lying shore, and she looked up at the sails and prayed silently for more speed. Arthur worried over her drawn and pallid face and said, deeply anxious: "We must go below, my love, you must lie down . . . you *must!*"

Faye shook her head. The pain was wracking her body, and her vision was clouded; she dabbed at the perspiration on her forehead with her sleeve and whispered: "No, my time is not yet, not yet . . ."

He felt her agonies and trembled for her, but she would not leave the deck nor take her eyes from the fringe of palm trees, a shore so very like the one they had recently left. She was terribly desperate when she watched the sails coming down and the tiny figures of the sailors on the footropes as they furled them. She heard the welcome clatter of the anchor dropping, and suddenly she screamed, quite uncontrollably, and bit her lip to stifle the sound. Arthur's arm was around her.

Captain MacCrimmon was beside them, scowling; he had left his post on the bridge in the hands of the mate at this crucial time and was in a savage fury. He shouted to Arthur: "Get her to y're cabin, man! Can ye no' see the state she's in? Have ye no' eyes in y're head?"

Arthur was taut with his fears, but he shouted: "No! I will not! It shall be as she wants . . . !"

Faye was moaning, held up only by her husband's arm, and she was trying to whisper: "The lighter . . . in God's name . . . quickly . . ." But the only sound that came from her throat was a rattle.

She was trying to stand on her own two feet, but she could not, and as the plank went down, Bidasso, a strong and angry man, was thrusting all contention aside as Arthur swept her up into his arms like a baby and stumbled down it with her; her body was thrashing in his arms. There were surprised hands waiting below to help him aboard the boat, and he heard the captain's roar behind him: "Then get her to the wharf! Quickly!"

Eight pairs of oars were bending furiously, and Arthur screamed: "She's delivering! God help us all now!"

One of the oarsmen, older and wiser than the others, himself a father of thirteen children, shouted: "Hold on, ma'am! Hold the little bugger there in comfort. We'll have you home in two minutes now!"

They were rowing like demons. Almost lost on the wind was Captain MacCrimmon's shout: "Look for my woman, Mr. Entwhistle! Look for Mrs. MacCrimmon waiting there! She's a midwife!"

Faye was twisting and turning her body in her agony, and Arthur could do no more than hold her tightly and try to stifle his emotions. He saw the crowd on the wharf, thirty or forty men and almost as many women, and he shouted urgently: "Mrs. MacCrimmon! Are you there? We need you now!"

As the lighter came in close, a plump and dour-looking woman was shouldering her way through the crowd to stand on the edge of the wooden wharf and look down on them. She was dressed in black, a kerchief over her graying hair. She saw what was happening and stared only momentarily.

Arthur had cradled his wife in his arms and was slowly, laboriously stumbling his way up the rope ladder, rung by rung, with infinite care, and he looked into Mrs. MacCrimmon's gray eyes and whispered: "In God's name, ma'am, your help now . . ."

She was a woman of very strong character, and as Faye was laid out on the rough timbers of the wharf, she crouched between her legs and muttered: "I came here to welcome my man, not to deliver a poor wee bairn who by rights ought to be dead . . ."

She raised her virago voice and shouted: "Stand back! Stand back, all of ye!"

Her trained hands were very soft and gentle as she worked the tiny head from side to side, and in a little while she said quietly: "A knife, someone . . ."

One of the fishermen gave her his clasp knife, and she cut the umbilical cord and tied the knots, and in a moment she stood up, holding the wet, slimy infant by its ankles, slapping at its back till it started howling vociferously.

She got to her feet and held the child out to Faye, and she said gruffly: "Unbutton y're blouse, woman, ye've a fine wee boy to put to y're breast now."

On the twenty-fifth of October in the year of Our Lord 1864, on the hard, bare planks of a Florida wharf, Faye Entwhistle was successfully delivered, only a little prematurely, of a strong and vigorous seven-pound boy who seemed, from the very moment of his birth, to be ready to fight against the whole hostile world.

He was Richard Peter Hayes Livingstone Entwhistle; and he was the first of the family born on American soil.